Praise for George V. Higgins and Outlaws

'A picture of a traumatised society. Its voices, caught here, have a disturbingly truthful ring'   *Guardian*

'Higgins writes some of the best dialogue going, with pit-of-stomach laughs or a cold gasp of dawning implications' *Observer*

'Higgins is my favourite. No, he doesn't learn from me, I learn from him'   Elmore Leonard

'Uniquely blessed with a gift for voices ... each as distinctive as a fingerprint'   *New Yorker*

'George V. Higgins is a writer of genius'   *Washington Post*

George V. Higgins was a lawyer in the Massachusetts Attorney General's office, in the Organized Crime section and the Criminal Division, and an Assistant United States Attorney in Boston. He then founded his own private practice, defending Watergate conspirator G. Gordon Liddy and Black Panther Eldridge Cleaver. Described as 'the Balzac of the Boston underworld', he wrote more than twenty novels, including a number of lowlife masterpieces constructed almost entirely out of pitch-perfect dialogue. He died in 1999.

By George V. Higgins

OUTLAWS

George V. Higgins

An Orion paperback

First published in Great Britain in 1987 by
André Deutsch Ltd
This paperback edition published in 2013 by Orion Books
an imprint of The Orion Publishing Group Ltd
Carmelite House, 50 Victoria Embankment
London EC4Y 0DZ

An Hachette UK company

3 5 7 9 10 8 6 4 2

A CIP catalogue record for this book is
available from the British Library.

ISBN: 978 1 4091 3818 1

Typeset by Input Data Services Ltd, Bridgwater, Somerset

Printed and bound by CPI Group (UK) Ltd, Croydon, CR0 4YY

The Orion Publishing Group's policy is to use papers
that are natural, renewable and recyclable products and
made from wood grown in sustainable forests. The logging
and manufacturing processes are expected to conform
to the environmental regulations of the country of origin.

www.orionbooks.co.uk

OUTLAWS

ONE

1

At about 9:50 in the morning the Brinks armored truck carrying its driver and two guards, all in uniform and armed with Smith and Wesson .38 caliber revolvers, arrived at the Danvers Mall branch office of the Essex Bank and Trust Co. The cargo consisted of forty thousand dollars in small bills and coins. A light mist was falling. The driver parked the truck in front of the free-standing brick building that housed the bank on the westerly side of Route 128, apart from the stores in the mall. The guard in the passenger seat of the cab was Harold McMenamy, 48, of Brighton. He emerged and locked the door. He unsnapped the protective strap on his holster and scanned the parking lot. He walked quickly to the glass door of the bank. He rang the night bell on its frame. A woman in her early fifties parted beige curtains on the inside door and peered out at him. He nodded. She grinned and unlocked the inner door.

McMenamy returned to the truck. He knocked twice, then once, on the rear door. Inside the truck Donald Fish, 39, of Bridgewater, unlocked the door and opened it. He gave McMenamy a red two-wheeled handcart and unsnapped the protective strap on his holster. McMenamy put the cart on the ground. Fish handed him two grey bags of currency and four grey bags of coins. McMenamy stacked the bags on the cart. Fish emerged from the truck and locked the door behind him. As McMenamy pushed the cart to the outside door of the bank, Fish followed, scanning the parking lot. The woman inside opened the door with a key and admitted McMenamy. Fish stood outside the door watching the parking lot, while she locked it behind McMenamy.

At approximately 9:55, the woman unlocked the inner door and then the outer door of the bank. McMenamy followed her with the cart, his body bent to exert the force he needed to push a cargo of twelve grey bags. The woman locked the doors behind him. Fish walked beside him as he grunted against the load. 'Hell is this?' Fish said.

'Goddamned sale,' McMenamy said. 'Asked her the same question. Some bright-eyed bastard inna mall had this great idea: Have the back-to-school sale two weeks before everybody else does, and get all the people's money. Run a goddamned raffle, so that everyone, gets lucky when they ring up fifty bucks, gets everything he bought free, plus a brand-new fifty, too. And damned if it didn't work. Four hundred thirty-three large.'

The green Chevrolet Impala sedan entered the parking lot from Route 128 at moderate speed; it veered toward the front of the truck when the Ford Country Squire station wagon came from the northwest back corner of the lot, appeared at the southwest corner of the bank and stopped behind the truck.

The passenger from the front seat of the Squire had an M3 .30 caliber grease gun. He spattered a six-shot burst off the back of the truck. 'It's loaded,' he said.

The female passenger from the left rear seat of the Country Squire had an M16. 'So's hers,' the man said.

The male passenger from the right rear seat of the Country Squire had a sawed-off shotgun. The male passenger from the right front seat of the Impala pointed an M79 grenade launcher at the windshield of the truck.

Fish and McMenamy clasped their hands on their heads.

The male with the sawed-off shotgun stuck it through his belt and went to the cart. He took it from McMenamy and wheeled it to the back of the Country Squire. He threw each of the twelve bags through the open back window. He returned to the car. 'Set,' he said.

The man with the grenade launcher hung on the door of the Impala until the Country Squire pulled out fast from the back of the Brinks truck and headed out of the parking lot, south on 128. Then he lurched back into the Impala, slamming the door, and it spun away fast, burning rubber, going north on 128.

Harold McMenamy expressed his resentment in the same terms to police and reporters. 'They were kids,' he said. 'They were nothing but damned kids. The guy with the grease gun – Christ, I had a goddamned grease gun once, and it wasn't anywhere near as good's a damned M-Three carbine. He was nothing but a damned kid. Got those crummy little granny glasses, and the hair all over the place, and naturally he looked like shit. You wanna know something? Even at my age, damnit, if he didn't have that gun, I could take that little punk. I could take him myself. Looked like a goddamned hippie. Army jacket, jeans, the boots, all that friggin' crap. And I'll bet the little bastard didn't weigh a hundred fifty, even with the gun.

'And the other one,' McMenamy said, 'the one with the sawed-off. Now he was a little bigger. He was *big*, in fact. Prolly twenny-five years old, maybe twenny-six, and I think he was a black guy. Looked like one to me. Got the Afro and the same clothes. And the broad. Same age. Looked like a filthy pig. I mean, what the hell is going on? What's the story here? These people, they're not robbers. They're not dangerous. What're they doing this stuff for? What the hell is going on?'

On the evening of September 13, 1970, the Ipswich Ensemble presented an all-Mozart program in the main auditorium on the Anchorage campus of the University of Alaska. The event was reported in the Anchorage *Times* for the 14th.

'The most striking thing for many in the large and attentive audience was not the complete professionalism of the musicians, but the realization that this internationally known orchestra is made up entirely of amateurs. Students, teachers, their husbands and wives, only a very few of whom stay with the group for more than one or two years.

'"We do have a small nucleus, a few people who've been with us since we began," Mrs. Claire Naisbitt said. With her husband, the Ensemble's famed musical director, Prof. Neville Naisbitt of the mathematics department of Ipswich University, and co-founder of the group, she has been one of them. "But apart from providing continuity, you know, perhaps a sort of ballast for the younger people, that's about all we do." Hard for the listener to believe, perhaps, after her thrilling soloist performance last night of the 17th piano concerto, but the gracious Mrs. Naisbitt does insist: "When Neville and I began this, twenty-five years ago next January, we did it to bring together students and teachers from Ipswich, interested in music, of course, with people like them from all around the world. That was our ambition, and any pride we feel, well, it is pride in them. For a year or two, three at the most, they're able to indulge themselves almost entirely in their music, before setting out in their careers in science, or the arts. How many do you think," she said, "how many of our students otherwise would see Alaska? Ever see its beauty? How many would see California, Santa Fé, New Orleans? Very few, I think. But because of the Ensemble, they make their way to Ipswich, and we take them to the world, and bring the world to them.'"

'And, she might have added: How many young Alaskans like talented Fiona Campbell, formerly of Wasilla, would have had the opportunity to travel the world playing their music in Rome and Tel Aviv, and revisiting her home?

'"We lived here when I was growing up," Campbell said. "My father," Maj. Andrew D. Campbell, USAFR, "was in the Judge Advocate General's office at Elmendorf. When he retired, and we moved back to New York for him to practice law," the lovely young Wellesley junior said, "I really didn't know if I'd ever see Alaska again. But now, here I am.

'"It's something I'll remember all my life," Fiona said. "I hate to see it end. It's good to come home again, nice to come back, and in some ways, I'd like never to leave again. But all of us, the ones from England, my friends from Florida and Kansas, all of us know that getting chosen for an Ensemble Year was the most exciting thing that's ever happened to us. It's really been wonderful.'

'The Ensemble will play an all-Bach program tonight at the Anchorage campus before moving on to Seattle, first stop on its eleven-city itinerary through the Lower 48.'

customers told the men in the truck they were giving them.

'Now,' Richards said, 'if we assume also that none of those customers actually knew the truck was going to be knocked off yesterday, had advance knowledge so they could fill up a couple sacks with newspapers and then claim insured losses that they didn't actually incur – and we don't have any indication of that – then the total was five-sixty-five, seven-fifty.'

'Wow,' the District Attorney said. The other four men at the table exchanged glances and small coughs.

'Well,' Richards said, 'yeah. It is a lot, and you combine it with the four-thirty-three plus they got in Danvers two years ago, same MO and some IDs, you can see why they don't have to do it very often. These folks've scooped almost a million bucks. They aren't doing this for thrills, and they're not the kind of people like your usual robbers that go out and blow the loot in Vegas or someplace like that two weeks after they get it. These people are doing this as an occupation, and like everybody else, they don't work any more often'n they absolutely have to.'

'How many of them, John?' the DA said.

'We think,' Richards said, 'we think probably a total of eight. Which, if we're right, is down one from two years ago. *If* what we got out of the witnesses then, if that was correct: that there were four people in the car that came up behind the truck there. This time there seems to've been three. You've got the two men and the woman in the car that takes the money. This time it was a Pontiac wagon they used, stolen in Middleboro Tuesday night. We've got a partial on the plates, four of six digits we're sure of, and if they're the ones we think they are then they were stolen on Newbury Street in Boston sometime between ten and eleven last night. So anyway, that's three in the car behind the truck.

'You've got two more in the car that blocks the truck from the front,' he said. 'This time they used a Buick Electra, stolen off a dealer's lot in Maynard. Didn't get a reading on the plates. Should have one by this afternoon. We're assuming they were stolen too. Probably from some car at the airport or something, where the owner's not back yet so he doesn't know.

'So,' he said, 'we've got the three people in the Pontiac, and the woman and the guy riding shotgun with the woman in the Electra.'

Capt. Ralph Fraley of the Brockton Police Department raised his left hand. 'We are sure of that now, John?' he said. 'We're satisfied now that the second driver's definitely a woman?'

'Yup,' Richards said. 'This truck driver's certain. The guy in the Danvers job was so impressed with the grenade launcher it never really occurred to him to study the face of the driver. And of course there's no guarantee that this was the same individual behind the wheel at Danvers. But this time, yeah, we're sure. This is definitely a woman.' He paused. 'An ugly woman,' he said, grinning. '"Face like a potato," was what the trucker said, but definitely a woman.

'So,' he said, 'that gives you five at the scene. They leave, the two cars follow the same escape plan they used at Danvers. Go barrel-assing out onto Twenty-four, one goes north and one goes south, and all of us go apeshit, stepping on our own dicks and falling down a lot. So they get away. We found the Pontiac in Bridgewater, parked on a nice quiet lane and just as empty as could be.'

'Prints?' Ward Keane said.

'Nope,' Richards said. 'We don't think so, anyway. Oh, we'll probably find latents of the rightful owners, mechanics, that kind of thing, if we look hard enough. But everything you could reasonably've expected the bastards to touch in the couple days since they've had it – rear bumper where they attached the plates, steering wheel, door handles, window cranks, all that kind of thing – is cleaner'n a nun's imagination.

'So,' Richards said, 'either the Pontiac was dumped next to an empty car, or else the Pontiac and the switch car arrived at the most a few minutes apart. Which we think is probably how they did that. Because if they left another car there unattended, somebody might come along and spot it for a hot one, and have it towed away. And this group's methodical. They time every-thing, and they execute it according to plan, and they don't take any unnecessary chances. Unless you count threatening people with machineguns and shotguns and grenade launchers is taking chances, which I happen to, myself, but that's another story. But anyway, now we're up to six perpetrators, and we've still got to account for the man and the woman in the Buick.

'The Buick we found in Randolph this morning. Same kind of thing: secluded lane. No apparently useful prints. No witnesses to the switch. Therefore, same conclusion: at least one more driver who meets them there with the next car. We're assuming, by the way, that the switch cars are both legal. That if you stopped them, all the papers are in order. We're now up to seven participants.'

'So why do you say "eight"?' Fraley said.

'Because of the precision, Ralph,' Richards said. 'For robbers, these are very careful people. What's that line about genius? "An infinite capacity for taking pains"? That's what these people show. There's at least one genius involved, and the bastard's not only giving us pains but he's taking them himself. And he's got his people drilled so that they don't screw things up after he maps them out. Very good discipline. Which means, not so incidentally, that the rest of this bunch are no slouches either, when it comes to thinking and doing. We're not dealing here with a group of retards, my friends. These are sharp minds we've got on our hands, making these withdrawals. We're not going to catch them in the process of pulling their next job, two years or so from now, unless we happen to get awfully lucky. Which means we'd better catch them before, if that is possible. I'm not sure that it is.' He made eye contact with each of the other men before continuing.

'Anyway,' he said, 'people like that're not going to take a chance that someone might have their safe-house staked out by the time they get back. So that they walk into our fond embrace when they get back to it. They're going to have somebody babysitting that place, listening to a scanner, and probably ready with a CB radio to warn them off if it sounds like we've got a tail as well. So there's your eighth member.

'I'm not saying here,' Richards said, 'I'm not saying here that eight's the most that it could be. Could very possibly be more. But almost certainly it's at least eight, at least two of whom are females. The rest we do not know.

'Which of course is also unusual,' Richards said. 'I know we've all heard about Bonnie and Clyde, and all that stuff. Ma Barker, broads like that. But just the same, it's not very often these days that we see women robbing armored trucks. They've got easier ways to get lots of money.'

'Unless,' Fraley said, 'the one that's the driver is as ugly as you say. Then she wouldn't have.' The other five men laughed.

'Well, I didn't see her myself, Ralph,' Richards said. 'I'm just going on the driver's, the truck driver's word. But yeah, that could be, I suppose.

'Next thing that sort of sticks out in this one,' Richards said, 'is that while we don't know yet what denominations of bills they got this time, and we may never know, we were able at the time to reconstruct the deposits they swiped in the Danvers job. And that was a peculiar job from that point of view, because it included an unusually large number of fifty-dollar bills. About ten thousand dollars" worth of brand-new fifties that the stores handed out in raffles to promote this early sale. Your cash receipt came out with a red star on it, and you'd spent at least fifty bucks, the purchases were free and you got a crisp new fifty, too. Which naturally the lucky customers spent just as fast as they could, before they left the mall. So they were in the bank's deposits when the thieves showed up.

'Those fifties hadn't been circulated,' Richards said. 'The Federal Reserve had records of consecutive serial numbers. So naturally we said: "Aha," and put the usual guys who buy hot money under more surveillance'n the President gets. And we circulated the list to racetracks and casinos and other joints like that, where the big spenders go.

'Got nothing,' he said. 'Came up as empty as a pail. Which means that the people who took the money either didn't have or didn't choose to use anybody's cut-rate laundry service, and did have the self-control either to hold onto those fifties until they cooled off and the lists came down, dumped them in some country abroad, or maybe never parted with them at all. Or destroyed them. Which is also possible. Like I said, they don't take risks.'

'So what?' Fraley said.

'So this,' Richards said. He began ticking off points on his fingers. 'This gang does not include anybody with a record. If they've done this before, except for Danvers, using a different MO, they haven't been caught doing it.

'Therefore,' he said, 'we're not going to get anyplace boiling informers and torturing the usual ham-and-eggers 'till they talk, because the usual ham-and-eggers don't know these people either. Tendency we have – and I include myself in this – the tendency we have is to look at cops and robbers like it was a monopoly. Like the cops know all the robbers, and the robbers know the cops, and all you have to do when a robbery's committed is figure out which robbers are the ones did it this time. We work like the line-backers in football: when the ball's snapped, charge right in and start picking up bodies until you find the one that's got the ball. Throw that one on the ground, and then your job is done until the next play begins. No trick to it at all.

'Usually we're right,' he said. 'Which is why we are compla-cent, and why a bunch of amateurs – in our terms, that is – why a bunch of amateurs can pull off one of these raids every couple or so years, and then sit back and laugh. We may *say* we're looking for the robbers, but we're not. What we're doing, what we gener-ally do, is inspecting the selection of robbers we know to see if any of them look like the particular robbers that we want. And these characters don't. If we saw them on the street, walking right outside this building, we'd ignore them unless they carried signs confessing.'

'If they're not robbers,' the District Attorney said, 'just what are they, John?'

'Longhairs,' Richards said. 'They're a bunch of goddamn long-hairs that got bored with protesting the war and branched out. That's the only way you can account for all of it. The descrip-tions: fatigue jackets, hiking boots, beards, the granny glasses, the presence of females – no self-respecting chap from Charlestown'd get himself up like that, even to confuse us. And if he did, he'd give it away. Wear a couple gold chains around his neck. And he wouldn't show his face, either. He'd wear some sort of mask. And he would fence the money, and he'd blow it on a horse and a couple high-priced whoors. And furthermore, it has to be, this has to be the explanation, because it's also the only way you can account for the planning, the precision. These are novices. They're at most in their middle twenties or so, and so far as we know, yesterday's job was only their second. But they pulled it off just like they did the first one. Split-second execution. Got to have brains for that, gentlemen. Got to be intelligent. And where do bright young minds go these days to learn about fascist dictatorships and capitalist dogs? To colleges is where they go, and that's where ours came from.'

'So what do we do, John?' the District Attorney said. 'Plug the NCIC computers into the College Board records and pick out the brightest ones?'

Richards laughed. 'Yeah,' he said, 'we could do that. See if they've started testing for aptitude in military tactics. Those will be our friends. But, no, Ward, that won't work. What we have got to do is sit down and do something that we don't enjoy that much, which is think very hard about how they manage to schedule these jobs to the second. How long before the cars roll up and the guns come out do they start collecting information? How do they go about it? Are they staking out these banks, timing the deliveries? That's what we've got to do.'

'That isn't going to be easy, John,' Fraley said. 'You're not saying what I came here to hear you say, that we will catch these bastards, no matter how long that may take. What you're saying is that they'll not only probably, but certainly, commit the third one before we figure out the second.'

'Oh,' Richards said, 'if I gave you a different impression, I certainly didn't mean to. That's exactly what I'm saying. But look at it this way, all right? We've got two years to think.'

Late in the afternoon of October 19, 1972, Florence Amberson Walker in a seminar room at Marble Preparatory School in Manhattan addressed nineteen young men and women responding to an invitation to discuss 'International Vistas in Music.'

'All of you were invited,' she said, 'because each of you has shown not only special ability in one or another of your academic fields, but because each of you has also shown that you have talent in music as well. One or two of you, in fact – and I think this is ironic – have so much musical talent that, your teachers tell me, now and then it's interfered a little with your regular studies.

'I am not here to tell you that you should forget about your plans – you, for example, Rodney, to attend Caltech; you, Jane, to go to Vassar – or in any way relinquish the great opportunities you have before you in your fields. In fact I will be the first to say that unless you have musical talents bordering on genius, it would be folly for you or anyone else to follow them exclusively.

'What I am here to tell you, to make you aware of, is that there are programs available that can enable you to enjoy and make use of your talents in music while interfering only slightly, if at all, with your studies and career plans. Programs that will let you use your abilities to enrich your intellectual lives, expand your knowledge of the world, make friends you'd never have. And I'm not speaking here just about the various university choral groups and orchestras, the bands and the other organizations that will certainly be recruiting you when you matriculate next fall. I am talking about an organization that probably few of you have heard of, that can and will provide to some, perhaps to some of you, a year of travel, cultural refreshment and excitement you'll remember a long time.

'This is not,' she said, 'this is *not* a program primarily intended for people who expect to make their careers in music. How many of you know who Tom Oates is?' Nine hands were raised. 'Of course,' she said 'Probably one of the most provocative young personalities in television today. Tom makes all of us think, every night that he comes on. But we who support the Ipswich Ensemble, well, we like to think perhaps some of his awareness, whatever you may think of his position on Vietnam, that some of his fire and conviction come from the year he spent with the orchestra, while he was at Dartmouth. Music, well, I'm sure Tom would be the first to admit that music was not his métier. But he was good enough, and bright enough, to qualify for the Ensemble, and it broadened his outlook. And that's what I'm talking about. If my daughter does end up teaching music, her life will have been enhanced by her year. And that's what we're offering to you.

'Now I know,' she said, 'I know that many of your parents have made sacrifices, big sacrifices, to get you to this point. And I know that no matter how many scholarships you may have, how many loans there are, you have to think, they have to think, about the cost of things. And some of you might say: "Well, Mrs. Walker, that's all well and good for you, to talk about a year off and go around the world, but there are other things, you know, we have to think about." And I want to answer that.

'The organization I'm referring to is called the Ipswich Ensemble. It exists to find, attract, *and support*, young people like yourselves. Young people who have more to offer themselves and the world than just the intelligence they can bring to engineering, or chemistry, or medicine, or physics, or literature – whatever you'd care to name. It's under the auspices of the University of Ipswich, in England. If you're lucky, and are chosen, it provides you with a year of study there – with credits you can transfer to virtually any American college or university, so you won't lose any time – and, without any expense to you, travel throughout the world, for one simply glorious year. Next year's tour, starting in March, has visits scheduled to Vienna, Milan, Madrid, Bermuda, Miami, California, Mexico City, Caracas, Melbourne, and then a stop in Hong Kong before returning home.' The students exchanged grins. 'When Christina toured,' Walker said, 'well, if you're excited, hearing about it, you can imagine how she felt, appearing as a soloist in Toronto, Chicago, Mexico City, all along the West Coast, Manila, Canberra and then Cairo.

'But I'm sorry to say you're all too late for next year's trip,' she said, smiling. 'And you're probably, unless you're taking early admission in the second semester this year, probably too late for the tour we're already planning for nineteen-seventy-four.' They looked crestfallen. 'But don't be discouraged,' she said. 'We've, well, the Ensemble's been doing this now for twenty-seven years, and the only comment I've ever heard *any* of the musicians make, when they visit New York or the East, is that whatever trip they've happened to be on, it was "the best one yet." If you're chosen, well, you may not get to Tehran, in your particular year, but that will be only because Frankfurt, or Brussels, or Oslo or Kyoto, or maybe even Rio, made that impossible.'

The students looked happy again. One young man with dark curly hair raised his hand. 'Question?' she said. He stood up.

'Darren Jefferson,' he said. 'Mrs. Walker, I have two questions. First, I wondered whether Tom Oates, well, if his being Carl Oates's son had anything to do with him being selected.'

She smiled. 'Do you mean, Darren: "If your father's Carl Oates, and you're a famous broadcaster, does that give you an advantage?"'

He shrugged. 'If you like,' he said.

'No,' she said, 'it did not. Tom applied, and auditioned, and he was chosen. As I've tried to suggest, while some musical ability is necessary, it's not the paramount concern. Nor is your family tree.'

Jefferson nodded. 'Okay,' he said. 'And the second thing is: I just wondered: Is there any chance this orchestra would go to Peking or Moscow? Because I'm thinking of specializing in Russian and Chinese studies, and something like that would help.'

'Where?' she said.

'I'm not sure,' he said. 'U of Chicago, most likely.'

'We've had several Chicago students in the Ensemble,' she said. 'One of them, from Boston – Alton Badger is his name – one of them's a private investigator. Another of them's a member of the Society of Jesus, and two have gone on to work with the Department of Defense. In various capacities. So it certainly wouldn't do you any harm, a year with the Ensemble.'

'That isn't what I meant,' Jefferson said. 'I meant: I want to see those places. Visit them. And I'd like to know whether the Ensemble's ever gone there. To Russia or China.'

'I don't believe so,' she said.

'Why?' he said. 'Do you think it ever might?'

She didn't answer for a moment. Then she shook her head slightly. 'There's no,' she said, 'there's no policy I know of that

21

would rule that out. But neither, so far as I know, has such a visit ever been made. Whether it's because of visa problems, or language barriers, or what the reason is – I really don't know.'

'So the orchestra just doesn't travel to the Iron Curtain countries?' he said.

'It has not,' she said.

'And,' he said, 'do you think it will?'

She sighed. 'No,' she said, 'I don't.'

3

At 2:00 P.M., Atty. Gen. Colin Reese of Massachusetts suggested that the five executives representing Brinks, Wells Fargo and Purolater take chairs on the window side of the long conference table in his State House office. He placed his Deputy Attorney General, Paul Green, on his right, and the Chief of his Criminal Division, Andrew Boyd, on his left.

'And Lieutenant,' he said to John Richards, 'why don't you sit next to Andy, there. And you, Ward,' he said, 'next to John.' He addressed the courier executives as his visitors took their seats. 'I was unable to reach the District Attorney of Norfolk County after your call yesterday. Mister Osgood's office informed my office that he's attending the funeral of a relative out of state, and won't be back until Wednesday. Peter Mahoney, District Attorney Peter Mahoney of Essex, would like very much to be with us today, but his wife's having a baby, and he said if he knows what's good for him, he'll be in labor too. So he asked to be excused.' He grinned and the executives forced smiles. 'Guess even dedicated public servants should get days off for stuff like that.'

Reese, at thirty-eight, two years before had parlayed his ability to use his physical presence (he was six-two and weighed a solid hundred and ninety pounds), his handsome features and resonant voice into an unexpected election victory over an incumbent Democrat who dismissed him as a 'pretty boy' and campaigned listlessly. Disparaging Reese as a man whose chief accomplishment was 'looking better in a blue suit than Ted Williams did in red socks,' he had given Reese the opening to unveil a ready wit. Reese took it, saying his opponent's record for errors in office was the worst compiled in Massachusetts since Dick Stuart stopped playing first base for the Red Sox, and made himself a favorite politician among TV news reporters. Holding as the result the highest elective office of any Republican in the State, Reese was widely, publicly and correctly assumed to be planning not only his campaign for re-election as Attorney General in 1976, but a 1978 campaign for the US Senate.

Ward Keane, like the other District Attorneys of the Commonwealth (all of them Democrats), regarded Reese with a complex mixture of feelings: envy of his relatively youthful success; fear of his state constitutional authority to supersede them in any case that he might choose; secret hope of replacing him if he won the Senate seat; and wistfulness that he and the other DAs had in two years been unable to maneuver Reese into accepting responsibility for investigations that looked hopeless to their eyes.

Keane had called Osgood's office after he received Reese's invitation. Osgood's secretary gave him the number of the hotel in Manchester, Vermont, where Osgood stayed when he took his wife to the races at Saratoga. 'You know, Dave,' he said, 'if that bastard Reese finds out what you're doing, he'll leak it to somebody. Guy gets shot in a robbery in your district, and where do you go? To the track. Will not look good in the papers. Won't look good at all.' Osgood had replied first that he had in fact attended the funeral of a distant cousin the preceding Saturday in Woodstock, Vermont, and secondly that if Reese wanted to start 'that kind of pissing contest, I'll tell a few folks what I know about him, and where he stays when he rambles.'

Keane had then called Peter Mahoney. 'Whaddaya think, Pete?' he had said, and Mahoney in his Salem office had said: 'You mean: 'Is he gonna take this goddamned pile of turds off our hands?" The answer is: he's not. He's gonna feint and jab and dance like hell, and when the meeting's over those armored-car guys're gonna go out of there just as pissed off and mad at us as they'll be when they go in. But not at him, Ward, not at him. You'll be going back to Brockton with your three pounds of shit in a two-pound bag, and I'll be back up here, with my bag of shit, and when Dave gets back from losing his customary five hundred bucks on the ponies, his shareshit will still be there, in the middle of his desk. And debonair Attorney General Gene Kelly'll be tap-dancing his way through the six o'clock news, singin' in the fuckin' rain that's fuckin' drowning us.'

Graham Foster, regional security manager of Purolater, appeared to have been designated the chief spokesman for the courier executives. Nominally ranked below Edward Mackiewicz, the regional general manager to his left, Foster's twenty years' pre-Purolater experience as an FBI Special Agent gave him a superior familiarity with law enforcement matters that the other managers lacked. 'General,' he said, 'Lieutenant, I'll be brief and

25

I'll be candid. Brief because we didn't ask to come here today in order for you to hear what we've got to say. You can guess that, and you have. Brief, also, because what we did come here for was to hear what you have got to say. And candid because as everybody in this room knows, every single one of us has got a damned big problem here and we've got to figure out what to do about it. We've got a twenty-four-year-old kid lying in the Brigham today with two bullets in his spine. He's going to live – if you call what a twenty-four-year-old paraplegic does for his next fifty years on earth a form of living, I don't, but many do – but that's just a matter his having been a little bit luckier than he might have been. Sooner or later, whether it's my company, or Jake Nolan's here, or Tom Hammond's here, or someone else's company that hasn't been hit so far, sooner or later one of us's going to wind up going to a funeral for some hardworking family man that never did a damned thing in the world except try to feed his wife and kids, guarding other people's property. So, what are we going to do about it? Or maybe I should begin by saying: 'What are *you* folks going to do about it, since it's your jobs to do it? And when is it you plan to start?'"

The Attorney General looked stern. He folded his hands on the table. 'Now Graham,' he said. 'I hope by my seating arrangements here you didn't get the idea I wanted or expected this to become an adversarial proceeding. Because I don't see it as that at all, and I didn't when I welcomed Ed's request for it. Basically the reason that I asked Ward, and Peter, although he couldn't come, and Dave, who couldn't be here either on notice as short as this, and Paul and Andy here, and of course, Lieutenant Richards who I understand's been coordinating all of these investigations into these things, that reason was my belief that the government and the private sector, representatives of the private sector, need to have these meetings when they have a common problem. To see what each of them can do to correct it. Not to blame each other for the fact that they've got it, and exchange heated accusations.'

Foster held up his hand. 'Let me interrupt, if I may, General,' he said.

Reese smiled. 'Go right ahead,' he said. 'That's what we're here for.'

'The fact of the matter,' Foster said, 'and I don't want any of us to lose sight of this, but the fact of the matter is that we do *not* have a common problem. We have different problems. Yours is that you happen to be the chief law enforcement officer of this Commonwealth. That's the job you sought, and that's the job you've got. Our problem is that you, and the people who work for you and Mister Keane and the other DAs, aren't doing that job. Not saying that's your fault, or that all of you aren't trying. But, fact remains, jobs're not getting done. If they were, our problem wouldn't exist.'

'Is that a fact?' Reese said. 'Do you honestly think your man got shot yesterday in Braintree because the Attorney General was busy with something else? That's ridiculous. Let me ask you something: Why did he draw his gun? Why was he even carrying a gun in the first place, as far as that goes? My clear recollection from my days in the General Court is that there've been repeated, numerous, almost annual pieces of legislation intended to reduce the number of non-law enforcement personnel allowed to carry guns, and every time one of those bills's been offered, your people have been among the loudest in their opposition. And the argument's been made, time and time again, that sooner or later one of these amateur – and I use that word deliberately – amateur cops that thinks he's Wyatt Earp is going to get himself into a gun battle that'll end up with him or some other innocent person getting badly hurt or killed. And you, not necessarily you personally, but your industry, you've rejected it, rejected it, rejected it. Time and time again.

'Well,' Reese said, 'what happened last Thursday at the South Shore Plaza is the proof of the pudding, I see it. A young man who overestimated his ability got himself badly hurt. Just as all those people you opposed, predicted for so many years. What's bothering you gentlemen here today – and I mean no insult by this because it's bothering me as well, I can assure you – but what's really on your mind here today is that you're, Purolater is, you're going to end up paying a multimillion dollar judgment, or settlement, to this paralytic. And you know just as well as I do what the grounds of that lawsuit're going to be: that you failed to give him proper, adequate training; that you did give him a firearm he did not know how to use; that you should've foreseen what would happen, even if you didn't; and now he is crippled for life.

'Now,' Reese said, 'my position on the necessity for cooperation between the private sector and the government is well known. Where it doesn't exist, I want it to begin. Where it does exist, to continue and improve. That is what I want.'

Foster, looking grim, opened his mouth as Reese shot his left cuff, looked at his gold watch, and stood up. Foster closed his mouth. 'Now,' Reese said, buttoning his jacket, 'I'm afraid I must ask you gentlemen to excuse me. I have a commitment of long-standing to be in the House at two-thirty sharp. One of my former law partners is being sworn in as a probate judge, and I simply must be there. So, you gentlemen make yourselves at home here, stay as long as you like, and see what you can work out as our response to this thing. Paul and Andy here have my complete authority. And I assure you, gentlemen,' he said, slapping his right hand on the table, 'I assure you that whatever plan you come up with will have my own, personal, full, complete, and unstinting support.' He strode from the room.

Foster leaned back in his chair. He looked at Richards. He looked at Green and Boyd, who shifted uneasily in their chairs. He looked at Keane. He looked back at Richards. 'John,' he said, 'tell me something: Does somebody breed those guys? Like fancy dogs and horses? Is there some farm somewhere that grows them, attorney generals, US attorneys, all those guys like that?'

Richards laughed. He shook his head. 'He's all right, Graham,' he said. He nodded toward Boyd. 'I'll vouch for Andy,' he said. He nodded toward Keane. 'And for Ward, too.' He smiled at Green. 'Paul here I don't know too well,' he said, 'since we just met when I got here today. But he's probably all right. And Peter, Peter's wife really is having a baby. So, don't take it so hard. The people you've got to work with, we're all in the room, and that guy that left'll back them, just like he said he would.'

Foster stared at Richards. 'Huh,' he said, 'sure. And when I get home tonight my wife'll be the spitting image, Gina Lollobrigida.'

Richards glanced quickly at Green and Boyd. Green's young face was troubled. Boyd, at thirty-two, four years younger than Green, was harder. His jaw was set and his eyes were narrow. Richards nodded. 'Okay,' he said, looking back to Foster, 'lemme ask you a couple things, so we can see where we go. You talk to Matt Lund about this problem?'

Foster blinked. He worked his mouth. 'I don't see what that's got to do with this,' he said.

Richards said: 'Uh huh.' He leaned back in his chair and

massaged his ear with the first two fingers of his left hand. 'Tells me what I want to know, though, doesn't it? Tells me that before you came in here, breathing fire and smoke, telling everybody where to go and how to get there, tells me you called up your old pal, the Special Agent in Charge, and you bounced this difficulty off of him. And I bet I can almost imagine what you said to him, can't I? You said: "Hey Matt, old pal, old buddy, this stuff got stolen from us, it was moving, interstate commerce. We had checks and stuff aboard, you know, in our custody, from other jurisdictions. And those deposits, they're from federally insured banks. So how about the FBI comes in on this with us, give us a little hand? How's about banging it past the USA and getting authority, investigate interstate transportation, stolen property. Or theft from federally insured banks."'

Foster looked uncomfortable. Richards leaned forward in his chair. 'And I bet,' he said, 'I would just bet that one of two things happened then. Either Lund said he would do it, bounce it off the US Attorney, and then got back to you and said you know what a bastard the guy is, he won't turn the Bureau loose. Or else he told you the truth, which is that he would rather go rub shit on his head'n have to explain to Washington how come he got the Bureau involved. I bet I could almost quote him, couldn't I. I bet he said something like: "Jesus H. Christ, Graham, you gotten simple since you left? Bureau only wants the cases it will *win*. Screw this package, buddy. I wouldn't touch this one with a goddamned barge pole."'

Foster chuckled. 'Pretty close,' he said. 'Pretty goddamned close. He did the first bit. Took it the US Attorney, and USA turned him down.'

'Sure he did,' Richards said. 'And I believe him, too. He went over to the courthouse and said to the man in there: "Graham Foster's got this cockeyed idea we ought to get ourselves in this mess the State boys got, and I think if you okay it you should be committed for a nice long rest in a very quiet place." And the USA said: "Thanks for the advice, Matt. Blow it out of here."'

'So,' Richards said, 'since you discovered you're not going to get Matt on the evening news reading one of those stirring statements about how the FBI is throwing its unmatched resources into the armored-car robbery investigation ... Would Matt say "investigation", Graham? Or would he say "manhunt"?' Green and Boyd were grinning.

'He would say "investigation"', Foster said, smiling. 'The press would say: "manhunt."'

'Right,' Richards said, 'of course. But anyway, since he isn't going to do that, you decided you'd come in here today with a broomstick up your ass and see if you could bully the AG into doing what the Bureau will not do. Which is get the heat off you at headquarters by having Mister Reese go out in front of the cameras and get their minds off you. And because people like you always get stuffed by Mister Reese, you now have the feeling that you have just had six pounds of breadcrumbs rammed up your ass.'

Foster joined in the laughter. 'All right,' he said, 'all right.'

'Now,' Richards said, 'if we can all conduct ourselves in these palatial quarters like we actually belonged here, maybe we can actually get something done. Let me tell you what we've actually got, and then if you've got something we don't have, you can tell me that.'

He glanced around the table at the prosecutors. 'I can at least finally tell all you guys that I think we're making some progress.

Since the last one, down in Brockton, we're pretty sure we've gotten hard IDs on the two ringleaders. Well, the ringleader and the assistant ringleader.'

'Excuse me, John,' Keane said, 'but how'd you manage that?'

'Stopped doing what wasn't working,' Richards said, 'and started trying to find something that would. Years ago, I was down in the Norwell barracks, met this kid that used to hang around the Waterford police station. Name of Alton Badger. Bright as hell. Think he was about fifteen, he went to college. And he was a cop buff. So through him I got to know his uncle, Larry Badger, runs this industrial security outfit over the Prudential. And I called up Larry and I said to him: "Larry, you guys ever do any work, any these defense contract types that had trouble with the longhairs?" And he said: "Sure. And Alton, he probably knows even more'n I do. He had the Dow Chem and the Dupont disturbances, the defoliant and napalm protests. Come by and have a chat. Give you anything we've got."'

'So I did,' Richards said. 'Alton runs about two, three hundred names he's got through his goddamned machines, comes up with couple names he remembers always on the violent fringe. Days of Rage and all that shit – he was in Chicago, at the University. Knew the troublemakers there, plus the visitors, and kept up his collection when he joined his uncle's firm. And he says these guys fit our bill. Big one comes from around here, and he's dropped out of sight. Matches the description, right age and all that stuff. So that's what we're going on.

'Ringleader's a young charmer named Samuel F. Tibbetts. Born, Newton Wellesley Hospital, March ten, nineteen-forty-seven. Parents Walter J. Tibbetts, Ellen Davis Tibbetts. Father's employment: research chemist. Then for W.R. Grace Company,

Cambridge. Now for Monsanto, Springfield. Members, Saint Mark's Episcopal Church, which our young Samuel attended faithfully and assisted on the altar. Graduated Newton South High School, nineteen-sixty-four, very highest honors. Editor of yearbook, varsity letters all four years in cross-country and track, All-State and All-New England band clarinetist, senior class treasurer, National Merit Scholarship winner, all-round American boy who would've almost certainly made Eagle Scout, and I'm not kidding here, if he hadn't've decided to use that scholarship, plus one he got from Stanford, move out to the west coast. Graduated Stanford, nineteen-sixty-eight, *summa cum laude*. Entered graduate school, Berkeley, same year, advanced fellow in mathematics. Candidate for Ph.D. First term, completed first quarter of that year. Did not enroll for second term, January nineteen-sixty-nine, and has not done so since.'

'This is a robber?' Foster said. 'This is a goddamned highwayman? Why the hell's he stealing, pointing guns at people? All he's got to do, have money thrown at him, was keep on the way he's going, and he'd swim in the damned stuff. If my kids'd had what he got, got and threw away, the whole family would've been delirious with joy.'

'Good question,' Richards said. 'I don't have the complete answer, but the question's very good. Apparently what happened was that studious young Sam got himself pretty heavily involved first in the uprisings against Lyndon Johnson, while Sam was still at Stanford. Then that summer, sixty-eight, he's down in Central America someplace, probably playing kissy-face with some goddamned guerillas, filling up his impressionable young mind with a load of communist shit. And then when he came up to Chicago to riot, Democratic National Convention, and went

33

on to Berkeley, the process just sort of continued. And he went from being against Johnson, because of the war that of course Sam didn't have to fight, being Two-S and all, to being against the whole, just society in general. And naturally Nixon, and anything else that anybody brought to his attention. Stopped reading his math books and started spending all his time with the radicals, getting himself a late education in Marxist theory and so forth. And by the time Christmas rolled around, and his papers in math were due, there was no way he could pass. So he just dropped out. Started this group Alton thinks they call "Bolivian Connection." "Contingent." Some fool thing like that. Ended up becoming the intimidating fellow with the thirty-caliber grease gun that we all admire so much. The one that paralyzed your guard there, what I understand. And in other ways, as well, no longer a model boy. Stopped writing to his parents, even calling them. Tell me they haven't heard from Sam – and I believe this, Graham – tell me they haven't heard from Sam in almost six years now. Don't know where he is. They have no idea.'

'Well,' Foster said, 'that last part, you may believe that, but I don't. The father may not know, but the mother does. The mothers always know. And the mothers never tell.'

Richards shrugged. 'Could be,' he said. 'I doubt it, but it certainly could be.

'Second guy,' he said. 'Deputy ringleader. James M. Walker, a.k.a. "Beau James." Born, New York Memorial Hospital, January ninth, nineteen-forty-five. Father, Clayton D. Walker, MD, then staff cardiologist, Columbia Presbyterian, now chief cardiologist, New York Memorial. Mother, Florence Amberson Walker. She's about half, maybe a quarter, black, I'm not sure which. Jamaican parents, one of them, at least. Born in London, where she met

Clayton during a research year. Naturalized American citizen. Concert cellist before her marriage. What I'm told, a very striking woman still. James has one sister, Christina, born nineteen-fifty-three, said to be an extremely beautiful young woman. Whether she's involved in this hootenanny, that I do not know. None of the descriptions we've been able to get of the women involved in these heists even remotely suggests that one of them's good-looking.

'James is quite dark,' Richards said. 'He's six-three, goes about two-ten, two-twenty. Supposedly very handsome, and not stupid, either. Apparently had some difficulty, though, deciding just exactly what the hell he was. Collegiate prep school in New York. Pretty good athlete, pretty good student, but never really distinguished himself, either line of work. Kind of kid everybody looks at and they're so impressed maybe their expectations for him're just impossible. So they're always just the littlest bit disappointed by what turns out.

'Anyway,' Richards said, 'James went to Columbia College for two years, starting in sixty-two. Did indifferently. Dropped out. Bummed around, apparently, until sixty-five, when he turns up on the coast. How he did that, without getting drafted, nobody seems to know. Establishes residence and then applies to San José State, where he graduates in sixty-seven, degree in mathematics. Heads for Berkeley where he gets into the graduate program for high school math teachers. Fiddles and diddles around, just scraping by on his grades, getting involved in all the demonstrations and stuff, probably doing some drugs. Getting laid a lot. And that's where he is when Sam Tibbetts arrives the next year. A natural follower, looking for a natural leader. Natural second-in-command, who has found his commander.

'Now,' Richards said, 'there are at least two, perhaps three, other

35

white males about the same age as these two monkeys that've been involved with them in the past. One of them's a kid whose last name's Mackenzie, we think. Reports we've got of some disturbances Sam and James were involved in on the campus at San José State have this kid named Mackenzie, Glenn Mackenzie, supposedly from Boston, listed on the arrest forms. But somehow the little bastard, if he's ever had his prints taken, they don't show up. Didn't register the draft, I assume – we're checking that as well. And when he was arrested, he wasn't carrying any ID. So all we really know's that a kid with blond hair and kind of a scraggly-assed beard was seen and arrested with Sam Tibbetts and James Walker at San José in May of nineteen-sixty-nine. And that he jumped bail. And we also know, as I say, that there's at least one and maybe two other white males whose names we do not know.

'Then we got the broads,' Richards said. 'I'm expecting verification that their names are Jill Franklin and Kathie Fentress. When I get it, I'll go to work on them. It is possible there's another one, name of Andrea Simone. And we understand there's one, name of Emma Handley, same status as far as we're concerned. We're working on them.

'The problem we've got here,' Richards said, 'well, there's several of them. Inna first place, these folks're cute. Banks have cameras inside. No cameras outside. Your normal bank robber goes in and either has his picture taken with a mask or without one, and we've got something to go on. But these people stay outside, so the only way we can get descriptions of them's by talking to civilians that were terrified, and guards scared out of their wits, as to what the bastards look like. So we're always piecing things together, never sure we've got them right.

'Then there's the other problem. None of the regular people

we've got who hear things hears things about this group. They're not part of the underworld network. They're hermetically sealed off. They're ideologues. We think they're common criminals, but they think they're revolutionaries. We can't nail down locations. The only thing we ever get is old, stale news about where they used to be, some time ago. Not where they might be now. It's damned hard work, I can tell you. Very frustrating. It's taken us four years to get even this far. We've made some progress, sure, but it's awful time-consuming. That's what the problem is, and that's why your man's lying in the hospital today.'

Mackiewicz cleared his throat. 'How can we help?' he said.

Foster cut in. 'Let me see if I can expedite things,' he said. 'Our three companies have discussed, and we're prepared to offer, a reward in the total amount of fifty thousand dollars to the person or persons coming forward with information leading to the arrest and conviction of these bandits. You think that might help?'

'It's worth a try,' Richards said. 'It certainly won't hurt. These buggers're crafty, but they've also been lucky. Could be one of the rascals that was in one stick-up but not the others might get talkative for that. Maybe there's one of them, feels left out. Might like some revenge. Especially if he got paid. These're not professionals. Not all of them, at least. They don't understand the rules. It could help a lot.'

'All right,' Foster said, 'then we'll do that.' He glanced at Green and Boyd. 'When we came in here today, what I hoped to do was have the Attorney General announce the reward offer.' He looked at Keane. 'Now I feel differently,' he said. 'Those punks nearly killed one of our men and stole four hundred thirty-eight thousand dollars from our truck last Thursday in the South Shore Plaza. Since Mister Mahoney can't be here today, and Mister Osgood isn't, and they're the other DAs whose jurisdictions are involved, I'd like you, Mister Keane, to announce this reward tonight.'

Keane looked worried. 'Graham,' he said, 'look. I'd like to do it. But a day won't make any difference, will it? Don't you think it might make more sense to wait until I can round up Dave and Peter, and have a joint appearance?'

'In other words,' Foster said, 'you're afraid your colleagues'll think you're grandstanding.'

Richards was watching Green and Boyd. Green was frowning, turning a pencil end for end, over and over, on the table top. Boyd's face was set. 'Andy,' Richards said, 'you've been awful quiet. Let's have some input from you here, you and Paul as well. How would you rate the chances that when Colin gets back from his ceremony and finds out about this, he'll call a press conference this very afternoon to announce this big reward? You wanna tell me that?'

Boyd looked at Green and grinned. 'Couldn't speculate, John,' he said. 'You wanna take a shot, Paul? Tell him what you think?'

Green stared at Foster. 'Everything you got today came from John Richards,' he said. 'John Richards works for the AG, coordinating this investigation. If Mister Keane, Mister Osgood or Mister Mahoney with their investigators or local police, if one of them cracks one of these things, Mister Reese will not interfere with that prosecution. But if Lieutenant Richards puts it together before any of them does, then Mister Reese's office will prosecute.'

Foster cleared his throat. 'You understand that, John?' he said.

'Certainly do,' Richards said. 'What Paul means is that if your companies want maximum exposure of your good news to your employees, and the families of employees, you'd better stand up beside Colin Reese on tonight's news. And if you don't want that,

I do, because Colin gets coverage. The more drifters, longhairs, and other bums that get a chance to hear what he's got to say, the better the chances something will come out of it.'

Foster looked at Green and Boyd. 'Makes sense,' he said with distaste. 'When'll the bastard be back?'

Green looked at his watch. 'I told the media this morning,' he said, 'we might have a thirty-second bite for them at four. If you can wait until then, I think he will be back.'

4

In the early morning, Lawrence Badger in a dark blue suit nipped at the waist was escorted by a captain in the bar of Boston's Ritz Carlton Hotel to Florence Walker's table at the southwest corner window. She had a martini and small carafe in front of her, and was nibbling salted peanuts. She stood up, smoothing the rose silk of her dress over her hips, and offered her cheek for his kiss. He sat down, glancing at the captain and nodding toward her drink. The captain went away.

'I rapped at you on the window,' she said. 'I forget about the dark glass – some see out but none sees in.'

He smiled. 'And no one sees through clearly,' he said. 'How've you been keeping, lady?'

She shook her head. 'Fairness is lacking,' she said. 'I suppose it's the sins of my scarlet past, but somehow it seems unjust to me that the older I become, the more problems I seem to have.'

'You and time,' he said. 'You remind me sometimes of Alton. When he was a little boy, and used to visit me, every night before bedtime, had to chase the bears away. And I finally said to him: 'Alton, not to make fun of your game. But there aren't any bears in here, you know. Never have been, never will. Is it really necessary for me to get under the bed and shine a light like this? We've never found a single bear, and I'm getting old, you know." And he said: "That's why we haven't, Uncle Larry – they know we're watching out." And that's how you are with the ravages of the years – you think if you talk about them all the time, none will ever come.'

She smiled. 'Your hair seems darker than I recalled it,' she said. 'And I notice you're thinner, as well.'

He returned her smile. 'Well,' he said, 'each of us deals in our own way with time. And I must say, on what I see, your methods seem to work well. You look all right to me.'

'Well, I don't feel right,' she said. 'I do not feel right at all.' A waiter delivered a second martini and poured it from the carafe. She pushed the peanuts away from her. 'I don't know why I eat these things,' she said. 'Take them away from me.'

Badger put the nut dish on the window ledge. He sipped his drink. 'All right, tell me,' she said. 'Tell me what's going on.'

'You're sure?' he said. 'Jet lag and all, it won't bother you?'

She made a dismissive gesture. 'Not coming this way,' she said. 'I was exhausted, the first day in London,' she said, 'but after that I was all right. Of course Clayton's upstairs, snoring away, else he'd never be able to have dinner tonight. But I feel well enough.'

'Maybe I should wait 'till Clayton's up,' he said. No use going through all this twice.'

'Larry,' she said, 'spare me this elaborate charade of including Clayton in on everything. Why do you think I asked you for

41

drinks? So he wouldn't be here, of course. You tell me what you've got to tell me. I'll decide what Clayton needs.'

'He's well?' Badger said.

'Clayton's Clayton,' she said. 'He had a lovely time for himself, posturing and prancing all over London, half the English doctors fawning on him, half the Americans looking pained. Claire and Neville came up from Ipswich, and of course we had a lovely time with them, and then Carl Oates, whom I *cannot* stand, came through with this year's bride, and so of course they joined the group.'

'Which one is this?' Badger said. 'I think I've lost track.'

'Yes,' she said, 'well, easy to remember – you've had two, so double that. And if you don't hear from Carl for another year, well then, triple it. That's how you can keep track. If only they didn't keep getting younger. This one can't be more than twenty-five. I'm sure she's a perfectly delightful child, but my goodness, when she joins the ladies we just have an awful time. She must be younger than his son. Surely he wouldn't bring Tom along, and expect him to join Clayton and Neville for cigars. It really isn't fair, not to her or us.'

'I heard he and Tom were at odds,' Badger said.

'"Odds"?' she said. '"Odds"? They were at daggers' points. We saw Carl in Paris last year – he was on his way to cover something at Geneva, or he'd just come back, or something – and so of course nothing else would do but that we get together at the Lipp for dinner, and Carl and Clayton got positively stinking drunk, as they always do, and they went through all that boring rot you people like to do about the good old days of war, brave comrades in arms, and then when that was finished, Carl … well, Clayton said something, I don't know what it really was, and somehow

Tom's name came up. And I gather, well, apparently Tom'd still not made his peace with his father about their views on Vietnam. And Carl was perfectly awful. Yelling and screaming about this cowardly son he'd had, "never speak to him again," all that sort of thing. Although from what I could gather, it did seem to me that Carl's anger was more that Tom'd contradicted on *his* show what Carl'd been saying on *his* show – that it was more one of those old-stag, young-stag battles than what Carl made it out to be. Which was patriotism. So, when we got to London, naturally I saw Claire, and asked her, and she said he'd been the same way, out in San Francisco when the orchestra was there. So, yes, they had a falling-out all right. But that at least didn't come up, at least not this time. This time it was just Carl and his fresh wife, and the other four of us.'

'You and Claire had time to talk?' Badger said.

'We were hampered by the showgirl,' Walker said, 'but yes, we did find time.'

'Because I wasn't sure how to reach you,' he said, 'and not wanting to take chances, I thought the best thing to do was just brief Claire enough so she could alert you, and see you when you got back.'

'Yes,' Walker said. 'Well, that was nice, and right, of you. It's the police, I take it? They're finally after James?'

'Put it this way,' Badger said, 'if they're not today, if they weren't when I briefed Claire, then they will be very shortly.'

She grimaced. 'I've been expecting this, of course,' she said. 'But it doesn't make it easy, just the same.'

He looked worried. 'You understand,' he said, 'it wasn't anything we volunteered. Anything like that. That we have to cooperate with the cops.'

'I know that,' she said. 'Up to a point, at least.'

'Up to a point,' he said. 'Which point they haven't reached, as yet, so we're cooperating.'

'But you're still free to talk to me,' she said. 'You can still tell me.'

'Up to a point,' Badger said, 'up to a point, I can. And I can certainly tell you things, that I might not tell them. Nothing that will hinder them – that's too dangerous. But things that wouldn't help them, really, that might be embarrassing? Those I hold back, best I can.'

'Like what?' she said.

'Well,' he said, sipping again, 'like the Ensemble. The minute that my friend the cop opened up his mouth, I could see it hanging there like that old blue banner with the gold Neville used to cart around. So I told Alton, when he was making his runs, to purge any files he got. Keep the Ensemble out.'

'I don't see,' she said, 'I don't see what the Ensemble's got to do with anything. It was years ago when Sam played, and James never did. I don't see it in there.'

'I don't either,' Badger said. 'That's just what I meant. Lieutenant Richards is looking for some armored-car robbers.'

'One of whom is James,' she said.

'That's right, and one is Sam,' he said, 'but they don't know where they are. They will, of course. Depend on that. John Richards will find out, just as he should do. That we cannot prevent.'

'But still,' she said, 'the Ensemble – how are they related? I mean, by now I'm certainly resigned to it, what James has been doing. And if he's caught, well, then he's caught. Nothing I can do.'

'Christina,' Badger said. 'We cleansed the Ensemble Year from Sam's profile. It reeks of CIA. We hadn't done that, first thing the cop would want to know is what the hell it was. And if we didn't tell him, well: A, he'd know we lied; and B, he would find out what it is, because they have computers, too; and C, he would be angry at us, telling misleading stories. Because if he ran the Ensemble through one of his own banks, or perhaps the FBI's, he would get Christina's name, and start tracking her at once, see if she'd lead him to Sam. And also to dear James, of course – let's not forget him. And how far would they have to look? Right in their own back yard. You'd have more cops cruising around the Conservatory than patrol the Combat Zone.

'Now,' he said, 'now that she's back in school, finally, and may be getting straightened out, I assume that you and Clayton, that you'd probably prefer that she was not disturbed.'

Walker shuddered. She drank some of her martini. 'Absolutely,' she said. 'If we can at least salvage Christina out of this horrible mess, well, that would be something. Something more than I feared we had – a total disaster.'

'Well,' he said, 'that was my theory, and that's why I did that. Let the cops find them – sure, of course, but keep her out of it.'

'Then you don't think,' she said, 'you don't think she was mixed up? In spite of James and Sam?'

He shook his head. 'I can't say that,' he said. 'I think she was, if we still deal in facts, as we have these many years. Question's whether they can prove it. That I tend to doubt. Nothing in the descriptions I saw puts her on the scenes. But: did she know? Was she around? You bet your life she was. Her brother and her boy-friend, but she stayed innocent? She would've had to be, to be in on it. I don't think the cops'll chase her, unless they decide she's bait. I *do* think they'll decide she's bait, though, if they do find out.'

Walker shivered. 'We've got a lot to answer for,' she said. 'What we've done to our kids.'

'Oh,' he said. 'I don't know about that. We had good intentions. Happens Alton's turned out well. So have most of them. 'S too bad that one who didn't was your James, and also Sam.'

'I was to blame for that,' she said. 'I was to blame for James, and then I was to blame for just sitting idly by, while he took up with Sam.'

'Doubt you could've done much,' Badger said. 'Kid that age, impulsive, headstrong: not much you can do. Why do you think they draft kids? Just because of that. "Charge machineguns"; "Fall on grenades"; "Go attack a tank": no sane adult would do those things, or order someone else. And just the same way, if you'd told him, "Stay away from Sam because he's nuts, the way he acts," he would not have listened, Florence. He would not have heard.'

'You're probably right,' she said. 'It's just that all these things that we did, with the very best intentions? Suddenly it seems as though we did the devil's work. When Claire and Neville came last spring, when they were in New York, one night after dinner Clayton took him to the club to see Carl, after he finished work. More old war-buddy talk. And Claire and I sat there and talked ... and I'm just so afraid. You know what I fear, Larry? Do you know what's in my mind? That one of these days, or some night, it's all going to explode on me, and that finally I'll have to do a thing I really dread to do.'

'I know that,' Badger said.

'I blinded myself,' she said. 'I saw the capacity for evil in that young man. I saw the effect that he had on James, and I ignored it, and when Christina became involved with him, I foolishly told myself it was for the good, because he had talent, because he had brains, because he had magnetism.' She sighed. 'And now it's harvest time,' she said, 'now it's time to reap.'

'Not just yet,' he said.

5

Richards entered the office of Dist. Atty. David J. Osgood of Norfolk County at 4:20 in the afternoon. The District Attorney at forty-four had the gaunt and harried look of a man so distracted by unmentionable, secret, insoluble dilemmas that he slightly neglected his personal appearance, did not eat properly, did not sleep restfully and shaved hastily, missing small patches of stubble on his neck. He was slumped in his chair when Richards came in, and he did not get up. 'John,' he said wearily, 'how the fuck're you?' He lounged forward and extended his right arm across the desk.

Richards shook the DA's hand and sat down in front of the desk. 'Moderately pissed off,' he said. 'Since you ask. Not seriously pissed off and not monumentally pissed off, but moderately pissed off. And I've got a right to be. At least I think I do, and that's good enough for me.'

The District Attorney rested his chin on the heel of his left hand. 'Join the majority,' he said. 'So is everyone. Any particular reason for your personal complaint? Or is it the same as everybody else's – just general dissatisfaction. "Life sucks, and then you die."'

'It's a little more specific'n that,' Richards said. 'I try to be a cheerful person. Keep myself occupied. I was growing up, I was about fifteen, I got this mad passion on me that I hadda have a self-winding watch. The only thing I had to have. And I asked for one for Christmas. Only thing I asked. And I didn't get it. And I asked my father: "Why?" And he said: "Fellow your age needs something to do, keep himself occupied." And he said: "Secret of life, son, no matter what else you may hear: always be a cheerful person, and to do that, stay occupied." So I took his advice and joined the Marines, and that's the way it's been.

'Now,' Richards said, 'now what I'm occupied with's mostly this gang of galoots that's been running around all over the country-side generally raising hell and robbing armored cars when they get the urge. I believe you have heard about them.'

The District Attorney nodded. 'I think something crossed my desk,' he said. 'Someone may have said something, 'fore I went out of town.'

'That they did,' Richards said, 'and quite a lot more when you *stayed* out of town, while all the rest of us're jumping through hoops and waving bandannas and throwing our sweaty nightcaps in the air, trying to stem the fucking stampede that followed the latest commotion.'

The District Attorney made a feeble waving motion with his right hand. 'Uh, uh, John, won't work,' he said. 'You got me confused with someone else. I don't feel guilty. That's a different guy.

Those're different guys, and what we do is bring them in, and we make *them* feel guilty. Me, all I do is what I do, and every six years or so I go out in front the public and say, "This is what I've done," and if they like it, they reelect me, and that's all there is to that.'

'You all right, Dave?' Richards said. 'You pardon me for saying so, but you don't look so good.'

The District Attorney sat up and clasped his hands on his desk and shook his head, blinking his eyes. 'No, John,' he said, 'I'm not all right. I'm not all right at all. Joan's got pancreatic cancer and about eight months to live. Woman's thirty-nine years old. She'll be dead by forty. And before she gets to be dead, there'll be several weeks, the very least, of perfect agony.' He stared at Richards. His eyes were dull. 'You know what she wants me to do, John?' he said. 'You know what she's asking me to do?'

Richards winced. 'Well,' he said, 'I don't know her. I've only met her once. Didn't spend much time with her, so I can't say I know her well.'

'Well,' Osgood said, 'if I were to tell you that she thinks a lot like you, that even though the two of you don't know each other at all, I like being married to Joan for the same reason I used to like working with you, with the few guys like you, would that help you to guess what she's asking me to do?'

'I think it would,' Richards said.

Osgood spread his hands, palms up. 'So, what do I do, John?' he said. 'Tell me what to do. What would you do, in my place, if she were asking you?'

'I don't know,' Richards said. 'My head, I would agree with her. I would think she was right. And if I were in her position, that's what I would want. But in my guts? A different matter. Don't know if I could. And you, you know, another thing you got to keep in mind: guys like us, we're not supposed, let people break the laws they think they got a right to break. Or help them do it, either. Even if they are convinced that they've got a good reason. That's not in our contract, to excuse people like that. You think because you're the DA, that does not apply to you? Does Joan think that, far as that goes? Does she honestly think that?'

'I don't know,' Osgood said. 'She says she does. To me. Does she believe it? I don't know. We're both of us, we're just frantic. Totally panicked. Like a couple, little kids, confronted with the biggest monster from the worst nightmare we had, but this time the monster's real and Dad and Mom can't help us.' He sighed. 'John,' he said, 'in Korea I was scared. I was really, truly scared. When we got up near the Yalu and found ourselves, all of a sudden, with a hundred million Chinamen coming at us with bayonets, there weren't enough bullets in the world to shoot them all, and I knew I was going to die.

'Well,' he said, 'I didn't. Either I was lucky or God didn't have my room ready, but that day I was lucky, and I didn't die. And I thought when I got out of that, I'd been through the worst. That nothing life could throw at me would frighten me again.

'I was wrong,' he said. 'Oh, boy, was I, *wrong*.'

'I don't know what to tell you,' Richards said.

Osgood sighed again. 'I don't know what to tell me, either,' he said. 'I don't know how to tell the kids, and Joan does not know, either. No one knows what to tell us. No one in the world.' He shook his head again. He coughed and cleared his throat. 'Fuck it,' he said, 'fuck it all. Fuck it to goddamned hell. What's on your mind, bucko? Get mine off of this.'

Richards rearranged himself in the chair. He crossed his legs. He frowned. 'Jesus, Dave,' he said, 'I feel a little silly now – that's the only word for it. Coming at you like I did, I really didn't know ...'

'No,' Osgood said, 'you didn't. I just laid it on you now. So forget about it, all right? Give me the reaming you came in to do, maybe clear my head.'

'That body they found on Sunday,' Richards said. 'The girl in the reservation up on Chickatawbut Road? Identified as Emma Handley? You had time to get up, see the reports on that case?'

Osgood nodded. 'Briefly,' he said, 'very briefly, John. What I saw, there wasn't much. Didn't look like much. Dead three days, shot in the head, probably while kneeling. Twenty-four or -five years old. Female. White. No record. Family lives in Randolph but had not seen her in years. College dropout – U Chicago, sixty-six? That's about all I know. I assumed: some drug thing, you know? That's what I assumed. Coroner found needle marks, so that's what I assumed.'

'That's what most people would,' Richards said. 'And most people would because that's the easiest explanation and the simplest, easiest explanation's always the one that that stupid, lazy bastard picks. So he can wrap the case up quick and get back home to sleep. Just like the fucking dormouse – only time he's happy is when he's in his teapot, fast asleep. And that's the only time he isn't dangerous – when he is asleep.'

'John, John,' Osgood said. 'I know what you think of Howard by now. Everybody I know does, and most agree with you. But nobody had any choice. The MDC cops called this office because it's in my jurisdiction and they thought I'd want to know. Howard's the lieutenant here. His brain may be the same size as my cat's, and he does sleep about as much, but he's also got the same authority you have, the same authority, and the same right to exercise it and take charge, at the scene of a homicide. I maybe don't have my mind on things like I should, right now, but if I didn't have a care in the world, I couldn't've kept Howard from being the ranking officer at the scene where a murder victim's found in Norfolk County.'

'I could've, in any county,' Richards said. 'I've got time in rank on Howard.'

'And he's afraid of you,' Osgood said. 'That I also know. That's why he badmouths you so much. He's intimidated by you, and he thinks by running you down that way, he protects himself. But fact the matter is, John, you know, you weren't at the scene. So Howard didn't have to step off to the side. He was the man in charge.'

'And therefore,' Richards said, 'all I can tell you now for sure is that I can't be sure, but I suspect that girl was killed for giving information. Or for looking to her killers like she might be getting ready, getting ready to come in. And if she was, if that was the reason they had, they might've left something or she might've had something in her clothes or around her, that'd tell me where she'd been recently, and suggest who she was with.' He paused. 'You want to estimate my chances of finding something like that now, after Howard's been through the scene like a swarm of fertile turtles?'

'Oh,' Osgood said, 'I'd say small, I guess.'

'Mine's 'none,' Richards said. 'And that's really too bad. Because somebody was getting ready to come in. And that someone was a female. Called three times in three days, the beginning of last week. Wouldn't identify herself. Wouldn't say why the hell else she'd be calling the informer number, if it wasn't to inform. And gave us absolutely nothing. But wanted to know if we'd protect her completely, never let on how we'd found out. And I said "No," naturally, because I'm not going to lie to her – "We don't capture you and prosecute you along with the rest," I said, "which I doubt you want us to do, they're going to know who it was. And if they can't figure it out, we may need you to testify at trial. So I can't promise you total and utter and complete protection. All I can promise you is that we can guard you and hide you until you testify at trial, and afterwards we'll relocate you, and we'll change your name. You'll have the fifty large to tide you over, help you to get settled down, and you *won't* be in prison. Where you *will* be for a long time," I told her, "if somebody else turns first."

'Now,' Richards said, 'was this the broad? The one that talked to me? Well, I don't know, but the last call I got was the day before the doc says she died, and I haven't had one since, so all I can do is guess. Because I wasn't called. When I should've been.'

Osgood shrugged. 'Well, if you should've been,' he said, 'I apologize. But nothing, nothing gave me any reason, think that you should be. You really think this kid's the one, with the armored cars?'

'I don't know,' Richards said. 'I *don't* know, and I *should* know, and I *won't* know, because once Howard gets through trampling through a crime scene like a herd of fucking elephants, nobody ever knows. I swear, Howard's the only man I know that I think probably reduces the net supply of human knowledge just by entering a case.'

'Well,' Osgood said, 'be that as it may, he did it and it's done. What can I do now, help you make it right? Anything? I'll do anything you say.'

'Yeah,' Richards said, 'there is. There's something you can do. I want you to get together with Ward and Peter, and the three of you guys make a public statement the effect that you've asked Reese to designate a man in his office, in his Criminal Division, to do nothing but oversee this case. With me.'

'But we haven't,' Osgood said. 'You think Reese'll fall for that? He's awful cute, you know. If he hasn't figured out what a mare's nest this thing is, cagey Paul Green'll tell him 'fore that leaky balloon's half in the air, and he'll shy away from it.'

'No, he won't,' Richards said. 'When he grabbed the handle on the big reward story, he didn't notice it had sticky stuff on it. He seized it with both paws, and he can't let go of it now. You guys present a united front and go in there and say: "Look, Your Eminence, or whatever you got people calling you today, we need another shot, publicity, remind the general public we're all working on this case and that there's a big reward. Like you told them two months ago. And this is a good gimmick which'll make them think we're hard at work, making progress here. Besides, who knows? Might work. Can't do any damage and might actually work." And he will go for that. You can bet your ranch he will.'

'You got anyone in mind for this prosecutor type?' Osgood said, looking wistful.

Richards laughed. 'You'd love to do it, wouldn't you?' he said. 'I can just see the nostrils flaring on the old warhorse, smells the gunpowder.'

Osgood grinned. 'Well,' he said, 'I did. I did like that stuff. Trouble with running the show's that you have to give up playing with the tigers when you become ringmaster.'

'Well,' Richards said, 'there's nobody I'd rather have, Dave. But we both know you can't. Too much else on your mind. And even if there wasn't, you have to run this office and you haven't got the time. And neither does Peter Mahoney, and neither does Ward, and that's why all of you need somebody, somebody with the time.'

'Anybody special?' Osgood said.

'Yeah,' Richards said. 'I think, there's a kid named Terry Gleason in the Suffolk DA's office that I think can do the job. He's got about seven years in, getting itchy. Wants to start his own practice. But even though he's been trying homicides and major felonies the past four, five years, nobody's heard of him. Judges think he's good. DA loves him like a son. Thirty-two or three, and hungry. Hungry as a wolf. So I got to thinking. If Andy Boyd was one of Reese's actual gunners, not bogged down in the office all the time with a bunch of paperwork, I'd never get this by him. He'd want it himself, and I'd be happy with him. Andy Boyd is good. Hard as fuckin' goddamned nails, he gets on a case. But Andy knows, just like I do, that what he's got under him in that stable's pretty soggy stuff. Brown and wet and smells like horseshit, all politicos. Spend all their time in the SJC arguing habes and logging all their Superior Court time prosecuting Walpole inmates for hurling their turds at the guards. Put them in a trial situation against some mean bastard on the other side, they would soil their knickers. Andy and I get along good. If I ask Andy to get Gleason appointed a Special Assistant, Andy can sell it to Green, and he will, and Colin'll do what Green says.'

'Sign me up,' Osgood said. 'I'll get in touch with Ward and Pete. I'll talk to you tomorrow.'

Richards stood up. 'Beautiful,' he said. He and Osgood shook hands. Richards frowned. 'The other thing,' he said. 'I'm really sorry, Dave.'

'I know you are, John,' Osgood said. 'That's the trouble with this work, the kind of work we do. We get to thinking evil is just something people do, and if we catch enough of them, there won't be any more. And then real evil hits us, plain damned random sadness that we can't cure or prevent, *and there's no one we can punish*. No one to hold responsible and no one we can kill.'

6

Terry Gleason was in a bad mood. He warned Richards when Richards picked him up at the corner of Ashburton and Bowdoin Streets in Boston at 9:20. He slouched into the passenger seat of the ivory Ford sedan and shut the door hard. As Richards headed the car down the hill toward Cambridge Street, Gleason said: 'I really like having a good fight with my wife, mornings when I have to go to work. You think about it and it's absolutely perfect, you know? The two of you have a good yelling match, and the only thing it accomplishes is to get you all upset – does not resolve a thing. Then you go out the door because you've got to go to work, saying the nastiest thing you can think of when you slam it shut behind you, and you stew about it all day. And while you're doing that, making your dramatic exit, she's screaming the most hateful thing she can think of at you, so's to get herself all worked up to the point where she spends the whole day steaming about you. So by the time you get home at night, worn out, the pair of you're feeling like two tubs of rancid butter, and neither one of you'll speak, and what started out like a simple disagreement turns into a full week of the damned sulks.

'I tell you,' he said, 'I hate it. The only thing I can think of that'd make it worse'n it is anyway'd be spending the day going to Providence. Why're we going to Providence, John? Do we really know? When we find the frozen carcass of a leopard up on top the mountain, do we ever stop to figure out what the leopard was doing there? Have we actually sat down, separately or together, or in groups of up to five, and worked out the metaphysics of this excursion? Determined the eschatological and scatological implications of our actions? Considered the moral consequences of our conduct, and weighed the ethical choices that it necessarily demands? Do we know what we're doing, John? Do we really know? Or: Do we merely imagine that we know? Tell me the meaning of life.'

'It varies,' Richards said, turning left on Cambridge Street. 'The meaning of life varies. That's why so many are confused. They seek a single meaning, when in fact there are millions. Millions and millions of meanings. Enough for every single one of us to choose at least one for himself, and be perfectly contented, sitting in the shade of his personal tree. It's being pernickety, people being jealous of other people's meanings, and deciding that their own's not as good. That's what causes war and other tribulations – athlete's foot, pyorrhea, dandruff: stuff like that.'

'You're sure about that,' Gleason said. 'Millions and millions of meanings, enough for every manjack that ever wore shoe leather?'

'I'm fairly sure,' Richards said. 'I could be off a little bit, maybe two, three hundred thousand. Either way. But there's at least a good dozen that I know about, I have personally seen.'

'What's yours?' Gleason said. 'I promise I won't covet it.'

'And you won't steal it, either,' Richards said. He took the Storrow Drive ramp at Charles Street Circle and headed west along the river, blue in the clear morning.

'Absolutely not,' Gleason said. 'I'm too exhausted to steal anything. These conjugal battles whip me all to shit.'

'Assist me in your guidance,' Richards said. 'The most useful knowledge is that which we acquire by ourselves – good examination of conscience, all that kind of stuff. What was the fight about?'

'The usual thing,' Gleason said, '"the usual thing" being some perfectly harmless-sounding remark that one of us makes and the other one takes as a mortal fucking insult and war's declared at once. I got out of the shower and I'm getting dressed, and she asked me what time I'd be home. And I said I didn't know, because I hadda go down to Providence today with John Richards to see the AG there. And I didn't know how long that was going to take – which I don't – but however long it takes. And add another hour to get back here. Plus another hour for dinner, if it runs for a long time. Plus about an hour for me to get my car here and back home.'

'And she got mad,' Richards said.

'Yeah, she did,' Gleason said. 'But Barbara's got this little trick she uses. She's very smart. She knows she gets mad at me for things that I can't help. And when she does that, I just ignore her. Like I would've done this morning, if she'd lighted into me for not knowing how long the Rhode Island AG's gonna want to talk about their little robbery. Or for not moving Providence closer to

Hanover, so I could get home earlier. Or for not moving Hanover closer to Boston. You follow? What she does, when she gets mad like that about something that there's not a damned thing in the world that I can do to change it for her, she lies in ambush for me. Waits for me to make some innocent remark she can deliberately misinterpret, and then bushwacks me. Supposedly over that, but really about what she doesn't dare to say's the real reason. So I won't be prepared.

'Now,' Gleason said, 'keep in mind that I knew, when she asked me what time I'd be home, I knew she was asking because she was looking to have me pick up Terry Junior at gymnastics up at Rockland. And he gets through at six. Which is precisely when Joanne's swimming class starts at the Norwell Health Club. What she had in mind was for me to collect Terry on my way home, and she would take Joanne, and her life would be easier. And maybe I'll be able to do it for her tonight, things work and we get back.

'So,' he said, 'knowing she's disappointed, and also sympathizing, I say while knotting my green tie: "I'm really sorry about this, you know, but I have to go. I wish I didn't have to, and that John could go alone, and I don't think I'm going to add much to the festivities, but Reese wants me at the briefing with the Rhode Island AG and that means I have to go."'

'Reese didn't,' Richards said, 'Reese doesn't know anything about your going down. This was entirely Boyd's idea. He's the one who called. Reese is in Hawaii, chasing maidens of dusky hue. Andy is the one who thought, this might be a good idea.'

'Yeah, yeah,' Gleason said, 'I know. But I'm just telling you what I said to her, all right? And she said, she's got this murderous soft voice she uses when she's winding up to throw a beanball right straight at my head. And she said: "Then why go?" And I said, sarcastic naturally, I said: "Well, darling, because I work for Mister Reese. That's why he pays me money. And when Mister Reese says: 'Gleason, go to Providence,' I have to go to Providence." And she said: "You don't have to. You told me, it was almost a year ago when you left the DA's office for this big wonderful new offer that'd make you a big star, you told me then that you and John, you'd have the birds in custody within a couple months. And you'd try them, and convict them, and then the clients would be beating down the doors to get you to represent them when you resigned right after that to open your own office. Well, as near as I can see, you haven't made it happen yet, and I don't think you're gonna. All that you've accomplished is another year of low-pay work, but this one with no trials. If most people didn't know you when you were in court every day, those who did will have forgotten, time this's over with.'

'Well,' Gleason said, 'what do I say? The truth? "You might be right, dear, that I made a big mistake? But if I did, I'm stuck with it? I can't go back and change it now?" No, that is not what I said. What I said instead was: "Look, we are partners. This is the way you wanted it, when I got out of school. You couldn't wait to quit your job and start having the kids. You didn't want to stay with Jordan's. You were adamant. I told you then, I tell you now, we could've used that cash. You'd worked for three or four more years, and we'd saved your pay, the things that we can't afford to buy now we'd already have. I know you're jealous of Susan Hemmings, and Sheila, and all those other ladies whose husbands're pulling down the heavy bread in private practice. I envy them myself. But you've got to keep in mind that Don Hemmings was editor of *Law Review*, and I wasn't, and Ted Feeney's father's a founding partner in that firm, and mine wasn't, and if being the wife of a guy like that is what you had in mind, well, you should've married one."

'And then I said some other things,' Gleason said. 'I dunno. I'm worried, John. I can see us just getting further'n further apart, like two kids with a play telephone made of two tin cans and a string, seeing how far apart they can get before they can't hear each other any more, and never realizing that the only reason you can make a play telephone out of two cans and a string is because smart kids never use a piece of string that's long enough to let them get out of earshot.'

'I don't know what to tell you,' Richards said. 'Back when I was a sergeant, down the Norwell barracks, I had this trooper under me, real nice kid named Colby. And his work started going to hell. No attention to detail, listless on the job, making dumb mistakes. And I called him in and sat him down, and I said to him: "Well, Tim, what the hell is going on?" And he told me a story lot like the one you're telling me. And I was sorry I asked. Wife didn't, she liked the idea, him being a trooper, when the two of them got married. But then she had the experience of him living at the barracks the days he was on duty, and the kids're driving her nuts, and she began to think, you know, this grand design they had – of him being a State policeman for enough years so he could grab off a chief's job in some small town – maybe wasn't going to work.'

'What ended up happening to him?' Gleason said.

'They got divorced,' Richards said. 'And I'm sorry you asked me that, too, but that is what they did.'

'Did it help?' Gleason said.

Richards turned off Storrow Drive at the entrance to the Massachusetts Turnpike in Allston. 'Gee,' he said, 'you've got a positive genius for the toughies this morning, haven't you, my lad.

Yes, it seemed to, as a matter of fact. Helped *him*, at least, quite a lot. Got the shit beaten out of him on the alimony, the support, naturally in those days – judge just hoovered him. But he was a lot more relaxed on the job, and took a lot more pleasure in life. Yeah, I'd say it helped. Had a nice, uneventful ten or twelve years in the uniform, picked off a chief's job that opened up in Amesbury, I think it was, collected a new wife along the way. Yeah, things turned out for him.' Richards paused.

'Lemme say, Terry,' he said, 'it's easy, me to talk. I put in the day on the job, which I like, and I go home at night. That I also like. Angela's all day at the library, which she likes to do, so she's busy and she's occupied and she isn't, when I get home at night she hasn't been by herself all day long in the house just waiting for me to get home so I can tell her all about what happened in the great world that she missed. Some new book came in that day, she thinks that I might like, she brings it home for me to read before she logs it in. And she's of course reading all the time, because that's her job, and I tell her what's happened on my job that day, she tells me about hers, and we get along. One of us cooks and the other one sits there in the kitchen and the whole thing works out good.

'Now,' he said, 'there's a lot of choices in there that don't, aren't obvious. Angela and I got married late, I didn't meet anybody until her that I was interested in marrying. Fucking, yes, marrying, no. And Angela, after her first husband she was not that keen on putting up with another one. Only reason we got to know each other was that I was in the place she worked so much, this was when she was an assistant and she hadda work nights, we got to know each other. And that took us a long time. And she didn't want to have children. She was forty-one years old when we got together.

And that was all right with me. I was used to living alone. I was thirty-nine. Come home at night, it's quiet, have something to eat and read while you listen to some music and perhaps sip a little light table wine? Very pleasant life I had. Idea having a bunch of kids running around and screaming through my evenings? Did not appeal to me.

'See, what we did,' Richards said, 'what Angela and I did was merge two lives that were working all right separately. And which happened, on which the gears luckily meshed. The only real adjustment we made was giving up our separate places, her apartment and mine, and getting a house. Which we set up the way we wanted it set up, and it was nicer'n what we'd left. We'd already developed our own lives, and we just kept on living them, but with some improvements.

'They can't,' Richards said, 'you can't live your whole life through another person. It doesn't work, that's all – it simply doesn't work. Nobody's up to that, living the life that he's got plus living the life that his wife hasn't got, and I don't care how sincere anybody is that claims they're going to do that, it cannot be done. And that is exactly what all you starry-eyed guys do, that get married young. And that's why there's so much trouble.'

'And that's the meaning of life,' Gleason said.

'No,' Richards said, 'that's the flotsam of life. The clutter. The stuff that keeps getting in your way and you have to kick a path through it. The meaning of life for you today is that the AG in Rhode Island's got a vicious little problem that he didn't have a week ago, but we've had for five years. Which is how to catch some guys 'n gals that're doing bad things in unconventional ways. Since it's almost certainly the same set of bad people that belted the Brinks truck in Warwick on the fourth that started belting

65

trucks on us in Danvers back in nineteen-seventy, the Rhode Island Staties figure maybe we know more about them here than they know about them there.'

'So give it to them,' Gleason said. 'Makes them happy? Very fine. Doubt it'll help them catch the bastards, since it hasn't helped us much, but if they feel better, great. This world's a gloomy place. One must help one's fellow man.'

'Already gave it to them, Terry,' Richards said. 'That is not the point. Point is the AG down there needs something, put inna papers. And you know our Mister Reese. Does not miss a bet. They read the Providence papers in Attleboro and the Massachusetts towns in the Blackstone Valley. Nice if they see Mister Reese's cooperating with Rhode Island authorities to collar the perpetrators. Mister Boyd, who can read Mister Reese's mind from a distance of thousands of miles, therefore dispatches me and you to Rhode Island for a conference with the AG and his cops down there. This will enable the people from the TV stations and the papers to write stories about how the two AGs are cooperating, because the fact that they can take pictures of us there proves it. Everyone will be pleased.'

'Hah,' Gleason said. 'Barbara will not be pleased. She will not be pleased tonight, when I get home too late, and if those guys from out of state catch a break and grab the robbers, she will really be pissed off.'

'They won't,' Richards said.

'No,' Gleason said, 'they probably won't. If we can't catch them, with what we've got, they probably can't catch them, working from our stuff.'

'They haven't got all the stuff,' Richards said.

'You said you gave it to them,' Gleason said.

'I said I gave them what we know,' Richards said. 'I didn't say I gave them what we think.'

'What do we think?' Gleason said. 'You wanna let me in on it, so I'm not caught with my thumb up my ass when you mention it today?'

'I'm not mentioning anything today,' Richards said. 'What I am doing today is getting information, not giving it. The giving part is over – getting's what we're doing. And if what I think we're going to get's what we turn out to get, then I will have enough for me to think that we can catch these folks.'

'And what is that?' Gleason said.

'I thought of this the other night,' Richards said. 'I was copying the files for them, and naturally I'm reading them over again, and I kept coming back to the same thing: the fucking precision of these punks. Every time they do it, it comes off like clockwork. Almost like an inside job. They know when those armored cars're coming, and they know when they're going to be fullest when they go away. But every time they do it, it's in a different place. And when we check out the bank employees, there's never anybody missing, might've been in league with them. There's not the slightest reason to suspect anyone in the banks or the courier companies or anywhere else of being in cahoots with them.

'And then I thought,' Richards said, 'then I thought: "Aha. You have been an asshole." The reason there's never been anybody in the banks or in the trucks that looked like they had a hand in this stuff is because nobody in the banks or the trucks had a hand in it. And how could they? These're deposits *from* the banks that the punks're stealing, not shipments *to* the banks. The people in the banks don't know how much they'll have on hand to ship out when the next truck comes. The people on the trucks don't know what they're going to pick up. So, who the hell does know? Well, someone in the shopping plazas, someone in there every day. Someone who can not only keep a little log of when the truck comes, for a couple months or so, but also knows, from personal observation, when the stores in the malls're doing a land-office business. So that when the truck does come, next time, it's going out chock-a-block full. Someone, in other words, who's not only watching the bank, but also watching the mall. They're putting a spotter in the mall, and taking careful notes, and then when they see a big haul coming up, they know when to strike.'

'So where does that get us?' Gleason said.

'We'll know today,' Richards said. 'My guess is that we'll find out there's some kind of a fast-food joint somewhere near the bank, where the people working mornings, when it's generally slow, had a very good place to watch the trucks come to the bank.'

'Hamburgers?' Gleason said. 'These things're morning jobs?'

'The burger joints serve breakfast now,' Richards said. 'You weren't so uxorious, staying home to fight with your wife every day, you would know that. Doughnut shops serve breakfast. Pancake houses? They serve breakfast. Every fucking fast-food restaurant in the whole fucking world, now sells fucking breakfast. Some day when I retire and have a lot of time, I am going to figure out who the hell is eating all those goddamned awful-looking slimy eggs and that greasy bacon, and the wet pancakes and fatty saus-ages with soggy rolls for breakfast. Obviously someone is doing it. Lots of someones. Otherwise normal-looking people're getting themselves out of warm beds every morning sooner'n they have to, every day, so they can get in their cars and drive several miles to pay money to eat food nowhere near as good as they could have at home, and do it every day. Thousands of them. Hordes of the bastards. Every fucking day. Because those restaurants're in business for money, and they're all selling breakfasts. We've got a whole underclass of people ruining their digestions every morning with stuff I wouldn't feed to my pet pig, and a whole class of other people making money off them.

'Most of those other people,' Richards said, 'are making the minimum wage. I'm talking about the slaveys here, the high-school drop-outs and the elderly ladies and the rest of society's rejects that can't get any other work and have their mornings free. I figure this way: the lumpers working the griddles're too busy to watch banks. But the people on the counter jobs, after the morning rush ends and they're mopping up the tables and emptying the trash, those counter people have the time to watch the fucking bank and see when the truck arrives.

'Since those jobs're minimum wage,' Richards said, 'they've got two features, one of which appeals to the longhair punks, and one of which should've appealed to us a long time afuckingo, if I'd've had the brains of your average household plant. The feature the bandits like is the fact that those jobs're always open. Joints're always looking for help. So for them it's not a matter of finding an opening in some deal-'em-off-the-arm, quick-'n'-dirty, happens to be near a bank; it's a matter, finding a bank, near a quick-'n'-dirty. Once you spot a bank in a mall, with a joint across the way, you can always get somebody in there, watch the goddamned bank.

'Now,' he said, 'the feature that appeals to *us* is that the joints have to keep records, prove they're paying the minimum wage, and who they're paying it to. 'Cause they got to file W-two forms and all that shit with the IRS and so forth. So that means when they hire somebody, or somebody leaves, they got to have records, when that person come on and when that person left. And that person's got to have, Social Security number and some identification. May not be the right SS number. Maybe false ID. But something, true or false, that shows who they are. Which means that if you go back and check on who started work a month or two before the job, and who stopped showing up either just before or just after, you know who the spotter was. And what the spotter looked like. And from talking to people working there then, maybe some things the spotter said, just happened to drop, that might tell you something about who they really were.

'So,' Richards said, 'this finally dawns on me, on Monday, this is what's going on, I took a little ride for myself yesterday, just refresh my recollection. In other words: to see if there was something I should've noticed at the scenes of these hold-ups a long time ago. And there was. There's a doughnut shop in Danvers with a direct view of the entrance to the bank across the way. There's a burger joint across from the bank in Brockton. There's a tire store across the street from the bank in Braintree, at the plaza, which is not the same thing as a fast-food joint, but hires the same kind of people. And what I'm betting is that there's some kind of similar business operating across from the bank in the Warwick mall where the evildoers struck last Thursday, which is what we find out today.

'Now if we do,' Richards said, 'if we do find that out, tomorrow or the next day you are going to sit down in your chair behind your desk and make out some subpoenas for me. And I am going to slap those little devils on the personnel managers of the restaurants and the tire store, and they are going to complain bitterly about me asking for books and records from five years back, and I am going to say: "I won't tell you why. Just get the stuff together and haul your ass in before the grand jury like Mister

Gleason says. All right?" And they will do it. Because we have the majesty of the law on our side, and we can drive them crazy if they feel like thwarting us. And then we will find out whether my theory is correct. And if it is, my friend, we will have something to work with. Not much, maybe, not the Rosetta Stone, but more'n we have got now, which will make us better off.'

Gleason sat up on the passenger seat. He grinned. 'You know,' he said, 'there are moments when I really like this job.'

'A few,' Richards said. 'They come along. Every now and then there's one of these little breaks in the clouds, sun comes peeking through, and tally ho, my lads, it's time to flog the steeds.' He slapped Gleason on the left knee. 'Don't,' he said, 'don't spend your whole life, every goddamned day of it, always thinking about how what you do today's going to make tomorrow better. Think about, at least sometimes, how today is pretty good.'

TWO

7

Daniel Flynn died on May 6, 1967, in his eighty-second year, at the Veterans Administration Hospital on the VFW Parkway in the Jamaica Plain district of Boston. Surviving him were two sisters, Margaret Flynn, 84, and Emily (Flynn) Kenney, 85, both of his late residence at 41 Talbot Street, Dorchester. The principal asset of Daniel Flynn's estate was the first-class liquor license issued by the Licensing Board of the City of Boston to Daniel J. Flynn, doing business as Broad Street Grille. It permitted him to offer for consumption on the premises at 23 Broad Street, Boston, all varieties of alcoholic beverages, provided he sold food. The license had been in his continuous possession since Prohibition ended in 1933. The lease of the premises had two years to run, but was subject to termination at the option of the landlord upon six months' notice in the event of the demise or retirement of the lessee, Daniel J. Flynn.

The landlord, Horace Evans Properties, exercised that option on June 2, 1967. Evans, owner of several large office buildings in the financial district, was queried about the reasons for his decision by a *Boston Commoner* reporter when 'it became known that the fifty-three-year-old landmark Broad Street Grille would close.' Through his attorney, Harold Silverman, Evans issued a statement: 'Dan Flynn was the landmark, not the Grille. Dan Flynn is gone. The city is changing with the passage of men like Dan Flynn, and the rest of us have to face up to that fact and keep pace with it. Twenty-three Broad is no longer the place for a bar-room to operate, not without Dan Flynn.'

Harold Silverman had known Daniel Flynn for more than twenty years. Off the record he told the reporter that 'the explanation, the real explanation for the decision, is that a man like Mister Evans felt, always felt comfortable doing business with Dan Flynn. Because you always knew if Dan Flynn was the guy selling liquor in your building, things would not get out of hand. You could bring your mother in that place, or your sister or your wife, and day and night, it didn't matter. The two of you could have a sandwich and a beer, and she'd never hear an off-color remark or be bothered in any way. And there was no gambling going on, none of that stuff at all. Dan Flynn ran a clean operation. You weren't, if you were Horace Evans and you owned the property, you could go to bed at night knowing you weren't going to wake up in the morning to a big story in the papers about how the cops'd raided one of your buildings the night before.

'Well,' Silverman said, 'you can't do that anymore. Now you've got all these kids coming along, and they're selling marijuana, and this and that, and a tenant with a liquor license, unless it's someone like Dan Flynn, just isn't the kind of risk you want to take. There aren't many like Dan Flynn,' he said. 'They don't come along every day.

'Of course the funny thing is,' Silverman said, 'the funny thing is that if Horace Evans'd owned the building back in 1921, when Dan first leased the space and moved his so-called restaurant operation into it from LaGrange Street, the chances are Horace would not've let him have the space. Because that "restaurant," unless you were a total idiot, you knew what it was. It was a speakeasy. The Congress passed the law you couldn't legally make or sell booze, and all the people like Dan who'd been making and selling booze – well, not all of them, of course, but a good many of them – all of a sudden, overnight, they became "restauranteurs." And what they used to serve you in glasses, before you had your meal, they now served to you in coffee cups, before you had your meal. But only if they knew you, of course, or if you came recommended by somebody else they knew.

'I'd drop in to Dan's place many nights after work,' Silverman said. 'He had no illusions. Absolutely none. "Who am I, indeed," he'd say, "who am I to say a man's not good as me? That Army doctor? I fooled him. Didn't want to fight for England. Fight for England, that was hunting down half my friends and relatives? Not on your life. Not on mine, anyway. Do you know what it does to your lungs, you inhale eight cigars every day for a week? Well, I do, and fortunately for me, the Army doc did not. And, I could've gone to prison. Broke the law for thirteen years and knew I was doing it. Cops knew I was doing it, too, and not every one of them that looked the other way always looked the other way without first getting something in his pocket for his wife and family. So that's another thing."'

Silverman laughed. 'I must be getting old,' he said. 'I must be getting on in years, when I miss the old outlaws. Old Dan was like a lot of us, I guess. Always obeyed the law. Except when he thought the law was wrong; or he didn't have any choice.'

Atty. Dennis M. Keohane, with offices at 1012 Dorchester Ave., Boston, represented the Flynn estate. Late in the morning of June 19, 1967, he received a call from Atty. Philip Ianucci, representing Joseph Nichols and Joseph Abbate. He made their offer to purchase the liquor license held by the Flynn estate for the sum of thirty thousand dollars, subject to approval of its transfer to the Downtown Social Club, Inc., a close corporation in which Nichols held forty percent of the voting stock, Abbate held thirty-five, and the remainder was divided among members of their families.

'Look,' Keohane said, 'obviously we're going to sell. My two old ladies aren't about to run a barroom. Although if you ask me, old Emily could do it if she set her mind to it. Old Emily could ramrod a trail drive through the Panhandle. Thing of it is, though, and I assume you want a transfer, the thing I got to know is whether all your guys're clean. Because if they're not, and the cops find out, and they start making calls, the next thing you know, everybody's getting jumpy at Licensing, you know? And we do not need that shit, Phil, where we got this thing all tied up while those jerks investigate, and hem and haw and jerk around, deciding what to do.'

Attorney Ianucci assured Keohane that neither of his clients had a criminal record, 'except for Abbate got some speeding tickets. And Nichols, I think he had a drunk-and-disorderly beef from about nine years ago – walloped some cop in Somerville after the cop started a fight.'

On December 5, 1967, the Licensing Board of the City of Boston approved the transfer of the Class A license issued to Daniel

Flynn, d/b/a Broad Street Grille, to Downtown Social Club, Inc., for the sale of alcoholic beverages to be consumed on the premises where common victuals would be offered, at 34 Randolph Street in Boston, the location being on the ground and basement floors of an eight-story masonry building two blocks south and one block east of the old Broad Street Grille.

Downtown Social Club, Inc., doing business as The Friary, had a pre-opening celebration on Wednesday, March 6, 1968. Among about eighty attending were a retired first baseman for the Boston Red Sox, two former Celtics guards, three members of the City Council, two priests active in CYO sports programs and a jockey under ten-day suspension at Suffolk Downs for rough riding. The rest of the invited guests enjoying a buffet of shrimp, roast beef, ham, and crabmeat, with an open bar, were men between the ages of twenty-eight and fifty who worked in offices near 34 Randolph Street, and women between the ages of nineteen and twenty-six employed by various airlines and modeling agencies in Boston. They mingled among heavy oak tables and sat on bentwood chairs in cosy beamed alcoves where the back walls were studded with protruding half-barrels charred with brands that said: port, and malmsey, and sherry. Jolly Falstaffs and rollicking monks were the subjects of the murals on the spackled plaster walls. Music was provided by the Donegal Fiddlers.

On March 7th the official opening again featured the Donegal Fiddlers and drew one hundred and thirty-two paying customers. Business picked up after that; Friday, the eighth of March, showed a gross of $3,591.75.

For the next nine years, The Friary prospered. The luncheon menu, served from opening at 11:00 A.M. until closing at 1:00 A.M., offered six-ounce hamburgers with a variety of improvements

79

and side-dishes that appealed to many. Clam chowder, heavily floured, and simple fish plates kept hot in steam tables, satisfied customers uninterested in quiche or omelettes. The Friary was closed on Sundays, but by popular demand maintained during the week a blackboard updated daily with listings of Las Vegas odds on NFL football games in the autumn, NBA basketball and NHL hockey games in the winter, and major league baseball in the spring and summer. There were pools on the Boston Marathon, the Stanley Cup, the All-Star Game, big fights, Olympic matches, college football, the World Series and the Super Bowl. A prominent member of the Massachusetts State Senate was arrested for driving under the influence on his way home after one of many political fund-raisers held at The Friary. A second-string running back for the Boston Patriots was sued for battery by a young man; he alleged that the athlete had slugged him in a dispute concerning the chastity of the young man's female companion.

Joseph Nichols was the chairman of the 1974 Handicapped Games, held at Boston College's Alumni Field. Interviewed by Channel 49, which carried the games live, he said: 'Look, we all know Ethel Kennedy's got her thing going there, with the Special Olympics and all. And it's good. She should do that. Bobby, you know, would've liked it. But we also got, we got a lot of kids around this town that don't get involved in that, in anything that's got "Kennedy" on it, one reason or another, which reason is usually busing and how Teddy stood on that, and they ought to have fun too. So, we're doing this.'

Joseph Abbate was the subject of a *Boston Magazine* profile in a series about the city's eligible bachelors; he was quoted as saying: 'I'm thirty-six years old, right? I had a wife already. A wife is what sits up 'till two and asks how come you're late, when you're running a saloon. Sandy's a nice kid. I'm not lying to her. She asks the question, I give her the answer. Woman's entitled to that. "I was getting laid, all right? That's why I am late." She didn't like it. She divorced me. I don't blame the lady, right? I'd do the same thing. But getting married again? Uh uh. Not in this life here. Joe and I're on a roll. We know what we're doing now.'

8

Peter Walmsley, 29, of 73 Walk Hill Street, Jamaica Plain, unlocked The Friary back door opening on the alley off 34 Randolph Street at 9:45 A.M. on Monday, May 5, 1977, as usual forty-five minutes late for his work as clean-up man, and confident as usual that Nichols and Abbate would not show up until at least 11:00. The lunchtime cook, Janet Iverson, would be in around 10:15; she would know that he had not reported on time because the dishwashers would still be hot and full. But Peter knew Janet would not tell because he also knew that she was having an affair with one of the waitresses, Diana McKechnie; Nichols, who hated queers, would fire both of them if he found out. Walmsley locked the alley door behind him and groped through the dim passageway between the cases of liquor until he reached the light switch on the partition next to the interior door leading into the main room. He switched on the light, opened the door, and went into the dim public space. He turned on the lights. Later he gave a statement to Boston Police, which he repeated for reporters.

'Everything looked just the way it always does. I didn't see a single thing that tipped me off that something must be wrong. And at the same time, you know? I knew that something was. It was like, it was like you could smell it. That something was definitely wrong. And I didn't know what it was. I looked at the bar thing they got there, with the glasses inna racks over your head, and like usual it was pretty empty, because all the glasses naturally're in the washers, right? And I think: "No, that's not it. Must be something else." And I go around behind the bar, and all the time I'm sniffing, you know? Gas leaking or something? And it isn't that. And I look, I look down at the floor there, when I get behind the bar, because I'm expecting, maybe, I will see water there. And I don't see any water, like I would've if we had a leak or something from the pipes, or Rickie left his towel in the sink or something, and he didn't shut the water off when he got off work. And it isn't that.

'Now I'm like, you know, really I am baffled. "What the hell is wrong here?" That's what I am thinking. And I go around and I check all the booths, you know, see if maybe someone's in them, maybe sick or something. And there's nobody there. I'm thinking of all kinds of things, like maybe rats got in, ate the wiring or something and the place is going up. And still I don't see nothing, don't smell nothing, don't hear much – except for the refrigerator and the freezer there, which always hums.

'I go inna Men's,' Walmsley said. 'Nothing there. I go in the Women's, and also nothing there. Not even faucets running or the flushes might've clogged. Just: Nothing, you know? Nothing. Nothing out of line. And still I know that something is. Something's

83

out of whack. Something isn't like it should be. I can, like, *sense* it, right? I can tell that something, something's definitely wrong. And then, all of a sudden, I know what it is. It's Walter and Frieda. The two fuckin' dogs. Usually, always when I come in, the first thing I got to do is calm down Frieda and Walter. Two big fuckin' German Shepherds. Because the first thing they want to do is eat me. And they're not around. So: where the fuck are they?

'I go in the office, and I see that I am right. Something's definitely wrong. I knew that right off. Inna first place, well, I hadda, hadda hit the door. Because it wouldn't open, all right? When I turn the knob. And naturally it wouldn't, right? Because Nick Nichols is against it and I guess he must've crawled there, trying to get out. And I seen them all in there, the five that was in there. It wasn't until afterwards, when the cops get here, they go into the freezer and they find the other two. Along with the goddamned dogs. I didn't see them other two. I didn't see the dogs. I didn't want to, either. All I saw was those five that they killed inside the office. All of them was on their stomachs, and their legs're bent. Except for Nick, who like I said was up against the door. And there was not a lot of blood, which sort of surprised me, you know? Because I knew they were dead. They had, there was a smell in there. It wasn't very nice. There was definitely a smell, and if I don't smell that again, it will be all right with me.'

Suffolk County Medical Examiner Charles J. Fox, MD, with Stephen M. Fratus, MD, Assistant Medical Examiner, conducted autopsies on seven corpses received at the Southern Mortuary on May 5, 1977. Their findings were reported to Det. Lt. Insp. John D. Richards of the Massachusetts State Police, at his office at 20 Ashburton Place in Boston. The findings read in part:

'The bodies of two well-nourished white females found in the walk-in freezer on the premises at 34 Randolph Street, Boston, have been identified from dental records and by relatives as those of Diana McKechnie, age 34, of 131 Hanover St., Boston, and Janet Iverson, age 36, of 1870 Commonwealth Ave., Boston. Death in each instance was attributable to multiple gunshot wounds (two) inflicted behind the left ear, victims kneeling at the time. Death occurred between 6:00 A.M. and 12:00 P.M. on May 4, 1977.

'The bodies of two well-nourished white males, two well-nourished white females and one well-nourished black female found in the back room or office of 34 Randolph Street, Boston, on the morning of May 5, 1977, have been identified by dental records and by relatives as those of: Joseph Nichols, age 41, of 121 Williams Drive, Canton; Joseph Abbate, age 39, of 1030 Memorial Drive, Cambridge; Maureen Wilkerson, age 26, of 368 Hancock St., Quincy; Helena Gross, age 27, of 1238 North Main St., Randolph; and Doreen Alexander, age 24, of 28 West Newton St., Boston.

'Each of the persons found in the office or back room of the premises at 34 Randolph St. suffered death as the result of multiple gunshot wounds (two) inflicted behind the left ear. The wounds were caused by a .22-caliber weapon fired from behind the victims, who were kneeling. Lividity and other factors warrant the conclusion that death occurred between 10:00 A.M. and 4:00 P.M. on May 4, 1977.

'Each of the victims tested positively for traces of narcotics. The two females in the freezer had used heroin within the twenty-four hours preceding their deaths. The five persons found in the office had used cocaine within the twenty-four hours preceding death.'

Aware that Asst. Atty. Gen. Terrence Gleason was on annual leave to attend the funeral of his brother-in-law in Seattle, Detective Lieutenant Richards prepared his own report as a cover to the findings, 'while my thinking is fresh,' and attached it to the documents from the medical examiners. It included these observations:

'There was no indication of forcible entry. The establishment was not open for business on Sunday. Keys found on the person of Janet Iverson included one fitting the lock on the door to the alley. The dogs, of course, knew Iverson. The coroner's report fixes her time of death, and that of Diana McKechnie, approximately two hours before the deaths of the five persons found fatally shot in the back room or office. Informant JDR4 advises Iverson and McKechnie were promiscuous lesbians. "They liked each other best, but they also cruised around."

'Nichols and Abbate maintained a checking account in the name of The Friary at the branch office of the Charter National Bank at 53 Broad Street. Their customary practice was to deposit receipts in the night deposit box at that branch. No deposit was received for the nights of Friday, May 2, or Saturday, May 3, the last night before the murders on which the establishment was open. I am confidentially advised that receipts for Friday nights customarily totaled in the neighborhood of $4,500, and those for Saturday nights approximately $2,800. A subpoena directed to the Keeper of the Records, Charter National Bank, will substantiate that advice.

'Informant JDR4 advises that one Michael Bendictson, a.k.a. Mickey the Dunce, a.k.a. Mickey Quiet, operated a handbook on said premises, specializing in sports booking. NCIC advises Michael Bendictson three times convicted setting up and promoting a lottery, served eighteen months, MCI Concord, on conviction 6/9/64. Subject missing from usual haunts, but Informant believes that he is all right and lying low.

86

'Informant JDR2 advises Nichols and Abbate heavily engaged in large-scale narcotics trafficking, and participated as well in "Mickey's" profits. Unable to substantiate. Informant JDR2 has in the past furnished information which subsequent investigation has not substantiated.

'No spent cartridges were found at the scene. At least eighteen bullets were fired. Preliminary results from autopsies and ballistics indicate that all were fired at extremely close range from the same weapon.

'In conjunction with Det. Sgt. Maurice Hogan, BPD Homicide, I am proceeding on hypothesis as follows:

'1. Victims Iverson and McKechnie entered the premises before Victims Nichols, Abbate, Wilkerson, Gross and Alexander, and either admitted or had previously provided duplicate keys to Tibbetts's molls, Fentress and Franklin. They were put into the freezer and killed. While informant JDR2 alleges Nichols was "violent," "quick-tempered," and "hated queers," and suspects Nichols killed the two women in the freezer after he found them on the premises, he is probably wrong. Nichols would not have shot his dogs. The killer or killers of the two women murdered them and the dogs, and then either hid on the premises or left them temporarily, until Nichols and party showed up.

'2. The body of Nichols when found was clad only in undershorts. The other four victims found in the back room or office were nude. Clothing found folded and piled on the sofa in the back room or office suggests that it was removed voluntarily by the owners. Informant JDR2 advises that Nichols and Abbate "had orgies after hours there when no one was around." Informant JDR2 uncertain whether Nichols and Abbate habitually used the premises on Sunday mornings for such purposes,

87

but believes they may have done so. Victims Wilkerson, Gross and Alexander have criminal records including several apprehensions for solicitation.

'3. The back room or office furniture included two lockable steel four-drawer filing cabinets. One of them was found locked and secure. The other had been forced open. The bottom drawer was pulled out and empty. Informant JDR2 alleges Victims Nichols and Abbate "put their cash in that drawer that they didn't give the bank." JDR2 alleges further that said receipts greatly exceeded sales at the bar. The contents of the locked cabinet have been inspected. They consist solely of records. The person or persons who forced the first cabinet either knew, or obtained by threat, the information that caused them to select it.

'4. What JDR2 knows is known on the street. It seems evident that neither Nichols and/or Abbate voluntarily admitted a person or persons unknown, whom he or they were expecting, and that said person or persons, having gained admission, murdered those present and stole the cash and the drugs. It seems likely that said person or persons unknown are not now and have never been active in the Boston underworld.

'5. Unidentified male caller employed hotline number morning of press reports. Agitated voice. Inquired whether armored-car reward still in effect. Said I didn't know. Asked for number to reach him. He said he'd get back to me P.M. Checked with Foster: Still in force. Payment okayed if Friary killers identified though not convicted of robberies. Unidentified male caller checked in P.M. Information conveyed. Said he would "think about it."

'6. These are the same guys, Terry. This is the same band of brigands that's been robbing the armored cars. They're branching out from their old tricks, and that is why they haven't hit the shopping center banks again. Somehow they got wind of the fact that we'd identified Simone, Handley and Fentress from the fast-food joints, and Walker from the tire store. My guess is that Fentress made a friend of like mind down in the Warwick lunch spot, and the friend tipped her off. My guess is also that either Franklin or Fentress, or maybe both of them, were getting it on in round-robins with McKechnie and Iverson, and that's how Tibbetts and the rest of them found out about the coke and cash. If we could only find these bastards, we could hang them high. See me soon as you get back.'

9

At 10:40 on the morning of May 3, 1978, the regular grand jury impaneled for Suffolk County concluded its thirty days of service. Accompanied by Asst. Atty. Gen. Terrence Gleason, the grand jury delivered its last batch of indictments into the dim courtroom of the otherwise idle Second Criminal Session on the eighth floor of the New Courthouse at Pemberton Square in Boston. The only people in the room were the judge, the clerk, the stenographer, the prosecutor, and the twenty-three grand jurors overcrowding the sixteen-seat jury box and occupying chairs inside the bar normally used by counsel and defendants. A court officer stood outside the doors to turn away any buffs or reporters who might arrive.

Assistant Clerk Michael Fournier accepted a thin sheaf of papers from the foreman and handed them up to Judge Donald Kittles. The judge inspected the seven papers folded twice and noted that they were marked 'Secret.' He glanced inquiringly at the foreman, frowned, looked back at the papers and unfolded the one on top. As he read he pursed his lips. He put it down and took up the other six in turn, his frown remaining. When he finished reading the last of them, he nodded. Groping for an elastic band at the front of the blotter on his bench, he peered over his half-frame eyeglasses at the prosecutor. 'Mister Gleason,' he said.

The prosecutor stood. 'Your Honor,' he said.

'Yes,' Kittles said. 'Warrants to issue?'

'If your Honor please,' Gleason said.

'Documents to be impounded?' the judge said.

'So moved, pending apprehension,' Gleason said.

The judge snapped the elastic band around the seven documents. He handed them over the rail of the bench to Fournier. Fournier opened the top fold of each of the papers in turn and copied the name typed in after the printed legend reciting that the grand jurors for the Commonwealth had alleged that person guilty of a crime. Then he put the papers in a white envelope which he sealed. He took a stamp from the top drawer of his desk and marked the front and back of the envelope in black ink: 'SECRET.'

'Motion granted,' the judge said. He turned his gaze to the grand jury. 'Mister Foreman, ladies and gentlemen,' he said, linking his hands on the blotter and hunching forward, 'I understand you have completed your service.'

The foreman was a white man in his late fifties. 'We have, your Honor,' he said.

'It is customary,' the judge said, 'for the judge who accepts the final report of each grand jury to extend in turn the thanks of the Commonwealth for your devoted service. That is my function now. We are aware that your service comes at considerable personal cost and inconvenience to yourselves, and applaud you for your dedication to your civic duty. The foundation of our system of justice is that no person shall be called upon to answer to a charge of felony, or punished thereon, except that such charge shall have been presented by a grand jury of his peers. Who have determined there is probable cause to believe that such crime has been committed, and that he or she, the person named, is who committed it. This is a serious responsibility.

'You, as members of the grand jury, are the living barriers between citizens and tyranny. I am sure as you have come here for the past six weeks in the New England springtime, your thoughts and inclinations have often been elsewhere. With your work. With your families. With your daily concerns. With those blasted Red Sox.' The jurors smiled. 'But nevertheless you have come; you have listened; you have deliberated.' His face creased in a grin. 'And you have lost wages by the bucketful.'

The grand jurors beamed at him.

'Mister Gleason,' he said, nodding toward him, 'is but one of the capable prosecutors who have depended upon you to, in effect, try his case before it is tried in court, before a petit jury. These are important matters you have reported on today, and all the other days when you have come into this session. Your impartiality in weighing the evidence they have presented to you is the ornament of our system at law. You have served well. You are dismissed. Go with our thanks, and God bless all of you.'

Gleason shook hands with each of the grand jurors as they left the courtroom. He waited in the corridor by the elevators as they entered the cars. Then he turned to his right and went into the stairwell opening beyond the men's room. He descended the metal steps – enclosed on his left by cyclone fencing material installed after one desperate defendant attempted to escape returning to his holding cell by jumping to his death – and descended to the seventh floor. He emerged into an identical corridor outside the busy courtroom of the First Criminal Session, made his way through the crowd of lawyers, defendants and cops outside the doors of the courtroom on his left, and entered the internal corridor behind the northerly elevator banks. There were small offices along it, occupied by younger Assistant District Attorneys handling arraignments, bail hearings, defaults and other minor matters before the First Criminal Session.

The door to the third one on his right was open. He went in. The desk was cluttered with files, but the chair behind it was vacant. He went behind the desk and sat down. He picked up the phone. He dialed four numbers. He said: 'Gleason. John there?' He waited. He drummed his fingers. He said: 'John. Yes, the newspapers were right: snow was general over Ireland. You said *you* believe Mackenzie? *They* believe Mackenzie.'

He paused. He laughed. 'Of course they went for it, John. How could anybody disbelieve you. We got 'em. Go get 'em.' He listened. He laughed again. He said: 'Of course they were satisfied, for Christ sake, John. I told 'em when I came in. I said: 'Awright. You folks, I dunno what you folks've heard about grand juries. Prolly that you're rubber stamps for the prosecutors. Well if you have, it's true. That's what you're supposed to be. You think I come in here looking for you to indict cases I can't win in court, you're nuts. You think I come in here wanting you to tell me I can't win a winner? You're wrong. When I come in here with the papers, what I have got in mind for you to do is sign the papers, and unless you think I'm clearly crazy, that's what you should do. Because I do know my job, folks. I do know my job." So go and get the bastards.'

A slight white man with wispy grey hair, a sallow complexion and stooped posture entered the cubicle as Gleason hung up the phone. He was carrying four thick brown cardboard accordion folios tied with faded red ribbons. He stared at Gleason. 'Hey,' he said, 'you're not Harrington.'

Gleason sat back in the chair and clasped his hands behind his head. 'Got me there, Bill,' he said.

'You, you're Gleason,' the man said.

'Got me again,' Gleason said.

The man frowned. 'You're supposed to be gone,' he said. 'You were supposed to leave.'

'I did,' Gleason said. 'I left four years ago.'

'So,' the man said, 'how come you're in here, then?'

'Using the phone,' Gleason said.

'You ask somebody?' the man said.

'No,' Gleason said. 'I remembered how to do it.'

'Not supposed to do that,' the man said. 'Guys in private practice, not supposed to come in here and use our telephones after they're not with us anymore.'

'I'm not in private practice,' Gleason said. 'Still a prosecutor. Different kind of prosecutor. But still a prosecutor.'

'That's why you left?' the man said. 'I never heard of that. Nobody ever leaves here, and when they do, they leave. You one those federal guys or something, did a thing like that? That isn't very smart.'

Gleason stood up. He hitched up his pants. 'I know it,' he said. 'You got me again.'

*

Det. Lt. Insp. John D. Richards in his office at 20 Ashburton Place a block away put the handset down and sat back in his chair. He clasped his hands across his stomach and stared at the woman sitting in front of the desk. 'Now you're sure,' he said.

'I'm absolutely sure,' she said.

'Because this is a volunteer assignment,' he said. 'You haven't been a trooper that long. Things could get a little hinky out there, we go in on this.'

'I know,' she said.

'You've never shot a man,' he said. 'The other five guys on this job're all combat veterans. They have shot other guys. But you, you've never shot a man.'

'I hope I never do,' she said.

'But you wouldn't hesitate to shoot one,' he said.

'No, I wouldn't,' she said.

'One these sons of bitches comes busting out of there and starts making loud noises with a gun,' he said, 'you're not going to duck down and cover up now, are you?'

'Certainly am not,' she said. 'If I'm the sixth gun on this job, it's because the job might need six shooters. I knew that when I came in.'

'And you still want to do it,' he said.

'Lieutenant,' she said, 'the way I get it, three of the suspects are women.'

'That's correct,' he said. 'Well, we're really not that sure. We think they may've replaced Handley, but they may not've. Gleason got a second Jane Doe indictment to be on the safe side.'

'And those women,' she said, 'those women've been in on the robberies and in on The Friary killings right along with the men.'

'We're not charging the robberies here,' Richards said. 'Just The Friary. And, you want my honest opinion, we're not all that fat on evidence even for that. What we're basically hoping here, we're hoping to get lucky, so that afterwards Gleason and I can turn one the bastards. Maybe then we get the robberies. But for now all we're hoping is to immobilize the bastards. The Friary case's thin, but it's also all we've got.'

'Well,' she said, 'but if Tibbetts and Walker and the John Doe trust them, trust the women enough to shoot, don't you sort of have to trust me? Too?'

Richards grinned. 'June,' he said, 'no, I don't. I don't have to do a damned thing that I don't want to do. What Miss Gloria Steinem and that gang say about how you got equal rights – none of that applies here. Doesn't matter if it's right. The reason you're being considered is that I think if this thing works, it's gonna work because those guys've been on the run so long, and succeeded at it, because they're used to keeping their eyes peeled for guys in uniforms and guys that aren't in uniform but wear suits like uniforms. They think they know what cops look like, and so far they've been right. Reason I want you in this patrol is that you don't look like a cop to me, so I think you won't to them. You do not look like a cop.'

She blushed and looked down at her lap.

'Now,' Richards said, 'the reason that Sara Kindred and Molly Dennis're not sitting where you're sitting now is that – and you'd better not tell them this, because they're mad enough at me as it is, and they're good troopers that I don't want any madder – but it's because the only difference between them is their heads. You could swap their heads – take Sara's head and put it on Molly's body and Molly's head on hers – and the only way anybody'd be able to tell the switch was made'd be if the stitching wasn't good. They may be real ladies, but they look like cops to me, and they would to someone else. Big, tough cops.'

She coughed to hide a laugh.

'Those bodies,' he said, 'those're not the kind of bodies that a couple guys with a nice houseboat on the river'd invite on a little cruise on a summer's day.'

She looked up at him. 'No,' she said. 'And you'd better not tell them that I said that, either.'

'I won't,' he said. 'You still signed on?'

'I'm still signed on,' she said.

'All right,' he said. 'Now, here is the procedure. We rendezvous tonight at twenty-hundred hours at the Black Horse Inn on Route Sixty-three north of Greenfield. The rooms're all booked in the name of Commonwealth Construction Company, me as Richard John being the president. I'm sharing a billet with Sergeant Martin Rowley of Troop B, whom you probably met in training.'

'The armorer, uh huh,' she said. She grimaced.

'You found Sergeant Rowley somewhat abrasive, did you?' Richards said.

'That's a mild way of putting it,' she said. 'He got very put out with me when, my first try with the machinegun, I didn't fire short bursts.'

'Most do,' Richards said. 'Find him abrasive, that is. Some even find him abusive. Most also fail to fire short bursts their first try with the machinegun. But Sergeant Rowley remains convinced that skill with firearms is an essential part of the accomplished trooper's repertoire, and that's why he acts that way.

'Sergeant Tom Morrissette from Foxboro,' Richards said, 'will bunk with Corporal William Hanson of Holderness barracks.

97

Hanson knows the river, because he grew up there. Sergeant Morrissette and Corporal Hanson, you probably don't know. Sergeant Morrissette was a Recon Marine in Korea. He looks and sounds like the second curate in a three-priest parish, and his specialty was killing silently. I tell you this because Sergeant Morrissette will not. He is not generous with insights about himself. I think he believes the savages have something when they refuse to have their photographs taken: because the camera will steal their spirits. I believe he collects and personally destroys all his nail clippings and whiskers lest some witch doctor get hold of them, and use them to get power over him. Sergeant Morrissette is a formidable man. With him in back of you, you need not fear the hostiles.

'Corporal Hanson,' Richards said, 'was Underwater Demolition with the Navy. Frogman. Expert with explosives. Very fine pistol shot.

'You will room alone, of course,' Richards said, 'and so will Trooper Frederick Consolo. Trooper Consolo is a recent recruit to our ranks. He comes by way of the Metropolitan District Commission force, where he distinguished himself by shooting a rattlesnake. He did this on horseback while his mount was rearing in fear of the snake, thus demonstrating that he is an expert horseman, a crack shot with the revolver, and unimpressed by wildlife regulations declaring the rattlers in the Blue Hills Reservation an endangered species. That disrespect got him reprimanded and suspended for two weeks with no pay, which in turn pissed him off enough so that he applied to us. Trooper Consolo was a sniper with the Green Berets in Vietnam. He has the reputation of being among the, shall we say, sexually more aggressive members of the young male bachelor set. He is rich, by our standards, at least, and he is personally well groomed. I'm told that many young women find him attractive. At the risk of offending you: You are not to do so, at least on this assignment.'

She sighed. 'Lieutenant,' she said, 'I met Cowboy Fred at Framingham one night and he put a move on me. I dusted him off then. If he does it again, I'll do it again. You have my solemn word.'

'Fine,' Richards said. 'We'll meet for dinner at the inn at twenty-thirty hours – civvies, naturally. Those who wish will have a couple beers or other refreshments after dinner, and that's *all* that they will have. We will retire at twenty-two hundred hours. Wake-up time tomorrow will be oh-five-thirty hours. Breakfast. Jump-off to the marina at oh-seven-thirty hours. From the marina: oh-eight-fifteen hours. I want to be off the beach from that little retreat before nine-hundred hours, and we are going to do it. I want our subjects to be still in the middle of their Cheerios and herbal tea when we arrive to see them.

'It is very important,' he said, 'and I can't emphasize this enough, that we keep the element of surprise on our side. Tibbetts and Walker are very dangerous men. The only reason they didn't kill anybody until three years ago was that they apparently didn't think it was necessary. They left a young man paralyzed on one of the armored-car robberies – that at this time we can't prove, and if hearsay was good evidence we'd be able to prove they killed one of their own people when they decided she was ratting out on them. The only question in my mind about the part they played in The Friary murders is whether we can prove it.

'The way we got this indictment, these indictments,' he said, 'was we finally got a blabbermouth, a stinking sewer rat, and he for money told us what his old pals've been doing. Some of it, at any rate. He held back what he did with them, when he was doing it.

'The rat did this for money,' Richards said. 'Did it for a reward. Naturally he's a bit nervous, lest his old chums find this out. He's afraid that they will kill him, and I must confess, I see his point. That would be my inclination, so I assume it will be theirs.

'There's no question,' Richards said, 'that we've got enough on this guy's statement to go into some convenient District Court and get complaints and arrest warrants. But if we'd've done that, once we arrested the bastards they'd be entitled to a probable cause hearing. And those things're dodgy. First thing you know, you've got some antic judge up there, letting them go free. Not only're we not gonna see them again, because they're gonna vanish like Ariel, into thin air, but they're gonna figure out how we snapped them in the first place. So Terry says to me: "Fuck public probable cause. Fuck hearings. We'll put the guy's statement into the grand jury, through you, which is *prima facie* probable cause, and then they'll be indicted. And then by the time they get their first crack at deducing who the polecat is, they will be in custody. And he'll be safe from them."'

'So what we did was have me go into the grand jury after some other, minor witnesses, and I read what this guy told us, from the transcript of our talk, and I said I believed it. Without giving them his name. And Terry said that's good enough. They could indict on that.

'Terry Gleason's a son of a bitch in court,' Richards said. 'And he's our son of a bitch, and he says he can do it. So I have to believe him. But I'm not as confident as Terry, on the state of the evidence as we've got it now. Still, I can see why, after four years of doing almost nothing but going after these birds, he's getting a little impatient. And since I've got eight years in on it myself, I guess maybe so am I. But there's a real question whether we can surface our informer in this case, when it comes to trial, and a real question whether his testimony'll stand up if we do surface him.

'So,' Richards said, 'it's a matter of crucial importance that when we go in tomorrow morning, we hit that place like a battering ram and prevent them from getting rid of anything that might link them to this fucking slaughter that they did a year ago. I'd imagine any coke they got is probably long gone. If they didn't snort it, they sold it. The money? Well, unless Nichols and Abbate had it labeled as theirs, and the labels aren't gone, finding it may not help us much. If there's any left. We'll therefore be looking for twenty-two caliber automatic pistols, High Standards, at the most two of them. And also for any little sentimental keepsakes that the ladies may've saved from the dalliances they had with the cook and the waitress in The Friary. Because according to our source, that's how Tibbetts and Walker first found out about the booty, and how to get into it.

'When we go cruising down the Deerfield, tomorrow bright and early,' he said, 'you and friend Consolo in your bathing costumes will be lounging on the roof of the houseboat in such manner and position as to suggest to the casual observer that you are utterly engrossed in each other's physical attributes.'

'I see,' she said.

'I'm sorry,' Richards said. 'It's necessary. You saying you find Trooper Consolo's prospective attentions more disagreeable than you find the prospect of filling someone's belly with lead?'

'In a word, yes,' she said. 'The guy's got more hands'n a damned watch factory. The night I ran into him in Framingham, and we were both in full pack uniform at the time, I felt like I'd bumped into an octopus.'

Richards nodded. 'Well,' he said, 'keeping in mind that I've now told you too much to let you out of this detail, I guess you're going to have to grin and bear it.'

'Only this time,' she said, 'in a bikini.'

'Well,' Richards said, 'I suppose it doesn't have to be that. But it's got to be something along that line, because otherwise you won't look like what I want you to look like when we show up at that cabin.'

'Which is … a tramp,' she said.

'That's correct,' he said. 'Harsh, but still, correct. When Hanson runs that craft aground the sandbar he says is there, and you and Consolo jump off the roof with your sidearms in plastic bags, and the rest of us come out of that cabin like bats out of Hell, I want any chance spectators to be absolutely stunned.'

She nodded. She took a deep breath. 'Okay,' she said, 'but I'm going to tell him, you know, if he touches the wrong place, I may blow the whole patrol and use the gun on him.'

Richards gazed at her. 'You can tell him you're going to do that,' he said, 'but you'd better not do it.'

She returned his gaze. 'How about,' she said, 'how about if I don't do it until after the arrests?'

He grinned. 'Satisfactory,' he said. 'That I'll tolerate.'

'Deal,' she said.

He stood up behind the desk. 'Okay,' he said, 'let's go get our stuff together, and meet the other kids.'

10

John Bigelow's office occupied three hundred square feet of trapezoidal space on the second floor of the townhouse at 91 Beacon Street in Boston owned by Damon, Bigelow & Connors. It overlooked an alley, and the bay windows were sun-blocked by the townhouse at 93. Bigelow at fifty-one inhabited the space like an orderly bear, his clean antique cherry desk located precisely in the window bay so that he presided with his back to the dim light over the leather armchairs for clients and the fireplace behind them. There were floor-to-ceiling bookcases on each of the walls except at the base of the trapezoid, where the fireplace was surrounded by portraits done in oil or photographed by Bachrach. There was a worn Aubusson rug on the parquet floor. His voice initially seemed too soft for a man of his size; he reserved volume to make emphases.

When Clayton and Florence Walker were settled in the chairs,

Bigelow took his own and cleared his throat. 'I've found it helps,' he said, 'if everyone is candid. As candid as possible, at least. At your request, through Mister Badger, I have seen and talked to James. I can give you my impressions of him and his case, and I want to do that, as I told you on the phone, before you see him yourselves. But I cannot divulge what he said to me, or any responses of my own that might suggest – except in the most general terms – what he said.'

'We quite understand that,' Clayton said. His white hair was tousled and matted, dampened to his skull by the early summer humid heat of his walk across the Public Garden. His face was flushed and he was flustered. 'I assured Mister Badger, as I am assuring you, that we fully comprehend the relationship between you, and appreciate very much your willingness to see us at all.' He paused and frowned. 'We're new to this,' he said, 'this terrible sort of thing. Any help that you can give us, much appreciated.'

'I'm afraid it won't be much,' Bigelow said. 'As much as I sympathize with you in your predicament, as much as I truly think that the people paying the bills are entitled to all the solace the lawyer can provide, there simply isn't a great deal that I can say to comfort you. James is in bad trouble. It's made worse by his attitude, his perception of it. He was hostile toward me when I arrived. He was hostile when I left. He'd already refused to see Mister Badger – both Mister Badgers, in fact, despite the fact that they'd arrived on short notice, interrupted their weekend, at your express request. Why he consented to see me, I do not know. The Charles Street Jail's not a pleasant place to stay – perhaps by the time I showed up, he'd become tired of his cell. I can only speculate.

'He appeared to be in relatively good physical shape,' Bigelow said. 'Fatigued, truculent, "defiant," one could say. But in full possession of his faculties. Not that that's a plus.'

'Why is that?' Florence said. 'I should think that would be good. If he has to face this case.'

'Ordinarily it would be,' Bigelow said. 'Ordinarily a client in a disturbed state greatly complicates his lawyer's job. But in your son's instance, given the extreme gravity of the charges against him, some agitation at least would be appropriate.' He paused. 'You're familiar, I'm sure, Doctor,' he said, 'with the "Fight or Flight Syndrome"?'

'I am,' Clayton said. 'But James has always had what we call a "low-affect personality."' He scowled. 'Unlike his sister, who's if anything too resourceful. But James, James lacks motivation – self-motivation, at least – unfortunately he was all too responsive to the kind of stimulus Tibbetts was able to give.'

'Well,' Bigelow said, 'that's my point, then, in a nutshell. James fails to manifest either of the symptoms appropriate to animals under stress. It's almost as though he perceives his situation as irrelevant.'

'Well,' Florence said, 'is that because he thinks he's going to go free?'

'I really couldn't say,' Bigelow said. '*I* don't, if that's what you mean. The Commonwealth's case, what little of it I've been able to glean from cursory examination of the documents that they've filed, certainly isn't airtight. And it deserves the suspicion appropriate to all evidence that hasn't been tested. Liars sometimes look like bishops, swearing affidavits.

'On the other hand,' Bigelow said, 'although it isn't ironclad, the Commonwealth's case, it's certainly substantial enough to warrant serious apprehension by the persons facing it. Murder in the first degree's equaled or excelled only by treason in the popular mind in gravity of offense. Jurors on such cases tend to take themselves very seriously, and no matter how often they're told that the defendants are presumed innocent, conclude from the mere fact that the cops believe them to be killers that they must be pretty bad actors. And James and the others are alleged to have killed not one, but seven. So that indigenous suspicion will be multiplied. It's one thing to look at a drunken-driving charge, say, and say: "Well, even if I lose, what's the penalty? Lose my license for a while. Let's go – let's take the shot." It's quite another thing to say: "Murder One? They can't prove that." But if they do, it's life.

'So,' he said, 'under the circumstances, I would have expected the defendant to welcome the visit of the Badgers, which he did not, and to be, if not gladdened, then at least relieved when I showed up to see him. And he definitely was not.'

'Well,' Clayton said, 'nevertheless, we want to do everything we can for him, and we want you to do that, too.'

'Doctor Walker,' Bigelow said, 'Mrs. Walker, that may well be my point, if I do represent your son. It may be – and forgive me for this observation if you find it offensive – but it may be that you've hit upon precisely the thing that bothers me the most about this very troublesome case. And this equally troublesome young man. If what the Commonwealth alleges is correct, he and his co-defendants have voluntarily, and as openly as you can without being captured, lived outside the law for the better part of six years. *At least* six years. Mister Gleason – Mister Gleason is the prosecutor – Mister Gleason is a very artful man. I know him well, have faced him many times. While it's of no concern to you or James, we don't like each other. But that does not cause me to underestimate him. He knows how to plant mines in a case, so that one false step by an unwary defense counsel sets off an explosion that destroys his client's cause. Experienced as I am with Mister Gleason's – I don't want to call them "tricks," although I think I'd be justified – I've learned to read his documents very carefully. He may not have as much as he'd like, but he may have more than he needs, and something in reserve as well, to spring a trap on me.

'To avoid those traps, I'm going to need full client cooperation. The sullen submission of a young man whose parents – and now lawyer – want to "do everything we can for him" will not suffice unto the day. I can spend your money without stint, my time heedless of expense. But if he persists in his current attitude, I will be helpless; he will be convicted, and you will be distressed. Under the circumstances, as much as Larry Badger cherishes you, and as greatly as I sympathize with any friend of his, I really hesitate to tell you that you'll get your money's worth. James is entitled to a public defender. He's of age. He says he has no money. Your circumstances are immaterial. Speaking forthrightly, I must tell you I think that might be best.'

'You don't want the case,' Clayton said.

'Doctor Walker,' Bigelow said, 'any criminal lawyer who tells you that he "doesn't want" a first-degree murder case calling for a fifty-thousand-dollar retainer up-front, from people who have the money; any trial lawyer who tells you that he "doesn't want" a murder case in which funds for investigation, and resources to conduct them, are unlimited – any criminal lawyer who tells you that will tell you next that calling horses "plovers" enables them to fly. Do I make myself clear?'

'Impeccably,' Florence said.

'The question for you, therefore,' Bigelow said, 'is not whether

I will put up with your son for the money, the aggravation the experience will bring – of course I will. The question is whether my aggravation, in and of itself, will satisfy you that you've been well served, in the light he is convicted. As he probably will be. That question is for you.'

Clayton sighed. Florence gazed at him. She looked back at Bigelow. 'You and Larry do your damnedest,' she said. 'I think it's conscience money.'

Bigelow took a pen from the holder at the front of his desk. He opened the left top drawer and took out a legal pad. 'Mrs. Walker,' he said, 'we will. You may be assured of that. But because James, I fear, will not do *his* damnedest, I'm forced to rely upon you for investigative leads I'd normally expect from my client.'

'I'm afraid we don't know much,' Florence said, her lips tightening. 'James has been very elusive, for several years. At least as far as we're concerned. We saw him only seldom, after he moved to California. When we did, he was not communicative.'

'Not about his friends?' Bigelow said. 'His associates, and so forth?'

'No,' she said firmly, 'not at all.'

Clayton looked troubled. 'Well,' he said, 'there was, there were one or two, at least, that we knew about. There was the Simone girl – what was her name, dear? Audrey or something?'

'I really don't recall,' Florence said.

'Well, you met her,' Clayton said. 'She stayed at our house. With that young Mackenzie fellow, the one that always looked startled if you spoke to him.'

'Oh, for heaven's sake, Clayton,' she said, 'that was *years* ago.'

'Andrea,' Clayton said. 'Andrea Simone. That was that girl's name. She had money,' he said to Bigelow. 'He did not. I recall one night when I got home very late, some emergency or something, and they were both up, in the library, having an argument. I thought James was with them – he turned out not to be. And they seemed like nice young people, idealistic, quite in love, and I said to them: "Now, what can be this important, to carry on like this?" And he said – I can recall this vividly; it seemed to me so odd – "Her loyalty is to the State, no matter what she says." And, it's coming back to me now, her father was a physician, out near San Francisco somewhere, and I said: "Her loyalty is to her family, also probably to you." And he glared at me, just glared at me, and said: "Of course you would say that."'

'He was probably drunk,' Florence said. 'Whenever James brought friends home, which wasn't very often, the first thing that they did was raid the liquor cabinet.'

'Do you know what the young man's first name was?' Bigelow said to Clayton.

'I will,' Clayton said, 'if you give me a minute.'

'While you're taking it,' Bigelow said, 'how about the two women arrested with Tibbetts and James? The Fentress and Franklin defendants? Ever meet them? Any facts on them?'

'None whatsoever,' Florence said. 'Never heard of them in my life.'

'Glenn,' Clayton said. 'The Mackenzie fellow's name was Glenn. I think he came from around here. Or he was going to school here or something. In Boston.'

Florence sighed. 'He was going to law school,' she said.

'Do you know which one?' Bigelow said. 'We do have a number here.'

'Boston University,' Clayton said. 'At least he'd been at Boston University. I think that was where it was.' He paused. He shook his head. 'No,' he said, 'no, I don't. The women, I don't. The women, I don't know. Can't say that I met them.'

Florence shook her head. 'Afraid I can't help you, either,' she said to Bigelow. 'I've never heard their names.'

'Handley,' Bigelow said. 'Ever hear of her? Girl named Emma Handley?'

Florence shook her head. 'Means nothing to me.'

Clayton scowled again. 'Wait a minute,' he said, 'just a minute – that does sound familiar.'

'Clayton,' Florence said, 'no one named Handley was ever in our house.'

'No,' Clayton said, 'no, I wasn't thinking that. But Emmy Handley. That I've heard. That name is familiar.' His expression cleared. 'I know,' he said to Florence, 'Christina mentioned her. Christina, when Christina came home one weekend from school here, right after she went back, you and she, you were talking about someone named Handley. Christina was upset.' He looked at Bigelow. 'Several years ago,' he said. 'Three or four, at least.'

'Emma Handley's dead,' Bigelow said.

'Then what help could she be,' Florence said, 'if she's not even alive?'

Bigelow raised his eyebrows. 'Not everything that's helpful to know would be helpful to put in evidence,' he said. 'Larry tells me she was murdered, perhaps by the Tibbetts gang. If Larry suspects this, so does Gleason. But the Handley homicide – that's precisely the kind of bombshell that Gleason likes to set off. I want to be ready to spike any effort he makes to sneak her into this case. So, if James was acquainted with her, if they were associates, it has to influence significantly how I try it. *Two* pairs of kid gloves, not one.

'Your daughter,' he said. 'Christina? What would she be likely to know?'

Clayton looked at Florence. 'Nothing, I should think,' he said, redirecting his gaze to Bigelow. 'She had … she did have a brief romance with Tibbetts – isn't that so, Florence?'

Florence sighed. 'She was in the same places he was in, for a year or so. She was young. Much younger than James and the rest. She had a soloist's appointment with an orchestra from the University of Ipswich, and the tour, they went on a tour that stopped in California, and she, naturally she got in touch with James, and saw him, and he introduced her to Sam. And later, later she brought, or James brought, or they both brought Sam to our place, and he stayed with us. That was probably the second or the third time he'd been there.

'She was very young, Mister Bigelow,' Florence said. 'She was prematurely sophisticated, or believed she was, and Sam was older, and glamorous, so she was vulnerable. They did have a brief fling. But that was *years* ago. I don't believe she's had any contact with Sam for years.'

'Would you know?' Bigelow said.

Florence considered her answer. She moistened her lips. 'If,' she said, 'if Christina thought I should know, or that I had found out, yes. If not, then no.'

'She's secretive?' Bigelow said.

Clayton cleared his throat again. 'Everyone has secrets. Bargains they have made, sometimes, that they shouldn't have.'

111

11

Trial of *Commonwealth* v. *Samuel F. Tibbetts, et al*, was scheduled to commence at 10:00 A.M. on Thursday, September 7, 1978 in Courtroom 6 of the New Courthouse at Pemberton Square in Boston, Judge Howard Bart presiding. Judge Bart was fifty-four, a graduate of Holy Cross College and the night law school at Boston College. John Richards learned of Bart's assignment to the case on the morning of September 5th. He complimented Terry Gleason.

'I assume this was not luck, Counselor,' he said. 'I assume Black Bart with his portable gallows and his extra coil of rope did not just fall from the sky to sit on this case.'

'No,' Gleason said. 'No, as a matter of fact, Judge Bart just concluded a civil motion session down in Barnstable. My understanding is that last spring he miscalculated the length of the summer – decided it'd probably start to get cold about now. Therefore he told the assignment judge that as soon as he finished up his summer on the Cape, and closed up his house in Eastham, he wanted to get back to Boston and his house on Com. Ave. And since nobody crosses Black Bart – unless they're ignorant or crazy – comes Labor Day and here's Judge Bart, looking for something to do.'

'Interesting this's what they found for him, though,' Richards said.

'Well,' Gleason said, 'it sort of figures, right? He likes criminal better'n civil. I was having a drink with him down at Chatham Bars Inn at the spring Bar Association do, and he was griping about "goddamned civil cases. Never any fun. The hell can you do in a civil case? Jury has all the fun. Sit up there on your arse like Mary on the Half Shell and a blue floodlight at night on some goddamned ghinny's lawn, and the only thing you get to do's yell at some stupid bastard lawyer, doesn't know a damned thing about the rules of evidence. I like," this is what he said to me, "what I like to do is *decide the goddamned case*, goddamn it." I saw him this morning, his way up the Hill, and he said: "Any chance they'll waive jury, you think?" Told him I doubted it.'

Richards laughed. 'Right,' he said. 'I can just see John Morrissey and Bigelow waiving jury so Black Bart's the whole show. Yes, I can imagine that. I can also imagine John Morrissey appearing bare-ass in the courtroom to concede his client's guilt. Well, we caught one break, at least. Maybe this is a good omen.'

At 10:10 on the morning of the seventh, Judge Bart surveyed the perspiring courtroom crowd. A venire of sixty potential jurors filled all but the first row of benches behind the railing that enclosed the bar.

'Ladies and gentlemen of the venire,' he said. 'The lawyers and the clerks and the bailiffs know the reason why we're all so hot today in this air-conditioned room. They know because they're familiar with this old barn and its peculiarities. And also, also familiar with mine. My peculiarity is a strong belief that the lawyers, and the jury, and the judge, as far as that goes, should be able to hear what the witnesses say on the stand. Counsel may now and then doubt it, but I also believe it's useful if the judge on the bench can hear what the lawyers have to say. Critical, in fact.

'The legislative branch, in its wisdom, has not seen fit to replace the air-conditioning units since they were installed – shortly after the siege of Vicksburg, I believe it was. It is true that they remain in good enough repair to alleviate the discomfort of the heat, but at the same time they drown out any sound originating more than six feet away from the person trying to hear it. So I, and most other judges who share my bias in the matter, order them shut off when we begin a trial. We will run them during recesses, during the luncheon recess, and all night when we recess at four each afternoon. That will help a little. But otherwise, I am afraid, you're going to have to sweat.

'Second in the Churchillian trinity,' he said, 'second comes the tears. Those of you who are selected to serve on this panel will be sequestered. This means that we are going to lock you up, in no uncertain terms. You will be billeted at a reasonably comfortable hotel, fed reasonably good food, permitted to receive clothing and toilet articles delivered by your loved ones – or picked up by court officers, if you live alone – and generally treated as if you were in quarantine with some loathsome disease. You will not enjoy it one bit, and we all know it, and we will do the very best we can to see to it that you endure the ordeal in the best comfort possible. Which isn't, to be honest, very much.

'We are doing this because the remaining item in the

Churchillian trinity – the blood – is very much a part of the evidence in this case. I will address questions to all of you – and I beg each of you to answer if you find any or all of them pertinent – intended to ascertain whether you have formed any opinions that might hinder or prevent you from reaching, *on the evidence and the evidence alone*, a fair and impartial verdict in what can only be fairly described as a lurid case. I neither can, nor wish to, exclude the media from these proceedings. I think extremely high risks must be demonstrated to warrant closure of criminal proceedings, and I don't see them in this case. What I do see, since I read the papers every day and often watch TV, is a certain appetite among the members of the press for stories such as I expect to develop during these proceedings. Often I have noted a certain tone in such reports which suggests to me that the reporter has personally formed an opinion of the guilt or innocence of some defendant. We don't want you to suffer such intervention in your deliberations. We don't want any seepage of opinions, or judgments, made by other people, to contaminate your individual judgments in this case. So, because we don't want that to happen, and we can't muzzle the press, we're going to lock you up. We will let you read the papers, and let you watch TV, but the papers that you get your hands on will be clipped of any reports of this trial, and TV news is out.

'Now,' he said, 'I'm going to ask each of the defendants to rise as I call their names, and each of their lawyers to rise also. Then I will ask the prosecutor and his assistant to do the same thing. After each of them has stood, and sat – because I and the witnesses are the only ones in this room who get to sit down while we talk – after that is over, I will address you generally with the question: "Do you, any of you, know any of these people? Have you ever had any personal dealings with one or more of them which would make it unlikely that you could render a fair and impartial verdict, solely on the facts as they appear from the evidence?

'Now, I'm not talking here about whether any of these people looks vaguely familiar. Or whether you've ever said "Hello" to one of them, or passed them on the sidewalk. What I want to know is whether you've ever done any sort of business with any of the defendants, or any of the lawyers, or any of the police officers, that will be involved in this case. And if so, whether you formed any relationships or opinions that would bias you, either in favor of, or against, any one of them. I expect you to tell me the truth. I not only expect you to tell the truth if you hate one or more of them – most of you might be tempted to say that anyway, even if it was not true, just to escape sequestration – but also to tell the truth if you love one or more of them. We want a fair shake for everybody here – the defendants, the Commonwealth, and each and every citizen who goes about his daily business in what I at least hope is the assumption that what passes for justice in American courts really amounts to that. Am I understood?'

The members of the venire nodded in unison. The judge addressed the lawyers. 'Any problems with that, gentlemen? Anything I've said so far?' The lawyers, remaining seated, shook their heads. 'So far, so good,' Bart said.

'Mister Samuel Tibbetts,' he said. Tibbetts – 'looking maximum meek,' John Richards whispered to Gleason at the prosecutor's table – stood up. He wore a dark blue suit, a white shirt, and a red knitted tie. His reddish-blond hair receded from his forehead. He wore octagonal eyeglasses with gold wire frames. 'Please face the rear of the courtroom, Mister Tibbetts,' Bart said. Tibbetts turned and faced the venire.

'Mister Tibbetts is represented by Attorney John Morrissey,' Bart said. 'Mister Morrissey, if you also would confront the venire.' Morrissey did so.

'Mister Tibbetts is a native of Newton,' Bart said. 'Mister Morrissey lives in Weston and has practiced law here in Boston for many years. Is any member of the venire aware of any reason which might prevent him or her from rendering a true verdict in the proceedings against Mister Tibbetts?' There was no response. 'I should add,' Bart said, 'that the charges against Mister Tibbetts, and each of the other three defendants are those of murder in the first degree.'

Four men in the venire immediately got to their feet. 'Uh, huh,' Bart said. 'I haven't even gotten to the question about whether your views on capital punishment would prevent you from reaching a just verdict, and you're already on your tiptoes. How many of you work for the Massachusetts Bay Transportation Authority?' Three of the men raised their hands.

'For the benefit of newcomers to our criminal justice system,' the judge said, 'the personnel of the MBTA are all but universally so morally and philosophically opposed to capital punishment that their revulsion precludes them from sitting as jurors in murder cases.' The lawyers, policemen and bailiffs grinned, along with the clerk. The civilians behind the bar enclosure looked puzzled. 'Some are so cynical as to allege that senior MBTA employees instruct all novices that such a pang of conscience will get them excused from jury duty, which pays nowhere near as well as the jobs on the MBTA, and urge them to develop such attitudes in order to avoid losing wages.' He paused. There was audible laughter. 'Telephone company employees, on the other hand,' he said, 'are nowhere near as sensitive. Some allege this is because the phone company not only allows its employees to keep the meager wages that jury duty pays, but also continues their regular salaries while they do their civic duty.

'You three bozos are excused,' he said. They picked up their newspapers quickly and started for the door. 'Hey,' the judge said, 'don't think you're going home. Or off to Suffolk Downs in time to dope the daily double. Report back to the jury pool. Somebody somewhere in this building'll find some work for you. I hope. The other fellow there – what do you have to say?'

'I'm a conscientious objector,' the man said. He was about forty years old. 'I was, I did my military as a medic. In Vietnam. I'm not, I'm not just trying to get out of something I don't want to do. That's not how I do things. It's just I think it's wrong to kill, for any reason. And that's all.'

'What do you do for a living?' the judge said.

'I'm a steamfitter,' the man said. 'I work for Malachy Construction, over Somerville. Been with them eight years now.'

'You're excused,' the judge said. 'Back to the pool. Anybody else?' No one else responded. 'Anybody got some feelings, hard or soft, about either Mister Tibbetts or his lawyer?' There was no response. 'You may be seated, gentlemen,' he said. 'Record will show that the venire stands indifferent.

'Mister Walker, Mister Bigelow, if you two would get up now and present your smiling faces to the potential jurors.'

James Walker wore a white tee shirt not quite large enough to accommodate his biceps and pectorals. Over it he wore blue and white striped overalls. His hair stood up in an Afro cut. He had a small goatee. He bowed his head and raised his right fist in the Black Power salute.

John Bigelow wore a grey suit and an expression of weariness. He closed his eyes and shook his head as he stood up.

'Mister Walker,' the judge said. 'This isn't Nuremberg, or Rome. It isn't Mexico City. You're neither war criminal nor Olympic medal-winner. You're here to be tried on murder charges, not to make statements, oral or symbolic, about any of your views. Put your fist down, square your shoulders, look the jury straight in the eye.'

Walker turned and faced the bench. He glared and gave the judge the finger. 'Fuck you, fascist pig,' he shouted.

The judge sighed. 'Very good, Mister Walker. Now you can sit down.'

'I don't want to sit down,' Walker said. 'I want to say publicly what everybody knows. That this whole system was designed to silence dissent, and stifle debate, and stop the oppressed from getting their rights. I want to stand on my feet like a man and declare that the whole American system was designed and operates to enslave the poor and black. That you and these two men at the other table there, that all of you are trying us on charges of crimes that you know we did not commit, because we oppose oppression. That you have trumped this up. Fascist bastards.'

'Bailiff,' the judge said, 'escort Mister Walker to the holding cells. Make the customary arrangements for proceedings in this room to be amplified in a secure place elsewhere in the courthouse, where Mister Walker can monitor them apart from the rest of us.'

'Fuck you,' Walker said, as the court officers approached.

'And my very best wishes to you, sir, as well,' Bart said. Walker was led away. 'Mister Bigelow,' the judge said, 'for the record, do you wish to make objection to my order?'

'So objected,' Bigelow said. 'Rule against me.'

'Done and done,' Bart said. 'Your exception to the ruling will be noted as well.

'Ladies and gentlemen of the venire,' Bart said. 'This happened a little sooner in this case than I expected, so I find myself obliged to make up ground. You are not to draw any inference, for or against, any party in this case, because of any non-testimonial conduct which the party may commit. If you find someone's behavior personally disagreeable, you are to put it from your minds when you weigh the evidence. Now: does any one of you have any recollection of any dealings whatsoever with Mister Walker or Mister Bigelow which would prevent you from doing that?' There was no response. 'Venire stands indifferent.

'Miss Fentress,' the judge said, 'and Miss Veale. If the two of you would stand, please, so the people can see you.' Fentress came out of her chair fast and wheeled to face the venire. She was blocky under her dark grey muu-muu. She had pulled her long black hair away from her face and secured it with an elastic band in a pony tail that hung down to her waist. Her eyes blazed. She folded her arms under her breasts and planted her feet splayed. Carolyn Veale in a dark blue coat dress stood demurely behind the bar. 'Anybody out there know either of these ladies?' the judge said. 'Any reason to believe you might be prejudiced?' There was no response. 'Ladies,' he said, 'you may be seated. Jurors stand indifferent.'

'Fuck you, they are,' Fentress said, sitting down again.

'Record will reflect defendant Fentress has availed herself of the common misapprehension that every dog gets one free bite,' the judge said. 'Record will also reflect that defendant Fentress has been, and is being, warned, that another such outburst will have her in the pound. And not the same pound as defendant Walker, either. Understood, Miss Veale?'

'Understood, with objection,' Veale said.

'Overruled, exception noted,' the judge said. 'Moving right along here, folks – Mister Klein and Miss Franklin will please stand and face the venire?'

Morris Klein was overweight, about five-seven. He wore a tan corduroy suit, a red and yellow plaid shirt, a black knitted tie and a long salt-and-pepper beard. He was bald. Jill Franklin wore a long white cotton dress with small roses in its pattern. Her face was mottled under her long blonde hair. In a voice barely audible she said: 'Power to the people.' In a much louder voice, Klein said: 'Power to the people.'

'That will do,' Bart said. 'Record will reflect same warning to Mister Klein and his client previously issued to Miss Fentress. Anybody ...'

'Objection,' Klein said loudly.

'Overruled,' Bart said. 'Exception noted. Please sit down. Your client, too. Anybody on the venire have any personal problem with these two? Keep in mind that private views about mannerly conduct are not to be considered. Record will reflect no response. Venire stands indifferent.

'Mister Gleason,' the judge said. 'Get up on your hind legs. Face the venire please. Introduce your companion, if you would.'

Gleason stood up. Richards stood up beside him. 'Detective Lieutenant Inspector John Richards will assist me with the paperwork in this trial,' he said. 'He will also testify.'

'Objection,' Klein said.

'Overruled,' Bart said. 'Exception noted.'

'I wish to be heard,' Klein said.

'Life is hard,' Bart said. 'Anybody know Mister Gleason, Special Assistant Attorney General Gleason, that is? Or Lieutenant Richards?'

'I object to Mister Richards being described by his official title,' Klein said.

'Overruled,' Bart said. 'Exception noted.'

'I object to your refusal to hear me,' Klein said.

'Overruled,' Bart said. 'Exception noted. Off the record.' The stenographer stopped typing. 'Sit down and shut up.'

'I object to that as well,' Klein said.

'We're off the record, Counselor,' the judge said. 'If we go back on, and you continue, the next thing the record will reflect is that you've been cited for contempt. Now, you wanna try this damned case, or you want your client's trial severed? You can take your choice.'

'I want the case tried,' Klein said. 'But I want it tried fairly.'

'That's what you're going to get,' the judge said, 'whether you like it or not. Now: sit down, and shut up. Back on the record. Record will reflect venire stands indifferent to Mister Gleason and Mister Richards. We'll take the morning recess.'

12

At 3:15 in the afternoon, Carolyn Veale stood and said that defendant Fentress was content with a fiftyish black woman named Mabel Wright who had been seated, subject to challenge, as the sixteenth person to serve on the panel hearing the case. 'Thank you, Miss Veale,' the judge said, 'Mister Klein?'

Klein stood up. 'Defendant Franklin challenges for just cause,' he said loudly. He was wearing the same suit and what appeared to be the same shirt and tie he had worn on the previous days of the trial. 'And may I be heard, your Honor?'

Bart shook his head. 'Mister Klein,' he said, 'are you going to try to make that silly argument again? Because ever since you ran out of peremptories on Friday, you've been boring us all breathless with it. Won't you just incorporate it by reference, and I'll rule on it again, so we can complete this panel?'

'It's *not* the same argument, your Honor,' Klein said. 'Those other times I was challenging for cause, I was doing so on the premise that any proceeding, in any part, is a violation of my client's rights, because these are criminal charges brought against her, serious criminal charges, and ... '

'I know, I know, I know,' Bart said, slapping his open right hand down on the top of the bench, 'and your claim is that this is essentially a political trial. If that's to be your argument now, then no, you may not be heard. Challenge for cause is overruled. Objection noted. Exception noted. Now let's get on with this case here so these poor people in the jury box don't all become eligible for Old Age Benefits before we hear opening statements.'

'That is not my argument this time,' Klein said smugly. 'That is what I was trying to explain when your Honor once again rudely interrupted me.'

'This is the fourth time I've had to warn you about that kind of comment, Mister Klein,' Bart said. 'I've overlooked a couple others, which was clearly a mistake. Provocative remarks, intended to incite the trial judge into a display of temperament, won't do you a gnat's breakfast worth of good before the Appeals Court, or the Supreme Court – if this case should go to appeal.'

'I submit to your Honor,' Klein said, 'that that remark itself is gravely prejudicial, displaying as it does this Court's blatant bias against my client. You've just implied to this panel that you expect them to convict in this proceeding, and invited them to infer that my expectation is the same, because I'm laying the foundation for appeal. I submit that the panel as constituted is therefore indelibly stained and tainted, and that each of them now sitting should be dismissed for cause, and a new panel selected, with the parties each enjoying the same number of peremptory challenges as we had when we began.'

'Denied. Objection overruled. Exception noted,' Bart said. 'I move for mistrial,' Klein said.

'For the record,' the judge said. 'Henceforth in the course of this trial, when the Court responds to some oration from Mister Klein by uttering the word "doe," it shall be understood by all attending that the word does not refer to Bambi's girlfriend, but in this proceeding is an acronym for "Denied. Objection overruled. Exception noted." At least maybe I can save some time, even if Mister Klein refuses. Motion for mistrial is denied. Objection overruled. Exception noted.'

'Move to strike that entire last comment from the bench,' Klein said. 'And again for mistrial and for you to recuse yourself, ground that the court is showing blatant prejudice by ridiculing counsel in open court, and by suggesting that counsel in protecting his client's rights on the record is engaged in dilatory tactics.'

'Mister Klein,' Bart said, 'I don't know how many more dilatory motions you've got there, but I'm very happy with your choice of that adjective to describe your tactics.' He turned to the jury. 'So that the record will be clear, Ladies and Gentlemen – regardless of whether it is ever made the basis of an appeal – I am stating it right here that I consider Mister Klein's tactics to be dilatory. I am further stating that his stalling and his argumentativeness on matters he knows to be frivolous are part of a deliberate strategy on his part to goad this Court into committing reversible error.

'I emphasize that I make those statements for the record, Ladies and Gentlemen,' Bart said, 'because I don't want you to draw the inference from the fact of my making them that I think you're too stupid to have figured these matters out for yourselves.'

Klein opened his mouth. 'Keep still,' Bart said, 'I haven't fin-ished. You are not going to hogtie this court and paralyze this system by continuous repetition of trivial, frivolous, weightless arguments and objections. The record will reflect that I have concluded from your current lack of substantial reason to warrant your challenge of Mrs. Wright for cause, that you have no cause to challenge. I therefore rule for the record that the defendant Franklin, having exhausted her peremptory challenges and having shown no cause to exclude Mrs. Wright from service on this panel, shall be deemed to have accepted her, and recorded as content with the panel as now constituted. Mister Klein, sit down. Mister Gleason?'

Gleason stood up. 'Commonwealth content, your Honor,' he said.

Bart exhaled loudly. 'Thank heavens, it's over,' he said, smiling at the jurors, who grinned back. 'Now, the clock on the wall says it's only twenty minutes until this long and rewarding workday comes to an official close, and I don't see much point in having Mister Gleason spend it giving you what I would anticipate to be about a third of his opening argument before I'd be forced to interrupt him. So I'm going to recess now until ten A.M. tomorrow, when we'll all meet again, tails bushy and eyes bright after we've all had a couple drinks, those who desire such refreshments, a good dinner, and a good night's sleep. I understand the court officers have arranged for you to see a movie tonight, those of you who wish to. Then tomorrow they will bring you back to the jury room upstairs, where I'd like you to clear your minds of all miscellanea and get ready to hear what I'm sure will be a very interesting case.' He stood up and, as the bailiff chanted that the court was adjourned, disappeared into his chambers.

*

At 5:15 that afternoon, Terry Gleason removed a stack of plastic cups and a quart of Jack Daniel's from the right bottom drawer of his desk at 20 Ashburton Place. Tpr. Fred Consolo looked worriedly at Richards and at Tpr. June McNeil. 'I still wish we wouldn't do this,' he said.

'Oh, for Christ sake, Fred,' she said, 'don't start that again. It makes you nervous to splice the main brace here, then don't do it. Take the elevator down and go have a drink somewhere else.'

'Not supposed to keep or consume liquor on State property,' he said.

'Just keep pouring,' Richards said to Gleason. 'I think this old paddy earned a double on this day.'

'The regular measure for me,' McNeil said. 'Was it really that bad in there?'

'Yup,' Richards said, picking up his cup.

'It was moderately awful,' Gleason said. 'Klein's bound and determined he's going to get Black Bart enraged enough to do something that'll kiss-of-death the thing on appeal.' He poised the bottle over an empty fourth cup and raised his eyebrows at Consolo. Consolo shook his head. Gleason shrugged and capped the bottle, taking the third cup for himself.

'How long's he gonna keep wearing that same suit and shirt?' Richards said.

'How long's the trial going to last?' Gleason said. 'It's part of his schtick. He cultivates this image of himself as the defender of the oppressed. Know what his luggage is? He calls it, with egregious self-deprecation, "a Puerto-Rican overnighter." It's a shopping bag. No matter where he goes – and the bastard's everywhere there's a headline to be grabbed – that shopping bag and his old briefcase are the only things he's got. Doesn't use hotels. Moves into crash pads with his clients. Or their friends. Is it the same shirt, every day? I don't know, he might have two. But he claims he rinses his shirt out every night, and that's how he does it. Supposed to get sympathy from juries. I don't think it works, but how much do I know? He's always confident.'

'Think he managed it today?' Richards said. 'What he set out to do?'

'He came pretty close,' Gleason said. To Consolo and McNeil he explained: 'Klein, ever since Klein got that Chicago case, the bombers, his own client acquitted and the record so fucked-up the other guys got blown out on appeal, he's been using this same tactic. Even though I don't think it's ever worked again. What he had going for him out in Chicago was this federal judge that everybody – prosecutors, defendants, agents, court officers, jurors, *and* the Circuit Court of Appeals – that everybody who'd ever met him absolutely hated. Autocratic son of a bitch on the bench. Rude, domineering: a total bastard. So, Klein being desperate, he put on a show, and as much as I'm sure the jury disliked him, they disliked the judge more. At least Klein was standing up to him. And jurors aren't stupid, you know. You get a dozen people in a room, who really don't like somebody, and if you give them time enough, they'll find a way to fix him. And that's what happened out there. They came back with a verdict that was so inconsistent – acquitted Klein's guy and then turned around and convicted the two other guys on exactly the same evidence – that the judge got the bird twice. Once with the verdict for Klein's guy, and once again when the Circuit threw the whole thing out and wrote one of those opinions about the judge that'd raise blisters on a teak wall.

'What Klein's overlooking here,' Gleason said, 'or at least I hope he is, is that this here is a different situation. Bart's rough on sentencing, but he's fair during trial. And he's nice. He goes out of his way to see that the juries are as happy as they can be, and he makes it clear to them that he really is interested. He's polite to the lawyers, and pleasant to the court officers. He doesn't browbeat; he's kind to witnesses – Howard Bart is a nice man. I don't mean he's weak, which Klein should know now he is not, if he did not before, I mean he is *good.* So I don't think Klein's gonna make himself any large point totals with the jury, goosing this judge. I think he's losing them. Klein's smart. He'll figure that out. Couple days, he'll stop.

'The points he raised? I don't see much trouble there. The political persecution argument doesn't cut the ice now, way it did, Dick Nixon was in office. And the only way Klein or any of them can make it is by confession and avoidance – admitting their clients robbed The Friary and killed the people, but saying the victims were bad, which they were, and deserved it, while their own motives were pure. To save the world by financing the armed fight against capitalism.'

'I can't see John Bigelow doing that,' Richards said. 'No matter what his batty client says. Bigelow's a prick, but even I feel sorry for a guy who's defending James Walker. Guy looks like a maiden's nightmare of a Mau Mau rapist. Even the black folks on that jury shy away from him.'

'I agree with you, John,' Gleason said. 'Now, Morrissey for Tibbetts? Well, what John Morrissey says he's gonna do, that is what he's gonna do. He told me, before he filed his notice told me he's gonna do it, he's going to put his man on the stand and Tibbetts is going to testify he's been out of his tree for the past

129

several years. Freaked out on drugs. About friends he had that made the mistake of taking LSD four or five flights up, and trying to fly out the window to the street below. About mescaline and magic mushrooms, and God only knows what all. And he'll say before he went to the ashram in LA – which is where he'll say he was the last year or so he's on the run – the reason he went to the ashram was he realized he had to get his act cleaned up.'

'"Temporary insanity,"' Richards said, sipping his drink.

'Think it'll work?' Consolo said nervously.

'No, I don't think it'll work,' Gleason said. 'It's ingenious, and it's about all Morrissey's got, and it's a hell of a lot better'n what Bigelow or Carolyn Veale've got to work with, but will it convince the jury? I doubt it. I had Tibbetts examined, soon's I heard. My doc says he's fine, and most likely always has been. That he's probably lying now about the amount and variety of the drugs he says he used, and that they should disregard. His doc of course will say the opposite. That Tibbetts is back from the dead, like the Doctor in *Two Cities* – who was that, John?'

'Doctor Manette,' Richards said. '"Returned to life."'

'Right,' Gleason said, 'and that's essentially the claim that Sam Tibbetts has in mind.

'Now,' he said, 'will it sell? Can John Morrissey make that leaky boat float? I dunno. I've been trying cases for a long time now. Learned the first time out that you never predict what a jury's going to do, how a jury will react.'

'Mackenzie can sink it,' Consolo said. 'You get him up there on the stand, Mackenzie can sink that. He can tell how Tibbetts planned all of those damned jobs. He was there. How his brain was working fine.'

'Oh *God*,' McNeil said.

'Please, Freddie,' Gleason said, 'don't start that again.'

'I don't care,' Consolo said. 'It's the only way to do it. You got to have Mackenzie testify about Tibbetts's condition.'

McNeil shook her head. 'Won't work, Fred,' she said. 'Even if Terry could do it, which he can't, Glenn's not up to it. You've seen him, just like I have. All he does is talk about his girlfriend. "Goddamned Andrea. Ballbuster." Then he starts to cry. This guy, if this guy can stand up to even one day on the stand, it'll be a miracle.' She looked at Gleason. 'If you think,' she said, 'if you think you can possibly get through this thing and prove your case, without putting Glenn on the stand, I would do it that way. This kid, he's a spaceshot. He makes Apollo Three look like a Harley-Davidson.'

'He isn't doing good, June?' Richards said.

'He wasn't doing good last night,' she said. 'I had the detail with Sara Kindred, down at Osgood's summer house. Had to get him out the motel, he was so ditzy there. The gist of what he says last night is that he's got to see Terry. Doesn't matter what you say: "Terry is on trial, and he just can't come down here." Nope, he's got to talk to Terry. Tell you what he thinks. That his partners, his law partners, that they're going to figure out where he is, and why he is there, and they'll tell Klein or someone else, and he will get knocked off. I personally think he's full of shit, and that what he's really doing's setting the stage to back out the deal. But he's not stupid, and he puts on a good act, and I wouldn't bet my lunch money he won't get up and blow it, if you get him up at all. If he's not getting close to becoming a basket-case, he does a good impression of a man who is.'

'I don't care,' Consolo said. 'Whatever anybody says, the only way we're going to hook this bastard Tibbetts is by getting

Mackenzie up there. And when you've got him up there, nailing down this fucking sanity thing.'

'I can't,' Gleason said. 'I've told you that before.'

'You've got to,' Consolo said. 'You don't have any choice.'

Richards put his cup down on the desk. 'Fred,' he said, 'I've made a decision. You're going to have to go to law school.'

'I don't want to be a lawyer,' Consolo said. 'I've got *some* pride, some integrity, you know.'

The other three laughed. 'Not your pride we're concerned about, Fred,' Gleason said.

'No,' Richards said, 'anybody spends as much on clothes as you do, he's either got a lot of money, lots of pride, or a lot of both. It's your ignorance that concerns us.'

'I know,' Consolo said. 'You talk about me starting in again ... '

'Well, but that's the point,' Richards said. 'That's exactly what I mean. Three or four times now, Terry's explained to you precisely why he can't do what you've got in mind. And that it wouldn't work if he could. Mackenzie wasn't around Tibbetts just before The Friary. Not enough to be able to form a firm opinion as to his sanity. And Tibbetts isn't charged here with the armored cars, which was when Mackenzie was around – only with The Friary. So, in the first place, Mackenzie doesn't have much help for us, on insanity. And in the second place, if he did have it, we couldn't use it. This game that we play, Freddie – the rules of evidence control it. You may not like them, and that's okay, but if you're gonna prosecute people, you really ought to know them.'

'It's a stupid game, then,' Consolo said.

'It is if you play it like a man who can clean both ears with one Q-tip,' Gleason said, 'just by pushing it through. But it's not supposed to be.'

13

At 10:03 in the morning, Judge Bart nodded toward the prosecutor's table and said: 'Mister Gleason?' Gleason thanked the court as he came to his feet. He wore a blue poplin suit, a white shirt and a red and blue striped tie. He approached the rail of the jury box. He rested the heels of his hands on it and delivered the customary cautionary remarks disclaiming any intention of appearing to present evidence. 'This is merely a prediction,' he said, 'of what the Commonwealth expects to prove. What you hear from the lips of the witnesses, see in the physical exhibits – that is the evidence. Not what I say now. Or what Mister Morrissey, Miss Veale, Mister Bigelow or Mister Klein choose to say when they in their turn address you.'

'Just remember the rule,' Richards had said to him the night before, when McNeil and Consolo had left, '"If you aren't sure you can prove it, put it in the opening. Hope the jury remembers, and everybody else forgets."'

Gleason began by describing the discoveries made by Peter Walmsley. 'You will hear what he found, on May fifth of last year,' Gleason said. 'He will describe it in detail – sight, smell, everything. You will see the color photographs taken at the scene. Those taken in the office, where five victims were found. Those taken in the freezer, where two victims – and the two guard dogs – were found dead as well.'

'Objection,' Klein said, standing up. 'No allusion yet to any evidence of homicide. Matter for the jury, whether anyone was killed.'

Judge Bart sighed. 'Excuse me, Mister Gleason,' he said. 'Just let me deal with this nuisance, if you will?'

'I didn't say ... ' Gleason said.

'I know you didn't, Mister Gleason,' Bart said. 'Mister Klein,' he said, 'Mister Gleason said the human victims and the dogs were found, quote – dead – unquote. Not quote – killed – unquote. I take it there's no dispute that the seven people found at the establishment, and the dogs as well, a year ago last May fifth were, in fact, quite dead?'

Klein looked confused. 'No, your Honor, none,' he said. 'I must've misunderstood.'

'And conveniently, too,' Bart said. 'Your misunderstanding enabled you nicely to interrupt Mister Gleason's train of thought. Which, I'm sure, was all you had in mind.' Klein sat down. 'Mister Gleason,' the judge said, 'sorry for the delay.'

'You will hear next,' Gleason said, 'from two doctors. Doctor Charles Fox was the medical examiner for Suffolk County then – since retired. Doctor Stephen Fratus, then his assistant, has now replaced him in that job. Each is a doctor of medicine. Each is a forensic specialist. They will testify to what their post-mortem examinations of the victims disclosed. Each of them will testify that in his opinion death in each instance was caused by gunshot wounds in the head. Also appearing will be Doctor Alfred Ketchum. His doctorate is in veterinary medicine. He will report to you on his post-mortem examinations of the dogs. He will state his opinion that the death of each dog was caused by gunshot wounds to the body.

'Each of those witnesses,' Gleason said, walking slowly toward the end of the jury box furthest from the judge, 'each of them will identify among other things – photographs, articles of clothing, results of chemical tests – certain objects he removed from the bodies he examined. Those objects will be offered as exhibits. The next witness will be Lieutenant Edmund O'Malley, who will state the credentials that accredit him as an expert in ballistics. Lieutenant O'Malley will testify that in his capacity as head of the Ballistics Lab of the Massachusetts State Police, he received the objects removed from the bodies of the humans and the dogs, and examined them microscopically. He will testify that he studied a total of eighteen bullets, that he found each of them to be of twenty-two caliber, manufactured by Remington Arms, and that each of them showed markings consistent with having been fired from one of two High Standard, twenty-two caliber, automatic pistols.

'My colleague at the table,' Gleason said, gesturing toward Richards, 'has already been introduced to you. Detective Lieutenant Inspector John D. Richards, Massachusetts State Police. Lieutenant Richards will take the stand to describe a cruise he took last May fourth on the Deerfield River, with five other

135

members of the State Police, for the purpose of effecting arrests ordered by warrants issued by this court, subject to the indictments now before you for trial. He will tell you that they arrived at a cabin in a secluded area, that they disembarked, apparently unnoticed by the cabin's occupants, and that they surprised four persons sleeping inside. He will identify those four persons as Samuel Tibbetts, James Walker, Jill Franklin and Kathie Fentress, and will tell you that the persons seated at the bar are the persons they arrested.

'He will describe and identify as well,' Gleason said, 'certain physical objects we will offer as evidence. These will include photographs taken at the cabin, and objects seized from it. Several of those objects are firearms. Two of them are automatic pistols, caliber twenty-two, manufactured by High Standard. Lieutenant Richards will tell you that each of the weapons was carefully handled to preserve any possible latent fingerprints. He will tell you that extra magazines – ammunition clips and several boxes of live cartridges, in several calibers – were handled with the same caution. To preserve any latent fingerprints that might be on those items.

'Sergeant William Ford of the Massachusetts State Police, assigned to the Criminal Identification Unit, will describe his credentials as a fingerprint expert. He will tell you that he examined each of the weapons – including the pistols – for latent prints, and found on them three from each of two defendants, and four from each of the other two. He will tell you that cartridges found in the clips of the guns – they were fully loaded when recovered – and cartridges found in those magazines and other clips, also loaded, carry clear fingerprints from each of at least one of the defendants.

'Lieutenant O'Malley will be recalled to the stand. He will identify those two automatic pistols as weapons he test-fired at the Ballistics Lab in order to obtain exemplary rounds. He will tell you that the markings on the test-fired slugs were identical to the markings on the slugs recovered from the victims of The Friary incident. He will tell you that in his expert opinion there is no reasonable possibility that any of those bullets recovered from those bodies could have possibly been fired from any pistols other than the two High Standards recovered from the cabin.

'Now, Ladies and Gentlemen,' Gleason said, 'this is an uncertain world. You heard his Honor warn you yesterday that I'd talk for an hour today. And I considered doing that. But as I told you at the outset, you're not getting any evidence, while I stand here shooting off my mouth. So I have given you the bare bones of what the Commonwealth expects its evidence to be, and if uncertainty occurs, I hope you will forgive me if I offer some that I did not just predict. Hold me, hold us, to what I have predicted we'll produce, and I have every confidence that after this is over, when you have retired, your deliberations on the evidence will prompt you to conclude, beyond a reasonable doubt, that the proper verdicts in this case require you to find ...' he wheeled and pointed toward the defendants, his voice dropping to a growl, 'Samuel F. Tibbetts, the missing James Walker, Katherine Fentress and Jill Franklin, guilty on each of the seven charges against each of them, of murder in the first degree – that on or about May fourth, nineteen-seventy-seven, at Boston, in the County of Suffolk, these four persons did with malice aforethought, and in the course of and for the purpose of committing a felony, to wit: robbery while armed, intentionally assault and beat Joseph Abbate, Joseph Nichols, Maureen Wilkerson, Helena Gross, Doreen Alexander,

Diana McKechnie and Janet Iverson, by shooting them, with fire-arms, and did cause their deaths.' He turned back to the jury and nodded. 'Thank you,' he said. He returned to his place at the table. He looked inquiringly at the judge. 'May I call my first witness, your Honor?' Judge Bart said: 'Proceed.'

At the luncheon recess, Gleason, Richards and O'Malley sat with their legs cramped at a small wooden table in an unused office on the seventh floor of the courthouse. On the table were waxed papers under the remains of the delicatessen sandwiches, cans of Coca-Cola, and two torn bags of potato chips. O'Malley was a beefy man in his late forties. He sat back from the table and belched. 'What I like best about these testimony things,' he said, 'what I like best is the fuckin' fine table you bastards always set. I wanna tell you, boy, this is really great. I mean, if I could get food like this alla time for lunch, you know what I would weigh? I would weigh about a hundred and eighteen pounds, is what I would weigh. I would weigh the same weight that I used to weigh when I was in the seventh grade. Cripes, what a spread. Here's the guys on the governor's detail, and what do they get for lunch? Lobster salad, naturally, sent right up from Dini's. Where they go for dinner, nights? Anthony's Pier Four, of course. Jimmy's Harborside. Few raw oysters, piece of swordfish, but no rich des-serts – I bet. And these're ordinary troopers. What the hell they know? Here I am, a damned lieutenant – I'm a famous man. And what do I get for my chow? To eat the damned phone book. Piece of ham and a piece of cheese on a roll that's tougher'n I am.'

''S good for you,' Richards said, leaning back. 'Make you a better person. Little privation, little fasting? Give your bowels a rest, for Christ sake. Seek an inner peace.'

'Right,' O'Malley said. He reached into his shirt pocket and took out a pack of Luckies.

'Gimme one of those,' Richards said, reaching for the pack.

'I think I'll have one, too,' Gleason said.

O'Malley pulled back. 'Jee-*zuss*,' he said, 'you fuckin' guys, you fuckin' guys're cheap. Have to buy my own lunch, buy my own drink, and now you're bummin' my butts. I hope you got gas in your fuckin' car, John. I don't plan on driving you home.'

'Just shut up and gimme the butt,' Richards said. 'Give my mouthpiece a cigarette too. Got to keep the bastard happy. Ball's in his court now.' Each of them lit up.

'I thought you did good this morning,' O'Malley said, through the smoke in the small room. 'I thought you did real good this morning. Kept it nice and short? I sat there lots of times in court-rooms. wait to testify, see these fuckin' bastards get up, talk for days and days. Just love the sound of their own voice, don't they? Think it's Beethoven. Stand up, say what you got to say, and then sit the fuck down. That's what I admire.'

'Thanks,' Gleason said.

'I'll amen that,' Richards said. 'Although of course I got to say, Fred's going to be upset.'

'Who the fuck is Fred?' O'Malley said.

'Cowboy Fred Consolo,' Gleason said, stretching and rubbing his eyes. 'Fred's got reservations about my approach to this case.'

Richards laughed. 'Fred,' he said to O'Malley, 'Fred's got reservations about everyone's approach, to every goddamned case. I bet Fred in this one, I bet if you went up to Fred and asked him what he thought, he'd tell you confidentially he thinks we also should've grabbed these bums, thrown in cruelty to animals, shooting the goddamned dogs. Fred wants all the stops pulled out. He thinks Terry's tanking it. That's what Terry means.'

'That asshole?' O'Malley said to Gleason. 'Asshole Fred Consolo? Who cares what he thinks? The fuck do you care? Who the fuck's trying this thing? Asshole Fred?' He shook his head. He looked back at Richards. 'Uh uh. This is your case, John, yours and Terry's here. You guys try the fuckin' case. Let Fred go pound sand. Lemme tell you something, all right? Lemme tell you something. I testified, I have now testified over two hundred times, in six goddamned States, all right? And I sat on my ass at least four hundred days, sat on my ass in courtrooms. Because I'm the fuckin' cop, and they know they can get me, so all the docs and all the hotshots, they get to wait on call, get their own work done. But all the guys that try these things, I know what they think. They think: 'Oh what the hell, what if we need, we need a witness fast? Better have the cops come in, sit down on their ass. 'Cause they will get paid anyway, and they're too dumb to care." That is how they think.

'Now,' he said, 'I watch things, while I'm doing that, sitting on my ass. And I've seen a lot of trials. And one the things I learned about trials is that trials're just like fuckin'. The most people that can do it at once, the way it's supposed to get done, is: two. Not three, not half a dozen, not a rifle platoon. Two people is the most that can try a goddamned case. You get more'n that involved in the action, somebody's always getting pissed off, feeling like they've been left out. And all of a sudden you're doing things you didn't want to do, because some jerk's feelings got hurt and you want to cheer him up. And that is a mistake. That is always a mistake.

'Generally speaking,' he said, 'and I hate like hell to admit this, but generally speaking, the guy who's likeliest to try the best case is the lawyer trying it. Not some cop – no offense, John – who's even there, and certainly not some other bastard, *isn't* even there. You start lookin' over your shoulder, Terry, taking free advice, worrying what people think, you'll get in the shit.'

'Yeah,' Gleason said, 'but the thing of it is, I am worried.'

'Why?' O'Malley said.

'Because Fred,' Richards said, 'Fred doesn't know squat about trying cases, but he's identified a problem and there's no doubt about that.'

'What's the problem?' O'Malley said. 'Something I can do?'

'Nope,' Gleason said. 'Nothing anyone can do. John Morrissey's come up with this insanity defense. The only witness we've got who could even come close to rebutting it – and he probably couldn't do that – has come down with a bad case of testicular insufficiency.'

'Ah,' O'Malley said.

'Well,' Gleason said, 'it's as bad as it sounds, but it's no worse'n it was. He couldn't've done much anyway, and if Morrissey beats me, well, I'm not the first guy he's beaten, and I certainly won't be the last. And, quite frankly, I never wanted, put this punk on the stand in the first place. He's got a lot of weasel in him. And he's gotten a reward. So already, before he started tossing, turning in his sleep, I had big problems letting Morrissey loose to cross-examine him. Now he's got cold tootsies, and he's jittery, and Big Mo can spot jitters like a wolf smelling fresh lamb. So, why do I need this? So John and I decided: Well, let's try it slippery-stones. If you've got to put flat stones down in the creek to get across, the water's gonna make them slippery, and the more of them you put down, the likelier you make it that you're gonna slip on one. So, if I can get away with it, I'm not gonna put El Ratto on the stand.

And if I can't, I still might not. That's why I'm doing this. But Fred is gonna be pissed off. And if I lose, quite loud.'

'Fuck him,' O'Malley said. 'On to more important matters. First thing: Who'sa broad?'

'What broad?' Gleason said. 'I didn't see no broad.'

'In the audience,' O'Malley said. 'I seen her come in when I did. Just ahead of me. Young. Really beautiful. Gorgeous-looking kid. Looks like a mulatto. Sat up in the front row. Next to this old couple. Like they knew each other.'

'Got me,' Gleason said. He looked at Richards. 'This after, all right? Check that out? While I got my back turned?'

'Naughty, naughty,' Richards said. 'You're a married man.'

'I'm a worried one, as well,' Gleason said. 'John Morrissey's got it in mind to run pool on me. At least I'd like a little notice, where he's getting any cues.'

'Point well taken, Terry,' Richards said. 'Should've thought of that. Tomorrow morning, maybe, we'll put June out at the door, couple metal detectors? Say we know they all got checked, when they came in downstairs, but we're checking anyway. Get IDs from all the folks – get 'em all pissed off, and see what that smokes out.'

14

Judge Bart emerged from chambers at 10:05. Spectators filtered slowly into the back of the courtroom. James Walker had been brought down with the other three defendants on John Bigelow's promise to the court that his client 'says he'll behave himself, your Honor, and that's all I can represent.' The jury box was empty. The bailiff directed all to draw near and give their attendance, promising that they would be heard. The judge sat down. He said: 'Good morning. Yesterday I decided not to bring the jury down until I had put a minor matter to the Commonwealth and the defense, on the record. This morning I was informed that Mister Morrissey wishes to file a written motion, and be heard on it, so yesterday's was a prescient decision on my part.

'What concerned me,' he said, 'was the information I received from the court officers to the effect that they propose to take the jury, or as many of them as wish to go, to a Red Sox game. In my experience, at least, nobody actually at Fenway Park ever concerns him or herself with so trivial a matter as a first-degree murder case, so I think it unlikely that any of the jury will be contaminated by attendance. But I wanted to have it on the record, in case any of you think otherwise. And, of course, if you do, then that will be the end of it.'

John Bigelow stood up. 'Your Honor,' he said, 'this is more or less just out of curiosity, because I can't imagine why my client or I would have any objection to this jury going to the ballgame. But I do have two questions. The first is: How the dickens are you getting them in? This is the hottest ticket in town.'

The judge smiled. 'I don't know, Mister Bigelow,' he said. 'The court officers tell me they can lay their hands on a block of tickets. I decided a long time ago never to ask court officers how they manage such magical things.'

Gleason stood up. 'Is there any chance they could get six or eight for us, your Honor?' he said.

Bart shook his head. 'I'd think not, Counselor,' he said, grinning. Gleason sat down.

'My second question,' Bigelow said, glaring at Gleason, 'is whether the jury knows that the Court has given counsel veto power on the issue of whether they get to go to the ballgame. Because, if you have, I think you've put us in one hell of a spot, and I hope it doesn't happen again.'

Bart's face hardened. 'The answer to your question is: No, Counselor. Now,' he said, surveying the lawyers again, 'I'll put my original question: Any one of you object to the jury attending the ballgame? I see no objection, and hear none. Jury can go to the ballgame.

'Now,' he said, 'Mister Morrissey has a motion?'

Morrissey, burly in a dark grey suit, stood up and walked to the clerk's desk. He placed one sheet of paper before the clerk and returned to counsel table. He picked up copies and delivered one to each of the other lawyers. The clerk read the paper, made a notation on it, and handed it up to the judge. The judge scanned it and put it down. He folded his hands. 'Mister Morrissey?' he said.

Morrissey cleared his throat. 'Your Honor,' he said, 'as we all are aware, there has been a major question in this case since its inception. The question is now by way of becoming a problem, and I think we have to deal with it – this Court has to deal with it – before it becomes any larger. Because it's a serious problem.

'The Commonwealth secured its indictments on hearsay. Now I'm well aware that the grand jury is within its rights to return charges on pure hearsay, if it believes the hearsay reliable. And in this instance, clearly, that is what they did. But the petit jury is not entitled to base its verdict in any way upon hearsay, at least as the term is traditionally understood.

'The grand jury minutes, which Mister Gleason promptly furnished as soon as the defendants had counsel, those minutes consist almost entirely of testimony delivered by Lieutenant Richards – for whom I have the utmost respect – reciting, or reading from reports of information given to him from confidential informants. I have no reason whatsoever to doubt the Lieutenant's veracity in telling that grand jury that *he* believed the statements he was relaying to be truthful and accurate.

'But I can't cross-examine the Lieutenant on the underlying truth and veracity of those statements, your Honor. To do that, I need to have before me, up there on the stand, the person or persons who made them to him in the first place. It may very well be that that person or persons would be able to substantiate every detail of what he or she told the Lieutenant, and that my client and I after interviewing them would either decide not to expose them to the jury, or deeply regret it if we decided otherwise.

'Point is, your Honor, neither my client nor I can make that decision, precisely the sort of critical, strategy decision that we have to make, if he's to have a fair trial, without knowing who those informants were – their names – and their current whereabouts.

'Now,' he said, opening his coat and hooking his thumbs in his belt, 'I listened very carefully, very attentively, to my learned brother's opening statement yesterday. Just as I listened, in the pre-trial hearings on this motion I'm renewing now, to his statements made at those. In July, when I asked for the names and addresses *of all possible witnesses* – anyone he knew of who might have any information germane to the trial of this case, whether probative of innocence or probative of guilt – Mister Gleason put me and this Court off. He said that he would timely serve a list of prospective witnesses as soon as it was ready. And he did. And it was not helpful.

'When he made his opening,' Morrissey said, 'when he made his opening statement yesterday, the roster of witnesses he gave mirrored the one he served timely. Which is of course to say that he has made a decision – he and Lieutenant Richards have made a decision – not to call any of the informants – however many there are – to testify in this case. So that is what prompts me to renew, this morning, my motion for those names and addresses.

'Your Honor,' Morrissey said, 'we have a definite *Brady* v. *Maryland* problem here. Again emphasizing that I in no way question the integrity of the prosecution team, that I know them to be fine, upstanding gentlemen, from long experience, and that I have had – except for this exception – only the finest and most cooperative relationships with them, I have to point out to the Court that if any of those informants was lying, if any of them has now changed his or her mind and now has exculpatory evidence to offer, evidence that would suggest to the jury that my client was indeed – as he also claims, along with his alternative defense of incapacity – framed, I need to have access to it. If Mister Gleason doesn't want to call these anonymous accusers, if he doesn't want to put himself in the position of propounding their testimony to the jury in this case, well, that's certainly his right. I think his choice to exercise that right may imply something about his – and the Lieutenant's – current estimation of their veracity, but that's another matter. Point is, and I say it again, if he's not going to produce these faceless, nameless accusers, and let us cross-examine them, at least give us the opportunity to decide for ourselves, as is our right, whether to expose them ourselves.'

'Mister Gleason,' Bart said.

Gleason stood. 'Your Honor,' he said, 'I am sensible of my brother's concerns. My natural inclination would be to accede to his motion. Indeed, I have known Mister Morrissey so long, and have opposed him so many times, that as he will, I'm sure, agree, discovery motions in our cases have become formalities. So, why won't I give him the names? Simple: we have four defendants on trial here. By order of this court, on agreement by counsel, the indictments were retyped from the originals, which accused seven persons, three of them John and Jane Does. This Court, and each of the attorneys representing defendants here, is aware of the background of this case. In the interest of fairness to these defendants, at this trial, the Commonwealth not only agreed to expunge the Does, lest this jury conclude that others are still at large, and dangerous, but in fact proposed the amendment. As

Mister Morrissey and his colleagues on defense are aware, and as this Court is aware, the Commonwealth remains concerned that such persons are still at large, are armed and dangerous, and may retaliate against persons whom they know to have provided us with information. Or, against officers of this court.

'Now,' he said, walking around the prosecution table to the front, 'I will state for the record, and I will, if requested, either ask Lieutenant Richards to take the stand, or file an affidavit, stating that all our evidence, with the exception of the names and current whereabouts of informants, has been provided, lock, stock and barrel, to each defense attorney. We don't have anything else. If there's anything that the jury might even remotely deem exculpatory in our evidence, defense counsel has it. All they need to do is read it.

'The law is well settled that the trial court and jury may not look behind the motives of the grand jury issuing indictments. The grand jury may indict on whim, in anger, or in appalling ignorance, and woe betide the prosecutor who conducts a public trial of an indictment so returned. But unless the prosecutor chooses not to proceed on an indictment, after its return, unless he decides to *nol pros* the charges, then the only issue is whether the prosecutor has sufficient evidence to back up the grand jury's charges. Not whether it's the same evidence. Not whether it's all the evidence. Not whether the grand jury was wise in its indictment. No, the issue at trial is whether the Commonwealth can back up its charges. Whether it has the goods.

'Mister Morrissey's question,' Gleason said, 'Mister Morrissey's question today was raised by him, and raised by each of the other counsel, at hearing on the motions to suppress the physical evidence that we seized in the cabin. The issue then was whether the Commonwealth had probable cause sufficient to justify those seizures. The Court found we did. I submit Mister Morrissey's motion today falls under the heading of "Matters already decided." Against him. That he has no right, though every reason, to attempt to determine what direction or what strategy the Commonwealth shall take in this prosecution. His motion should be denied.' Gleason returned to his chair and sat down.

Klein and Veale were coming to their feet. 'Miss Veale,' the judge said, 'Mister Klein. And Mister Bigelow, as well. I assume you wish to join in Mister Morrissey's motion?' Each of them nodded. 'Record will reflect,' Bart said, 'that each of the defendants renews his or her motion to compel disclosure of names and addresses of confidential informants known to the Commonwealth. Court has carefully considered arguments of counsel on each side of the issue. Court finds no substantial reason to believe that the Commonwealth is withholding, or has in the past withheld, exculpatory matter. Court further finds merit in Commonwealth's contention that protection of innocent persons is a legitimate concern in this matter. The motion to compel disclosure is there-fore denied, as to each of the defendants. Objections are recorded, and exceptions noted.' He handed Morrissey's motion down to the clerk. 'Bring the jury down,' he said.

Klein stood up. 'Your Honor,' he shouted.

'Oh, dear,' the judge said. To the bailiff, whispering into the courtroom telephone at his desk, the judge said: 'Hold it, Harry. Don't bring the jury down. Mister Klein wants to declaim.' To Klein he said: 'Okay, Mister Klein, what's on your mind?'

'I haven't a written motion,' Klein said. 'The reason I haven't a written motion is that I didn't know the grounds for it until I got off the elevator half an hour ago. My motion is for mistrial on the grounds of the Commonwealth's prejudicial action in installing metal detectors and searching spectators outside this courtroom this morning.'

The judge looked at him and nodded. 'Yes,' he said, 'I saw that when I went into chambers this morning. I must admit, Mister Klein, that while I didn't think a great deal about it at the time, I did share your basic curiosity. Why you doing that, Mister Gleason?'

Gleason stood. 'Basically, your Honor,' he said, 'for the same reason we're so tightlipped about the identity and location of informants. I can go into further detail if you wish, but we do have the media here, and I'm not sure whether it might not be better to review it with counsel in camera? But I'm agreeable, either way.'

Bart rubbed his chin. 'Yeah,' he said, 'Counselor.' He paused. 'You said "review," Mister Gleason – that deliberate?'

'Yes, your Honor,' Gleason said. 'The reason's no different today than it was when the motions to suppress were brought. No different, and no less.'

'You,' the judge said, 'you're not searching jurors, I hope.'

'No,' Gleason said. 'Just spectators, sir.'

'Yeah,' the judge said.

'I protest, your Honor,' Klein said. 'When the jurors come down, sooner or later, they're bound to see those machines. Their certain inference will be that these defendants are dangerous, or have dangerous friends. Or both. And that is prejudicial.'

The judge nodded. 'I agree with you,' he said, 'it is. On the other hand, as Cardozo said, defendants are entitled to fair trials, not perfect ones, and we have to do the best we can, under the circumstances. Far as prejudice's concerned, on the danger-ous people thing, well, you've heard, and they've heard, the

Commonwealth's attorney here allege that these four defendants killed seven people, not to mention two dogs, in cold blood. So the Commonwealth's opinion that they're dangerous people, and may have dangerous friends, made manifest by the security outside this courtroom – that probably isn't going to come as news to them. To the jurors, I mean.'

He shook his head. 'No,' he said, 'I see the reason for your concern, Mister Klein. I even share it, to an extent. But this courthouse's been bombed once, which is why we have the security in the lobby, and while I'm sure neither you nor any other of defense counsel wishes me to recapitulate the discussions we all had in chambers pre-trial of this case, I want you to know I also have that in mind. I think the Commonwealth is being reasonable and prudent in ordering additional security for this case.'

'But your Honor,' Klein said, 'the police are taking names. They're checking IDs as a condition for admission to a public trial in an American court of law. This is unconstitutional, and it is unjust.'

The judge leaned on the bench. 'Mister Klein,' he said, 'you know just as well as I do why the cops're taking names. They're still looking for some people that might know your clients here. You want me to go further on the record with that? Is that really what you want?'

'No,' Klein said, shaking his head. He sat down.

'That's what I figured,' the judge said. 'All right then, off we go. Record will reflect each defendant joins in Mister Klein's motion. Denied for reasons stated. Objections and exceptions noted.' To the bailiff he said: 'Harry, bring the jury down.' Klein stood up. Bart held up his hand. He shook his head. 'Nope,' he said. 'No more on that. We've got a thrilling day ahead of us, way I understand

151

it. Two forensic pathologists Mister Gleason has scheduled for our entertainment here. Can't keep the docs just sitting around – they've got bodies piling up. Lots of color photographs, maybe even a ballistician. No more arguments this forenoon. Bring the jury down.'

15

Tpr. June McNeil crowded her way into the small office along with Gleason, Richards and O'Malley during the luncheon recess. She looked at the sandwiches wrapped in waxed paper on the table, and the three cans of Coke. 'You guys,' she said, 'you guys didn't get me a sandwich?'

Richards looked sheepish. 'Didn't think of it,' he said. 'Sorry – I'll split mine with you, you like.'

'Don't do it, babe,' O'Malley said. 'You haven't had one these sandwiches. Somebody forgets to get you one of these, you should count your blessings.'

'That bad, huh?' she said. 'Well, I should watch my weight anyway, I guess.'

'Oh, I don't know,' O'Malley said, looking her up and down. 'You look pretty healthy to me.'

She patted him on the right shoulder. 'Now, don't get piggy, Ed,' she said. 'You know I've always looked up to you as my father-figure. Don't go and spoil it all now.' Gleason and Richards laughed.

She removed a small spiral notebook from her purse. 'Okay,' she said, 'since there's no sandwich – might as well go to work. Here is what we've got. The girl, the young woman, is Christina Walker. New York driver's license gives her DOB as March eighth, nineteen-fifty-three. Address Two-twenty-one Sutton Place. Has an outdated Student ID card, New England Conservatory, Music. Also current telephone bill addressed to her, One-eighty-nine Commonwealth Avenue. No car registration – in her bag, at least. Height: five-five. Weight: one twenty-eight. Eyes: brown. Same color hair.' She looked up at the men. 'Uses Clinique cosmetics and Ortho contraceptive foam. I wasn't able to get her measurements,' she said. 'We were kind of pressed for time, and I didn't want to make it seem like I was nosy, or something.'

The men snickered. 'Brazen little hussy, isn't she?' Gleason said.

'Or a Girl Scout,' McNeil said. 'We like to be prepared, too, you know. And besides, when we go out in the morning, we don't usually expect some cop to go through our bags that day.

'Now, I'm assuming she's the defendant's sister,' she said. 'Cowboy Fred's running her, NCIC, this afternoon. He already ran her, Ten-ten's computer, and came up dry – no record here, at least.

'The older couple,' she said. 'Walter J. Tibbetts. Mass. driver's license DOB March fourteen, nineteen-seventeen. Home address Twenty-one Larch Street, Longmeadow, Massachusetts. Also has employee ID card, Monsanto Company. Weight: one-sixty-five. Height: five-ten. Hair: grey – and losing it, I might add. Must wear corrective lenses. Woman: Ellen D. Tibbetts. No driver's license. I asked her about that and she said it makes her too nervous when she drives – had one, but gave it up two years ago. Showed me a Mastercard with her name on it, and an ID card from the BayBank Hampden County, same address as Walter's. Both of them very scared. Timid. Nervous. But also bold. Wanted to know why I was writing all this stuff down. Told her it was so we wouldn't have to ask for ID every time anyone passed through – that the people we'd IDed could just walk through the detectors, once we had their names. She wasn't pleased at all. Grabbed her handbag back, gave me the gargoyle stare, went inside. I'm assuming these're the defendant's mother and father, so I didn't bother to have Fred run them. Think I should do that?'

Richards glanced at Gleason. 'Nah,' he said, as Richards shook his head. 'I don't see any point. I would like as much as you can dig up on the girl, though – wouldn't you say, John?'

'Uh huh,' Richards said. 'Could be one those females we never did catch up with, identify, on the early robberies. Or one the support staff. She decides, Morrissey or one of them guys decides might be a good idea, put her on the stand, maybe bolster Sam's claim of being nutty, or strung out on drugs, could be very useful – a good dirty file on her.'

'Such as, her sex life?' McNeil said. 'You would do that, Terry?'

He shrugged. 'If I thought it'd help? Sure. She gets up there on her nice legs and starts telling lies for one these bastards, it'd be real helpful for the jury to know if she used to spread them for him.'

'Or for one the women, too, far as that goes,' Richards said.

'Nice to know what nice fellas I'm working with,' McNeil said.

'Nice to keep in mind, too,' Richards said, 'what kinda nasty bastards the fellas that you're working with're actually up against.

You think a murderer'd shrink from perjury, if he thought it'd help?'

McNeil drew a deep breath. 'Okay,' she said, 'there's a friend of mine – when I was auditing that criminal law course at Northeastern Law, I met this Fiona Campbell. We used to have coffee. She's with the Bureau now. I could just romp on over to Government Center this afternoon. Or call her up. See what the Feds've got.'

'They won't give it to you,' Richards said. 'If they haven't, if it's not in NCIC, and they've got it, then they're either not sure enough of it to let it out – and they're afraid if someone else gets ahold of it the Bureau'll look silly – or they're hoarding it because they think it might make them a splashy case or two.'

'Oh, John,' McNeil said, 'they're not like that anymore. They don't hoard stuff now.'

'Not much, they don't,' Richards said. 'You can tell me that all you want, June, and I'll never believe it. The only change there's been is that now they *claim* they're sharing, which they didn't used to do. And, which's supposed to make us feel so good we won't pay attention, catch them holding back, just the same's they've always done. They haven't gotten different – they're just craftier.'

'Fiona wouldn't do that,' McNeil said. 'Fiona's a friend of mine. We play on a level field.'

'I know who she is,' Richards said. 'Met her one day, over Larry Badger's place. She was sucking his brains out through a little silver tube or something she'd inserted in his ear, and Larry – good old Larry – hasn't changed a bit. You ever start getting concerned, Terry, when you get a little older, that your dick might start to get as old and soft as your brains're getting, go over and see Larry. Smart as hell, even though I don't think he can actually read ...'

'He can't *read*, John?' O'Malley said. 'This's Larry Badger that we're talking about here, and you're telling me he can't read? Guy's a fuckin' genius. If Larry Badger doesn't know it's going on, it's not fuckin' going on. And his nephew's maybe even smarter. Don't tell me they can't *read*.'

'Ed, you know,' Richards said, 'you oughta let me finish, all right? Larry's got a, he's got one of those learning disability things they're always hollering about all the time. He's dyslexic. I didn't say he was stupid – I said he can't read very well.'

'Anyway,' Richards said, 'I went over there, nothing much on my mind. Shoot the shit with Larry, see what he's following. Larry calls us now and then; we call him now and then. So I'm showing the flag. And this Fiona babe is in there, giving him the treatment, purging his fuckin' brain, and him just loving it. You show Larry Badger a good-looking woman, boy, and Larry'll give you the store, plus the shed out in back to go with it. Absolute slave to his pecker.'

'Well, there now, you see?' McNeil said. 'She's doing the same kind of thing you do, and you don't think she's smart?'

'You're worse'n O'Malley, McNeil,' Richards said. 'You got to learn to pay attention. She may be smart enough – I don't really know. All I'm trying to say here is, I was not impressed. Woman doesn't have to be very smart to figure Larry Badger. Mae West's old line? "You carrying a revolver or are you just glad to see me?" That's the way he is.'

'Well,' McNeil said, 'if you don't know her well enough to say whether she's smart, why don't you like her?'

'Didn't say I didn't like her,' Richards said. 'Just said I was not impressed. And that, that's I guess because she struck me as a dilettante. I bet it costs more to dress her'n it costs to rig Consolo, and that, friends, is a lot. I don't like rich people, men or women, who come into my line of work and start foolin' around in it, killing some time, just because they happen to be rich, and they're bored, and they think they'll play policeman for a while – just to get cheap thrills and kicks. Dabblers. Not reliable in a pinch. You can't count on the bastards, any line of work – and I don't care what it is – where you've some fuckin' hobbyist messing around on a serious job.'

'Well,' McNeil said, 'but she *is* rich. What's she supposed to do? Hide it? Dress like a bag-lady, so the rest of us that have to work for a living won't be envious?'

'No,' Richards said, 'I'm not saying that. It's just ... I don't trust her, I guess. I'm saying I don't trust her. She's too, she's too damn slick, and too damned smooth, and she makes it just a little too apparent that she's just slumming for a while in this darling little trade.' He shifted to an adenoidal honk. 'I can just hear her telling some hoity-toity dinner table in New York: "But Muffy, *really*, dear. They're all *so* original. I mean: *truly*, Muffy, *truly*, simply fascinating."'

O'Malley and Gleason were laughing.

'But that's exactly what I mean, John,' McNeil said. 'That's why I mentioned her. She's from that Walker world. The one that old James used to live in, anyway – before he became a robber. All those people know each other. If Christina's kept her name off the blotters in the precinct houses, and I'm betting that she has, the only way we're going to get a decent file on her is talk to people who know where she's been, what she's been doing, for the past few years. Has she been out of sight? Did she bag out for a while?

I don't move in Muffy's circles. If Christina took a sabbatical for a while, to go rob armored cars, and no one managed to catch her; well, wouldn't it be interesting to know?'

Richards gazed at her. He nodded. 'You know, Trooper McNeil,' he said, 'you have got the makings of a pretty damned good cop – unless you let some old Loot that thinks he knows everything, go and screw up your head. Yeah,' he said, glancing at Gleason, who nodded. 'Yeah, go and see Fiona. See what kinda lint you pick up on this Creole-looking kid.'

16

O'Malley completed his second appearance as a witness in *Commonwealth* v. *Tibbetts* at 3:55 in the afternoon. He left the witness stand and Gleason returned to the prosecution table. 'Mister Gleason,' Judge Bart said to his back, 'do you have another witness?'

Gleason turned. 'I'm sorry, your Honor – may I have a moment?'

'Certainly,' the judge said.

Gleason leaned over the table and whispered to Richards. 'Well, John, whaddaya think?'

'That's what I'd like to do, Terry,' Richards said. 'Lock it up for the day. Go back the office. Have a pow-wow. He nails you to do it, though: I'd rest. True artist is the one who knows when to stop. That's what I would do.'

Gleason turned and faced the bench. 'Your Honor,' he said,

'Lieutenant O'Malley was the Commonwealth's last witness for the day.'

Bigelow was on his feet at once. 'Your Honor,' he said, 'is the defense to conclude from that that the Commonwealth has rested?'

'Oh,' the judge said, 'I shouldn't think so. Mister Gleason seems fairly articulate. I imagine when he rests his case, he will so state in plain terms. He hasn't done it yet, though – at least, that I have heard.'

'Because,' Bigelow said, 'while I have several motions to present as soon as that does happen, and wish to be heard on them, and assume other defense counsel will also have such motions, it would be helpful for all of us in planning for tomorrow if the Commonwealth would specify whether it intends to present further evidence. In the case-in-chief.'

'Seems reasonable, Mister Bigelow,' the judge said. 'Care to respond to that, Mister Gleason?'

'Happy to, your Honor,' Gleason said. 'What I'd like to do, with the Court's permission, is hedge a little bit. We're close to the regular hour for recessing for the day. With the Court's indulgence, therefore, and in the belief that it's unlikely to prejudice any rights of the defendants, I'd request that I be permitted to defer until the morning my decision on whether to rest.'

'You may wish to call further witnesses?' Judge Bart said. 'My notes indicate you've presented all those you enumerated in your opening statement.'

'In answer to your question, your Honor,' Gleason said, 'I may. In response to your observations, I have. I will state at this time, as courtesy to Mister Bigelow and other counsel, that I do not at this time contemplate calling further witnesses. In all probability, the Commonwealth will rest tomorrow morning. If I do decide to offer additional evidence, it will be brief.'

The judge nodded. Bigelow said: 'Well? Which is it, then? Is he is, or is he ain't?'

'Ain't's the way I take it,' the judge said.

'Well, that's not fair,' Bigelow said. 'How're we supposed to plan, what we're going to do, if we don't know what he is? How can we do that?'

'Mister Bigelow,' the judge said, 'you have adequate information. Mister Gleason has said he thinks he'll rest, first light. But that if he does not, what he offers will be brief. Therefore I should think what you'd do, and the others on your side, would be to call a huddle tonight – get your ducks into a row, and who will do it first. If you think you'll need witnesses tomorrow, after you've done that, by all means, call your witnesses, and have them sitting here.'

'That's not much help, your Honor,' Bigelow said.

'Well, I'm sorry if you think that, Mister Bigelow,' the judge said. 'I'm sure Mister Gleason intended to be helpful, and I know that I did. But this is an imperfect world – it's possible we've failed. And I want to add, for the record, and for the jury to hear as well, that I thank each of the counsel for their economical approach to cross-examination, and their evident effort to avoid duplication in the questions they have put. Now, is that all, Mister Bigelow?'

Bigelow scowled. He nodded and sat down.

The judge turned toward the jury. 'Now, Ladies and Gentlemen,' he said, 'as you've just heard, the Commonwealth's just about finished presenting its case, and as far as I'm concerned, everything's just gone along perfectly so far. I have a few more housekeeping conversations to conduct with counsel, for which there's no need that you be present, so I'm going to excuse you now until tomorrow. The officers tell me that you're all going to the ballgame tonight, which indicates to me that you are either very courageous men and women who are able to handle dismay, or that you suffer from the same morbid curiosity that I have – which is how on earth a team fourteen-and-a-half games ahead at the All-Star break can find itself engaged in a bitter pennant fight in September. If any of you figures that out tonight, please address a note to me through the bailiff.' The jury grinned. 'Jury's excused,' the judge said. 'Court will remain in session.'

'Now,' the judge said to the lawyers, when the jury had filed from the room, 'I know all of you are hardworking, diligent people, and I respect you for that. Respect you enough so that I'd like to spare you unnecessary labor, and going without sleep. I've kept careful notes of the evidence presented by the Commonwealth. While I neither wish nor expect to discourage any of you from filing motions for directed verdicts of acquittal, based on insufficiency of the evidence, I think you should know that I've already decided the Commonwealth has made out a *prima facie* case. Viewed in the light most favorable to the Commonwealth, the evidence presented in the case-in-chief, together with all inferences reasonably to be drawn therefrom, would warrant a reasonable man or woman in finding each of the defendants guilty as charged, beyond a reasonable doubt. I'm not saying they will, that this jury will so find – I am saying that if they do, they have the grounds to do so. In other words, Mister Gleason in my estimation has lobbed this one over the rail. There will consequently be no directed verdict of not guilty. This one's going to the jury.'

Gleason and Richards stared straight ahead.

'If you have other reasons to cite for a directed verdict,' the judge said, 'I will hear them with great interest. Because insufficiency's the one I'm most familiar with, and you haven't got it there. Present any papers you have, tomorrow, and if you've already prepared briefs, submit them. But understand, as you do so you're traveling uphill.

'Now,' the judge said, 'how else may I be helpful?'

Bigelow stood. 'Your Honor,' he said, 'I intend to ask the Court tomorrow to permit Mister Walker to make an allocution to the jury. Not that the Court permit Mister Walker to do it tomorrow, but that the Court put it on the record that you intend to allow Mister Walker that opportunity at some point before this matter goes to the jury.'

The judge's eyebrows went up. 'Do I have your word, Mister Bigelow,' he said, 'that he'll behave himself? Because you, and he, have my word, Mister Bigelow, that if he does not, if he takes this as another opportunity to put on a display similar to the one he started this trial with, I will have him clapped in irons and carted away, in full view of the jury. Is that understood?'

'Ah,' Bigelow said. 'Well, put it this way, your Honor: I've mentioned that problem to him, that it could be a problem, and he's assured me that it won't.'

The judge nodded. 'Mister Gleason?' he said, 'your comment on that proposal?'

Gleason got slowly to his feet, glancing at Richards as he did so. 'Your Honor,' he said, 'ordinarily agreeing to an unsworn statement, by a defendant to a jury, not subject to cross-examination – ordinarily that would be anathema to me. But since I have asked Mister Bigelow and his colleagues for their indulgence of my hedging, overnight, on whether I will rest first thing, I suppose that in the spirit of harmonious compromise I should defer to him. So I will. Commonwealth has no objection.' He sat down.

'Very gracious, Mister Gleason,' the judge said. 'Any other matters we can get rid of here?'

Carolyn Veale stood up. Her hands trembled. 'Your Honor,' she said, 'may counsel confer in chambers?'

The judge looked startled. 'Well,' he said, 'usually ... Yes, Miss Veale.' He stood up. 'Court will be in recess,' he said. 'Court will see counsel in chambers.'

'The fuck was that about?' Richards said at 5:40 in Gleason's office at 20 Ashburton Place.

Gleason shook his head and smiled. He looked up at McNeil and Consolo. 'Funny world,' he said. 'Wanna tell all you great people: It's a funny world. Kathie Fentress told her lawyer that she's gonna fuck her. Or whatever it is, that broads do to broads. Goes up to see her in the conference room this morning, try to keep her bucked up and so forth, and Kathie says to her: "You know, Carolyn, Jill and I've been separated for a long time now. I can't even get a man in this damned joint. You're beginning to look kind of good. Let's get it on." And Carolyn, naturally, is horrified, but tries not to show she is. And Kathie says: 'I could rape you, you know. I'm, I bet I'm stronger'n you. And I really need some sex. Sick of fingering myself.'

'Carolyn is worried,' Gleason said. 'Wants out of the case, pronto. Judge's not about to let her out, not at this late stage.' He sighed. He reached toward the bottom right-hand drawer. He stopped. He looked at Consolo. 'You gonna start in again?'

Consolo looked puzzled.

'He's gonna get the whiskey out again, Fred,' McNeil said. 'And not a moment too soon, either. He wants to know: You gonna pull your Carrie Nation routine on us again?'

'Because, if you are,' Richards said, 'you can fuckin' *leave*.'

'I don't like to see people short-changing the rules,' Consolo said. 'I don't care who they are.'

'You didn't answer my question,' McNeil said.

Consolo crossed his legs. 'Oh,' he said, 'go ahead. I won't say anything.'

Gleason resumed his motion. 'Actually, what Carolyn is, Carolyn is scared,' he said. He brought out the bottle and the plastic cups. He began to pour. 'I don't envy her, either. Privilege says the client and attorney meet alone. Sure, Carolyn gets attacked, and she can holler loud. Get someone to rescue her. But who the hell wants to go through that?'

'So what'd the judge say?' Richards said, reaching for his cup.

'Said he'd post a stout matron – no reflection, June ...'

'Shut up, Terry,' McNeil said.

'... outside the conference room, armed with a truncheon or something, and if Kathie gets consumed by passion, Carolyn should scream and Grendel's mother'll rescue her. Doesn't sound too promising to me, but Carolyn seemed satisfied.'

'Well, then,' Richards said, raising his cup as Gleason poured the third half full for himself, '"over the rail," my friends. Congratulations, Terry. Like O'Malley said, you tried it smooth and true, and superfine. I myself personally thought it went in like a ... well, never mind. But very nice. You're a good trial lawyer.'

'Like a what, John?' McNeil said.

'Like a slick dick,' Richards said. 'Nice job, my man. Nice fuckin' job.'

'Thanks,' Gleason said, 'but I ain't finished yet.' They drank.

'You rested?' Consolo said. 'Did you rest today?'

'No,' Gleason said, 'I didn't. But I certainly will tomorrow. I'm just waffling tonight. Making Big Mo and them wonder, what I'm going to do. Screw up their sleep a little bit at least, huh John?'

'Yours isn't gonna be too peaceful, I miss my guess,' McNeil said.

'Well,' Gleason said, 'when I say I'm gonna rest, I don't mean I'm finished. There's still work to do.'

'You got that right, my friend,' Consolo said. 'You got that last part right.'

'Fuck're you talking about?' Richards said.

'You shouldn't've, you shouldn't rest,' Consolo said.

'Fred,' McNeil said, 'willya? All right? This's a strenuous life around here. Strenuous enough's it is, 'thout all your commentary.'

'He rests,' Consolo said, 'he rests without puttin' Mackenzie on, then the next thing that's gonna happen is that Morrissey does exactly what he says he's gonna do, what he said he's gonna do, and Tibbetts and his doctors're gonna get up there, and lie and lie, and then Tibbetts'll go free.'

'Fred,' Richards said, 'not again, all right? Terry tried the case tight. They get out of it? They get out of it. You got to learn to have some understanding of this life. The best you can do is the best you can do. It's not good enough? Then it wasn't. But it's all you can do.'

'Not if you leave half the laundry on the floor,' Consolo said. 'Not if you say: "Well, this here's a little chancey, so I think I won't

167

do that." This Tibbetts guy's a fuckin' menace. He's got to go away. This guy's the fuckin' mastermind, and you're giving him ways out.'

'He's worse'n Klein,' Richards said to Gleason.

'No, he's not,' Gleason said. 'What Fred is, is concerned. And I sympathize.'

'Well then,' Consolo said, 'do something, will you?'

'Doing all I can, Fred,' Gleason said. 'Doing all I can.'

'Look,' McNeil said, 'lemme jump in here, all right? I got two things to talk about, and I got to start in now. Because I got to call her. Call her before six.'

'Call who?' Richards said. 'Who you got to call?'

'Christina Walker, Terry,' McNeil said. 'She let everybody else leave, when the court shut down tonight, and then she came up to me for some private conversation. What she wants is: talk to you. Talk to you *alone*. Meet you someplace private, since she clearly can't come here. Ball's in your court, Terry – what do I tell her?'

'Well,' Richards said, 'the first thing you tell her's that Terry's not meeting her alone. That is flat, fuckin', *out*.'

'But he's got to meet her, though,' Consolo said. ''Less we really are, that all we're doing's, throwing in the goddamned sponge.'

'I agree with that, John,' Gleason said. 'Not the part about the sponge, but I do have to see her.'

'Wonderful,' Richards said. 'Then she either accuses you of rape, or she takes the stand and says you promised her something, she lies about her brother. Or Tibbetts. Or the dykes. Then what? You're a fuckin' witness. You're disqualified. What the hell do I do then, Terry? Start all this again? Is that what I do?'

'No,' Gleason said, 'you don't.' He looked at McNeil. 'Call her up, June,' he said. 'Tell her that I can't. Don't tell her why it is that I can't – just that it can't be done. And then do the best you can to see if she will talk to you.'

'Well, she won't,' McNeil said. 'Not if the second item, if what I got from Fiona today's the straight stuff. Way Fiona tells it – and she does know this family – way she tells it is that Christina's been the kind of kid you're glad other people had – not you. Very independent. Doesn't accept substitutes. If it's you she wants to talk to, she's not gonna talk to me – from what Fiona says. Ever since she's fourteen or so, this kid's been doing as she very well damned pleases. And apparently – she's very bright – apparently when she was about sixteen, seventeen, she went out to California or something, sees her brother. Supposedly. And she gets out there, and she meets Sam Tibbetts, who's about six years older'n she is and really radical. And she started fucking him, and her mother was scared shitless that Christina's father'd find out what his pride and joy was doing.'

'Is she still with him?' Richards said. 'This little honey tries bringing him a gun or something, things could get a little active up in Judge Bart's quiet court. Keep an eye on her, June, willya, while she's sitting behind us? Make sure there's no contact between them, no little packages.'

'Fiona,' McNeil said, 'Fiona says she thinks no. Her understanding is they came the parting of the ways about three, four years ago. Says she remembers being home for either Thanksgiving or Christmas, and she saw Mrs. Walker, and Mrs. Walker told her she was so relieved, because little Christina'd gone back to school and seemed to be settling down. Not doing hard drugs anymore, and sleeping around with Lenin. So, Fiona's not sure, but she thinks it's all over.'

'So she's no threat, then,' Richards said. 'On the sanity thing, I mean.'

'No threat either way,' Gleason said. 'She hasn't been with the guy since seventy-four, seventy-five? Her opinion's no better'n Mackenzie's. I think we give this babe a pass, June. Try to talk to her, still – there might be something there. But she's potential dynamite, up there on the stand. One defendant's sister and another's jilted girlfriend? Fuck that – Morrissey or Bigelow wants to load up that goddamned cannon, let 'em do it. Liable blow up in their faces. And if it doesn't, I'll spike it on cross.'

'You're throwing this case,' Consolo said.

'What?' Gleason and Richards said in unison.

'You guys,' Consolo said, 'you guys're either trying to lose this thing, or you don't care if you win. I don't know what it is. Maybe it doesn't matter enough, matter enough to you. But here you've got, you *know* you've got one guy, guy in custody, that at least knew Tibbetts sometime. And he can tell you that son of a bitch was as clear as a glass of gin. And now you've got, you've heard about, this broad, and she might have something, and you're just gonna pass it up. "Ah, hell with it – I'm tired."'

'Fred,' Richards said, clearing his throat, 'after this's over, matter how the thing comes out, I'm going over Ten-ten Com. and see if I can get you a nice comfortable position sorting paper clips and sticky tape, out in Framingham. Away from the public, away from trials, and most of all, from me. You ain't suited to this demanding way of life, I think. It strains your brain too much. You get all overheated and start making stupid statements. That is what you do.'

'You know,' Consolo said, 'I'm never going to forget any of this. The way you people've acted. Everything about it.'

'Good, Freddie,' Richards said. 'And if you learn even a little bit from what you've seen go on, well, that will be a bonus. And we all will be grateful.'

17

The jury came down at 10:08. The judge came out and sat down. Gleason stood up and said: 'Good morning, your Honor.'

The judge nodded. 'Your decision, Mister Gleason?'

'The Commonwealth has completed its case,' Gleason said.

The judge made a note. 'Very good,' he said. Gleason sat down.

'Ladies and Gentlemen of the jury,' the judge said, folding his hands on the desk and facing the box, 'the Commonwealth has rested. Given what I have to say next, it may seem to some of you rather silly that we brought you all trooping down here for that one piece of information, but it is a significant point in each trial, and I continue to believe that the jury's role in these proceedings is such that you should be present for all such ceremonies. Our rituals are important. They represent indicia of our civilization, emblems of our liberty, that so many have died for. And it doesn't do to sell them short.

'Now,' he said, 'normally the defense at this point presents motions and arguments for which the jury's presence is not required. So, having brought you down, we are going to send you up again. There being four defendants, each being entitled to present whatever questions the attorneys may deem significant, I expect those presentations will take the better part of the morning. So, if you wish to dawdle over your second cups of coffee, feel no compunction about so doing.

'Be assured,' he said, 'that we will not be dawdling down here. All of us know that some of you – those picked earliest have now been away from your homes, families and jobs for more than a week. And that you are anxious to return to them and resume your normal lives. So my practice, when the timing works out as it has in this case, is to move the luncheon recess around as necessary on the day when the Commonwealth rests, in order to make the best use possible of the usual court day. Your lunch will therefore be brought to you at noon. When counsel have finished their arguments, and the Court has ruled, and any other problems have been dealt with, the attorneys and the clerk and I will take one half-hour for lunch, instead of the usual hour, and whenever that half-hour ends, you'll be brought down again. That way, I hope, we can pick up an extra hour or so of work today, which is one less ahead of us the next time that we meet. Jury is excused.'

After the door had closed behind the last juror, the judge accepted sheafs of paper from each of the four defense lawyers. He heard arguments on motions: to dismiss; to compel disclosure of the names and addresses of informants; to renew motions to suppress; for directed verdicts; and to strike to certain evidence as unduly prejudicial. He denied all of the motions, noting objections and saving exceptions. At 12:10 he said: 'Any other necessary formalities, people?' There was no response.

'Very good,' he said. 'It must be my turn, then. Have the attorneys for the defense decided among themselves the order of their presentations?'

John Morrissey stood up. 'We drew straws, your Honor,' he said. 'Mister Tibbetts will go forward, followed by Mister Walker, then Miss Franklin, and finally Miss Fentress.'

The judge made notes. 'Each of you will make an opening statement, I presume?' he said. 'May I have an estimate of length?'

'I will need about twenty minutes,' Morrissey said.

'I think fifteen will be ample for me,' Bigelow said.

'Waive opening,' Klein said, 'if I may be permitted unlimited time for my closing.'

The judge's right eyebrow went up. 'Care to comment, Mister Gleason?'

'Well,' Gleason said, standing up, 'it's the Court's discretion and all, but I for one have no desire to see this turning into a rerun of the Lincoln-Douglas debates. I'll object to "unlimited." If Mister Klein wants to add, say, half an hour to whatever the Court sets as a limit for other counsel, if there's to be one, then I wouldn't object to that.'

'Well,' the judge said, 'I do like to have some sort of a ceiling. Suppose I offer this, Mister Klein: Each defendant to have a maximum of one hour to sum up, except that in your case, an hour twenty minutes. And the Commonwealth to have a maximum of one hour and a half. Think that will be sufficient?'

Klein pondered. 'I believe so, your Honor.'

'Miss Veale?' the judge said.

Carolyn Veale stood up and tapped on the top of the defense

table with the eraser of her pencil. She frowned. She shook her head. She looked up. She cleared her throat. 'Your Honor,' she said firmly, 'we will waive opening.'

The judge nodded and made notes. 'Fentress waives opening. Any other matters?' he said. 'Before we break for our abbreviated lunch?'

'One, if I may, your Honor,' Bigelow said. He produced a six-page document which he delivered to the clerk. He gave copies to each of the other lawyers. The judge scanned it. He looked up. 'For the record: Mister Bigelow has presented a proposed stipulation of agreed facts, always appreciated in protracted cases. It's rather detailed. I'm therefore going to suggest that our truncated luncheons be extended for our study of this document over our sandwiches. When we come back, at, say, one P.M., I'll expect the Commonwealth's reaction. For your information, Mister Gleason, in case I haven't made it clear, I like these things. They can save a lot of time, if the parties can find some way to agree.' Gleason said he understood.

Gleason put Bigelow's stipulation on the window sill and unwrapped his sandwich. 'Fuck's he want?' Richards said, in the small office on the seventh floor. 'We agree that Walker's innocent?'

Gleason bit into the bulky roll. He shook his head. 'Uh uh,' he said. He swallowed Coke. 'Take a look at it, you want. It's reasonable enough. What he did was have the Badgers go back and track down every goddamned job that Jimmy's had since he got out of school. Must've cost 'em a fuckin' *bundle*.'

'What good does that do him?' Richards said. 'We never said the kid was lazy, we said he killed people.'

'What good does it do?' Gleason said. 'Does Walker very little. But does Bigelow a lot. Puts it on the record that Bigelow got something, all the money he laid out. That he was diligent, hardworking, that he really prepared his case. Anybody decides to come around a year from, James's doing time, and say John Bigelow did no homework, right there in the case file is Bigelow's retort – "An exhaustive defense. Investigation conducted by Investigations, Inc., the best in the whole world. No stone left unturned. Blah, blah, blah."'

'He's cute,' Richards said.

'Got to be cute,' Gleason said, 'you're charging fees like his. Course some of the time that he's being cute, he's not being cute protecting your ass – his client's – he's protecting his own. So you're paying him your money to protect *him* against *you*, not *you* from somebody else. Which doesn't seem quite fair.'

'You gonna do it, when you get out, Terry?' Richards said. 'On the other side?'

Gleason drank Coke. 'Uh huh,' he said. 'Bet your ass. Have to. Day, the way things are today, from the day your client walks in the office, you're laying backfires to ignite behind his ass, the day comes that he sues you. You think Consolo's bad? At least he's not going to file a complaint against me with the Board of Bar Overseers, and then sue me for two million on a malpractice complaint.'

'You gonna let Bigelow have it?' Richards said. 'His stipulation there?'

'Oh, sure,' Gleason said. 'I'm even going to add a little something – that none of the employments listed were the kind that would have required James to work on Sunday, May the fourth, nineteen seventy-seven. Then I'll argue: "No alibiin' this stuff, ladies and gentlemen."

'But I've got to let Bigelow have it,' Gleason said. 'He's got about a dozen witnesses there, every one of which he's got a perfect right to call. He could keep us here another three weeks – well, maybe only one – dragging all these Connecticut Valley tobacco farmers, and major appliance installers, and Pioneer Valley construction foremen, and all those other guys. Parading them up one after another to say James's worked for them and he's a good employee, too. I gather the defense is going to be that James never showed any indication to the outside world that he came into a share of a rather large sum of money, and a good-sized stash of cocaine, on the morning of May fourth. Which is all all right with us. Grand jury didn't say that James went out and bought a yacht. He isn't charged with using drugs, though I would bet be did. I thought when I first read it: 'Geez, I wonder if these people, if they've got attendance records. 'Cause I sure would like to know if he was absent on four specific days between October fourth of nineteen seventy and September fourth of seventy-five. When those armored cars went down. And if he wasn't on the job, well, we know where he was – he was on the *jobs*.'

Gleason stretched. 'Shit, I'm tired,' he said. 'I wish this was over with. And now I got this afternoon, all their ranting and raving instead of mine – which's nowhere near's much fun – and I know what Bart's gonna say, when four P.M. rolls around.'

'What?' Richards said.

'He's gonna say: "Tomorrow,"' Gleason said. '"We'll sit on Saturday." Because the jury's been locked up, and they are getting antsy, and he'll want to console them, and so that's what he will do.'

'But you're getting antsy yourself,' Richards said.

'I am,' Gleason said, 'but I am not, antsy, if you take a look at Barbara. Barbara is antsy like George S. Patton got antsy about Panzer divisions surrounding Bastogne. I miss about three more dinners, I'm not there at sun-up about two more mornings, she is going to have the bread knife aimed at my throat the next time I come home.'

'She'd better learn to live with it,' Richards said. 'This is how you do your job.'

'She *has* learned to live with it,' Gleason said. 'It's my life that's in danger.'

18

Morrissey intercepted Gleason on his way back to the courtroom on the afternoon of September 15th. He took him into the internal corridor leading to the judge's chambers and began a murmured conversation. McNeil, at the security table, glanced at them from time to time. She heard Gleason say: 'Okay.' Morrissey continued down the corridor and knocked on the door of the chambers. Gleason came toward her. 'Tibbetts gonna plead?' she said excitedly. Gleason looked mildly startled. 'No, no,' he said, 'nothing like that.' He went into the courtroom.

At 1:03 P.M. the bailiff noted the return of Carolyn Veale and rapped on the courtroom door of chambers. The judge emerged immediately and swept onto the bench. The jury box was empty. The defendants sat behind the rail. The judge sat down and clasped his hands. Morrissey was standing. 'You have some glad tidings for us, Mister Morrissey?'

'I believe so, your Honor,' Morrissey said. 'Inspired by my brother, Mister Bigelow's example, I sought out Mister Gleason at the luncheon recess and proposed a stipulation of agreed facts in the case against Mister Tibbetts. Mister Gleason, with the civility and fairness he's invariably showed me, in all our many confrontations, accepted my proposal. Time did not permit me to reduce the agreement to writing, but if the Court will permit, I can recite it for the record. If what I say varies in any way from Mister Gleason's understanding of our undertaking, I will bow to his correcting amendments.'

'Unctuous bastard, isn't he?' Richards whispered to Gleason. 'Shh,' Gleason said. 'It's part of his act. He'd wear a wig if he could.'

'As Mister Gleason has indicated to the Court,' Morrissey said, 'discovery motions in cases that he's prosecuted and I've defended have been mere formalities. Our custom over many years has been to swap as much of our files as the attorney-client privilege permits. Following that practice in the case at bar, each of us has a copy of the other's results of medical evaluation of my client, Mister Tibbetts. Mister Gleason knows what my doctor's going to say on the stand, and I know what Mister Gleason's doctor will say on the stand. Each doctor is Board-certified. Each has staff privileges at prestigious teaching hospitals. Each lectures on psychiatry at leading medical schools. And, as usual, they are diametrically opposed in their diagnosis of the state of my client.

'I, for one,' Morrissey said, 'have never been able to perceive how a jury benefits from such battles of the experts, each firmly nullifying the other's opinion. I suspect the jurors ignore both, and proceed on their gut reactions, but since I can't be sure, I always offer what I have. Mister Gleason and I both know that neither of us is going to shake the other's expert on cross. Therefore, in hopes of expediting this matter – and also saving a few dollars in expert-witness fees – we have agreed to offer each of the reports in evidence, and to ask the Court to tell the jury they may take it as proven that if both doctors had been called, they would have testified according to the tenor of their reports. Which, if the Court so allows, will almost certainly enable the defendant Tibbetts to complete his case this afternoon.'

'Or maybe around midnight,' Richards whispered, 'if Big Mo talks much longer about all the time he's saving.' Gleason hid his grin behind his hand and looked down at the table.

'Mister Gleason,' the judge said, beaming, 'any variance between your understanding and what Mister Morrissey has said?'

Gleason cleared his throat, and his face of expression. He stood up. 'No, your Honor,' he said. 'Mister Morrissey with his inveterate succinctness, brevity and wit, has accurately described our concord.' He sat down. Morrissey grinned.

The judge coughed. 'Yes,' he said. 'Well, nevertheless, the Court appreciates the effects of this cooperation among counsel, and so states on the record. Any other good news for me?' There was no response. 'Bring the jury down, Harry,' he said. 'Let's get cracking here.'

Morrissey told the jury that the case was 'very simple. We by no means concede any point that the Commonwealth has tried to make – indeed, that the Commonwealth must make – in order to support its allegations against Sam Tibbetts. We don't, in part – though only in part – because we can't. Our position is that Sam Tibbetts on the date in question was literally out of his mind, and we are going to prove that, on the evidence.

'Therefore,' Morrissey said, 'whether Mister Tibbetts's fingerprints were on a gun; whether Mister Tibbetts was found sleeping in a cabin; regardless of whether Mister Tibbetts ever in fact was in The Friary Bar and Grille: all of that stuff is irrelevant. The fact of the matter, as our evidence will show, is that Samuel Tibbetts on May fourth of last year was incapable of forming the intent that our statutes – and our Constitution – demand for the commission of a punishable criminal act. He was then, still, under the hegemony of dangerous drugs – as he had been, for nearly a decade. He was then, still, suffering delusions. Of grandeur. Of omnipotence. Of omniscience. He was, in other words, my dear Ladies and Gentlemen, not in his right mind.' He paused. 'And he will so testify.

'His testimony,' Morrissey said, 'will be preceded, the foundation laid for it, by that of his parents.'

'Oh boy,' Gleason whispered to Richards, 'I was afraid of this.'

'They will tell you what he was, before he went to the West Coast,' Morrissey said. 'They will tell you that he was a brilliant student, a conscientious young man, active in his church, a talented musician – in short, in every respect, everything a mother and a father could have wished an only son, an only *child,* to be. They will tell you about the sad changes they observed in his character. His inexplicable estrangement. How he became, in their words, "a different person." You have seen them every day, sitting in the audience. You could not know who they were, of course, but perhaps you yourselves have remarked the anguish evident in their faces. They will tell you, each of them, they will recount for you the torment – and the agony – of living through this horrifying deterioration of their beloved son.

'Sam will testify as well,' Morrissey said. 'He doesn't have to; no defendant does. He has a constitutional right to remain right where he is. Make the government prove its case against him – if it can. But he's waiving that right. He's saying to you: "No, I'm going up there. I'm going to tell these people exactly what happened. If they're going to judge me, then let them hear the whole story. Let them know all the facts. As degrading as they are."

'Now,' Morrissey said, hooking his right thumb in his belt, 'you are going to receive, as the result of an agreement between me and Mister Gleason here, copies of two reports by physicians. The report that we're submitting – Doctor Herbert Hamisch's, and he's an eminent psychiatrist at the Harvard Medical School and the Brigham Hospital – supports the facts I've just outlined. The other report – by Doctor Norris Alpert – contradicts it. We believe that what you hear from the Tibbetts family, on the stand, will lead you to agree with Doctor Hamisch's report, and that you will find Sam Tibbetts not guilty of these charges, by reason of insanity.'

'I think he mousetrapped you,' Richards whispered.

'No,' Gleason said. '"Sandbagged," maybe, but not "mousetrapped." He was gonna do it anyway, and I could not stop him. This way it's over quicker.'

Gleason was deliberate and gentle when he took Walter Tibbetts on cross-examination. 'I'm going to refer to some of the testimony you've just delivered, Mister Tibbetts,' he said, 'in response to Mister Morrissey's questions. And I'm relying of course on the notes I took while you were giving it. It's possible my notes are incorrect in some respects. So I hope, if I did misunderstand – or mis-hear – something, that you'll feel perfectly free to correct me. Tell me exactly what you said.'

'I understand,' Tibbetts said. He licked his lips.

'I know this is, this must be, an ordeal for you, sir,' Gleason said. 'I'll be as brief as I can.'

'I appreciate that,' Tibbetts said.

'You testified, sir, I believe,' Gleason said, 'that your son became estranged from you. I'm not sure I got the date. Could you tell me approximately when you first noticed that estrangement?'

'It was around,' Tibbetts said, frowning, 'I believe it was around the middle of the summer.'

'And the year, sir, if you recall?' Gleason said.

'Nineteen sixty-eight,' Tibbetts said, clearing his throat. 'The year he graduated from Stanford. Nineteen sixty-eight.'

'And you testified, sir, did you not,' Gleason said, 'that what prompted you to notice this, what excited your concern, was his failure to come home and visit you and his mother?'

'Well,' Tibbetts said slowly, crossing his legs, 'no. Not exactly. That was … Sam'd been away summers before and we were not concerned. He enjoyed working around the water, and since he was always, since he'd always been a very responsible kid, mature for his years, good judgment, we'd always felt comfortable, since he was about fourteen, allowing him to do that. He had jobs on the Cape, mowing lawns, doing gardening work, staying with friends of ours. And then, when he was sixteen, working at the marina in Edgartown. On Martha's Vineyard. We were accustomed to the fact that he was uncommonly industrious, and independent – self-sufficient – for a person of tender years.'

'And you were proud of him,' Gleason said.

'Oh, very proud,' Tibbetts said. 'It seemed like, it always seemed as though Sam was God's child, you know? I remember when he was a freshman at Stanford, he called us up, all excited, and said: "Can you believe it, Dad? The Ipswich Ensemble? That I'm spending second quarter, that I'm going to Egypt, and to Israel and Lebanon? Can you believe it?" And I said, I'm afraid

I was a bit complacent, I said: "Of course I can believe it. You're an extraordinary person. You have gifts. The only limitation on your future is your own imagination." And I meant it, every word.'

'I see,' Gleason said. 'Well then, if you can, sir, what was it, that prompted your concern about your son in sixty-eight?'

'Well,' Tibbetts said, 'we'd gone out there before, while he was at Stanford. Business trips, conventions in San Francisco, all that sort of thing. And naturally we always made time to see him. Take him to dinner at Jack's in San Francisco, him and whatever young lady he happened to be seeing at the time. And those were always very pleasant occasions, you know? Very nice occasions. And I suppose his mother and I were guilty of a little planning ahead, a little anticipation, when we'd meet a particular young lady. Looking forward to the day when he'd get married, settle down, start a family of his own. And the girls, the girls he introduced us to were always very sweet, very nice young women – we would have welcomed any of them as our daughter-in-law. So, when it came time for his graduation, I called him up – I suppose this would've been late April, early May – and I knew of course that Stanford being a big school, there might be trouble getting hotel reservations around graduation time. So I called him up to make sure of the date, because I wanted to reserve a room for us either at Ricky's Hyatt, near the campus, or, failing that, at the Fairmont in San Francisco, and he said: "Oh, Dad, I don't know. I don't think I'm going to it." And naturally I was surprised, and asked him: "Why?" And he said: 'Well, look. I know it's important, that you and Mom've looked forward a long time to this. But I've got this opportunity – some friends of mine're going down to Central America for part of the summer. Something like a Peace Corps

185

thing. Which I would like to do, the regular Peace Corps, but with Berkeley in the fall, I can't. So I thought, you know, I could go down there for the summer.'

'And we saw nothing wrong with that,' Tibbetts said. 'We were, as I've said, we were accustomed to Sam being away in the summer. Naturally we were a little disappointed not to see him graduate, but this did seem like a good opportunity. So he went off to Bolivia with our blessings.'

'Then what prompted your concern that summer?' Gleason said.

'His letters,' Tibbetts said. 'As in everything else, Sam was a very good correspondent. If we weren't seeing much of him, we always knew what he was doing, what was going through his mind. What he read – everything. And around the middle, I suppose it was July, but around the middle of the summer, his letters started to … well, they were disturbing.'

'In what respect?' Gleason said. 'Any one thing stand out in your mind?'

'More like two, I'd say,' Tibbetts said. 'Two things stood out. The first one, initially the first thing didn't concern me a great deal. Sam's major field was mathematics, but his interests were catholic – eclectic. His range of interests was very broad. So when he started writing about reading Castaneda, and various other – I suppose you would call them "seers," "gurus," "mystics," whatever – I wasn't immediately concerned. But then there began to creep in, really, what sounded to me very much like Marxist rhetoric.' He hesitated. 'I think,' he said, 'I think if it'd been either of those, what, enthusiasms, either one of them, I would not have been concerned. But the combination, the combination of visionary stuff and radical politics: that troubled me. And then I got – we got – a letter in early August which had clearly been written under the influence of something. It made no sense at all. Now he wasn't talking about reading about visions – now he was reporting visions that he'd seen. Himself.'

'Did you try to get in touch with him?' Gleason said. 'Find out what was going on?'

'We did,' Tibbetts said. 'It was impossible. By phone, at least. He was off in the mountains somewhere, and we couldn't reach him. We debated, we considered flying down there, both his mother and I did, but then we decided there was no point in that because we didn't, neither of us speaks Spanish and we didn't know where to find him. So, we put that aside and made plans to go out to Berkeley to see him in the fall.'

'And did you do that?' Gleason said.

'No,' Tibbetts said.

'The reason?' Gleason said.

'He,' Tibbetts said, coughing, 'he told us on the telephone he wouldn't see us if we came.'

'Did he give a reason?' Gleason said.

'Just that he didn't want us to come,' Tibbetts said, shaking his head and coughing. He removed his glasses and rubbed his hand over his forehead. He coughed again. He replaced his glasses. 'I'm sorry,' he said. 'He didn't want us to come.'

'That must've been very painful for you, sir,' Gleason said.

'It was,' Tibbetts said. 'Very painful.'

'And when was the next time you saw him?' Gleason said.

'When,' Tibbetts said, 'when he was arrested.'

'That would've been this past May?' Gleason said.

'Yes,' Tibbetts said.

'Did you have any other contact with him,' Gleason said,

'between that telephone call in the fall of sixty-eight, and when you saw him again, in custody?'

'Only the canceled checks,' Tibbetts said. 'For the first year he was at Berkeley, we continued to send him spending money. Trying to preserve whatever small link that remained Just small amounts – fifty, a hundred dollars a month – and the bank would of course include them in our statement. But then the envelopes, the envelopes started to come back – "Moved. No forwarding address" – after a while we just, I suppose we just gave up.'

'You didn't, then,' Gleason said, 'you had no contact with him whatsoever between, say, January first of nineteen-seventy-seven and the Fourth of July of that year?'

'You mean, last year?' Tibbetts said.

'Yes,' Gleason said.

'No, none,' Tibbetts said.

'Thank you, Mister Tibbetts,' Gleason said. 'I have no further questions.'

19

Each time Ellen Tibbetts answered a question from Morrissey, she glanced defiantly at Gleason. Each time Gleason stood and objected to her answer on the grounds that it was not responsive to the question Morrissey had asked, and moved that it be stricken, she clenched her fists and glared at him. Each time Gleason stood up, Judge Bart upheld the objection and ordered the jury to disregard the preceding statement by the witness, and Ellen Tibbetts glared at the judge.

'Now, Mrs. Tibbetts,' the judge said, 'we really do have to move along here. I understand your emotional condition.'

'My emotional condition is perfectly fine,' she said.

'In fact,' the judge said, 'all of us, here, understand how difficult this must be for you and your husband to go through.'

'Then why are you putting us through it, then?' she said. 'If, if you know how hard this is for someone, why do you make people do it?'

'Mrs. Tibbetts,' the judge said, 'you are up there on that witness stand because your son and your husband and your son's lawyer – and you, evidently – because each of you appears to think that you can contribute something to your son's defense. Something that will help the jury to decide one of the major issues in this case. Which is whether your son was mentally competent to commit a crime on May fourth, nineteen-seventy-seven. If you're uncomfortable, if you think it isn't fair for your son's lawyer to ask you questions, and for all of us – including Mister Morrissey – to require you to answer, not with speeches but with responses appropriate to the questions that he's put, then you shouldn't've gotten up there.'

She picked up her purse and stood up. 'Then I'll get down,' she said.

'Your Honor,' Gleason said.

Judge Bart made a small gesture toward Gleason with his left hand. 'I know, Mister Gleason, I know,' he said. 'I'll take care of this.

'Mrs. Tibbetts,' he said, 'you can step down if you wish. But if you do, before Mister Gleason has a chance to cross-examine, I'm going to have to instruct this jury to disregard all the statements you've already made. *All* the statements, Mrs. Tibbetts – not just the outbursts that you've seen fit to sprinkle in among the few responsive answers you have managed to give.'

She sat down. 'This is outrageous,' she said. 'There's no need of any of this. Happening at all. Absolutely no need.'

'Well,' the judge said, 'the grand jury disagreed with you there, ma'am. Seven bodies were found in that barroom, as you call it, and the grand jury concluded that your son, among others, was probably responsible for their murders. Now it doesn't matter what you think of the legitimacy of that view, of the grand jury. What matters is that you've chosen to get up there, and be sworn, and answer the questions that the lawyers put to you. And *only* those questions. Not what you happen to feel like blurting out. Just what the lawyers ask you.'

She pursed her lips. 'I think it's all ridiculous,' she said. 'They were, all of them were probably drug sellers and prostitutes. And anyone, anyone who knew Sam before all of this stuff happened, anyone would tell you that something'd happened to him. That he wasn't right. He was a different person. I think it was the drugs that did it. If he wasn't hypnotized.'

"'Hypnotized,"' the judge said. He sighed. 'Jury will disregard that last as pure speculation on the witness's part. Mister Morrissey, want to try again?'

Morrissey took a deep breath. 'Your Honor,' he said. 'I note that it's three-oh-five, and we have been underway for about two hours. May I have a short recess, to talk to my witness?'

Judge Bart stood up. 'Certainly,' he said. 'Court will be in recess for twenty minutes.'

McNeil came into the small office, giggling. 'He's got her out in the hallway,' she said. 'She's going at him like a she-bear. He's trying, calm her down, her husband's trying, calm her down, and all she keeps saying is that she doesn't care. "This is a travesty of justice."'

'You're gonna have fun with her, Terry,' Richards said grimly.

"'Fun"?' Gleason said. 'After the way the old man murdered me, you think I'm gonna touch her with fireplace tongs? The fuck

I am. You know what she's waiting for? She's waiting for me to ask my first question. Then will come the waterworks. Mary weeping at the tomb of Jesus. Morrissey'll turn into Joseph of Arimathea – the old goat's already delivered the centurion's line: that Sam is the Son of God – and the whole procession'll bear Sam out of the courtroom on their shoulders, Fentress as Magdalene. We go back in there, Morrissey's gonna say: "Nothing further, your Honor." Meaning: "I think I'll just hand Gleason here this fucking live grenade." And you know what I'm gonna say? "No questions, your Honor." No sir – it's one thing to get spattered with shit, while you're minding your own business and somebody throws it at you. It's another thing entirely, jump in the toilet bowl.'

'I thought you did pretty well with the father,' Richards said.

'You did,' Gleason said. 'You thought I did pretty well with the father? Is the heat too much for you, John? Lemme feel your forehead. You probably think Torrez can pitch, the Red Sox'll win the pennant, if you think that I did that.'

'He answered your questions,' Richards said.

'Damned right he did,' Gleason said, 'and there wasn't a way in the world I could stop him. He fuckin' killed me. Or came as close's he could, 'thout pulling a dagger. That fuckin' Morrissey – I give the bastard credit. If the witness's coachable, John'll make the world forget Vince Lombardi with the Packers, Miller Huggins with the Yankees, and whoever prompts Olivier when he forgets his lines. Only problem he's got with the dam in this case is: she's not as tractable's the sire. She thinks she knows more about the whole thing'n Morrissey does, so she's acting up. I'm not gonna touch the bitch. I know an ambush when I see one – she's not going to cry on me.'

*

At 3:30 P.M. the jury was seated and Mrs. Tibbetts returned to the stand. Her mouth was set and she was scowling. Morrissey said: 'I have no further questions of this witness, your Honor.' He sat down.

'Mister Gleason?' the judge said.

'No questions,' Gleason said.

The judge smirked and nodded. 'Now there's a surprise,' he muttered. 'You're excused, Mrs. Tibbetts,' he said. 'You may step down now.'

She stared at him angrily. 'In fact, Mrs. Tibbetts,' the judge said, 'you *must* step down.'

She clenched her jaw muscles and left the stand.

'Your next witness, Mister Morrissey?' the judge said.

'Your Honor please,' Morrissey said, 'and I'm only asking the Court's pleasure on this, but my next – and last – witness is the defendant, Mister Samuel Tibbetts. I anticipate that his direct examination will require at least an hour. Then of course there is the further possibility that Mister Bigelow, Miss Veale and Mister Klein will wish to cross-examine him, as well as Mister Gleason.'

'Yes,' the judge said. He mused. 'Ladies and Gentlemen of the jury,' he said, 'what Mister Morrissey has just said falls into the category of a friendly warning. And I've taken it in that light. He hoped to complete his defense today, but like most other predictions of duration in the courts, that proved to be somewhat more optimistic than subsequent events warranted. Now, all of us are sensible, as I've said, of the inconvenience to each of you, and we want to go as fast as we can without short-shrifting anything. I've already decided that we'll all come in tomorrow for a full day's work – unless any of you are subject to religious sanctions against work on Saturday?' He looked inquiringly at the jurors.

There was no response. 'Fine,' he said, 'so we'll plan to do that. And I have hopes – hopes which may turn out no better than Mister Morrissey's have been, but hopes nonetheless – that each of the other defendants will be able to complete their evidence then. Which would mean that unless the Commonwealth feels it necessary to offer rebuttal evidence, counsel will be able to make their final arguments on Monday. I would then charge you, give you my instructions on Tuesday, draw the names of the four alternates, appoint a foreman, and after that the schedule will be entirely in your hands.

'Now,' he said, 'the question Mister Morrissey is raising is whether defendant Tibbetts should begin his direct testimony today, since the lateness of the hour indicates he will not complete it before the regular hour for recess. Much less any cross-examination. So what I think we're going to do, unless there's some very strong reason offered not to, is suggest that we go as long as it takes today, to complete Mister Tibbetts's direct examination. And then, at whatever time that is, recess until morning. When we'll have the cross.' He surveyed the courtroom. 'That agreeable?' There was no response. 'Fine,' he said. 'Mister Morrissey, call your witness.'

'Morrissey did not look happy,' Richards said in Gleason's office, raising his cup at 6:35. 'Confusion to our enemies,' he said, before he drank.

'Morrissey was bullshit,' Gleason said, pouring his drink. He raised the cup. 'Up the rebels,' he said. He drank. 'I would've been bullshit myself,' Gleason said, 'Black Bart'd done that to me.'

'What difference does it make?' McNeil said. 'He starts today; he starts tomorrow: why does it matter?'

'You sure you don't want a drink, June?' Richards said. 'What're you doing? Filling in for Fred?'

'No,' she said. 'I'm sure. I've got a date tonight. Bad enough to get home plowed – shouldn't start out that way.'

'The Honorable Osgood again?' Richards said slyly.

She blushed. 'Yes,' she said. 'How you know about that, John?'

'I know everything,' Richards said, grinning. 'Don't get mad. I think it's nice. Nice for you and nice for Dave. He was really desolate when his wife died, there.' He hesitated. 'Guy who told me about it didn't think it was so nice, though – think he had his eye on you himself. Said he wasn't sure it was "right" for a lady cop to be dating a DA.'

'Fearless Fred told you?' she said. 'Oh, that son of a bitch. I'd go out with Dracula 'fore I'd go out with him. What'd you tell him?'

'Told him to go bag his head, naturally,' Richards said. 'Assured him Dave Osgood is chaste and pure in all respects – that the Honorable is honorable, in other words, and he should spare no fretting about your virtue in hazard.'

'Good,' she said.

'Then,' Richards said, 'then Fred said it wasn't your virtue that concerned him. That it was your life.'

'He did not,' she said.

'He did,' Richards said. 'He said: "And even if it was right, trooper dating a DA, that guy, he killed his wife."'

'I don't believe this,' McNeil said.

'That Dave did it?' Richards said. 'Neither do I. She did it herself. But that Fred thinks Dave did it? I believe that. "A week before she died," he says, "week before she died, when anybody knew a thing about how she was, knew she wasn't gonna last three weeks, Osgood goes out and gets thirty Seconals, a hundred milligrams.

Now why did he do that?" And I said: "Freddie, Freddie, the woman was in agony. He was just trying, help her with the pain. Doctor prescribed them." And Fred says: "Bullshit. Wasn't for the pain. Wasn't for the pain at all. It was to kill herself. I went down, I went down the drugstore, Dedham Square, and I checked all the records there, and there it was in black and white: a month's supply of Seconal for a woman that was lucky if she lived for two more weeks. And he hadda know that. Absolutely had to." And I said: "So what if he did? What difference it make? If she took the stuff herself." And Fred says: "Suicide's a felony. Accessory before the fact a felony, charged as principal. That's the goddamned law. If he didn't kill her, if what he did wasn't, didn't amount to killing her, then helping her to do it amounts to the same thing. Far as I'm concerned, at least."'

'Fred is,' she said, 'Fred is really nuts.'

'Yes,' Richards said, 'but not completely, and not always wrong. For example: I was certain I was lying when I said your virtue was safe. Least, I hoped I was.'

'Well,' she said, 'I don't know when you said it. But for a while you were right. He held out against my feminine wiles for several dates more'n I had in mind.'

'Atta girl, Junie,' Richards said. 'This's serious, then.'

'No predictions,' she said. 'I've had too many trophy heads escape. It's one thing if you decide you want to go through life intact, but it gets really frustrating if you make up your mind to put out, and you still don't get anywhere.'

'You husband-hunting, June?' Gleason said. 'That what it's about?'

'If it comes to that,' she said, 'yeah, I will take a husband. Marriage happens? Fine. But I'll settle happily for a reliable man.

That's really all I'm after. There's so many twerps around. Twerps, and gays, and guys cheating on their wives, and … and *Freds*.' She laughed. 'Assholes, in other words. One reason I got out of teaching was it had so many clowns in pants, lusting after sophomores and ignoring grown-up stuff. Very disappointing, if you're the grown-up stuff.'

'Well, I guess that rules us out, John,' Gleason said. 'Both of us're married men.'

'Well,' she said, gazing at him, 'it might not've, if the drought'd lasted a few more years.' Gleason blushed. 'I'm serious, Terry,' she said. 'All you people that just happened to get married, you bastards think *every*one's married. You go home at night and there's a set of compatible genitals with a person attached, waiting to rub your neck and blow in your ear, and tell you how fine you are. And it isn't like that, for most of us. It isn't like that at all.'

'Certainly isn't for me,' Gleason said. 'Time I get home tonight, there's no way I'm gonna let Barbara near my ears. I'll come in tomorrow with one bitten off, and a big bandage on the other one.'

'Well,' McNeil said, 'I've never been married. I've never even lived with a guy, for God's sake. So maybe my hopes're too high. But my God, there's got to be something better out there'n cruising the bars, and picking up stiffs, and warding off all of the Freds.'

'Dave's a nice guy,' Richards said. 'Sink the hook deep, play him carefully, lots of line, and then reel him in. He'll go quietly, and he's a fine catch. Very decent guy. But tonight either make him spend the night at your place, or get you home real early if you're going somewhere else. May be Friday, and all, but we've got a full day tomorrow.'

Gleason stood up and stretched. 'Yeah,' he said, 'and I've got a full night tonight. First I go home and get chewed out 'cause I'm late as usual. Then I eat cold dinner. Then I get ragged out again because the lady will not like it when I say I've got to work.'

'Work on what?' McNeil said.

'On *taking* advantage *of* the advantage that Black Bart gave me today,' Gleason said. 'Which was why Big Mo was bullshit. I've got all night to plan my cross tomorrow. 'Stead of having to get up right after Morrissey got through, and start winging questions at that little bastard, making it up as I go along, I've got overnight to do some planning. Think up really nasty things to harpoon the little prick.' He paused. 'Not that I've got much hope of really shaking the kid. He's good. He's very good. He's smart, and for all I know, he's telling the truth – maybe he had to be nuts. I've got to be really nasty.' He chuckled. 'Maybe I should let Barbara plan the cross. She's really good at that. It's her specialty.'

20

On Saturday morning the public halls of the courthouse were dim and silent. The jurors and the parties to the trial hushed their voices and behaved like trespassers. Christina Walker and the Tibbetts couple constituted half of the civilian spectators passing through the metal detectors under June McNeil's bloodshot gaze. Consolo came in behind the three reporters.

'Mister Tibbetts,' Gleason said, 'yesterday at the close of your direct examination, Mister Morrissey invited you to agree that you had told "a sordid story" of your life since nineteen-sixty-eight – do you recall that?'

'Yes sir, I do,' Tibbetts said. He wore a dark grey pinstriped suit, a blue shirt and a dark red tie ornamented by blue whales.

'And you accepted that invitation,' Gleason said. 'And you agreed with him.'

199

'Yes sir, I did,' Tibbetts said. He straightened himself in the chair. 'It was.'

'A story,' Gleason said, 'of contraband drugs. Of sexual promiscuity. Of sexual perversity. Of habitual law-breaking with respect to dealing in narcotics, harboring fugitives, attempting to subvert the government.'

'Yes sir,' Tibbetts said. 'What I can remember, at least. I did all those things.'

'And you admit having done them, now,' Gleason said.

'Yes, I do,' Tibbetts said.

'But – so we will all be clear on this – you do not admit planning and carrying out the robbery of The Friary on May fourth of last year,' Gleason said.

'No, I do not,' Tibbetts said.

'You do not admit causing the victims, Abbate and Nichols, to die of gunshot wounds,' Gleason said.

'No, I do not,' Tibbetts said.

'You do not admit causing the victims, McKechnie and Iverson, to die of gunshot wounds,' Gleason said.

'No, I do not,' Tibbetts said.

'You do not admit that you caused the deaths, by gunshot wounds, of victims Wilkerson, Gross and Alexander,' Gleason said.

'No, I do not,' Tibbetts said.

'You do not admit to any part in killing the two guard dogs,' Gleason said.

'Well, now,' Morrissey said, half rising, 'I think we'll object to that.'

'I'll withdraw it, your Honor,' Gleason said. Morrissey sat down. 'You do not admit, sir,' Gleason said, 'you do not admit that you and at least these three co-defendants, on May fourth, nineteen-seventy-seven, did forcibly or fraudulently obtain entrance to The Friary, with the intent to steal drugs and money, and that you, and at least these three co-defendants, in cold blood, murdered those seven people?'

'Now,' Morrissey said, standing up. 'I really do have to object here. This is repetitious.'

'And I object, as well,' Gleason said, 'to my learned brother's transparent effort to shield his client from rigorous cross-examination, by means of these frivolous interruptions.'

'I ask that my brother,' Morrissey said, 'be instructed to refrain from arguing his case to the jury under the guise of cross-examination.'

'Both of you: enough,' the judge said. 'The two of you are justly famous for your dog-and-pony shows. Some judges are even foolish enough to put up with them. This judge is not. Mister Morrissey, you will refrain from cluttering up the record with a lot of time-wasting foolishness. This is cross-examination. You put your client on the stand, Mister Gleason is entitled to have at him, and I have every confidence he will. Unless he makes the sort of blunder Mister Gleason rarely makes, you will maintain your seat. Clear?'

'Yes, your Honor,' Morrissey said. He sat down.

'Mister Gleason,' Bart said, 'you know just as well as I do that the sort of remark you just made in the presence of the jury is improper, regardless of how you are provoked. I not only suggest – I admonish you, that the prosecutor's responsibilities in this courtroom do not extend to reprimanding opposing counsel for infractions of decorum. And I further admonish you that counsel thus usurping the prerogatives of the presiding judge lay themselves also open to reprimand. Which is what I am giving you now – understood?'

'Yes, your Honor,' Gleason said.

'Now,' the judge said, addressing the jury, 'every so often, in this line of work, we find ourselves distracted from our common purpose by a little ego-tiff among the *prima donnas*. Some hair gets pulled, in the figurative sense, and there's a little scratching. But when that happens, as it did just now, we try to stop it short of biting and gouging. You are fortunate to be sitting on a case in which able, aggressive counsel are contending skillfully and strenuously for the interests of their respective clients. You are to ignore such exhibitions as just occurred – and which better not recur, gentlemen – when their zeal overcomes their judgment.

'Mister Gleason,' he said, 'put your next question.'

'Mister Tibbetts,' Gleason said, 'before you took the stand yesterday, you had long and detailed discussions with Mister Morrissey, did you not?'

Morrissey stood up. 'Objection,' he said. 'Clear implication, something improper in client conferring with lawyer.'

'Mister Morrissey,' the judge said, 'when I desire to know the reason for your objection, I will ask for it. Is that abundantly clear?'

'Yes, your Honor,' Morrissey said. He sat down.

'Stand up,' the judge said. Morrissey stood up. '*Unless* I ask for it, I do not wish to hear it. Understood?'

'Yes, your Honor,' Morrissey said.

'Good,' the judge said. 'You may be seated. Your objection is overruled. Your exception is noted. Mister Gleason, please continue.'

'Mister Tibbetts?' Gleason said.

'Yes, sir?' Tibbetts said.

'Answer the question, Mister Tibbetts,' the judge said.

'I don't remember it, your Honor,' Tibbetts said. He looked troubled.

'Oh, for heaven's sake,' the judge said. 'Mister Gleason: Put the question again.'

'Thank you, your Honor,' Gleason said demurely. The judge gave him a sidelong glance. 'Mister Tibbetts,' Gleason said, 'before you took the stand yesterday to confess your many transgressions – at least the ones you say you remember – you discussed your situation with Mister Morrissey, did you not?'

'Oh,' Tibbetts said. 'Yes. Yes, sir, I did.'

'And did you,' Gleason said, 'did you at some time – or maybe even more than one time; maybe several times – did you hear Mister Morrissey use this phrase: "Statute of Limitations"?'

Tibbetts frowned. 'I'm not sure, sir,' he said.

'You're not sure,' Gleason said, 'you're not sure whether Mister Morrissey, *even once*, said whether a given action that you proposed to admit, on that witness stand, was a serious felony, but that the Statute of Limitations had run and you could not be charged?'

'I'm not sure,' Tibbetts said.

'You're "not sure,"' Gleason said. 'Did Mister Morrissey by any chance happen to mention to you that you can't be charged with perjury if you say that you're "not sure"?'

'Objection,' Morrissey said, jumping to his feet.

'Sustained,' the judge said, 'jury will disregard. Next question, Mister Gleason.'

'All right,' Gleason said, 'let me ask you this: Did Mister Morrissey, Mister Tibbetts, assure you that each and every one of the actions you enumerated yesterday – the narcotics offenses; the intimidation of young women into acts of what amounted to prostitution; the extortion of monies from terrified or misguided young people; the advocacy of violent overthrow of the government; the travel in interstate commerce for felonious purposes; the purchase and possession of automatic weapons – that all of those felonious acts, *each and every one of them*, was now forever barred from prosecution by the Statute of Limitations?'

'I don't recall,' Tibbetts said.

'You, *don't recall*,' Gleason said.

Morrissey stood up. 'No need, Mister Morrissey,' the judge said. 'Spare us the heavier sarcasm, if you would, Mister Gleason.' Morrissey sat down. 'Just allow, if you will, the witness's answers to be entered on the record, without your marginal glosses. You may proceed.'

'Thank you, your Honor,' Gleason said. 'Well, Mister Tibbetts, allow me to test your memory in some other areas. See what luck we have there.'

'Objection,' Morrissey shouted, as he came to his feet.

Bart shook his head. 'Sustained,' he said. 'Enlighten me, Mister Gleason: What are we to do with you?'

Gleason looked offended. 'That was a perfectly innocent remark, your Honor,' he said.

'That was a perfectly snide remark, Mister Gleason,' Bart said. 'Now, I've told you before, and I tell you again: What you get away with in other courtrooms, does not interest *me*. You and Mister Morrissey may've enjoyed great success with your Frick-and-Frack routine before other judges. But I'm not one of them. I don't approve of it. I won't tolerate it. Phrase your questions neutrally. *Do as I say.*' He glanced at Morrissey, who was grinning. 'And you,

Mister Morrissey: Wipe that smirk off your puss. Keep in mind I know who started this commotion. One more peep out of you that's not called for, and we'll all have a little chat when this trial's concluded.' Morrissey looked solemn. 'Proceed, Mister Gleason,' the judge said. He slumped back in his chair. 'Honest to God,' he said softly.

'Beg pardon, your Honor?' Gleason said. Judge Bart feebly waved his left hand at him. 'Mister Tibbetts,' Gleason said, 'you were present yesterday, were you not, when your father testified about how smart you are?'

Tibbetts looked uncomfortable. 'Yes, sir,' he said.

'You heard him tell Mister Morrissey, here, and the members of this jury, that your test scores, and your grades, and all the other stuff, indicate to him at least that he fathered a genius?'

'Yes,' Tibbetts said, shifting in the chair.

'Mister Tibbetts, let me ask you,' Gleason said, 'are you one of those extremely smart people who goes through life in the belief that everyone else is stupid?'

Morrissey came out of the chair fast, as did the judge. 'We,' Bart said, gesturing at Morrissey, 'we will take the morning recess here. Jury will be excused. Counsel will repair to chambers, for a brief conference.'

21

'I was chastized,' Gleason said in the small office. 'Morrissey was chastized. Klein and Bigelow were invited – no: commanded – to benefit from our example by not imitating it when their turns come. Veale didn't get mentioned by name – I think her feelings were hurt. Anybody got a smoke?' He put his feet up on the table and closed his eyes.

'Virginia Slim, you want it,' McNeil said, opening her handbag.

'Gimme,' Gleason said. He opened his eyes and accepted the cigarette.

'I thought,' Consolo said, 'I didn't think you were being too hard on him. I thought the cocksucker deserved it.'

'Ahh,' Gleason said, accepting a light from McNeil, 'doesn't matter if I was. I wasn't getting anywhere. Making any headway. John Morrissey knows how to varnish his witnesses. If they're smart enough to pay attention, and cool enough to keep their wits, and this lad is very smart, with the guts of a burglar – which is why of course he's here – you can hose 'em as much as you want – fuckin' water just rolls off. Judge says to us in chambers – off the record, naturally – "I don't want any more shit from you two birds." Didn't matter to me. He hadn't called that recess, threatened me and John with contempt, I was gonna pull my horns in anyway. No use banging your head against a brick fuckin' wall. I can't crack the guy.'

'So,' Consolo said, 'what're you gonna do? Just roll over, then?'

Gleason exhaled smoke. 'Fred,' he said, 'two of you'd make a dozen. No, what I'm going to do is go back in there like Mickey the Dunce and let the goofball think the judge's got me buffaloed. And see if I can trick him into making some statement that's so obviously outrageous I'll be able to use it when I argue to the jury. John's talking to his client now, while I'm talking to you. Pumping him up. Telling him how the judge landed all over me. Good. Might make him cocky.

'But I will tell you something, Fred,' Gleason said, 'if I don't get him claiming that he personally talked to Jesus, if I don't sucker this punk into something totally preposterous, within ten minutes of the time when I stand up, I am gonna sit fuckin' down. I am not gonna have him doing a repeat performance of that choirboy routine he did yesterday. Jury hears that one more time, they're liable to fuckin' believe it.'

'I don't see how you can let Morrissey get away with this,' Consolo said. 'Morrissey knows he's lying.'

'Fred,' Richards said, 'I don't really have the time or the energy just now, take another crack at explaining the American legal system to you. Just take it on faith, okay? John Morrissey's good. That's why he gets all these cases, the real time-bombs and the unexploded mines, and all this other touchy stuff nobody else'd grab. Because he's good.

'Terry,' Richards said, 'I was, you know, I was thinking while you're up there, and I, I agree with you. Thing concerns me, you know, is that we're losing sight, our main objective.'

'Speak, sage,' Gleason said.

'No matter what you do to him,' Richards said, 'you eat the rug; you nice him to death; you punch his fuckin' lights out – it isn't gonna matter. The jury's still gonna have to decide: Was he nuts at the time? And the only way they're going to be able to do that is by guesswork. The only direct evidence they're going to have is his own say-so. To contradict that, we've got the circumstantial stuff that the job was pretty carefully planned; that it was carried out in obvious cold blood; that whoever did it knew exactly what they were looking for, and therefore must've been fairly well acquainted with the drug sideline Nichols and Abbate're fronting with the tavern – and consequently couldn't've been a good person himself. If the jury can look at what we've got, and if they think about the fact that this respectful, well-pressed lad has a very good motive to lie now, and say that he was nuts when he pulled off a major heist and then managed to avoid not only us, but all the regular hoods, for about a year – if that jury can say a guy who can do that must be nuts, then we are going to lose.'

'You think they can?' Consolo said.

Richards shrugged. '"Can"? Sure they can. Jury can do anything it wants, and most of them usually do. "Will they"? I don't know. And I won't know, either, until after they've done it. And neither will you, Fred, neither will you.' He looked at Gleason. 'Now, what I think, Terry,' he said, 'I think you've probably made all the money that you're gonna make on this kid.'

'Which isn't very much,' Gleason said.

'But still,' Richards said, 'all you're gonna make. And if you try to work him for any more, you're running the risk of getting Bart really pissed off at you. Which we don't want to do. Bart likes you. The jury likes Bart. If Bart decides he don't love you no more, you know just as well as I do he will let the jury know. And they will say to themselves: "Well, this nice judge, that takes such good care of us, he seems to think Mister Gleason needs a little discipline. So we'll do the judge a favor – we will punish the young man." And they'll do it, too. You rile up Bart to the point where he decides to whip out his dick and piss on your boots with that jury looking on, you're not gonna convince them that your pants're wet from rain. You could lose not only Tibbetts, on the insanity drill, but also the daughters of Sappho and the refugee from everybody's All-Star goon squad. Cut your losses, man. You sit down when you go out there, you'll catch Big Mo flat-footed. He's expecting you to open up a few more interesting areas for him to explore on redirect. Disappoint him. Man never got in much trouble, what he didn't say.'

'What you say makes a lotta sense, John,' Gleason said.

'I know it does,' Richards said.

'And as a result,' Gleason said, 'naturally, I'm not gonna do it.'

'Mister Tibbetts,' Gleason said, 'you testified yesterday about your third year at Stanford, and what happened to you then.'

'Yes, sir,' Tibbetts said.

'And, I believe, you compared your experience to that of a religious conversion,' Gleason said.

'Yes sir,' Tibbetts said.

'Would you elaborate on that for us, sir?' Gleason said.

Morrissey stood up slowly. He shook his head. 'Your Honor,' he said, 'when I don't understand the question, I have to assume my client can't, either. So I'm going to object.'

'It is a little broad, Mister Gleason,' the judge said. 'Think you could trim it down a bit?'

'I'll give it a shot, your Honor,' Gleason said. 'Mister Tibbetts, when you said that your experiences over nineteen-sixty-seven, eight, when you said they were comparable to a religious conversion, did you mean that you suddenly found yourself – and I mean no offense by this; I'm groping for my words here – did you find yourself, as it were, blinded by a revelation?'

Morrissey stood up. 'No,' Bart said, holding up his right hand, 'no, you wanted Mister Gleason to rephrase it, and he has. If the witness can answer it, I'm going to ask him to do it.'

'I can answer it, your Honor,' Tibbetts said softly. The judge nodded. 'I,' Tibbetts said, 'when I was growing up, I was raised in a strictly observing, God-fearing house. But, as I got older, it seemed to me that most of what we did in church, and in our daily lives, was ceremonial. Ritual. That there wasn't much substance to it. That we did it last Sunday, and we'll do it next Sunday, and the incense will burn and the singing will be nice, and we'll all feel peaceful inside. But nothing, nothing outside ourselves changes much. The poor are still poor. The blacks are still oppressed. We're still killing people in Vietnam, with whom we have no quarrel. We still have a president who believes that this is right. We feel contented in ourselves, because we've observed the patterns, but we're deluding ourselves. Making believe.

'I was young, Mister Gleason,' Tibbetts said. 'I was young, and passionate, and I saw injustice. In my first year away from home, for the first time I saw with my own eyes the disparity between the way that I had lived, the way my parents lived, the way I guess 'till then I'd assumed everybody lived, and how people in other places suffered under the most grinding poverty. I traveled, for the first time I traveled outside this country. I was invited to be a guest musician with what was – still is, I guess – called the Ipswich Ensemble, and we visited countries in the Middle East, performing for the élites, and aristocracies. The English couple that controlled it saw it as a showpiece, of our democracies. I was one of their show horses. I saw something else. All around us we saw the hordes of the poor, starving, begging, crying out for help. And I couldn't, I couldn't reconcile what I saw with what I believed that I believed.

'I went through what I'm afraid I actually called, then, "a crisis of faith." I counseled with a clergyman and asked him what to do. And he recommended that I search the writings of the mystics. And I did that. John of the Cross, especially. And I was moved by the holistic understanding of the unity of the universe that he expressed.' Tibbetts smiled sadly. 'One of my professors told me, in my sophomore year, that – I'm afraid I'd made him very impatient with some argument of mine – that the major symptom of pathologically persisting adolescence is the non-negotiable demand for a pan-explicative. And I became very angry, and said that the reconciliation of contradictions between what we, as Americans and as Christians, what we say we believe, and what we actually do, lends itself to but one explanation. Which is simply that we profess ideals we're not prepared to carry out. That simple.

'Until about the first part of sixty-eight,' he said, 'I was what I suppose would have been called "conventionally liberal." Protest marches, candlelight services, raising money for Cesar Chavez.

Very earnest, but very committed. Then, in April, Martin Luther King was murdered. And I was shaken. Then, in June, Robert Kennedy was killed. And what my teacher had said to me turned out, I guess, to be correct. In my despair I concluded that there must be some single explanation for this uncanny, seeming coincidence of murders. That there were dark forces at work to thwart any politically legitimate effort to turn the system around. To make it function for justice, and equality, and fairness. To make it stop killing people.' He hesitated. 'Do you follow me, sir?'

Gleason nodded. He retreated to the bar enclosure and rested the heels of his hands on the rail. Morrissey fidgeted at the defense table. 'I do indeed, Mister Tibbetts. Please continue.'

'I'd started using drugs,' Tibbetts said. 'I'd started doing drugs, mostly speed – amphetamines – at the beginning of my senior year. There was so much to do. There was a whole world of knowledge that I did not possess. I wanted all of it, and I wanted it all at once. Sleep was an interruption, a needless delay. So I was doing that. Then, then a friend of mine who was aware of my religious interests told me of the path to enlightenment that opened with mescaline. He told me about visions, about travel through the time and space continuums, about the personal experience of transcendence. I experimented. He was right – or at the time, at least, I thought he was right. I went on to LSD. I actually recommended it to others. Two of whom died, I should add. But my own experience was bliss. A mandala sense of wholeness, and unity and peace.

'I became convinced,' he said, 'that my father had been right. That the only limitation on my ability to do good, to accomplish much, to redirect the energies of this great nation toward the good – that the only limitation was my own imagination. And that the need to do it, the obligation to do it, was a moral imperative. That I had no choice.'

'A saviour complex?' Gleason said.

'Absolutely,' Tibbetts said, smiling and rueful. 'I know it sounds arrogant, when I say it now. I know it sounds juvenile and stupid. I know it sounds, even, crazy – but I *was* crazy, then. For several years, I now know, I was certifiably insane.'

'And this,' Gleason said, leaning his buttocks on the bar enclosure and folding his arms across his stomach, 'this would of course explain why you didn't run for president, do something along that line, instead of turning to violence? Because of your convictions that a moral imperative had been revealed?'

Tibbetts chuckled. He nodded. 'I guess it would, yes,' he said.

'And why you, instead of working in some anti-poverty group, or something like that, why instead you acquired a machinegun, and a sawed-off shotgun, and a few pistols and ammo – to arrange for social justice?' Gleason said.

'Mister Gleason,' Tibbetts said, spreading his hands, 'if you want me to tell, you know, that what I am accused of doing, that it makes any sense at all, well, I can't. Because it doesn't. Which is exactly what I'm saying, to this jury and to you. If I contemplate the life I led until this past winter – the way I treated my parents, tyrannized my good friends, abused drugs and all the rest – if I look back on it now, as I've had to do since I cleansed myself, I look and I'm appalled.'

'Understandably enough,' Gleason murmured. Morrissey stood up. 'What was that?' he said to Gleason. 'I didn't quite catch that.'

'I did,' Tibbetts said, smiling. 'He said: "Understandably enough." It's a reasonable comment, Mister Gleason.' Morrissey sat down, scowling. 'You have to understand the reinforcements

I received, for the course that I was taking. It was increasingly evident, to anyone paying even the slightest attention, that agencies of the government, of our own government, were engaged in domestic espionage. Spying on our own citizens. It was blatant that the Warren Commission had at best bungled its investigation of John F. Kennedy's assassination, or – at worst – intentionally fogged up the issues. It was plain that James Earl Ray could not possibly have subsisted on his own for a year or more, after his release from prison, before he turned up in Memphis to shoot Martin Luther King. There was no doubt in my mind that Sirhan Sirhan was a mere instrument, a tool, protecting others in the shadows. The inescapable deduction was that Chairman Mao was right: "The only power is the power that comes out of the gun."' He paused. 'So,' he said, 'so we acquired guns.'

'And used them?' Gleason said.

'I honestly don't know,' Tibbetts said, shaking his head sadly.

'You have amnesia, too?' Gleason said.

'I have,' Tibbetts said, 'I *now* have a clear understanding of the blackout effects of years of prolonged drug abuse. I know we had guns. I know we knew that people in Boston were preying not only upon addicts here, but upon oppressed peasants in Bolivia and Chile, to – in effect – steal cocoa from the farmers, and to victimize the poor here with the cocaine product. I recall discussions about taking direct action against these predators.'

'But you don't recall doing it?' Gleason said.

'No, I don't,' Tibbetts said. He looked wistful. 'If I did – and I mean this, Mister Gleason – I would admit it now. But I honestly do not.'

'Mister Tibbetts,' Gleason said, 'this will almost certainly be my last question to you ... No, on second thought, I've asked my last question.' He looked at the judge as he went back to his chair. 'No further questions, your Honor.'

Behind the bar enclosure, James Walker in his tee shirt and overalls stood up. 'Power to the people,' he said. 'Death to the traitor, Tibbetts.' He raised his fists above his head.

'Good God,' Bart said. He sighed. 'Mister Morrissey,' he said, 'any redirect?' Morrissey looked up. He shook his head slowly. 'Good,' the judge said. 'Mister Bigelow, Miss Veale, Mister Klein? Any cross from you?' Bigelow shook his head. Veale shook her head and Klein stood up. 'No, your Honor,' he said. 'No wisdom from me.' 'Good again,' Bart said. 'We'll take the luncheon recess.'

22

In the afternoon, Morrissey stood up and said: 'That is the case for the defendant Tibbetts.'

'Defendant Tibbetts rests,' the judge said, making a note. 'Ladies and Gentlemen,' he said, 'again let me anticipate the instructions I will give you before you retire. The case against Samuel Tibbetts – and the case *for* Samuel Tibbetts – is now closed. Anything that any of the other defendants may decide to offer, or that may be obtained from them on cross-examination: none of that may be considered for or against Mister Tibbetts. I know we're asking you to walk a conceptual tightrope here, but you have to manage it.'

'Mister Bigelow,' the judge said.

Bigelow stood up. 'Waive opening statement, your Honor,' he said. 'At this time, Mister Walker wishes to make his allocution.'

'Yes,' the judge said. He made another note. Walker stood up. He was wearing a dark blue tee shirt under his overalls. His face was impassive. 'Just a moment, Mister Walker,' the judge said. 'Ladies and Gentlemen,' he said to the jury, 'the defendant Walker, through his attorney, has asked the Court for permission to make an "allocution" to you. The Commonwealth has indicated that it does not object, and therefore I have granted the request.

'An "allocution" is basically an unsworn statement. Mister Walker will not take the oath. Or the stand, either. Mister Gleason will not have the opportunity to cross-examine him. You are therefore to take the statement in that light, and give it whatever weight, or none at all, as you deem it worthy of.

'Mister Walker,' he said.

Walker had a bass voice. It resonated in the uncrowded courtroom. 'Fellow citizens,' he said, 'Che taught that love is the only motivation of the true revolutionary. That whatever dedicated men and women do, in the name of the revolution, they do it out of love. And we – I – we were all filled with love.

'We were few in the beginning,' he said. 'We were young, and filled with hope. We had passion and intensity. We sacrificed for one another, and the proletariat. We made bonds with those in bondage; we enslaved ourselves to slaves. Where we saw oppression; where we saw despair; where we saw the hopeless, the bereaved, and the forgotten: there our hearts lay, and our spirits. There we cast our lot.

'Out of that commitment came the Bolivian Contingent. Still few. Without much money, except for what we had ourselves. But still, a growing cadre, a movement that had promise, a foundation for a future that would say to young, and dedicated peoples: "Yes, we are Americans. Yes, we are truly, free. Yes, we know what we are doing. We're not hypocrites," we said. "We do not forge chains. We break the chains that stifle progress, chains that weigh us down. We have the force of our convictions. What *we* say, we *believe*. And we are prepared to *act*.'

'Yesterday, and again this morning, you have seen disgrace. You have seen a husk before you, shaken out and thrown aside. You have seen a once proud man, once strong, and once a leader, piss on all that he believed, shit on all he loved. I am a strong man, and a leader, and I loved the man he was. I followed that man in the sunshine, followed him in rain. I took him as my leader. I took him as my guide. I, and many others, took him for our chief in battle, our consoler in distress. And now, because he is afraid, because he would deceive you – now he has betrayed us. And all we tried to do.

'I will be true to the cause that we embraced,' Walker said. 'I am not broken. I will not repudiate my brothers, and my sisters, and the poor. I will not stand up now and say that I regret my acts. I tell you proudly I was right, no matter who may cringe. I tell you that we gave ourselves entirely to the betterment of mankind, and that what we did was right.

'I do not acknowledge this court, that judge there, or you. I do not recognize your right to try me, shackle me or kill. I recognize the revolution. That and only that. The day will come when we are free. When all of us are free. And you will know then: I was right. And you will hang your heads.' He sat down.

The judge cleared his throat. He glanced at the jury. 'Um, yes,' he said. He looked back at the defense table. 'Mister Bigelow?' he said.

Bigelow stood up. 'That,' he said, 'that, ah, the defendant Walker rests.'

'Very good,' the judge said. He consulted his notebook. 'Mister Klein, I believe?'

Klein in the corduroy suit and the plaid shirt stood up. 'Your Honor,' he said, 'I have advised my client thoroughly of her rights. Miss Franklin has advised me that she has carefully paid attention to what she calls "this travesty," and does not wish to dignify it by active participation.' He turned and looked at Franklin. 'I have stated your position correctly, Jill?' She nodded, looking grim.

'Record will reflect,' Bart said, 'that the defendant Franklin has made a gesture of assent by nodding her head.'

'Therefore, your Honor,' Klein said, 'therefore with the Court's permission, defendant Franklin rests.'

'Franklin rests,' the judge said, writing. He looked up. 'Miss Veale,' he said, 'I believe that you're the anchor.'

Veale stood up. 'Defendant Fentress waives opening,' she said. 'Call defendant Fentress.'

'May be sworn,' the judge said. 'Please take the stand.'

Fentress in jeans and a khaki twill shirt with epaulets and two flap pockets strode toward the witness stand and stood in front of the chair. The clerk raised his right hand. 'Solemnly swear,' he said, 'that the testimony you are about to give will be the truth ... '

Fentress wheeled toward the judge, hawked phlegm from her sinuses, and spat on the judge's robe. She did a military right face and strode back to her chair behind the enclosure.

The judge looked down at the spittle on his robe. He looked up at Veale. 'Miss Veale,' he said, 'ponder carefully your answer. Did you know your client intended to do this?'

Veale shook her head. 'I,' she said, 'I wasn't sure, your Honor.'

'You "weren't sure,"' Bart said. 'Well, that's not half good enough, Miss Veale, I'm afraid. Be advised that I will take under advisement whether we will look into this matter in more detail in a separate proceeding. Now, have you any other delightful surprises up your sleeve?'

Veale cleared her throat. 'Defendant Fentress rests,' she said.

The judge nodded. He made a note. He looked up. 'Commonwealth,' he said, 'any rebuttal?' Gleason stood up. 'None, your Honor,' he said. He sat down.

'Excellent,' the judge said. He addressed the jury. 'The evidence is now complete,' he said. 'After nine days, those of you who were picked early, I'm sure you're all glad of it. What remains now are the final arguments, and the instructions that I give.

'This is not an easy case,' the judge said. 'I, when the jury is faced with decision of a complex set of issues, I like to give counsel overnight to prepare their closing arguments.' He smiled. 'Judges are former lawyers who are sure that we can all speak, off the cuff, without preparation, and do so effectively. But, when I was a lawyer, I always felt the jury had the benefit of better reasoning, and logic, when I had an evening – or a day – to marshal the evidence in my own mind, and make a couple notes.

'Tomorrow of course is Sunday,' he said. 'And I'm sure some of you will want to attend church services. And, quite frankly, I think we could all use a day of rest. We will resume on Monday morning. Promptly at nine-thirty. Mister Morrissey, Mister Bigelow, Mister Klein and Miss Veale will present their arguments. Mister Gleason will offer his. We will break for lunch. I will deliver my instructions, which will take about an hour. Then the names of alternates will be drawn; I will select a foreman, or forelady, and you will retire to begin deliberations.

'When you were impaneled,' the judge said, 'the clerk read the charges to you. Then he recited the words on a card. If you didn't catch them, that is understandable. But I think they are important, and I want to repeat them, now. He said: "To these charges, the defendants have said that they are not guilty, and, for their trial, have put themselves upon the country. *Which country you are*, and you are sworn to try the issue. If they are guilty, you are to say so. If they are not guilty, you are to say so. And nothing more. Jurors, hearken to the evidence."

'Keep in mind, during tomorrow's rest, that that command has echoed down more than three centuries of trials in Massachusetts. You have endured separation from your loved ones, deprivation of the most ordinary amusements, mediocre food,' the jurors smiled, 'and the ordinary, day-to-day association with your fellow workers that means so much to all of us. You have done so because this is America, and this is Massachusetts, and in this Commonwealth, at least, when we are sworn to do our duty, that is what we do.

'In eighteen-thirty,' Bart said, 'in eighteen-thirty, Daniel Webster arose in the Senate of the United States, to respond to an attack upon this Commonwealth. He said: "She needs no encomium from me. There she stands – behold her." And here you stand, today.' He stood up. 'Court will be in recess,' he said, and stalked off the bench.

'He ain't bad,' Richards whispered to Gleason. Gleason looked at him. 'ain't bad?' he said. 'He's fuckin' beautiful.'

23

At 5:20 on Thursday afternoon Gleason returned to his office at 20 Ashburton Place. McNeil, Consolo and Richards were waiting for him. 'Nothing,' he said. He collapsed into his chair. He massaged the bridge of his nose with both thumbs. 'Three fuckin' days, they've been out.' He looked at each of them. 'I will be god*damned* if I understand what the hell they're hung up on.'

McNeil looked disappointed. 'I thought,' she said, 'I thought for sure when you were gone, there must've been a verdict.'

'Ah,' Gleason said, 'no. That was just, Bart decided since we're all sitting around with our thumbs up our ass while those turkeys gobble, might's well dispose the side issue of whether Carolyn Veale gets hammered for her client spitting. So he had us all in to chambers, and he puts it on the record. He thinks Veale's suffered enough, that her client's already punished her enough for this world's tastes, so he kissed the contempt thing off. Wish the jury was as decisive.'

'They're hung up on Tibbetts,' Consolo said. 'They're hung up on Tibbetts because you didn't rebut all that bullshit about him being nuts. You should've called Mackenzie.'

'Another county heard from,' Gleason said.

'There's a hanger in there,' Richards said. 'There's one stubborn son of a bitch who's not gonna budge, no matter what anybody says. Or what the evidence is, either. It's probably that black broad Bart picked for foreman.'

'You think so?' McNeil said. 'She looked all right to me.'

'June,' Richards said, 'I had, Dave and I had a case once, back when he was, oh, I suppose he had about two years under his belt. He was one, Frank D'Amelio's assistants, and it seemed like Dave couldn't lose a goddamned case. No matter how bad anybody fucked it up, Dave'd find a way to yank a guilty out of it. He was like fuckin' Houdini. Guys, guys're camping out on the courthouse lawn to get in line so's Osgood got their cases. You'd run into some carnivore cop that never had a good word for anybody in his life, and he'd have the big shit-eating grin on his face, and you'd say to him: "Drew Osgood, huh?" And he'd just nod and grin some more. Your boyfriend there was one the hottest prosecutors I have ever seen.

'Well,' Richards said, 'I get this goddamned open-shut thing – three guys with records longer'n RCA Victor's decide they didn't like the food, this fancy joint, Cohasset, so they go in with guns to get *everybody's* money back. And we got tipped. So, we're waiting for the cocksuckers, and when they come out the door we do the classic "Get 'em up." And they did. Now, I guess Frank figures Dave's taken in so many toughies he is due for a free ride.

223

So here I have got this dead-to-rights sure winner, and Dave and I're walking arm-and-arm through life, singing songs from *The Student Prince*, and doesn't the fuckin' jury stay out *seven fuckin' days*? It was awful. "Where did we go wrong, Lord?" That is what we're saying. "Red-handed, Lord, You got that in mind? Red-fuckin'-handed. The hell's the matter?"

'Well,' Richards said, 'it turned out all right. They got hooked, all three of them, and the judge was old Rosie, Bill Rose, and if you had a gun in your hand when you got caught doing it, and old Rosie drew the case, well, forget about vacation plans because you went *away*. But Dave and I're curious, even after we finally win, and we go sneak around to one the jurors, and we ask her some questions. And she says it's eleven to one, guilty, five minutes after the instructions. The rest the seven days they hadda spend just wearin' out this one obstinate young bitch that took a dislike the foreman, the first day of the trial, and wasn't gonna do *any*thing he said, no matter how many other people said it, too.

'So,' Richards said, 'that is probably what we got. There is some stinker in that draw that's got a hair across his ass about something or other, that the person who did it probably even doesn't remember, and that bastard's gonna make everybody sit there until he makes his point. And all we can hope is the other folks don't weaken. Don't just get sick of it, give in so they go home.'

Gleason sighed. 'John,' he said, 'I hope you're right. But I doubt you are. I think for once Fred's probably right. Partly right, at least.'

'Well,' McNeil said, 'that'd hike your average, Fred.'

Gleason snickered. '"An ill wind that blows nobody,"' he said.

'Should've done what I told you,' Consolo said stiffly. 'Wouldn' have this problem now.'

'On another point,' McNeil said. 'She called me again. Said she really has to see you.'

'This would be Christina Walker,' Gleason said.

'Don't do it, Terry,' Richards said. 'There be dragons there.'

'She isn't going to stop, I think,' McNeil said.

'After,' Richards said. 'After the verdict, after it's over, you wanna jump inna shit? Go ahead and jump inna shit. But do not see this cupcake until the fuckin' trial is over.'

At 10:20 A.M. on Friday, September 22nd, Gleason received a telephone call from Bart's clerk. 'We have a verdict,' the clerk said. At 11:10 Carolyn Veale completed the array of lawyers. The defendants entered the courtroom and were seated. Behind them, Christina Walker, and Walter and Ellen Tibbetts entered and sat down in the spectators' section. Judge Bart came out of chambers and said: 'Harry, bring the jury down.' The jury was seated at 11:21. 'Jury will please rise,' the clerk said. They stood up. 'Madame Forelady,' the clerk said, 'Ladies and Gentlemen of the jury, you have reached a verdict?'

Mabel Wright looked stern. 'We have, your Honor,' she said. She handed documents to the clerk. The clerk scanned them. He handed them up to the judge. Bart scanned them. He scowled. He looked at the jury. He handed the documents back to the clerk 'Ask 'em,' he said.

The clerk cleared his throat. 'Members of the jury,' he said, 'hearken to your verdicts as you have recorded them. To so much of the indictment charging James Walker with seven counts of murder in the first degree, you have recorded that the defendant is guilty.' He looked up. He looked down. There was no sound from the back of the courtroom.

'To so much of the indictment charging the defendant Samuel Tibbetts,' he said, 'with seven counts of murder in the first degree, you have recorded that the defendant is not guilty, by reason of insanity.' A soft moan came from Ellen Tibbetts. Christina Walker gasped.

The clerk looked up again. He looked down. 'To so much of the indictment charging Katherine Fentress with seven counts of murder in the first degree,' he said, 'you have recorded that she is guilty, and to so much of the indictment charging Jill Franklin with seven counts of murder in the first degree, you have recorded that she is guilty.' He looked up again. 'So say you, Madame Forelady?' Mabel Wright nodded. 'So say you all?' he said. The other eleven jurors nodded. He handed the papers back to the judge.

Bart raised his eyebrows as he accepted the papers. 'Madame Forelady,' he said, 'Ladies and Gentlemen. It is customary at this time for the Court to express the thanks of a grateful Commonwealth for your unselfish service. I do so now. The jury system is the cornerstone of our liberty. To serve in it is always a burden – especially when, as in your case, that civic duty completely isolates those discharging it from their daily lives. We, all of us, thank you. And you are dismissed.' The jury filed from the room.

'Counsel,' Bart said, flipping through a calendar on his desk, 'I'm putting this down for sentencing ... ten A.M., October nineteenth. That bother any of you?'

Gleason shook his head dejectedly. Morrissey stood up. 'Your Honor,' he said, 'respectfully move that disposition in Mister Tibbetts's case be deferred, that bail be set, and that he be released pending psychiatric evaluation of his current mental state.'

'Nice try,' Bart said. 'Motion denied. Off the record. You've dodged another bullet here, John. Heard it said, many times: "Morrissey could walk through a rainstorm, 'thout getting wet." Appears to be true. Back on the record. Court orders defendant Samuel Tibbetts be committed, forthwith, to Bridgewater State Hospital, and there confined for psychiatric evaluation for a period not to exceed … Off the record. What the hell's the longest stretch I can order here, anyway?'

'It's indeterminate, your Honor,' the clerk said.

'Would've looked the damned thing up,' Bart said, 'I had the faintest inkling this was gonna happen. Back on the record. For such period as the superintendent of the institution thereof shall deem adequate and necessary for determination, the defendant's mental state. And, until such time as the superintendent thereof shall certify to this Court that the defendant, in his opinion, is not a danger to himself, or to society. When a hearing shall be held. But in any event, not to exceed ten years.'

He looked at the lawyers. 'That sound about right?' he said.

'Well,' Morrissey said, 'naturally, I want to object.'

'Your rights are protected,' the judge said. 'Mister Gleason?'

Gleason stood up. 'I'd like to object too, your Honor, but the people I'd like to object to've left the room.'

'I know, Mister Gleason,' the judge said, 'but you have to look at it this way: you rode a lame horse a good race, and you won most of it. Be grateful for successes, however partial they may be.

'Now,' he said, 'while the rules require I have to be punctilious about allowing the probation officers time to compile their reports, nothing in them says you folks have to be surprised when the day comes that I formally act. So, barring the discovery of some really astonishing fact in the pre-sentence reports, I now inform counsel of my intentions on the nineteenth.

'As to defendant Walker,' he said, 'defendant Walker will be sentenced to life in prison upon his conviction of the crime of murdering Joseph Abbate, and to life in prison on each of the other counts of murder whereof he's been convicted. Said terms to be served concurrently at the Massachusetts Correctional Institution, Walpole. Defendants Franklin and Fentress will be sentenced to life in prison at the Massachusetts Correctional Institution, Framingham, on their convictions of murdering Joseph Abbate, and to life in prison on each of the other counts whereof they've been convicted. All said terms to be served concurrently with one another.'

Gleason stood up. 'Your Honor,' he said, 'may I ask that the Court consider, that the terms be made consecutive?'

'You may ask,' Bart said, 'but I won't do it. This was one enterprise. These people were kind enough to take seven … Off the record. These people were kind enough to take seven skunks out of the garden. Fourteen or fifteen years in the joint are probably enough. Back on the record. Court therefore will deny Commonwealth's motion for consecutive sentencing.' He stood up. 'Counsel for the defense may file motions to reconsider sentence within ten days of formal imposition, and request hearing. Bail in each case to remain the same, pending actual sentencing. Defendants remanded to custody as previously ordered. Court will be in recess.'

THREE

24

Judge Bart emerged from chambers at 2:05, sneezing twice as he approached the bench. The bailiff called for order and directed all to sit. Richards and Gleason took chairs at the prosecution table. John Morrissey sat alone at the defense table. Samuel Tibbetts in a dark grey suit, white shirt and knitted blue necktie sat by himself with his hands folded in the chair behind the rail. There were no spectators in the courtroom. The jury box was empty.

'Matter of Samuel F. Tibbetts,' the clerk said. He gave the docket number. He handed papers to the judge, who sneezed again.

'God, I feel awful,' he said. He fumbled under his robes and produced a handkerchief. He blew his nose loudly. He thumbed through the papers quickly. He looked up. 'Who knew, thirty-one years ago, that the woman I'd picked to marry'd turn out to be a rose fanatic, and that I'd recapture the lost days of my childhood when my allergy to roses came back and I'd be miserable each spring?' He blew his nose again. 'Damn those indoor plant lights.' He coughed. 'Counsel will please identify themselves for the record. Moving party?'

Morrissey stood and gave his name and Tibbett's. Gleason stood and said: 'Terrence Gleason,' he said, 'Special Assistant Attorney General. For the Commonwealth.'

'And the gentleman beside you?' Bart said.

'John Richards,' Richards said, standing. 'Retired.'

The judge grinned. 'Congratulations, Lieutenant,' he said. 'Record will reflect that time in all its tuneful turning has taken Mister Richards from his former grace as Detective Lieutenant Inspector, Massachusetts State Police. And Mister Gleason, as far as that goes, from his, as full Assistant Attorney General of the Commonwealth, each being here as a courtesy and service to Attorney General Peter Mahoney, they being the gentlemen who prosecuted the criminal case underlying today's civil matter.' He sneezed again. 'Mister Morrissey,' he said.

Morrissey stood. Behind him, Cpl. Fred Consolo, Massachusetts State Police, entered the courtroom and sat in the back row of the spectators' section. 'Honor please,' Morrissey said, nodding toward the clerk, 'defendant has received and is informed that certified copies have been provided to the Court and counsel for the Commonwealth, documents containing findings by competent physicians on the staff of the Bridgewater State Hospital. Said documents representing that in the unanimous opinion of all physicians and psychologists inquiring into the present mental condition of Samuel F. Tibbetts, Mister Tibbetts is of sound mind. That he presents no danger either to himself or the community. And that he is unlikely to return to his former disturbed state in view of which he was formally sentenced October nineteenth, nineteen-seventy-eight.

'Whereupon, as counsel for Mister Tibbetts, I have filed the appropriate petition that pursuant to the terms and conditions of said formal commitment, that he has satisfied all burdens imposed by the Court upon the jury's finding in the underlying criminal matter, and have moved that the Court enter an order directing the superintendent of said institution to discharge him forthwith.' He sat down.

The judge frowned and nodded. He suppressed a sneeze. 'Mister Gleason,' he said. 'As you are aware, the Commonwealth has a right to call for a full evidentiary hearing on this application for discharge and permit you the opportunity to examine fully and completely all or any of these doctors, and Mister Tibbetts himself, if you so choose.' He grimaced. 'And take up days and days doing it, too, if that happens to be your mood.'

'I am, your Honor,' Gleason said.

'I must warn you, though,' Bart said, 'that if you so elect, you will face two more hard choices. My calendar is 'way behind. This wretchedness involving my breathing apparatus has forced me to suspend the afternoon sessions of the very complicated multi-defendant rape case I have underway three times in the past two weeks. My calendar, in other words, is not getting shorter, but longer. And I'm scheduled to open a criminal sitting in Barnstable the first of next month.

'So, Mister Gleason,' he said, 'if the Commonwealth wishes to exercise its right to a full hearing, it will have to decide whether it wants me to preside at it, some time in late June, early July, down on the Cape, or wishes to have the matter reassigned as promptly as possible to some other judge, sitting here.'

'Your Honor please,' Gleason said. 'The prospect of recreating in a new judge your Honor's detailed knowledge of the case is not a pleasant one. The Commonwealth notes for the record, as well, that in no instance within the memory of any member of the Department of the Attorney General has any judge found that the expert opinions of doctors in such matters, that they were so clearly erroneous as to warrant the court in substituting its own for theirs and overruling their recommendations. And finally, I might add, both Mister Morrissey and I're held for trial in *United States* v. *Ianucci, et al*, a long case before Judge Reese in the federal court, beginning at the end of this month. So neither of us'll be available, in all likelihood, until well after Labor Day. So, I've discussed the likelihood of this issue coming up today with Attorney General Mahoney, and I represent to this Court that I have his full permission and approval to waive the Commonwealth's right to full hearing and to join in my brother's request that the matter be disposed of, forthwith.'

The judge nodded. 'Record will so reflect,' he said. 'Record will reflect further that the Court has made a detailed examination of the documents forwarded by the superintendent, Bridgewater State Hospital, regarding and pertaining to treatment and examinations of Samuel F. Tibbetts. Reference is made to criminal case cited, *Commonwealth* v. *Tibbetts, et al*, and incorporation by said reference of that proceeding is herewith made.

'Court finds there is adequate evidence to conclude that defendant-petitioner is now of sound mind, represents no danger to himself or the community, and that there is therefore no reason to confine him further at said facility. Mister Morrissey,' Morrissey stood. 'Mister Morrissey,' the judge said, 'do you know, are you aware of any other process currently outstanding on your client?'

'I do not,' Morrissey said. 'I am not.'

'Mister Gleason?' the judge said. 'Have you made, or caused to be made, diligent search to determine whether any process in any other matter exists, whereby Mister Tibbetts should be held to answer it?'

'I have, your Honor,' Gleason said, 'and I have found none.' He sat down.

The judge nodded. 'Mister Tibbetts,' he said. Tibbetts stood. 'Mister Tibbetts,' Bart said, 'the gist of what you have heard is the consensus of those of us on this side of the fence – excluding, of course, your capable counsel – that you have managed to fool a total of at least eighteen total strangers – the jury who decided your case, and the six doctors who determined your fate. We are aware that jurors are often inexperienced persons, unsophisticated, and that sometimes they are misled, to the detriment of justice, by slick and crafty guys like you.' Tibbetts remained expressionless.

'In other words,' the judge said, 'you have beaten the rap. Not entirely, not entirely, but still you've managed it.

'We know how you've managed it,' the judge said. 'We are aware that the doctors at State Hospitals are underpaid, overworked, and often in despair at the number of patients they confront. So that they not only sometimes make mistakes, but sometimes do so on purpose, just to move the folks along. That was probably not the case in this instance, of course. I for one have no doubt whatsoever that you're as sane as an angel now, and that notwithstanding your virtuosity in applying your manipulative skills to the jury, with the same success you enjoyed among your loyal followers, you have in fact always been.

'Nevertheless,' the judge said, clearing his throat, 'the system that you so disparage – perhaps in the cynical but understandable belief that anything allowing you to escape full punishment, for heinous acts, must have much wrong with it – nevertheless, it is the system that we have. And it says you go free. I hope we never see you again, sir, and you'd better hope so, too. Because if there is a next time, sir, things will be different.' He nodded towards the clerk.

The clerk stood and informed Samuel F. Tibbetts that unless further process was outstanding against him, he was 'free to go without day.'

Bart stood up. 'Court will be in recess,' he said. The bailiff chanted, ending with: 'God save the Commonwealth of Massachusetts, and this honorable Court.'

'Yes, indeed,' Bart muttered, and vanished into chambers.

Consolo waited by the elevators in the corridor outside. The muscles in his jaw were bunched, and his eyes glittered. When Gleason and Richards came out of the courtroom, he slowly turned his back. Gleason looked at Richards, who shrugged. A car arrived containing an operator, one small pimp, two black whores and one white one – they were laughing about bail. 'You know somethin'?' one of the women said. 'You wanna bet some night some girl that he sets bail on's gonna make it back from him?' Gleason and Richards got into the car and faced front. The door slid closed. 'Or maybe these guys, Charlotte,' one of the other whores said. 'They might like a date.'

Richards turned slightly and faced her. The rest of the descent was made in silence.

25

Some months after Glenn Mackenzie died in the fall of '82, Andrea Simone began to talk about the way he'd treated her. On July 8, 1985, Andrea received a call at her office at WCTX in Brighton from a woman who identified herself as Molly Dennis of the Battered Women's Project. Dennis said that the office of the Norfolk County District Attorney was conducting a study of patterns in spousal abuse, in order to devise a program to combat its incidence. Andrea asked Dennis how she had secured Simone's name; Dennis told her that all the project's records and sources were confidential. Andrea agreed to take time from work to be interviewed on tape at 765 Providence Highway, Dedham. She went there the next day in the late afternoon and found the office in a cramped cubicle at the rear on the lower level of a shopping mall. Overhead there was a pet store. Andrea could hear dogs barking and people walking. She could smell something as well.

'At first I didn't want to,' she said. 'I didn't want to say a word. That I'd lived through it and everything, outlasted the guy, and now it was over. And: just let it go, you know? The dead bury the dead. But then all these people started coming up to me and saying, well, wasn't it a shame? And I started to think: "Hey, no, it wasn't." You know? It wasn't a shame at all. I wouldn't exactly say I was *glad* that he was dead, I wouldn't go that far. But if one of us had to be dead, well, I was glad it wasn't me. And kind of surprised it wasn't, too. Because it could've been. It could've been that way.'

She was five feet, nine inches tall and almost gaunt. She sat on the base of her spine in the wooden armchair with her legs spread out under her long grey cotton skirt and her bulky green cotton sleeveless sweater shapeless around her torso. She had long black hair with streaks of grey in it; she kept it back from her temples with gold barrettes over her ears. She let her hands dangle from the arms of the chair. 'I guess I thought, that I just assumed, you know, that because these were people that'd known us a long time, that they must've seen how he was changing, and what I was going through. And that they just hadn't said anything because I never did, and they assumed I wanted it that way. That I was handling it without any help from anybody, and I must not want any. And that was what stunned me, when they started coming up to me and trying to console me. See? That all these people we'd known for so long could've been so *stupid*.

'The first one,' she said, sitting up in the chair and fishing in her straw bag on the floor at her right, 'well, not the first one – because there were quite a few that I just thanked them and said, you know, it was a shock – but the first one that I guess actually got to me finally was Mary. Mary Battaglia. Now Mary wasn't one of our closest friends. Glenn went to BU with the guy she was living with, Homer, and Glenn sort of cultivated Homer afterwards because, well, you want the truth, I always suspected it was because Homer was black and Glenn didn't have any other blacks that he knew really well, or could say he did. And so he needed Homer for that reason. Some, if somebody said he was a racist: "No, I'm not. I'm pals with Homer." And I think one the reasons, that we didn't see that much of them after a while, was that Homer also suspected that was what Glenn was doing, and he didn't like him for it.

'But anyway,' she said, taking a package of Carltons and a book of matches from the straw bag, 'I was over in the Square one day about six months after Glenn died, just sort of poking around on a Saturday trying to find something I could get for my mother's birthday. Which I go through every March because she's so damned difficult to get anything for, and I never know what to buy. And I thought maybe there might be something she would like in one of the stores – like a book or a print or something. And I really didn't have any idea. And I ran into Mary coming out of that art book store there on Boylston Street up from the travel agency, and she said: "Let's have coffee; it's been so long; I've been meaning to write to you and have you over; and I feel so *bad*; and blah blah blah." Which is the way Mary is – that girl just never stops talking. She's a very nice person and she'd do anything for you, but Glenn used to say about her that she never learned sequential reasoning, never mastered it. Got all the way through Syracuse and never found out how you get to Point B after you start at Point A.'

She pulled a cigarette out of the pack and dropped the pack back into her bag. She lit the cigarette and dropped the matchbook back into the bag. She reached with her left hand for the amber glass ashtray on the table next to her and pulled it nearer. 'So, I was frustrated already. Before I ever ran into her. Because of my mother, you know, and trying to get something for her, and it was sort of drizzling and damp and cold out, and I said: "Why not coffee? Sure." And we went into this quick-lunch place across the street and sat in one of those little booths, and she just started pouring out her heart to me. All this sympathy, you know? And I said – well, I lost my temper, I guess. And it wasn't the first time I'd been tempted to, either. And I said: "Mary, what *are* you telling me? Don't you know what he *was*?"

'And she didn't,' Andrea said. 'She honestly did not. I said: "Mary, he changed. Glenn changed from when you first knew him and I first knew him, and all those good old days. When he found out, when they did the Plaza job there, and Sam and Beau James never even asked him, and he didn't even find out about it until after it was done, that was when it dawned on him that Sam actually meant it. That Sam, when he stopped consulting him in the spring of seventy-four, that it really was because Sam thought he was too soft. That he didn't have the balls, to be in the revolution. He was "too theoretical," Sam said. He didn't have the rocks. And I said to her: "Mary, that was over nine years ago, all that stuff went down. And you didn't see what it did to him?"

'And she said no, that she didn't. That Homer told her at least a year before that, when Sam threw Glenn out, that he was getting worried about some things that Sam was saying, and that Beau Walker was saying, and that Glenn Mackenzie was also saying at that time, and they were either getting too radical for him or else he was getting too old for them, and he was pulling out. "And I just assumed," she said, "I just assumed that was what Glenn did too, later on. When we didn't see Sam and Christina and Beau anymore, but we still did see you two. That Glenn'd just decided the same thing Homer'd decided, and he had pulled out too.'

'And I said,' Andrea said, 'I said: "Well, Mary, you were wrong. Homer resigned. Glenn was fired. And I said to him when the word got out, when it was in the papers and everything about The Friary thing, I said to Glenn: 'Are you *nuts*?' Because he was just moping around, you know? I said: 'All these years you've been going around, always looking over your shoulder all the time, someone knocks on the door and you jump, you talk in your sleep and I wake up and you're mumbling about them coming after you and catching you and that, and now you're *jealous* of these guys that they've got for murder? Is there something *wrong* with you?"' And she was absolutely stunned.

'And I said to her: "Well, Mary, that was what he was. He, it was like when they pulled the Warwick job, the one down in Rhode Island 'cause Sam thought it might be getting hot, here in Massachusetts, and Glenn didn't know or go, it was like he thought they'd really cut his balls off. Like he finally realized, he was really out. And he decided after that he had to prove he still had them. Still had his manhood and all. And the way he would do that was by force. By using force. On me."

'And she was the first one I told,' Andrea said. 'That was in March of eighty-three, and Mary Battaglia was the first one I told. And she was shocked. And so was I. She was shocked because she never dreamed, and I was shocked because she hadn't. And it started me, that started me on telling people, other people that knew us, that the Glenn Mackenzie they knew in the next eight years was not the Glenn Mackenzie I knew during those same years. That the one I knew used to tie me to the bed and hit me if

I refused to let him do it, until I finally let him do it so he would stop hitting me. And that he stuck things into me, and did things to me, things that were really awful. So that when he died, aged thirty-six, in nineteen eighty-two, it sort of came as a relief. Came as a relief to me.'

'Let me ask you something,' Dennis said. She sat on a secretarial chair behind a small grey metal desk. She wore a tan cotton suit and a white blouse with a brown knitted necktie. 'Since you knew what he had done, all the things he'd done before he left the gang ... '

'Why'd I stay with him for so long if he was doing that to me?' Andrea said. 'Why didn't I just leave him when that change came over him?'

'Yes,' Dennis said. 'And turn him in, as far as that goes. I mean, yours wasn't the usual case where the woman has children, or she thinks with good reason that the police can't protect her and the abuser'll get out and come back and beat her up again or maybe kill her. You, you had the means, right at hand. If you'd gone to the police and told them Glenn Mackenzie, about the things you knew he'd done, he would've been arrested, jailed, and then put into prison for a very long time. I suppose it doesn't matter now, since he's dead and gone, but why didn't you do that? Turn him in? Or at the very least just leave him, he was treating you like that?'

'She asked me the same thing,' Andrea said. She took a deep last drag on the cigarette and stubbed it out. She exhaled the smoke. 'Mary asked me that that day, and everybody I've told since, they have asked me too. Which I think's sort of made me, forced me to work it out in my own head, and I think I have.

'It was because,' Andrea said, 'well, in the first place it was because he didn't always do it. I mean, it wasn't like it was always happening. The first time – they had the Christmas party at the law firm, and I was working on some big deal production Buster Knowlton was behind schedule on at the station, so I couldn't go. Which was really all right with me because those parties'd become a drag. I thought they had, at least. Here're all these rads in flannel shirts and corduroys and workboots, standing around in these depressing offices they've got down in the South End, getting smashed or stoned or both, talking about justice for the poor. And their hair's beginning to fall out and they're getting middle-aged, whether they like it or not. And I just got sick of it. I don't mean they weren't sincere. I don't mean I didn't think what they were doing, what they wanted to do, wasn't good – and if they could actually do it, it would be wonderful. But I was sick of it, you know? All this crap about the establishment, and the government, and the stinking rich and equal rights – I believed it all, and I still do. Most of it at least. But I was fed up with hearing about it all the time, you know? I guess I was bored.'

'Do you know,' Dennis said, 'not that it probably matters, but did that law firm, so far as you know, did that law firm ever make money?'

'I don't know,' Andrea said. 'Well, I mean, I know there was a long time, it didn't, because Glenn never had any, and like when Zeke said it was time to pay the rent, or Glenn, when one of Glenn's tuition loan payments came due, he would come to me and ask me for another one, his "loans." Which he never paid back. And if I had it, which I usually didn't because I was, all the money from my job was going for the rent on the apartment and the stuff we ate and stuff, if I had it I would give it to him. And if I didn't, I would write, or call, and ask my father, you know, and like tell him it was for me, and I would give it to Glenn.

'But then,' she said, 'then it did start finally to make some money. The law firm, I mean. At least Glenn stopped asking me, so I assume he must've been getting it from the practice. And he actually, he actually paid the rent on the damned apartment a few times. And we bought this new car. Well, not new, but it was a pretty good second-hand Jeep. And Glenn paid for that. So *something* was improving.'

'And when would that've been?' Dennis said.

'Ohh,' Andrea said, 'this would've been … I'm not really sure when it was. Because whenever it was, it wasn't something like, that got announced. He was gone, this was in the summer, seventy-eight, and he was gone for a long time. And he told me, he said he had this hush-hush project somewhere down in Connecticut or something, I don't know where it was, and I wouldn't be able to get in touch with him. So I figured, with Sam and the others on trial, maybe he was afraid he'd have to testify, and he was cutting out. But I wasn't really sorry. That I'd never see him again, even if he didn't have the balls to tell me – anything that stopped him from hitting me. And then he came back, and I let him, and he did, he had stopped. And then I just sort of woke up to the fact one day that Glenn hadn't been asking me for money for quite a while. And I didn't say anything, because I didn't want to give him the idea maybe he should've been. And besides, I thought maybe he was robbing stuff again. That that was where he'd been. Off with some new guys. But I really don't know.'

'Did he leave you any money?' Dennis said.

Simone laughed. 'Well,' she said, 'if he did, I haven't found it. I don't know how much he had.'

'But it was after he started beating you up?' Dennis said. 'See, one of the things we're finding, often when the batterer's under financial pressure, the likelihood of that being a contributing factor seems to be fairly high.'

'It could be,' Andrea said. 'There could've been some of that. For a while, at least. But then, if it was that, just the money, well, it must've run out or something. Because he started whacking me again. No, it wasn't dough.

'The first time,' she said, 'I got home that night before he did, this would've been seventy-four, Christmas of seventy-four. It'd been a bad year all round, first with Sam just reading Glenn out of the Contingent, and then Glenn hearing about the Warwick job, and then when they killed Emmy in the fall. I mean, by then the only times I ever heard anything about what was going on, going on with them, I mean, was when Sam got bored or something, and decided to call Glenn up at the office and read him out for going soft. Tell him what a loser he was.' She paused. 'Which he was, of course, when I think about it now. But he didn't like hearing about it then. And then Sam would brag about all these wonderful things they were doing, that Glenn didn't have the balls. So I'm just really, I'm just assuming they killed Emmy, that it had to've been them. Nobody told me that. But anyway, I didn't feel much like Christmas and I got home and he wasn't there.

'And I really didn't mind. I suppose it was one or so, after midnight at least, and I was really beat. So I took off my clothes and I got in bed, and I was almost asleep, and that's when he came in. And he was *plowed*. I don't know what he'd had, or how he'd gotten home, but he was about one step away from where one more drink, or one more joint, or one more anything, and he would've just passed out. Which from my point of view, it would've been better if he'd had them, and not come home at all.

And he woke me up and started mauling me. That was the first time. Compared to the ones that came after, it really wasn't that bad. I didn't scream or anything, though I would like to've. But it was a nice apartment we had then, in Allston, and I was afraid if we started making a lot of noise, you know, the middle of the night, we'd get thrown out of it. So I tried to fight back and naturally he was too strong, and too big and too smashed, and he hurt me enough so I said to myself: "All right, this isn't going to work. Your roommate for some reason wants to rape you, let him do it. Deal with this in daylight when the bastard's sobered up." Because I'd never seen him like that.

'And I thought I did,' she said. 'I thought I did deal with it. The next morning was a Saturday and I got him up around noon and sat him down in the kitchen with his hangover and all, and I said to him: "All right, Glenn Mackenzie, now tell me what's going on." And he said he didn't remember.'

'Did you let him get away with that?' Dennis said.

'I certainly did not,' Andrea said. 'I gave him chapter and I gave him verse. I read him the riot act. I don't mean I was yelling, because I was not. I was perfectly calm. Well, maybe not calm. I was really very mad. But I was perfectly rational. I told him everything he'd done to me and I said to him: "Now Glenn, I want an explanation. Because I'm not going to take this kind of shit from you or anybody else. You want to stay out late and get shitfaced, go ahead and do it. You want to come home and get laid, even if you are shitfaced, you ask me nice and you know me, I'll probably go along. But I'm not going to have you knocking my teeth out because you did too much drugs or had too much booze before you got home. That I won't stand for."

'And he was very apologetic,' she said. 'Very contrite. Said he'd had some stuff, most likely acid in the punch or some fucking thing like that, and he'd never done it before and he'd never do it again.

'I took his word,' she said. 'What the hell did I know? When Glenn came out to San José State in nineteen-sixty-nine, and Beau and I met him, he was the nicest, sweetest guy you'd ever hope to meet. I don't mean how he talked, his rhetoric and stuff. He was just as wild and off the wall when he talked as the other guys were then. Maybe even wilder, because he was from the east but he didn't go to Harvard and therefore had more to prove. But personally he was a very sweet guy. And anyway, I agreed with all the stuff that those guys were saying then: Out of Vietnam, and justice for the poor. The talk did not scare me – any other kind of talk would've put me off. "If you don't worship Che, you know, I got no time for you" – I was nineteen years old, for God's sake. That's the way I was then. So, from the minute I saw Glenn, I just adored him. And I went and told Beau, who's only twenty-three or so himself and we're all consequently very dramatic about every-hing that happens, I went and told Beau I was not going to be available any more. Because that was one of the things at the time that everybody did: we were all against property. And that meant that whatever belonged to anybody else in the Contingent belonged to all of us. And that included each other. We were pure communists, pure in everything, and in our commune that meant that if anybody asked you to fuck, or suck, or anything else, and you weren't sick or something, you had to go through with it or else have a pretty good explanation for not following the party line.

'But I was brave,' Andrea said. 'I went to Beau and I told him. I said: "Beau, this doesn't mean, you know, that I'm not still committed to the struggle and everything. But from now on, you know, it's just Glenn." And he didn't like it a whole lot, Beau didn't, but he was also a nice guy, then, and he said all right, that if I wanted it that way he was a friend of mine and he would understand and mention it to Sam.'

'This would have been Sam Tibbetts,' Dennis said.

'Right,' Andrea said. 'Sam was the chief. *El Jefe.* We were all equal, and there was no cell hierarchy. But that always meant, from the very beginning, or at least since I came in, which was in the second year the Contingent'd existed, that always meant that Sam was the leader and the boss. You didn't have to do what Sam said, but if you didn't you were out.'

'And Sam approved,' the woman said. 'Approved of you going with Glenn.'

'Not actually,' Andrea said. 'He just didn't make a big stink about it. Probably thought, probably Sam thought even then that Glenn had no balls, and if I wanted to go with Glenn, I wasn't worth getting worked up about either. And Sam, too, I was putting a lot of money into that group, by comparison with the other people. "From each according to his means," right? Well, I didn't have much means of my own, but my father was doing a fair amount of plastic surgery up the road in San Francisco and he just couldn't deny me. So, I don't know whether Sam decided I didn't matter, so he'd let it go, or my money did matter so he'd have to let it go. But either way, he did. And the next semester I transferred east to BU. To be with Glenn. Not to get out of the Contingent. I was still in that. But now I was in the east coast branch, so I could be close to Glenn. And that was when we started living together. September of nineteen-sixty-nine.

'So, you think about it,' Andrea said, 'and I don't think it's too difficult to understand. We'd been living together with each other for over five years when he started hitting me. When Glenn first beat me up, I thought I knew the guy. I'd supported him in what he did, law school and everything. If he wanted to stay in the fight by fighting in the courts, I was all for that. He didn't have any reason to want to kick me around. He told me it was bad drugs that made him do it the first time? I believed the guy.

'About five or six months later,' she said, 'the bastard did it again. And this time he hadn't been anywhere else, hadn't taken anything I hadn't taken too – just some grass and beer on a Sunday afternoon, and there was nothing wrong with me. But all of a sudden he erupts and I'm getting it again. And I began to get scared, which of course I should've been after the first time, the first time he whacked me. And after he was finished and he went to sleep, I got up and cleaned myself up, and very quietly I packed some stuff and went to a hotel. And the next day he called me at work, and he's all remorse again. Wants me to come home. And I said to him, you know: "What is going on here? Why do you do this to me? I'm not coming home again until I find out these things, and if I don't like what I find out, then I'm *not* coming home."

'But I did,' she said. 'Naturally I did. I missed him. And I kept doing it, too, when it happened after that.' She paused. 'It was,' she said, 'it was all mixed up together. It was like all the excitement we had at San José, the way I felt when I first met Glenn and we were all going to change the world, well, it had to stay the same. Or as much the same as it could. Romantic, you know? Dedication. The way we felt about the world and the way we felt about each other, it meant that if I didn't see Glenn anymore, I was giving up all those other things too. And I didn't want to do it. Even when he hurt me. So I kept going back.'

'And you stayed with him, then, for eight more years,' Dennis said. 'After he started abusing you.'

'Yes,' Andrea said, 'I did.'

'Do you have any idea how many times it happened?' Dennis said.

Andrea shrugged. 'I don't know,' she said. 'Probably, oh, ten. Maybe a dozen. The year when the cops caught Sam and Beau, and The Friary trial and everything, after that spring he didn't hit me. I guess he had too much on his mind. And, he was away. But I know he was worried. What was going to happen to Sam and Beau and the women. How come Sam and Beau had, you know, how come they hired the lawyers they did, the establishment lawyers, and paid them, when they could've had Glenn and his partners for nothing. Solidarity and all that crap. Too depressed to hit then. Didn't have the strength. But all the other years, every so often, every six months or so, but it varied, he'd go off the handle and start beating me up.'

'Did you ever fight back?' Dennis said. 'Effectively, I mean?'

'Oh yeah,' Andrea said. 'Two or three times. I remember once – see I'd generally try to hide in the bathroom if I saw it coming on. Make enough noise so the neighbors'd call the police. But the police, the police in Boston aren't always on your block of your street when your roommate decides he'd like to change the way your face looks. So I was lucky once because Glenn passed out before they came. And the next day, after he went to work, I got a little purse-can of Mace from one of the girls at work, and the next time he came after me, I had it under the dirty clothes in the hamper in the bathroom, where I knew he'd never find it 'cause

I always did the wash. And I locked the door and he's pounding on it and I got that can of Mace out, and when he broke the lock I Maced him. That time he had to go to the emergency room. And of course I had to make up the story that it'd gone off in his face while he had the hamper open, because of the heat from the radiator next to it. So no one would know the truth. And another time – the last time, in fact, before he died – he came after me when I was cooking dinner in the kitchen. And I threw a roasting pan of hot pork gravy at him. At his crotch. He usually came at me, usually when he came after me he had his dick out. Part of his rape fantasy. So that stopped him, that time.'

'He died in nineteen-eighty-two, you said?' Dennis said.

'Uh huh,' Andrea said. 'October twentieth, nineteen-eighty-two.'

'What was it?' Dennis said.

Andrea snickered. 'You mean, "was it anything I did? No, it wasn't, although that's another thing that sort of came as a relief. Because the longer it went on, the more likely it was that I might kill him some day, by accident. In self-defense. So his dying saved me that.' She inhaled deeply. 'It was a stroke,' she said. 'A clot hit his brain and that was it for him. He was sitting at his desk in the office, and I was at the station, perfectly normal Wednesday of me busting my hump for Buster, which is why we call him that, trying to get the Friday-night magazine ready two days after it should've been done on Monday. And he keeled over. They took him to Boston City but he never regained consciousness. Died an hour later. Thirty-six years old.'

'It must have been difficult for you, all the same,' Dennis said. 'Keeping it secret, the way you'd been. I mean: with all the family and friends at the funeral.'

'Oh,' Andrea said, 'not all that difficult. It was sort of like …

What we're talking about here's my youth, you know? And that, when he died, it was the end of that. It was over with, and gone. And it hadn't really been that nice, you know? When you thought about it. So in most ways, I was glad.'

'Did you see any of the others?' Dennis said. 'At the funeral, I mean? Sam Tibbetts's old gang? I know he, Walker and Kathie Fentress and Jill Franklin, was it? They were still in jail, of course, but none of the others came?'

'The Contingent?' Andrea said. 'There wasn't anything left of it, by then. Just Sam and them. That I knew about, at least. It was over, too. After they did The Friary thing and after they were caught, I read about them in the papers and Glenn talked about them just incessantly, and I used to think: "Yes, and if I'd've been still with you then, and they had kept you in, you and I would've ended up in the same ditch with Emmy, probably the same day." But we didn't see them at all. I haven't seen them in years. About a hundred years, seems like. At least a hundred years.'

26

At 5:45 P.M., Terry Gleason told Det. Sgt. Fred Consolo he had failed to return the first two calls from Christina Walker. He gestured at the top of his desk, covered with piles of yellow paper, trial transcripts in blue covers, manila folders spilling documents and fat brown bellows files tied with faded maroon ribbons. His red and blue striped tie was down from the unbuttoned collar of his shirt; his bottom eyelids were also down, sagging under his bloodshot eyes.

'I figured,' he said, 'I figured, If I haven't got enough on my plate as it is, it's certainly enough to suit me. You realize how long it's been since I've had six – not eight but six – consecutive hours, sleep? It's been since Memorial Day. I keep telling myself: "This's the big time, Gleason, my man. This is what you wanted. The heavy-lifting, big-dough cases, ninety days of trial." And I guess it probably is. And I *am* enjoying it. But it's the same thing, you know, the tomcat said about the affair he had with the lady skunk. "I really liked as much of it as I could goddam stand."' He sighed. 'So,' he said, 'I got the messages. I knew she called. But I didn't call her back.'

Consolo had dressed impeccably in muted brown plaid sport coat, white button-down shirt, neat patterned tie in brown and gold, lightweight grey flannel slacks with welted seams and deeply polished brown loafers. His greying hair was trimmed and brushed back at the temples. He sketched deliberately on his notepad, making diagonal lines and connecting them into tiny trapezoids. 'You didn't have the time,' he said.

Gleason shook his head. 'Yes and no,' he said. 'If maybe you'd've come up here some evening, late afternoon, nothing special on your mind, if you'd've just come up here and said to me: "Terry, my friend, let us go and have a beer," I would've been out of here like a shot. Because there wouldn't've been anything complicated about that, you know? I would've grabbed the break. But Christina was a different story. That was complications.'

Consolo's left eyebrow went up. He made pentagrams. 'But if you didn't know what she was calling about,' he said, on a rising inflection. 'Since you didn't know *why* she was calling at the time?'

'Didn't matter,' Gleason said. 'I didn't have to know exactly what she wanted. All I had to know was that she was the one who wanted it. And that was complications.'

'I don't think I'm tracking,' Consolo said.

'Freddie, Freddie,' Gleason said, 'you gonna sit there and make me take you back to school? You know how I met Christina. You were around her brother's case. You were gaping her yourself. Everybody was. Don't start giving me that shit, you're not tracking me. You know exactly what I mean, why I shied away. Don't jerk me around.'

Consolo chuckled. He drew octagons. 'But that,' he said, 'that was, what, seven years ago? You gonna sit there and tell me, that still sits on your mind? You two haven't been an item for six or seven years.'

Gleason snorted. 'Not on the street, we haven't, maybe,' he said. 'There I agree with you. But in my happy home, we have, I can tell you that. Barbara is a jealous woman, and with the memory she's got, she should have a fucking trunk and be out hauling logs in Burma, getting jabbed in the arse by some *mahout* with a hooked pole, you know? In one large house that can get awful small sometimes, in scenic, serene Canton, Freddie, we're an item still.'

Consolo snickered. He drew small squares. 'But in any event,' he said, 'at some point, you did call her back. You called Christina back.'

'I did call her back,' Gleason said. 'Against my better judgment, but yes, I did call her back.'

'And you had some conversation,' Consolo said.

'No, we didn't,' Gleason said. 'All I did was, when she answered, I told her who it was, returning her call, and then we just sat there for fifteen minutes or so, breathing heavy in the phones, and then she said: "You give good phone," and we both hung up.'

'You're still a fresh bastard, Terry,' Consolo said. He made sharp, dark slashes on the pad. 'You're maybe getting old, and you say you're getting tired, but you're still a damned fresh bastard. Got to give you that.'

'Well, you should've known better'n to start in on that line,' Gleason said. 'The answer to your question is, 'Yes, I conversed with her, and she conversed with me. Now you satisfied?'

'Don't get all bent out of shape, Terry,' Consolo said. 'I'm just a working stiff here, you know, making a goddamned living, just doing my job. What'd you talk about?'

'That's what I meant before,' Gleason said. 'You know I can't tell you that. I was a lawyer the day you met me, and I'm a lawyer today. Conversation was privileged. I can't tell you what we said until she orders me to do so.'

'Which she's not likely to do,' Consolo said.

'I would guess not, no,' Gleason said. 'That's how I would bet.'

'At some time,' Consolo said, 'as a result of this conversation or for some other reason, did you have occasion to see her face to face?'

'Yes, I did,' Gleason said.

'And was that by prearrangement?' Consolo said.

'Oh, goodness, no,' Gleason said. 'I often get up at five in the morning, while I'm on trial in Boston, and drive twenty-eight miles down to Waterford and pull into the old high school parking lot, see if somebody turns up in the dawn's early light to have a little chat around five-thirty-five.'

'And you had some more conversation with her there,' Consolo said.

'Affirmative,' Gleason said.

'Keeping in mind,' Consolo said, squinting at his pad. He drew lines connecting the squares with the pentagons. 'Keeping in mind that the whereabouts of fugitives is not a confidential communication if the person knowing of them could be charged with harboring – having that in mind, and having also in mind the fact that the relationship of Christina Walker and Samuel Tibbetts was at no time one such as is recognized as entitling either party to withhold knowingly from law enforcement ... '

'You're really getting your money's worth at Suffolk Law,

Freddie,' Gleason said. 'You guys that go there nights really hammer those books, don't you?'

'... information that might lead to the whereabouts of the other party,' Consolo said, 'can you ... '

'She didn't tell me where Tibbetts was,' Gleason said. 'Assuming of course that when you use the word "fugitive," he is who you've got in mind.'

'He's the one,' Consolo said. 'He's the very one. You're a good guesser, too, Terry. Very intuitive.'

'"One of my many talents," he said modestly,' Gleason said. 'What I can't intuit, though, is why you think he's a fugitive. Fugitive from what? He did his bit. The jury said he was batty and the judge locked him up. Seven years later, docs said he was normal. And the same judge let him out. That's the way the law works, Fred. You were there that day. You heard what he said. Judge didn't like doing what he did any better'n you liked watching him do it, but that's what the law says. Guy's found NG by reason of insanity, he goes to Bridgewater. He gets better? He gets out. What've you got steaming around in that fevered brain of yours? You want to try him again for The Friary? See if you like it better, way it comes out the second time? Law doesn't allow that. Take the course in double jeopardy next time they offer it. Very instructive.'

'When I'm looking for a guy,' Consolo said without expression, 'that guy is a fugitive. What he's a fugitive from is something I decide. Not you. Not the DA. Not the governor. I'm the one that decides. When I find him, *then* all you guys can get involved, and tell me if we can arrest him, and try to stop me from convicting him. But not until I find him.'

'So he hasn't been charged with anything new,' Gleason said.

'He hasn't yet,' Consolo said. 'Like I say: When I find him, then I'll go to the DA and say: "This is what I've got, and here is where he is." And see if the DA wants to take what I've got into the grand jury, and indict him, and get me a warrant so I can go and get him.'

'And you think he will,' Gleason said.

'I know he will,' Consolo said. 'I told that little killer, the day that he got out, I waited for him in the hall, and when he came out, I said, to him and his slimy lawyer, I said ... '

Gleason held up his hand. 'I know what you said, Fred,' he said. 'John Morrissey told me.'

'I said: "Don't get the idea that you're free now, just because you've gotten out. You're never gonna be free, long as I am on this earth. I'll track you the rest of my life if I have to, or yours if that comes first. But I'm never gonna forget, and you just remember that."'

Gleason nodded. 'And John Morrissey quite properly called Peter Mahoney and said if you threaten his client again like that, or harass him in any way, he's gonna sue the ass off the Commonwealth in a federal civil rights case that'll set your hair on end.'

'He won't have much luck,' Consolo said. 'I get an indictment, which I am going to get, he can holler and yell all he wants – harassment that is not.'

'Yeah,' Gleason said. 'Well, good luck to you and the Red Sox, then. I still don't know where he is.'

'Did you ask her?' Consolo said. 'Did you ask Christina Walker where the gentleman might be? Where he went when he got out?'

Gleason hesitated.

'Also keeping in mind,' Consolo said, 'that there's a lot of other warrants out on this guy, that cops have got nothing to do with. He may not be technically, this minute, a fugitive from me, but there's a lot of private citizens who'd be very interested in finding out who his contacts've been since he got out. There's a lot of money lying around somewhere. Money that belongs to other people. Maybe they're not nice people, and they expected to get it by having Nichols and Abbate retail lots and lots of dope, but they think it still belongs to them, and I bet they want it back. Sam took their consignment, and that didn't make them glad. If he hasn't got the profits on him when he turns up – which of course he won't – anyone who finds him's going to be very hot to find out where he put them. I don't know if either one of you's figured this out, but if Sammy gets nabbed by one of his old victims before he gets collared by us, he could be a very dead Sammy before too much time goes by.'

'I should give a shit?' Gleason said. 'Sam Tibbetts to me is in the same basket with Abdullah Bulbur Emir. He's a bad actor. Always has been. Asshole buddies we are not. I get my preferences with him, I hope the wise guys get him first. Hogtie him with a fucking rope with his heels up his ass, so when he straightens out the legs, he shuts off his air supply. Throw him in his goddamned car and make him go to sleep. Second choice is: I hope you guys get him first, he resists arrest, and that you guys scrag him. That's the way I feel.'

Consolo smirked. 'Harsh words for a guy you helped so much, counselor,' he said, snapping the notebook shut.

Gleason scowled. 'You cocksucker,' he said. 'You still think I went in the tank on that case, don't you.'

'I didn't say that,' Consolo said. 'I just think it's awful funny, the way that things turned out. I wonder, you know – you've this busy practice now and you're doing pretty well collecting fees off the bad guys, and I wonder if maybe the fact that Sam got off the way he did, if maybe that didn't have something to do with this prosperity. Who's the other lead counsel on this *Ianucci* case? Don't I know him from somewhere?'

'John Morrissey's always represented the heavy hitters, Fred,' Gleason said wearily. 'John Morrissey's been the guy to get when you're in the deep shit since before the glacier went back.'

'Yeah,' Consolo said, 'but Terry Gleason didn't used to be their regular second choice. He was a prosecutor. Isn't it funny? Terry boots his last big case for the Commonwealth. To John Morrissey. Terry opens his private practice. He's barely got the lease signed when the heavy rollers're lining up around the block to give him fat retainers. Where'd they get your business card, Terry? Who might your rabbi be? John Morrissey, perhaps? Did John Morrissey promote you to those guys who hated you?'

'Sure,' Gleason said. 'Naturally he did. Hard's it may be for you to believe this, Fred, I'm a damned good lawyer. Multiple-defendant case, Morrissey doesn't want co-counsel that don't know what they're doing, screw things up for him. He wants people he can work with. Knew he could work with me.'

'I'll say,' Consolo said. 'And if he had any doubts, *Tibbetts* got rid of them. You worked real good with him on that.'

'Oh cut it out,' Gleason said. 'I'm really sick of this.'

'Here you got two men and two women,' Consolo said, 'on trial for seven murders, all done the *same* day, in the *same* place, for the *same* reason. The two broads get convicted and get life, and they're still in Framingham. The guy who pulled the trigger gets convicted also. The only change there's been in James Walker's address since seventy-eight was when they changed the name of

MCI Walpole to MCI Cedar Junction. And that's the only change there will be. At least 'till he either stops getting in fights, and losing his good time, or he *loses* one of those fights and six guys with a long black car take him to his next destination – which'll have a headstone on it and be his permanent address.

'But the guy that *planned* the whole thing, that put the group together in the first place to finance the revolution by robbing armored cars, the guy that smelled out the coke in The Friary safe, and the money in there with it, his lawyer at the trial puts in some perjured evidence that the boss of the whole thing's out of his gourd. And the prosecutor, which is you, the prosecutor doesn't even *bother* to rebut it. The *insanity* defense? For this mastermind? And it *works*? Incredible. Strange to me, back then – still strange to me today.'

'I rebutted it,' Gleason said. 'I had my doc's report in. What I didn't do was refute it – which I couldn't do because my doc didn't see Sam Tibbetts until over a year after The Friary. Which was not the issue. Whether he was competent to stand trial in nine-teen-seventy-eight – it was whether he was capable of forming requisite intent, in nineteen-seventy-seven. And my doc didn't examine him then. So, naturally, he would've had to say on cross he didn't know if Sam was crazy, thirteen months before he saw him. What else could he've said? He could only speculate.

'You know,' he said, 'and you really oughta think about this, Fred, but we did damned well to get any convictions in that case. John Richards at the time had his reservations about whether we had enough to go with. I was the one, talked him into it, and he told me afterwards: "Hey, never mind, Tibbetts cheats the hang-man. He only cheated him a little – he'll still do some time, and that's not the Ritz he's in. We broke up his fucking gang, and we did it mostly on your snow job. You should feel real proud."'

Consolo snickered. 'And a month after that,' he said, 'less'n a month after Christina Walker's boyfriend goes to Bridgewater – knowing all he's got to do to get out is play-act some more, and "recover" – three weeks or so after that happens, fearless prosecutor's banging Christina and having a high old time. Weirdness added to strangeness: that's the way I see it. Unless of course there's some simple explanation that makes it very plain. *And* understandable.'

Gleason sighed. He clasped his hands on the desk and shook his head. 'Fred,' he said, 'I've tried to like you. I heard all the stories, right after I met you, and I said: "Well, that's all right. Keep an open mind. See how he acts around you. Wouldn't be the first man, had a bad rap on him. Maybe he's just aggressive. That can be good in a cop."

'The trouble with you, Fred, though,' Gleason said, 'the trouble with you's you don't learn. You, Mencken was talking about you: For every complex problem there is almost invariably a simple explanation – that's almost invariably wrong. You get some half-baked idea based on partial ignorance, and you just wedge it edgewise into your brain, and it stays there. And after you get all the facts, after you cure your ignorance, if you ever do, you don't go back and dig out that wrong idea and get rid of it. It just stays there like some fucking dinosaur that's still roaming around and crashing into things, a hundred thousand years after all the dinosaurs died off. That's why you're dangerous.'

Consolo laughed. 'Think what you like, Terry,' he said. 'I've got my job to do, and I still get to decide how I do that job. Until somebody orders me not to. Which nobody's doing right now.'

'John Richards was right,' Gleason said. 'After that trial, I talked to the Loot, and John predicted, 'way back then, you'd never change your mind. "Fred's not reasonable," he told me. "Fred thinks he knows how the world oughta work, and how things should come out. Nice and neat and squeaky clean. And when things come out all messy and wrinkled and spoiled, like this case did, Fred gets all upset. And he starts thinking somebody fucked it up on purpose. Doesn't matter to Fred if they actually did. If he thinks they did, they did. And he does not change his mind. Fred's a stubborn lad."'

'My mother used to say that,' Consolo said.

'You should've listened to your mother more,' Gleason said.

'I *always* listened to my mother,' Consolo said. 'To everything she said. And one of the things she said was that I should stay stubborn, because my father was stubborn and he knew he could make a lot of money when people told him he was nuts. And he didn't listen to them, and that's exactly what he did. "What works with oregano and melted cheese," my mother used to say, "will work with something else. Stick to your guns and don't let anybody tell you anything you want to do can't be done. It almost always can."'

'Inspiring,' Gleason said. 'Words to fucking live by.'

Consolo shrugged. 'Works for me,' he said. 'Maybe I'm just lucky, but it seems to work for me.'

'Okay,' Gleason said, 'so have it your way. But I'm telling you: That jury convicted Beau James because Suffolk County juries back in seventy-eight didn't acquit big strong handsome niggers on murder charges unless those black men in the dock had their lawyers give those jurors plenty damned good reasons. And sometimes, not even then. And· Beau James's lawyer did not, because Walker wouldn't let him. John Bigelow's a son of a bitch to deal with, but even if he'd been an angel, he would've had to go with what his client gave him. Which was worse than nothing. Picture of arrogance. Supercilious Manhattan jigaboo, strutting around like he owned the place. The only thing he didn't do was dare the goddamned jury to convict him, but he didn't have to – they took it on faith.

'The two women?' Gleason said. 'California sluts. Kathie Fentress looked like Madam DeFarge, talked like Bela Lugosi, practically bragged she was a promiscuous bisexual, and then goes and spits on the judge. Jill Franklin had had Moe Klein to represent her, Moe with his head shaved and beard full of food, and his mouth full of revolutionary slogans. So they got convicted too. Those mostly good men and ladies true do not like folks like that.

'But Sam?' Gleason said. 'Sam's a nice boy. From Newton Highlands. Former Boy Scout. Good churchgoer, even if he was Episcopalian. Comes from a hardworking professional family. Mummy and Daddy're there every day, all four of their eyes filled with tears. Mom was a bit ineffective on the stand, but Dad was dynamite. Sam's lawyer's a Boston boy too, John Morrissey as I live and breathe, calm and polite and nice. Those jurors sat there and John showed them the truth about Sam. How he was always an honor student, this poor lad still small for his age. It was California that corrupted him, all those whores and whacked-out lotus-eaters, out at Stanford there, feeding on drugs and communist plots. Sam was led astray. Of course he was nuts when The Friary went down. He would've had to've been. Their hearts went out to him, and they let him off.' He paused. 'That's what happened, Fred,' he said. 'I'm aware you never liked it, but that's what happened. Just the same.'

'You should've put Mackenzie on the stand,' Consolo said. 'I said that at the time, and I'm saying it today. You should've said: "Fuck the agreement, I got to have him testify and he goes on the stand." Mackenzie could've told them what an animal Sam was. Behind the thin hair and the little gold glasses and the choirboy face, what a criminal genius there was. Mackenzie could've done that.'

'We disagree on that, Fred,' Gleason said. 'But even if he could've, next time John Richards, or the DA's offices, or any other law enforcement officer in Massachusetts ever offered a deal to an informer after I did that, he would've been laughed out of town. You can't go burning informers, Fred. No matter what's at stake. Even you know that much.'

Consolo shifted in the chair. He smiled. 'You're very persuasive, counselor,' he said. 'I can see why you make a good living.'

'It's easy to be persuasive,' Gleason said, 'when what you're telling is the truth.'

'I don't believe it, though,' Consolo said.

'I didn't think you would,' Gleason said.

'What I do believe,' Consolo said, 'is that she knows where he is. And furthermore, that that dark lady probably told you down in Waterford that morning. And I want you to tell me.'

'She didn't,' Gleason said. 'And even if she had, I still could not tell you.'

Consolo nodded. He stood up. 'I see what you mean about persuasion and the truth,' he said. 'I am not at all convinced.'

27

The store at the easterly end of the block on the north side of the Waterford Shopping Plaza was a big MediMart. Blue and white posters in its windows advertised a coupon sale of mouthwashes, panty hose, sanitary napkins, shaving cream and motor oil. Next to it there was a Dunkin' Donuts coffee shop. Two telephone company trucks, a blue and white police cruiser, a blue and white Ford Bronco II carrying police shield logos on its doors, a white US Mail truck and two private cars were parked in front of the doughnut shop. There were small clusters of two and three cars on the southerly side of the parking lot, near the entrances to the First National Bank of Waterford, the Omnidentix Clinic and the Commonwealth Savings and Loan offices. The rest of the lot was vacant. Flimsy pieces of waxed paper, discarded by doughnut eaters, lay silver in the sun on the pavement, stirring occasionally in the soft morning breeze.

Consolo at 7:45 parked his burgundy Mercedes Benz 450 SL in one of the spaces in front of the drugstore and shut off the engine. He got out of the car and locked it. He put the keys in his jacket pocket and hitched up his pants. He walked to the door of the MediMart and tried it. It was locked. He faced toward the parking lot. No one was watching him. He turned right and headed toward the easterly end of the building.

There was enough room between it and the sluggish brook coagulating beside the gravel upgrade of the westerly shoulder of Route 4 to accommodate six parking spaces and a large blue Dempster Dumpster. There was a white Chevrolet van parked in the third slot, between a black Ford pick-up truck and a blue Starion coupe, its grille facing the brick wall of the building. Consolo went around it to the passenger side and rapped twice on the windowless sliding freight door. He paused and then rapped twice again. He felt rather than heard movement in the van. He heard the latch being unlocked. The door slid open about an inch. He grabbed the edge of it with his left hand and slid it open just far enough to allow him to get in. He stepped up into the truck, stooping, and shut the door immediately behind him, making sure it latched. He locked it, groping for the lever as his eyes adjusted to the relative darkness inside the van.

The only light came from three ten-inch black-and-white television monitors on the shelf on the left side of the cargo bay. The only sounds were the intermittent squeak of a tape deck in need of cleaning and a beautifully rendered performance of Bach's Second Sonata for Unaccompanied Violin being received on a speaker with a weak treble range.

'Who's in here this hour?' Consolo said, squinting at the bulky figure sitting on the swivel stool in front of the shelf, staring at the screens. Consolo hunkered down and rested his buttocks on a large metal box against the partition closing off the driver's compartment. 'That you, is it, Peter?'

'Affirmative,' the figure said.

Consolo now could see well enough to count two cardboard Dunkin' Donuts containers near the right hand of the figure. 'One of those coffees for me,' he said, reaching for it.

The other man stuck his right hand out and spanned his fingers to cover both of the containers. 'Conditionally,' he said.

'Conditioned on what?' Consolo said.

'Conditioned on you not giving me a whole loadah shit about not going inna fuckin' coffee shop, the morning,' he said.

'You know my views on that,' Consolo said, grasping for the container nearest him and taking it out from under the fingers. 'You fuck up this detail getting chummy with the locals, eating crullers in the morning, drinking soup the afternoons, I will personally be glad to hash up your jacket with a memo stating how I told you not to do it.'

'Thank you very much, Sergeant,' the other man said. 'Want you to know: It's one the big pleasures in my life, working under your command and getting all the benefit, your vast experience. 'Cept the time Denise called up and told me we had herpes, and she knew hers came from me, it's about the most fun I have had since Vietnam.'

Consolo removed the plastic cover from the coffee container and sipped the contents gingerly. The coffee was very hot. 'It's such a pleasure for you, Peter,' he said, 'the fuck don't you get here in the morning, you're supposed to, 'stead of about two minutes ahead of me? If that?'

'Very simple,' the other man said, taking the other coffee

container and removing its cover, 'those of us have wives and kids, drive your basic junkers 'cause it's all we can afford – we now and then have the experience, the morning, where the fuckin' car won't start. Which mine did not, this morning.'

'You should plan your life better, Peter,' Consolo said, blowing on the coffee. 'Wasn't my decision, you know, you ought to get married and have about eight kids. I know love's grand, and all that shit, but you go around indulging yourself like that, it's pretty hard to swing the payments on that lovely German steel.'

'I suppose,' the other man said. Consolo now could make out the expression on his face in the light from the TV screens. It was one of distracted resignation.

'Well, Peter,' Consolo said, leaning forward to study the images, 'what do we seem to have here this fine day, for all our difficulties? Tell me everything you know. Don't leave anything out.' The screen nearest him showed the door to an apartment; it was numbered '2N.' The screen in the middle showed the outside entrance at the rear of an apartment building. The screen on the left showed the front entrance of an apartment building. There were no people visible on any of the screens. The music continued.

'I think she's getting dressed,' Peter said. 'Fitzy told me the radio came on the usual time, six sharp, and he heard the john flush and the coffee grinder. Hasn't been anything since then 'cept this fuckin' music she likes so much, and she hasn't been out for the paper. No calls, in or out. Just the goddamned fiddle music, sounds like somebody hurtin' a cat.'

'She's a music teacher, Peter,' Consolo said. 'Music teachers like that stuff. Their tastes're refined, you know? Very high-class stuff.'

'Yeah,' Peter said. 'At home I got Kerry, playin' Madonna, over and over again. I come to work on this detail, I get the classical shit. I dunno which I hate worse. How come I never get a detail, somebody listens the ballgame or something?' He changed his voice to falsetto and sang the same line twice, alleging that Consolo was an angel. 'And then the other one there, about how this is a material world, and she's a material girl. Which is, the both of them, I think, are about gettin' laid. Unless I don't speak English anymore.' He paused. 'Or they don't, which is possible.'

'Always like to see the young people enjoying themselves,' Consolo said. 'You think when she gets older, the convent isn't going to take her?'

'No,' Peter said. 'I think when she gets older some young stud is going to take her. Which will be all right with me, long's it's off my hands along with off her pants. It's just I think fourteen, you know, might be a little young to start having that in mind. Just the teeniest bit young. That's what bothers me.'

'She's not getting dressed,' Consolo said suddenly. He put the coffee container on the shelf and lifted himself into a crouch, going around behind Peter and using his left hand to grope for the receiver delivering the music.

'The hell're you doing?' Peter said.

'I'm turning up the goddamned sound,' Consolo said. 'That broad is not getting dressed. What she's doing, one of two things is going on here. She is either, she either got out again before you got here this morning, or else she's waiting for a phone call.' He turned up the volume so that the music was almost painfully loud in the acoustically deadened truck.

'She couldn't've got out,' Peter said with some agitation. 'Fitzy was here all night, just like he's supposed to. He told me this morning, Davis brought her in last night, and then she had a date with some guy that she calls "Marty," and Davis watched him leave about, she threw him out early, I guess, around ten fifteen, and then Fitzy come on and she didn't go out after that. She couldn't've got out.'

'She got out once before,' Consolo said. 'Keep that in mind, Peter. Old Fitzy there, nice guy and all, but he's got a tendency to nap, grab a few Zs now and then, when nobody's lookin' on.'

'That was when,' Peter said, 'that was when he was having them allergy treatments and the stuff was makin' him sleepy. That was when that was.'

'That was last fuckin' week, was when it was,' Consolo said. The music played on. He adjusted the volume upward again.

'You know, boss,' Peter said, 'you crank that thing up about one more red cunt hair, they're not gonna need to see me comin' inna coffee shop, know what we're doing here. They're gonna be able, hear what she's listening to better'n she can herself, while they're eatin' honey-dips.'

'Ahh,' Consolo said disgustedly. He turned the volume down slightly and crabbed his way back to the metal box. 'Most likely no point in it anyway, since she probably got out while Fitzroy was dreaming, dozin' away on the floor – got his head down on the shelf, something along that line. Only thing we're going to get here now's when she comes back. And we're gonna look damned silly, too, when she comes strolling in.'

'Look, willya?' Peter said. He manipulated keyboard controls under the screen in the center of the display. The camera focus zoomed back from close-up to wide angle so that the four parking spaces nearest the rear entrance of the apartment building were visible. As the focus changed, a man wearing a light-colored suit and carrying an attaché case emerged from the door and walked toward the camera. He turned to his left and walked behind a Ford Mustang convertible and then a silver Volkswagen GTI. 'See?' Peter said. 'There's her fuckin' car, all right? That's her fuckin' car. And that car, that fuckin' car was *not* there, the morning she got out.'

'She got a ride from someone, then,' Consolo said. He peered at the screen. 'Who's the fuckin' guy?' he said.

'She *didn't* get a fuckin' *ride* from *any* fuckin' body,' Peter said. 'She's inna damned apartment where we put her in last night and she had meatloaf with a guy. He was crazy about it. That, they had more talk about that meatloaf'n they did the fact we're prolly all gonna get blown up, nuclear holocaust. You're givin' this broad too much credit, is what you are doin'. I'm telling you, I'm tellin' you, this broad is not that smart. She's a fuckin' *music* teacher, not a goddamned Russian spy. She don't know where Tibbetts is. She hasn't seen the guy. She hasn't talked him, onna phone. He hasn't called her up. She don't know where to find him and she don't know where he is. And we are wasting our damned time here, in this fuckin' heat. Might as well go down the beach and take off all our clothes, and just go inna water, all the headway we make here.'

'A guy I know says that she knows,' Consolo said equably. 'Him I believe, not you. Who's that guy there?'

'Who's the guy where?' Peter said.

'The guy with the attaché case,' Consolo said. 'I assume Davis's got brains enough, he's already running the guy that had the meatloaf through the fuckin' magic box, I don't have to tell him that.'

'Well,' Peter said, 'he is. But frankly from the conversation the two of them had, I wouldn't get my bowels in an uproar, waiting see what comes out. The guy, the guy sounds like a teacher. He's a teacher too.'

'What's he teach?' Consolo said.

'What difference does it make?' Peter said. 'He's a fuckin' high school teacher. Who cares what it is?'

'Sam Tibbetts was a teacher, too,' Consolo said. 'That's something that Sam Tibbetts did, when he was just lying low. He had himself a nice, quiet job, teaching math in Brattleboro, all right? That is what he did. And now he's lying low again – maybe he's gone back to it. That's why it makes a difference, you're looking for some guy. Guys that do the same things he did, they might help you out. Might not mean to help you out, but that's another thing. And a guy that did something before, when guys were after him, he's liable do the same thing again, something gets him jumpy.'

Peter sighed. 'Right, Sarge,' he said. 'Chemistry or something, I guess. Didn't talk too much about that, but I think that's what he is from what I see on Davis's logs. Spent all the time they weren't talkin' about the meatloaf, bitchin', near as I could tell, gripin' how they hate their boss, what a prick he is.' He paused. 'Which I could relate to, you know what I mean.'

'Uh huh,' Consolo said. 'I hope you really like being a corporal, Pete Kelly. You're gonna be one, I would say, for a good long time.'

'Oh, big fuckin' deal,' Kelly said. 'I already been one longer'n JFK was president. You think that bothers me, that shit that you hand out?'

'You got me,' Consolo said. 'Mostly I don't give a shit, it bothers you or not. Try to stick to business here. Never mind your beefs. You want another line of work, go find one for yourself. Inna meantime, do your job. Tell me what I want to know. Who's the guy? The one the briefcase there? We got a make on him? Or is he just another bozo that we're planning to ignore, the same way we let her slip out when she saw Mister Gleason there?'

'He's,' Kelly said, 'he's a guy named Mister Thomas that works inna Consumer Protection Division, the AG's office. He lives by himself in number One-K, and he's probably a fairy, although we're not sure of that. You know how those bachelors are – most of them are perverts. Okay, Sergeant? That do it for you all right? Make you calm and satisfied?'

'For the moment,' Consolo said. The violin music ended. A radio announcer's voice replaced it, reciting the name of the selection and reporting that it was a performance by a Russian musician who had made several other Bach recordings not yet available in the United States. The announcer exhorted his listeners to write to the recording company and request importation of the other discs. The telephone rang in the apartment.

'Uh huh,' Consolo said. 'I was right. And she'll get it on the second ring, the latest.'

They heard the phone being picked up midway through the second ring. From the speaker that had delivered the music they heard a woman say: 'Hello.' Simultaneously from a second speaker that had been silent until then they heard her greeting and a male voice that said: 'Chris?'

'Ah hah,' Consolo said, leaning forward. 'Come on, Christina baby.'

'Yes,' she said hesitantly.

'Chris,' the male voice said with some urgency, 'listen: I can't talk here. Is there some way I can get in touch with you, see you so we can? I've really got to see you.'

She sighed. 'I can't go through this again, Dan,' she said. 'I've told you and I've told you, and I know it's important to you. But it's also important, it's also important to me, you know? It's very important to me. And I don't, I just don't feel the same way you do, you know? And I can't pretend I do. And I've got to hang up now, and I'm sorry, but I just do.'

'Shit,' Consolo said as the woman broke the connection. He leaned back against the partition. The only sound from the speakers was the opening movement of the thirty-fourth symphony by Mozart.

'That helps us a *lot*,' Kelly said. 'That's a real big fuckin' break we got there, that thing we just got. Spending the taxpayers' money, dig up something big like that, really makes it worthwhile. Makes you feel good inside.'

'Oh,' Consolo said, 'I wouldn't go that far. It's useful for us, know these things, dig up all we can. More we know about this broad, better our chances are.' He paused. 'Besides,' he said, 'that's not the guy. That was not the call she wanted.'

'What,' Kelly said, 'what's so goddamned useful? That this guy Dan Matteo's got the hots for her? So what? Everybody's got the hots for this broad, near as I can tell. So this guy that runs a record store, so he's one of them. What good does that do us? Can you tell me that? Taping people that take lessons, taping what she listens to, onna radio. Taping … No shower, right? That's how you knew, she was waiting for a call. She didn't take a shower.'

'Ah, Peter my boy,' Consolo said, patting him on the right shoulder, 'there are moments when you make the whole thing worth the effort. All the time and trouble I take, teaching you your job, I tell you, when you shine like that, you really make me proud. Now, tell me what you're hearing now.'

Kelly listened silently to the music. 'More goddamned classical shit,' he said.

'And that's all, isn't it?' Consolo said.

'That's all I hear,' Kelly said.

'Which means?' Consolo said.

'Which means,' Kelly said, 'she's still not in the shower. She's still waiting for a call.'

'You're a pistol, Pete,' Consolo said. 'You make me so proud.'

'Yeah, Sarge,' Kelly said, 'but suppose she doesn't get it? What if you're right, and that's what she's waiting for, but the call never comes through, all right? Or it doesn't come through to her here? Then what do we do?'

'Peter, Peter,' Consolo said, 'we're already doing, we're doing other things.'

28

When Barbara Mary (Donovan) Gleason was contented and composed, she was an attractive woman. She was forty-three years old. She had ash-blonde hair, carefully styled in a Newbury Street salon to soften her somewhat sharp features. She had grey eyes and she had had her teeth capped. She played eighteen holes of twelve-handicap golf in good weather, Monday through Friday mornings, late April through mid-November, at the Milton-Hoosic Club course in Canton. In the winter she kept fit and trim by playing indoor tennis – doubles – with three other women three mornings a week at the Blue Hills Tennis Center.

She considered gravity one of her two major enemies. It had relentlessly continued the bodily decline accelerated by the effects of four pregnancies – three carried to term; one surgically terminated in the first trimester when amniocentesis disclosed the substantial probability that the fetus, intentionally conceived when she was thirty-six, was afflicted with Down's Syndrome. She watched what she ate. In the summer she wore cool casual cotton skirts and shorts in pinks and greens and yellows, from The Talbots', and in the winter she wore brownish tweeds, muted plaids and clingy jersey from Orvis. She used foul-weather gear from L.L. Bean all year.

Her oldest son, Terrence Junior, was a senior at Boston College High School in Dorchester. Her daughter, Joanne, was a freshman at Milton Academy. Her younger son, Philip, was in the seventh grade at Briar Hill, a private school in Sharon for hyperactive and presumably disturbed children. Her father, Philip, was deceased. Her mother, Mary Barbara (Lynch) Donovan, lived year 'round in Connemara Town Estates, outside Orlando, Florida, in the retirement home she and her husband had purchased on the ninth fairway of the Emerald Club Golf Course. Barbara's brother, Timothy, was an office manager for Raytheon in Burlington. Her sister, Joanne, was the widow of Cmdr. Donald Welch, USN, who was killed in an attempted landing on the carrier *Saratoga* during exercises in the Mediterranean; she lived in Seattle. Barbara attended Mass alone on alternate Sundays at St Casimir's Church in Stoughton; it was not her parish – which Terry described as 'Our Lady of Perpetual Remonstrance' – in Canton, and she generally declined to account for her preference for it.

She volunteered the reason to Lawrence Badger, implying by it the identity of her second enemy: another woman. At 10:35 on the morning of July 16, 1985, she sat in front of his desk at Investigations, Inc., on the westerly side of the thirty-eighth floor of the Prudential Tower in Boston, overlooking Fenway Park empty in the morning sunlight, and with great exasperation in her voice told him she attended St. Casimir's 'because I don't think anybody knows me there. Where I know everybody knows me in my actual parish, and I can't hold my head up there. Not since nineteen-seventy-nine, when I became the last person, I believe, to find out what'd been going on.'

Lawrence Badger was sixty-two years old. He was small and slight. There were brown liver spots visible on his tanned face and under the long wisps of grey hair he arranged each morning on his scalp. He wore a dark blue shirt with a white, gold-pinned collar and french cuffs, and a bright pink silk tie. He steepled his fingers. He cleared his throat. 'Mrs. Gleason,' he said, 'I do hate to seem abrupt. But if you could tell me, please, the reason for today? Why you are here today? I take it you believe your husband's having an affair.'

She nodded. She moistened her lips. 'I do,' she said. 'Yes, I do. That's why I came here.'

'Yes,' he said. 'Well, as I believe I explained to you on the phone, Mrs. Gleason, our policy here is that only in very rare instances do we accept direct retentions by clients in such matters. We seldom, as a matter of fact, accept them at all. Even when they are proffered to us by practicing attorneys. Most of our work is in the area of industrial security – trade secrets, formulas, processes; items of that nature. We do very little work in domestic relations matters. They're not our cup of tea.'

She nodded. 'You did tell me that, Mister Badger,' she said. 'And, as I believe I explained to you, this is one of those rare matters. My husband is a prominent attorney. He's currently involved in a notorious case, involving notorious people. If,' she said, moistening her lips again, 'if … I don't hate my husband, Mister Badger. Even if he is cheating on me. I don't want to damage him, or damage his career.' Her eyes filled. 'If I go to an attorney, if I go to any other attorney, and tell him or her about my suspicions, it will be all over Boston by nightfall. My husband's told me about this town. Gossip is its stock in trade. Character assassination – all the rest of it. I don't want that to happen.'

'Mrs. Gleason,' Badger said, 'really, now. No lawyer that you consulted would dare to breach your confidence. It would be unheard of. It simply wouldn't happen.'

'The lawyer,' she said grimly, 'the lawyer might not talk. But you can bet your bottom dollar that his secretary would. What Terry Gleason does is news. Especially if it's scandalous.' She shook her head. 'You can talk to me,' she said, 'you can talk to me 'till you're blue in the face. You will not change my mind. I'm not going to a lawyer until I'm sure I have to. And I won't be sure unless and until I get someone like you to find out if I am right. And tell me so.'

She smiled. 'You must understand my position,' she said. 'Seven years ago this Christmas, Terry and I finally escaped from a dinky little three-bedroom colonial in Hanover. Into a twelve-room antique farmhouse behind a stone wall on four acres of land with a pond out in back. In Canton. I have a cleaning lady three times a week. In the summer I move to our cottage in Chilmark, as soon as the kids finish school. Well, I did until this year. And last winter, last winter we sent the kids to stay with my mother in Florida, and Terry and I took our vacation in Hawaii. We worked hard, Terry and I did, and we sacrificed and did without. And finally, finally it all paid off. I've earned what I've got, Mister Badger, every damned bit of it.

'But,' she said, 'the kids're growing up now. They're bored, just spending the summer with Mummy on the island now. Terry Junior's in tennis camp. Joanne's a lifeguard at the pool. Philly, I suppose, could go, but he's in a special summer program for kids who have his problem, over at Curry College. And besides, who'd be home with Terry Junior and Joanne, when they come back at night? So, I can't do that.'

She took a deep breath. 'I need to know,' she said, 'I need to know if I'm going to be completely alone. When they're all grown up. And, if I am, I have to start planning for it. Now. Before it happens. I haven't worked since nineteen-sixty-seven. The people who were in my field then're all on the management level now. If I went back, went back into buying, I'd have a whole new lingo to learn. And whole new groups of people to get to know. And that's assuming I could even get a job. Which is quite an assumption.'

She inhaled again. 'So you see, Mister Badger,' she said, 'I have to be very careful here, about how I approach this thing. I don't want Terry's business to be hurt, even if he is running around on me. It's bad enough if I have to divorce him, and face the rest of my life alone. Which is most likely what would happen to me, if I reached that point. That would be bad enough. But if I somehow, stupidly, if I do something that ruins his practice, I could find myself in a position where I'd have to go back to work. And I don't want to do that. Because I think I'll fail. If I've failed at one thing,' she said, 'if I've failed at my marriage, well, that's bad enough. I don't want to get into a position where I fail again. At my life.'

Badger studied her. 'You're very persuasive, Mrs. Gleason,' he said. 'You may not've worked for a good many years, but your mind has not been idle.'

'No,' she said, 'it hasn't. Now, will you listen to me, hear what I have to say?'

'No promises,' he said.

'I understand that,' she said. 'Except for secrecy, of course.'

'It won't leave these offices,' he said.

'Good,' she said. 'Ten years ago, my husband was an assistant district attorney in Boston. He'd been one for eight years by then, and he was good at it. He handled major cases – murders, robberies and that stuff. And he did well in court.' She hesitated. 'At the time, he left that job,' she said, 'I thought we were both agreed that it was, that he should leave. Because it didn't pay all that well, and both of us'd always wanted nice things. So I thought he wanted to do it. Wanted to leave. Now? Now I'm not so sure. When he was a prosecutor, we didn't have much money but he was always happy. He liked what he did. Now he makes a lot more, and I know he's good at it, but maybe we emphasized the material side too much.' She coughed. 'Anyway,' she said, 'I don't want to create any false impressions. Terry is a good man, and a fine lawyer.'

Badger cleared his throat. 'I'm familiar with your husband's work,' he said. 'Both sides: prosecution and defense. I've worked on cases that he was presenting for the Commonwealth, and for other lawyers on cases where he was on the defense team. He's a very resourceful lawyer. Very quick, very bright, very alert. Very hardworking, too. And, I must say, trustworthy. He keeps his word. If, as most suppose, John Morrissey is the dean of the Boston criminal defense bar, then he ought to know, and John Morrissey says Terry Gleason is the most capable trial attorney he's ever run up against. Anywhere.'

Her eyes narrowed. 'Oh,' she said, 'are we now getting to the real reason, you don't want this case?'

He looked puzzled. 'I don't think I've said that, in the first place. All I've said is that we seldom do accept such cases. Which is not the same thing at all. In the second place, I'm not saying that. All I'm saying is precisely what I've said. That I know who Terry

Gleason is. I've worked with him, 'though not for him. I know he's capable. I respect him for that.'

'Well,' she said, 'all right. Because he is those things. Very capable.

'Terry's last case, as a prosecutor,' she said, 'was The Friary shoot-out. The two men who ran it, and three women. Prostitutes. Found shot to death. Plus two other women as well. In a freezer.'

'We worked on that case,' Badger said. He frowned. 'Very troublesome case, that. For us, I mean. We had to walk a thin line. I'm still not sure we didn't slip.' He cleared his throat. 'We worked for Attorney Bigelow. One of the defense counsel.'

'John Bigelow,' she said.

'That's the one,' Badger said.

'Terry hates his guts,' she said with satisfaction. 'He says John Bigelow's the biggest snake that's ever been on earth. At least since the Garden of Eden.'

Badger put his head back and laughed. 'Doesn't surprise me,' he said. 'You should hear what Bigelow has to say about your husband.'

'What is it?' she said fiercely. 'Just what does he have to say?'

Badger held up his right hand and laughed, shaking his head. 'Easy, easy,' he said, 'I'm not going to tell you that. John Bigelow and your husband're both perfectly nice men. Men of integrity. John's a bit stuffy, perhaps, but basically a very nice man. Your husband's a bit of a renegade, but basically a very nice man. John and your husband: they just don't like each other. They have a personality conflict that makes them – when they rub up against each other, they tend to give off sparks.'

'Well,' she said, 'maybe, but after what Terry's told me about him, well ... '

'Discount it by thirty percent,' Badger said. 'It's just a personal antagonism. Just a normal human weakness. Go on with what you were saying.'

'One of the defendants in The Friary case,' she said, 'was a man named James Walker.'

'"Beau James," they called him,' Badger said. 'Very unusual man, praise God. He was John Bigelow's client.'

'So, you're familiar with him, then,' she said. Her eyes were very narrow.

'I wouldn't go quite that far,' Badger said. 'I don't think anyone was ever quite "familiar" with Beau James. Mister Walker ... Let's just say that Mister Walker was a man who guarded his privacy. Even from his lawyer, and his lawyer's investigators. Very complicated chap. Very complicated. It was hard to know how to defend him. He was so secretive with us.

'John Bigelow and I were quite frustrated,' Badger said. 'But we pursued the matter according to his wishes. He, after all, was paying us to chase down all those leads that didn't pan out. All the people who couldn't be found. Paying us a lot. We took his money. We thought he was a nut, but the checks were good.'

'I gathered he came from a very wealthy family,' she said.

'Um,' Badger said, '"well-to-do," I'd say. His father's a research cardiologist at New York Memorial. Very highly respected. Mother was a concert pianist before her marriage. And her father was a cellist for the London Philharmonic. Before he emigrated to this country to teach at Yale. Terribly, naturally, terribly upset about this thing. This squalid murder case? Absolutely horrifying. Father had a heart attack shortly after the boy was arrested. I don't think there's any question but that it was brought on by the ordeal.'

'He's a Negro, too, isn't he?' she said.

'I suppose,' he said. 'I suppose he'd be characterized as a black. His mother, James's mother, his mother was a West Indian. His putative grandfather was Spanish. James is quite dark.'

'Actually,' Barbara Gleason said, 'it's his sister that's more my concern.'

Badger pursed his lips. 'Ah,' he said, 'yes. Christina. To one degree or another, she was everyone's concern. Everyone connected with The Friary trial, at least. Remarkable woman. Very remarkable woman. How to put it? "Wise beyond her years," I'd guess. Wise beyond her years.'

'Mister Badger,' she said, 'my husband had an affair with that woman. She was almost the cause of the end of our marriage.' She looked down into her lap and gnawed her lower lip. 'I had,' she said, 'I had a really awful time, deciding what to do. For several months after I found out what was going on, I was just beside myself. And then,' she said, gasping once, 'then I made up my mind. And took him back. And I forgave him. I said: "All right, Terry. I guess I'm over it. I suppose every family, every couple has to go through something. Some men gamble; some men drink. Donald knew very well what a tramp my sister was, how she was taking on every man in Seattle while he was at sea, and he came to terms with it, somehow. And I guess, I guess I can do the same with you. I think I can live with it, what you've done to me, and maybe some day I'll even manage, manage to forget it. But if this ever happens again ... " I told him I didn't think – I knew, in fact – that I couldn't go through it again. And we even had – and this was his idea – we tried to have another child.' She stopped. 'But we couldn't. I was too old, I guess. I miscarried.'

Badger tilted back in his chair and clasped his hands behind his head. He smiled sympathetically. 'Mrs. Gleason,' he said, 'I've been married to the same woman for the past twenty-one years. Before that, I was married to the same woman for nineteen years. To my childhood sweetheart, mind you. And until I met my second wife, the thought of leaving my first wife never entered my mind. But the minute I set eyes on Martha, I knew without any doubt whatsoever I was going to divorce Sarah and marry Martha. I knew it, don't you see? Whatever it took for me to get her, that I was going to do.

'That was in nineteen-sixty-four,' he said. 'I was forty-one years old, and that was exactly what I did. It cost me plenty, I assure you, but I did it, and I paid it without a whimper.

'Fourteen years later,' he said, 'fourteen years after I married Martha, I went to work on The Friary. And naturally, in the course of my work for John Bigelow, I was introduced to Christina Walker.

'I was fifty-five years old,' he said. 'I don't by any means suggest I'd been a model husband to Martha before that – we're all prisoners of our own characters, and mine has at least the average number of defects. But there's a distinction that adults need to draw, I think, between the sort of transient infatuation that leads to little flings, and often can be explained by a disparity between the sexual appetites of spouses, and the overpowering urge to possess another person. Exclusively and permanently. Until I met Christina Walker, I had never felt the slightest temptation in that respect to leave Martha.

'Well,' he said, 'my age saved me from making a complete fool of myself. Time goes by, thank God, and we get too tired to repeat our mistakes. Morality often gets the credit for the effects of fatigue. Christina was, I think, about twenty-five then, give or take a year. If I'd been thirty-five, even forty-five, I think I would have gone completely rattraps over that young woman. No matter who I was married to, or what anyone else thought of my behavior. She was an extraordinary woman.'

'So I've heard,' Barbara Gleason said. 'So I've often heard.'

'Mrs. Gleason,' he said mildly, 'listen to me, please? I'm telling you this because I think – indeed, I know – that what your husband did back then was understandable. If you asked me to tell you then, why this young woman – this child, really – distracted as she was by the fix her brother was in, as baffled as the rest of us by his reasoning, and what he said – if you had asked me then to account for her enormous attractiveness, I could not have done so. I can't, adequately, to this day. But I can, what I can do is tell you that it was there. That it existed. It was powerful.'

'I've heard that, too,' she said.

'It's not,' he said, 'it's not that she's beautiful. In any conventional sense of the word.'

'No,' Barbara said. 'There I agree with you. I saw her. When I found out what was going on between her and my husband, found out who she was, my friend Rachel knew her. Knew who she was. Rachel's very active in her synagogue, always setting up recitals and so forth, and she knew who she was. She had heard her play. And Rachel knew what she was doing. That she was getting education credits at Bridgewater State, to get a teaching job. And Rachel, we went over there one day, and Rachel pointed her out to me. And I was astonished. I guess I expected some Miss America or something, someone with a big chest and blonde hair and stiletto heels, wobbling along in pants so tight her pulse showed, and here I saw this young Negro woman with kind of her hair in a bun, and wearing a baggy old sweatshirt and blue jeans and moccasins, and no makeup or anything, and I thought: "What on earth? What on earth is going on here? I am losing my husband to this streelish, black, *child*? How can this be happening?"'

'I'm sure you did,' Badger said.

She shook her head. 'I didn't understand it,' she said. 'I couldn't understand it. I still don't understand it. I'm, I take care of my appearance, Mister Badger.'

'I can see that,' he said.

'Even my friends,' she said, 'even my friends're always telling me: "Oh, lighten up a little, Barbara. Don't be so meticulous. You're too fastidious. 'Barbara has her hair done before she goes out to the mailbox.' Stop fretting all the time." But I was brought up, my mother always taught me to take care of myself. She told me, long before I met Terry, long before I was married, she told me one of the worst things a woman can do is let herself go, afterwards. And the night before I was married, she told me: "Now, you may not believe this, and I've never told you this before, but your father's no different from any other man, and neither is Terry, either. I like him, and I think you've made a wise choice for a husband. But husbands're always men. And men're all alike. Men do not keep promises, no matter what they say. They're always holding something back. Always hiding something. And when they say they'll always love you, and take care of you, what they really mean is that they'll do it unless somebody else comes along that they decide they'd like better."

'And of course I told her, little wimp that I was,' she said, changing to a singsong voice: '"But Mother, we *love* each other. I love Terry very much, and I know that he loves me."

'And she said,' Barbara said, 'she laughed at me. "You let him in," she said. "I don't blame you for that. Only a crazy man would marry a woman without getting into her first. Only a crazy woman'd hold out on someone that really interested her. And if the parts fit right, of course it must be love.

'"But that doesn't change the facts," she said. "Terry loves you now because he finally got you into bed. And he always will, too, if you remember they're all dogs. Every single one of them. Including your father. All men're dogs. And the only way you can be sure of keeping your dog at home is by giving him lots and lots of whatever he wants, whenever he wants it. He barks? Give him a treat. Any flavor. Because if you don't, kiddo, there's some dame out there who will, and the minute she offers it, he'll be off like a shot."

'I was embarrassed,' she said. 'My mother, talking like this? I said: "Mother, I am shocked." But I did it,' Barbara said. 'I did what she said.' Her eyes teared up. 'I'm not going to go into detail, Mister Badger, but I can tell you that Terry never wanted anything in the bedroom that he couldn't get from me. Anything. If I thought it was something, you know, that I even thought was degrading – if that was what he wanted, well then, that's what I would do. I didn't let it matter. I went along with it. There was just – there was simply no reason why he had to go looking somewhere else.'

She shook her head. 'That's why,' she said, 'when I saw her, I just couldn't understand. How was this insignificant little person doing this to me? It could not be happening. It simply could not be.' She took a deep breath. She snuffled. She dug into her purse and produced a handkerchief. She blew her nose hard. She shook her head again. 'It wasn't fair,' she said. 'It simply wasn't fair. I still don't understand it. She couldn't possibly've been giving him something with her body that he couldn't get from mine. If she'd've been some bimbo, some eighteen-year-old stewardess, I might've understood. He wanted something young and firm – I wasn't anymore. But this was just a child I saw. I couldn't understand.'

Badger cleared his throat. 'It's her eyes,' he said.

She stared at him. 'Her eyes,' she said in a flat voice.

He cleared his throat again. 'At first, I mean,' he said. 'At first it's her eyes. They change color. They seemed to change colors, at least. I don't know what any of us, any of the, well, older people involved in The Friary – I don't know what we expected to encounter when we came into contact with the people in that case. I know I expected, I guess I just assumed we'd be dealing with the detritus of an aberrant generation. A bunch of superannuated kids left over from a strange decade, obsolete debris. And most of them were – men and women in their thirties, still in adolescence. Cases of arrested development. But some of them, Christina, at least, had emerged from it. Evolved. And the reason, the reason that I, and someone like your husband, that we noticed those that had evolved, was usually something physical. And in Christina's case, it was her eyes. I don't really know what color they are. Blue. Green. Violet. Grey. I really don't know. They're hypnotic, though. Mesmerizing. You can sit there and have a conversation with her about some dreadfully dirty business that's got her terribly upset, and you as disturbed as she, and you find yourself thinking, at least if you're a man, you find yourself thinking, after a while: "My God, how does she do that? How many colors are there, that she can do with her eyes?" It's very unsettling. Most unsettling.'

Barbara gazed at him uncomprehendingly.

He coughed. 'Well,' he said gruffly, 'no need belaboring the point.' He rearranged his letter opener and pencils on the desk blotter. 'All I meant to say was that there was a certain fascination, for all of us, in dealing with the people involved in The Friary case. And none of us was prepared for Christina. So, if your husband later had an affair with her, well, I don't mean to make light of it, but you shouldn't feel too bad. He just happened to be the one that succumbed. Or "succeeded." That perhaps would be the word.

'The fact,' he said, 'the fact that you're married to someone, Mrs. Gleason, as I'm sure you are aware, that fact is not a guarantee that that person is therefore immune to human weakness. To temptation. Nor is it necessarily a safe-conduct pass for you, when that temptation strikes. If, well, if you put it behind you, as you appear to have done in that instance, then that's the sensible thing to do. A mature decision.'

He stopped. He frowned. 'Now,' he said, 'now if you suspect, he's being tempted again, if someone else, and new, has entered the scene, well, I suppose, that's a different matter. That you must weigh carefully. And, if you can't see your way clear to riding out this new storm, going through it all again, well, then that's a decision you'll have to make yourself. But really, Mrs. Gleason, I don't think your situation really requires the sort of service we provide.

'We're very expensive,' he said. 'We employ all of the most modern laboratory techniques and scientific devices available. The people that my nephew and I hire are the very best at what they do. And they're paid accordingly. I have to tell you, as I tell almost everyone else who comes to see me with a problem similar to yours – and I don't mean to sound as though I'm minimizing it – I know it's very painful for you. That you wouldn't be here if it weren't. But I also have to tell them, as I must tell you: It doesn't make good sense, economically, for you to seek out the kinds of services we offer, at the prices we have to charge, for what amounts, really, to a fairly simple surveillance exercise. If you want him followed and watched, there are dozens of other, smaller, operations, that're fully equipped to handle the job, and charge about a third of our normal fee.'

'Mister Badger,' she said, 'when I say it's started up again, I mean it's started up with her.'

'Oh,' he said. 'You, ah, do?'

She nodded. 'I don't know it for certain, but I'm pretty sure I'm right. It's started up again. With Christina Walker.'

His eyebrows went up. 'Oh, dear,' he said. 'Oh dear, dear, dear. How did this come about?'

29

Lawrence Badger late the same morning reached Alton Badger's office on the northerly side of the thirty-eighth floor just as Carla Hamilton emerged, closing the door behind her. She was in her early thirties, about five-seven, with a stocky body which she covered carelessly in cold weather with pilled, shapeless sweaters and sturdy tweed skirts, and in warm weather with tee shirts and polyester pants. She was wearing a white Mickey Mouse tee shirt and orange pants and she looked merry.

'What's he doing in there, Carla?' Lawrence Badger said warily. 'Is it safe for me to go in?'

'Oh,' she said, giggling, 'I think you'll be all right. He's having a wonderful time for himself.'

'Has he got someone with him?' Badger said, putting his hand on the knob. 'One of those crazy people from across the river there, playing with computers?'

'Oh, no,' she said, giggling. 'He's all by himself. He's playing baseball today. Really having a good time.'

'Baseball,' he said.

'Yeah,' she said. 'It's the interleague trading deadline, you know? It's midnight tonight. And I guess, well, I'm not really up on it and everything – I've been playing chess with this guy out in Norman, Oklahoma, and he's really got me so I don't know whether I'm coming or going, you know what I mean? Because he is really good. But I guess what it is is that one of the owners in the Ober League's in Hong Kong, and he's claiming a rules violation. Something about a trading deadline? Because it's tomorrow there.'

'I see,' Badger said.

'And the owner up in Ottawa,' she said, 'he's saying that the guy in Hong Kong deliberately went there and crossed the international dateline to invalidate the deal he wants to make today, and he's also filed a protest. And naturally Alton, as the commissioner, he has to decide.'

'I thought,' Badger said, 'I thought Alton was an owner.'

'Well,' she said, 'he is. But the commissioner, the regular commissioner was in that TWA hostage thing and he's still recovering. So Alton's filling in for him as interim, see? It's just 'till he gets out. The regular commissioner.'

'Do you think, Carla,' Badger said, 'you know him pretty well and all. Do you think there's any possibility actually that my nephew is, well, not in his right mind?'

She giggled again. 'Alton?' she said. 'Alton's fine. He's just enjoying himself.'

'Well,' Badger said, 'that makes good sense. Whistle while we work. Nice talking to you, Carla.' He opened the door and went in.

Alton Badger's office provided a view of Back Bay, the Charles River and MIT beyond. In the foreground along the windows there was a counter that ran the entire twenty-foot length of the office. On the counter there were six computers: three IBMs, two Compaqs and an Apple Macintosh. Each of them was connected to a phone modem next to it.

At the easterly end of the office there were two laser printers. The one nearest the corner was quiet. The one next to it was coughing out documents at the rate of eight pages per minute. Next to them there was a conversation grouping of four orange barrel chairs around a glass coffee table. On the wall behind the chairs were three large abstract posters in pastels advertising concerts at Salzburg in 1980, 1981 and 1982. They were framed in chrome.

Along the westerly wall, there was another counter holding two facsimile machines, an Associated Press silent teletype machine, a Telex receiver, a Dow Jones ticker and a large telephone console. Next to the counter, in the southwesterly corner near the door, there was a large Xerox copier. On the wall over the counter there was a map of the world eleven feet long by four feet wide.

Against the wall on the other side of the door there was a small refrigerator. Next to that there was a wet bar. Over the bar there was a large picture of Clayton Moore attired as the Lone Ranger, astride the great horse, Silver, with Jay Silverheels as Tonto aboard Scout, the paint, just behind him; the two men were looking intently at something that had caught their attention beyond the right margin of the poster.

In the center of the room there was a butcher-block table twelve feet long by four feet wide. There were draftsman's lamps clamped to each end. Over the center of it, suspended from the ceiling, was a circular fluorescent light contained in a brushed-aluminum conical fixture. Yellow plastic stars and white plastic comets were pasted on the fixture. On the table there were nine precise piles of documents, the complete Britannica Micropaedia, a Sony TV AM FM set with a three-inch screen, a rack of six meerschaum pipes with yellow stems, a tin of Cake Box tobacco, a green tin of Sail tobacco, a large glass ashtray with a cork pipe-knocker in the center, a small telephone console and two separate phones. There were backless posture chairs on each end and on each side of the table. In front of it there were two oatmeal tweed swivel chairs.

Alton Badger was standing at the Macintosh computer, staring at the screen. He was thirty-four years old. He had dark red hair cut moderately long, and a full dark red beard trimmed moderately short. He was five feet, ten inches tall. He weighed one hundred and sixty pounds. He wore a white broadcloth shirt with a gold collar pin and a nubby wool khaki tie. His trousers were tan chino. He wore brown jodhpur boots. He was chuckling.

Lawrence Badger cleared his throat. 'Uh, Alton?' he said.

Alton laughed delightedly. The laser printer nearest the corner of the room spat out a printed sheet. 'Come in, come in,' he said. He did not turn around.

Lawrence sat down in the swivel chair nearest the left end of the long table. 'What are you doing?' he said.

Alton turned around, grinning. 'Larry,' he said, 'it's beautiful. Yesterday there was a leak. Hans Lloyd up in Ottawa'd come to an agreement, secret, of course, after about three weeks of argle-bargle with Tom Denise down in Atlanta, where Tom will give him Dan Quisenberry in exchange for a player to be named later. And the two of them decide they're going to wait until today to announce it, so Bert Magazu won't find out about it and pull off something of his own to counteract it. Because of course the player to be named later was going to be Bill Madlock, who Bert doesn't want on Tom's team, playing in the same league as his.

'But,' Alton said, 'Hans can't keep a secret. Hans likes to gloat. He said enough on the phone to Harry Cohen in New York, so that Cohen figured out something was up. Harry got ahold of Bert in Los Angeles. Bert's on his way to Rio at the time. He can't make a deal of his own, and he can't claim Quisenberry on the waiver wire until Tom and Hans actually announce the deal. See, you have to waive down in your own league before you can ship a player to the other league. But failure to block a waiver deal – claim the player – is assent to it, and Bert has to catch a plane. If he does that, since it's a good long flight, by the time he gets himself checked in, in Rio, the league office here will be closed, and so will be the deal. So, you know what he did? He flew instead to Hong Kong, where it's tomorrow, and the first thing he did was get on the wire and file notice that no more waivers can be made because the deadline's past where he is. Which Hans in Ottawa said he couldn't do because the deadline isn't past where he is, and where Tom is. And Bert's manipulating the rules. At which point Magazu filed a protest of any deal that might be made here, today, under Rule 8A, which says the interleague trading deadline ends at midnight, July sixteenth, and it's now July seventeenth in Hong Kong. Which is where he is, and now we've got this great brouhaha over whether the league is in the eastern time zone of the United States, or wherever any owner happens to be at any given time.' He chuckled. 'So,' he said, 'I decided to suspend the transaction and gave both sides forty-eight hours to file briefs. And now Magazu's hired Flowers, Wilson and Malloy in Washington to present his case. And they've asked for extra time to master the league rules. Really wild stuff going on.'

'You spend your time on this,' Lawrence said.

Alton laughed again. 'My time,' he said, 'and also my money. You know where the Boston Badgers are now, even as we speak? First in the Ober League, is where, because of Carlton Fisk hitting homers like he has, and Gooden, naturally. This year I win the pennant. That's what I am going to do.'

'How much money's involved, again?' Lawrence said.

'Close to eighteen hundred bucks,' Alton said defensively, lowering himself onto the backless chair. The laser nearest the corner produced another document. The one beside it continued to disgorge sheet after sheet.

'Alton,' Lawrence said, 'is there any chance, perhaps, we might do some work today?'

Alton reared back. 'I'm working right now,' he said. He gestured toward the printer that was working steadily. 'I've got Cyclops on the Frolio case. Time you get back from lunch today, I'll have every nominal Model Nine-ninety owner between here and the Iron Curtain listed, catalogued, profiled, back-checked, with capsules of their key personnel.' He paused. 'I'm not saying,' he said, 'I'm not saying when we get all that data, we'll have the whole issue solved. That we'll know for sure exactly where the leak is, or which one those purchasers of record is the straw reselling them. All I've got for sure so far's a pretty strong link between an outfit called Dynamics A.G., Zurich, that I never heard of before, and a retailer in Madrid, name of Ashir Mohammed. And I don't know what use anybody named Ashir Mohammed in Spain could possibly have for twenty Model Nine-nineties. Only thing the damned things're good for's weapons design-slash-defeat. And the Spaniards aren't into that, least as far as I've found.

'But we've at least got a start on things, and by tomorrow we should have enough of a lead so the Bureau'll be satisfied Frolio's as concerned about this as the Agency is. Which for now's got to be all we can hope for – Jackie's company gets indicted for shipping those units to the East, he'll be in big-big trouble. They'll suspend all his government contracts until the case is tried, and by the time that happens, he'll be belly-up. There's no way to win that.'

'Is what you're doing legal, Alton?' Lawrence said.

Alton shrugged. 'Mostly,' he said. 'Obviously Frolio doesn't mind. He gave me their codes. The, ah, some of the others, well, they might not be *strictly* aware of what Cyclops can do, but they've got some idea. And they know I've developed it. I think, my guess is that as long's the Bureau and the Agency think you're probably on their side, they're not going to set up a stink. Unless you ask them if it's okay, browse a little in their files. In which case, then they would. But anyway, it doesn't, Cyclops doesn't leave a trace. No footprints, you know, Larry? Cyclops leaves no spoor.'

'So you've often said,' Lawrence said. 'But, if it did, if perhaps one of your, ah, sources, without your knowledge, has devised something that would let them know when Cyclops has been in, would we have a problem?'

'Negative,' Alton said. 'I reprogrammed Cyclops last month when I heard, maybe NCIC's putting in some kind of new detection. And what I did, I set it up so if Cyclops senses something wrong, which it would have to do, any system they might use, Cyclops terminates and calls for Morgan Le Fay. Which I've got standing by as back-up, set to go. Nobody can detect Morgan Le Fay, Larry. Nobody can find Morgan.'

'Then why not just use Morgan?' Lawrence said. 'Why take this chance you're taking?'

'Overkill,' Alton said. 'Morgan's too meticulous. Therefore, slow. And besides, she isn't that good at getting into things. Taking things out of things? Yes. Morgan's great at that. But getting access in the first instance? Morgan's too careful. Takes too long. We can't goldplate this stuff, you know. Time is money, Uncle.'

'Yes,' Lawrence said. He steepled his fingers. 'Alton,' he said, 'what I came in to see you for. I had a visitor this morning. Woman by the name of Barbara Gleason. Husband's name is Terry.'

'Ah,' Alton said. 'How is our old pal, Terry? Still dodging slanders from unkind persons, think he took a dive in The Friary case?'

'You think he did it?' Lawrence said. 'Got his hair wet, I mean?'

Alton shook his head twice. 'Uh uh,' he said. 'Terry's glands got the better of his judgment, sure, but he tried that case clean and mean. Wasn't anything he could do about Tibbetts. You and I both know that. It's just that it looked so bad when he got himself involved with Walker's sister. Very poor judgment, his part, but when his zipper's closed, Terry's an honorable man.'

'That's what I thought,' Lawrence said. 'That's what I told his wife. Who thinks he's having an affair. She said he's, they're living apart while he concentrates on that rackets trial in the federal court. "He claims it's because I'm a restless sleeper," she said, "but I know it's more than that. He's got another woman. He's at the Parker House."'

'Most likely, then, he is,' Alton said. 'Wives're good at finding out, little things like that. They're generally right. And he has done it before.' He paused. He studied Lawrence's face. 'You, ah, didn't take the case, I assume.'

'I'm not sure,' Lawrence said.

'Larry, Larry,' Alton said, his eyebrows going up. 'Domestic relations? Really, Larry. Has it finally happened to you? Have you finally lost your mind?'

'Well,' Lawrence said, 'I'm not really sure, but probably not. You see, some of the things she told me made me think that there might be considerably more going on, some greater implications in her husband's indiscretion, if he's being indiscreet, than she really understands. That might be of considerable interest to us.

'The woman in question, she thinks,' Lawrence said, 'is Christina Walker. Again.'

Alton's eyebrows came down. 'That *is* interesting,' he said. 'After all the hot water he got into before with her, why would he do it again? Guy's got a decent practice going now. Everything's nice and peaceful. What's he need another commotion for now? Is he that much in love, he looks her up again?'

'Or did she look him up?' Lawrence said.

'And if so,' Alton said, 'why? Why would she do that? He's still married. The wife smoked her out the last time she got hooked up with him. Lawfully wedded spouse won that one, hands down. Why seek more punishment? Christina shouldn't have a lot of trouble, finding a suitable man. Terry's a nice guy and all, but he's a good deal older'n she is, and she knows there's trouble there. Christina isn't stupid. Why do a thing like that, which is?'

'Well,' Lawrence said, 'what I thought might perhaps be the explanation is that she's not interested in resuming their romantic entanglement. That she might have something else in mind, and that he just happens to be the only person she could think of, or one of the relatively few persons, maybe, who could help her.'

'Where's her brother now?' Alton said. 'Is Beau James still in the pokey, or did he get out?'

'I don't know,' Lawrence said.

Alton made a note on a yellow pad. 'How about Sam Tibbetts,' he said, making another note. 'He got out, last spring. Do we know where Sam is these days?'

'No, we don't,' Lawrence said. 'Some of my old friends probably do, since they keep up with things. But we certainly do not.'

'You mean, Claire Naisbitt,' Alton said.

'Well,' Lawrence said, 'I would have *said* Neville, but yes, Claire would be who would know. Or Fiona, far as that goes. Either one of them could find out pretty fast.'

'Sam was Christina's main man long before The Friary case, and she got involved with Gleason,' Alton said.

'That is correct,' Lawrence said. The printer nearest the corner produced two more sheets of paper.

'But Sam was supposed to have a lot of money squirreled away some place, when he got put in Bridgewater,' Alton said. 'Armored cars from here to Rhode Island. Lots and lots of money, that nobody ever found.'

'So John Bigelow believed at the time,' Lawrence said. 'John was very exercised about that fact, when Sam was committed for observation instead of being convicted and put in prison for life. He calculated Sam's share of the Contingent's loot was over half a million dollars. And how much was the actual take from The Friary, all that dope and stuff? We never found that out, but it was over half a million. Almost had to be.'

'Probably 'way high,' Alton said. 'Still, though, certainly more than enough so that some people're still probably quite interested.

Longhairs shifted their attention from pouring chicken blood into Selective Service files, started knocking off armored cars and then stealing people's drugs, tacked a lot of people off. Even if the money's gone, they're probably still mad.'

'Now,' Lawrence said, 'given all that, plus the fact that Mrs. Gleason included in her tale of woe the fact that she suspects her home to be under surveillance by a party or parties unknown ... '

'Why would she be under surveillance?' Alton said. 'Is she fooling around some, too?'

'Assures me she is not,' Lawrence said. 'Her inference is that her husband is trying to fabricate a case of adultery against her, in order to block her in the event that she makes one against him.'

'Mexican stand-off,' Alton said.

'Something along that line,' Lawrence said. 'She says at least every other day, in the morning before her husband normally leaves for work, and around six thirty, seven in the evening, when he'd ordinarily get home, an unfamiliar car cruises slowly by their house. Which is in a secluded residential area where unfamiliar cars are uncommon. What she said to me is that the people who drive down their street are people who either live on their street, or are visiting people who do. It's not a street that anyone would use as a back way to Route Twenty-four, or One-twenty-eight, or anything like that.'

'And she thinks it's a private dick,' Alton said.

'I presume so,' Lawrence said. 'Given what I see in the case that she apparently does not, I'm inclined to think it may be someone rather more sinister than that. Someone who thinks that Terry Gleason sooner or later will lead him to Sam Tibbetts and his cache, if he tracks him long enough. I saw no reason to alarm her, though, so I kept that to myself. If some remnant of that Bolivian

Connection, or whatever they called themselves, is prowling around her property, better leave that quiet. At least for the time being.'

'She get a good look at the car?' Alton said.

'Yes,' Lawrence said. 'Not only that, but the first three digits of the license plate. It's a maroon Mercedes Benz, the two-seater, and the first three digits on the plate are two-nine-two.'

Alton laughed. 'It's the Cowboy,' he said. He slapped the table with his left palm. He stood up and jammed his hands in his pockets. He was grinning. 'It's Cowboy Fred Consolo,' he said. 'Freddie is a cop. Terry hasn't got a tail on his wife – the cops've got one on Terry.'

'So,' Lawrence said, 'what do we do now?'

'Talk to John Richards, I think,' Alton said. 'Go and see the man and find out what's going on.'

30

Alton Badger met John Richards late in the morning in the parking lot off Route 6A in Sandwich. They walked north along the beach toward the eastern end of the Cape Cod Canal.

'You know,' Richards said, 'I was a cop for a lot of years. Over half my life. Thirty-five diligent years. And I loved what I did. It was fun. It was fun in the beginning, fresh from the war. Being a cop's much better'n being a soldier; you're a soldier and the other guy's *supposed* to shoot at you, whereas when you're cop, he *may* shoot you, but he'd goddamned right well better not because some other cop will get him for it if he does. So you've got an advantage as a cop that you didn't have in the First Marines. No guarantee, but an advantage, and that was sort of a relief. Made things pleasanter.

'And the amazing part of it is,' Richards said, 'the completely astonishing part of it was that the day I decided to retire it was still fun. I didn't decide to hang it up because I'd gotten bored, or because I was forced to, reached a certain age, or, thank God, because I was sick. I just woke up one morning and said to myself: "This is the day. You've done it long enough, and now it's time to do something else." And I got dressed and I went downstairs and I said to Angela: "This is the day." And she said: "You're sure." And I said I was, and that was it.

'Now that was four years ago,' he said. 'Four years ago this September. We've got a quiet life down here. Take care of my investments in the morning, bother my broker, read the papers, keep myself occupied. Drive around in my Continental. You know that's the first new car I've ever actually owned? I told Angela that morning: "And here's another thing," I said, "ever since nineteen-forty-six I've wanted a Lincoln Continental, and tomorrow I'm going down to Fred Gillis's and buy me one of them." And she said: "Good. You've earned it and you should. But why tomorrow? Let's go down after dinner tonight."

'I usually have lunch at the club with the lads. Maybe play some cards in the winter afternoons. This time of year, if there's a breeze, take the boat out for a few hours. Angela's at the library four days a week in the forenoons, and at night we either stop for a bite at Tancredi's or I'll destroy a perfectly good piece of meat on the barbecue. Glass of wine, watch a little television, maybe read a book. It's a nice life.

'Gives you something I guess I never had before,' he said. 'Time to think. They'll tell you retirement's dull, that it's boring, and I think that's probably true, if *you* are dull and boring. But if you're like I was, and am, saw a lot of things as you went along that you would've liked to linger over a lot longer'n you had time to spare, think about what they meant, then when you stop working for somebody else and doing what they tell you's got to be done, you can go back over them and figure them out. It's a real luxury.

'Now this business that you're telling me about,' Richards said. 'This is the kind of thing that I've thought about in general terms, several times. Not The Friary gang, I mean, not in particular. But the whole general idea of what I was doing all those years, when I was enforcing the law. Or trying to, at least. Just what exactly was it? All those statutes and rules, and all that glossy shit, that we were out there running around like mad, trying to catch people and bash them on the head? What did it all mean? Assuming it meant something. Why were we trying to do this?

'And the reason was, I decided,' he said, 'we were trying to keep it down to a dull roar. What we *thought* we were doing, while we were working so hard at it we didn't have time to think about it – what we thought we were doing was maintaining the peaceable kingdom. Repelling the boarders, putting down mutinies, dispersing unruly crowds. But what it amounted to was keeping our eyes peeled for the guys whose behavior displeased us, assuming it must make everybody else mad because it pissed us off. And then hunting through the books for some law somewhere that said they couldn't do that. Then arresting them and putting them in jail. Peace officers: that's what cops were when Bobby Peel invented us, and that's what we are today.

'Now,' he said, 'when I was a peace officer, things like The Friary had a tendency to *annoy* me. *Personally.* It's not *right*, somebody should be able to come busting into a man's place of business on a Sunday when he's trying to relax with a few whoors and his pal. Sure, they were hookers, and Nichols and Abbate, they were pushers and bookies and pimps and bad boys. Father Flanagan was wrong – there *is* such a thing as a bad boy. Hundreds of 'em, in fact. But that doesn't give anybody the right to rob them, and *shoot* them, when they're indoors with all their clothes off, getting nice blow jobs and having a fine time. Anybody's going to interfere with them, while they're doing that, *we* should be the ones. And since we never had enough probable cause to go in and do that, nobody else should've, either. Usurping our power like that. Infringing on our jurisdiction. It really made me mad.

'Well,' he said, 'at the time that was good, that The Friary and all the other crimes we investigated made me mad like that, because I did a better job'n I would've if I didn't take them personally. But now when I look back on it, you know, I can see that some of the things about the law that used to exasperate me, make my life inconvenient, were actually good ideas. Sound reasoning, from wiser men than I am. Those armored-car heists that we know Tibbetts and his whole gang pulled, in the days when he had a whole gang and not just a few strays and crazies – by the time we made the collar, Limitations'd run. On the first two of them at least. Not on the second two, or the conspiracy that'd probably've let us charge them with the first two, but you get my meaning. And that was society's way of saying: "Okay, robbing people's a bad thing to do, but it's not as serious a bad thing as killing them. So, you cops there, you got six years to grab the guys that rob people, and if you don't catch them by then, we're gonna forget about it. But, you bad guys there, you'd better not kill anybody while you're robbing them, or just for the fun of it, because we're not gonna tolerate that brand of foolishness and if we *ever* catch you, you're gonna pay for it."

'It's a matter of proportion,' Richards said. 'It's maybe a good thing if you don't have a sense of it, or a highly developed one, at least, while you're still a cop, because you're not paid to be a philosopher; you're paid to catch bad guys. That's what the courts and the lawyers are for; they're supposed to deal with all that balancing shit. But where you've got a guy like Fred, who has no sense of it all, then it becomes awful important to have somebody over him that's riding herd on him all the time, making sure he doesn't get the bit between his teeth and just go galloping off in all directions at once, using his badge and his authority any way that suits him, so long as he likes the results.

'My guess,' Richards said, 'my guess is that since it's summertime and things're slow, and Dave Osgood's sent his life out to be rebuilt and gotten it back in better shape'n it was in the first place, nobody in the Norfolk DA's office's paying much attention to what Cowboy Fred is doing. Dave, well, he went through a lot, and I thought, I thought when he got married the second time, married June McNeil there, I thought that'd fix him up. That he'd get his grip back on things. And he did. But on different things – his wife and family – not his office. So now instead of being gone most of August, so you can't find him because he's at the track, now he's out of sight the whole damned summer. Down at his place on the Cape in July. Up at the track in August. Making up for what he missed, the first time around. So Fred, well, he lacks supervision, and when Freddie lacks supervision, things have a way of getting sideways.

'Fred was enraged,' Richards said, 'when Tibbetts got acquitted on that crackpot insanity defense, as everybody from the AG on down was, and now it's seven years later and all the rest of us've calmed down, and Fred is still enraged.' He sighed. 'That boy doesn't have enough on his mind. He needs to keep himself occupied, and he doesn't. What he does is all he ever thinks about.

Not what it means, or whether it's right, but how he's going to do it and how soon he'll get it done.

'You called me,' Richards said, 'and I thought about it, and I said to myself: "I think I will make some calls here and there, see what's going on." After all, God wanted us to be ignorant, He wouldn't've given us the phone. So I did that and I found out some things.' He began to check them off on the fingers of his left hand.

'The only file that's still open is the Handley murder case. Now you got to keep in mind that the way we finally bagged those bastards for The Friary, without getting anybody else killed, was by using blind informer evidence to get out indictments. And then getting damned lucky on the arrest and bagging enough circumstantial so we didn't have to surface the informer.

'Didn't have that option with the Handley killing,' Richards said. 'My old friend Howard fucked up the ballistics on that one bad enough so even though I knew it was one of those two twenty-twos that was used to shoot the girl, we couldn't prove it. To do it, we would've had to've had either an informer who'd stand up – which Mackenzie would not've – or a rat who was present when the foul deed was done. Which we did not have, and that's why the file's still open.

'That, I think,' Richards said, 'is what Fred has got. Or thinks he's got, at least. Fred thinks he's got a big fat rat, who will sink some long white teeth into Tibbetts, front a jury.'

'The girl,' Badger said. 'You think that it's Christina and that's why she's back with Gleason? To protect her from Fred?'

'No,' Richards said. 'We did a full-field on her when she showed up at the trial. She was nowhere near those birds when the Handley kid went down. Hadn't been away from them long, but she was back in school. Didn't see the murder, and no one confessed to her.'

'Then why's she seeing Gleason? And why's Gleason seeing her?' Badger said. 'Dangerous for him. No beach day for her.'

Richards shrugged. 'Mutual benefit,' he said. 'She's scared of something. He needs something. You've seen her. You know what temptation is. Terry's a good lawyer, but he's not perfect either. When she came in to us, after the trial, she was a frightened lady. Terry believed her, that the reason she was scared was Sam'd think she was the one that turned them in – that when he got out of Bridgewater, he'd have her killed. Myself, I agreed that she was scared, but I always wondered if maybe it was really us she feared.'

'Really,' Badger said.

'Absolutely,' Richards said. 'Abso-bloomin'-lutely. She was a beautiful kid, and she was obviously really upset. Brother convicted of murder? Ex-boyfriend in the booby hatch, or he would've been sunk too? Who wouldn't be upset? But I always kind of wondered if maybe what was bothering her mostly was that she'd been involved in some the shit that those guys pulled. The armored cars, I mean. And, maybe, the Handley killing. She knew we still had two Jane Does and a John Doe on the rest of that indictment – we could try it anytime, and if one the dykes'd decided to get even, nail somebody else, she could've been the one. That she was coming in and flinging herself into our arms so she could keep an eye on us, see which way the wind was blowing, give herself a little edge, time to get out if it seemed to be shifting in her direction.

'Those two dykes, you know,' he said, 'those two dykes did not like Christina a whole lot. She wouldn't fingerfuck them, I guess – they were not pals with her. If one of them'd had the brains, which neither of them did, to look at their situation realistically, and decide to see what she could get for spilling her guts to us, she probably could've put Christina in a mess of shit of her own. I think that's what Christina was afraid of. Not of Sam recruiting someone on the outside to kill her. Not of her brother getting life in the slammer. No, of us making a case against her that'd put her behind bars for a while. She was bawling her eyes out to us, and making eyes at Terry, because she needed information and that was a way to get it. That is what I thought.

'Terry didn't agree with me,' he said. He laughed. 'Stiff prick'll believe anything.'

'So, then,' Badger said, 'now we're seven years later, eight from The Friary, fifteen from the first armored car, and all of it's history long gone. Why is Fred tailing Gleason?'

'Fred thinks she's got the missing piece,' Richards said. 'The missing piece, his puzzle. I don't know what he thinks she knows, but he thinks he needs it. She evidently thinks so too. That's why she went to Terry. If Fred had any doubts before, that took care of them. Now he'll never let her go. Won't let Terry, either.

'Fred likes symmetry,' Richards said. 'He likes things to be perfect. Especially when they're not.' He laughed. 'It's funny,' he said, 'the different ways people react to things that they can't do anything about. Like time going by, and that stuff. The sensible ones, like me, of course, we pass our own private Limitations, and we say to ourselves after whatever number of years it is've gone past, we say: "Right. The hell with it. If I'd've had the chance to do something about it back in seventy-seven, or whatever year, I would've taken it. But now? Too late. Forget it." And that's healthy, I think. Restful, at least. Man has to get his rest.

'Fred,' he said, 'Fred came out of the MDC like some sort of moonshot, like they tied a rocket to his ass and launched him. And we, the State Police, were going to give him back the kind of hard-ass pride he'd had when he was Eighty-second Airborne. Kicking ass and taking names, but no prisoners. The first major assignment he was on with me, when we arrested Tibbetts and the rest of them. Floated down the Deerfield River in a houseboat with June McNeil stretched out in a bikini on the roof – Lord but she had the best tits I've ever seen on a cop – he thought he was back in Nam. Jumps in the water, over his head, carrying a twelve-bore, plus a belt, and a three-five-seven mag, with five speedloaders, in this goddamned plastic bag – *knowing* he couldn't swim. The bastard walked ashore. Surfaced like the Creature from the Blue Lagoon. Did it ever cross his mind, might be some sharp-shooter up on the sundeck with a sniper rifle crosshaired on his bubbles? Doubt it. I think he was disappointed. That we didn't fire a shot.'

Richards stopped and faced Badger. 'What else can I tell you?' he said. 'Every generation produces its own variety of freaks. I was, I suppose I was one the freaks of mine – Hitler and Tojo mutated us. We got the idea young, we're supposed to maintain order. And that is what we did, all the rest of our damned lives. Then came the one that developed Tibbetts and Cowboy Fred. One of them looks at Ho Chi Minh and sees the same Tojo I saw, and he goes overboard. The other one looks at LBJ and sees Hitler, and his porch light goes out. So they're that kind of freak. Fred's nowhere near as dangerous as Tibbetts was – maybe still is – and at least Fred's on our side. But he's whoopy, Alton, whoopy. Fred is still a freak.

'But freaks have a short useful life. Unless, at least, they adapt. All around us now, the whole damned world has changed.

Tibbetts, Walker, the girl, Terry Gleason, your uncle and I – does Larry still cavort with the spooks, the way he used to do? Of course not; he's too old. Everybody involved in The Friary trial's gotten older. We're all different now. We know it's not the same. The things we all saw that introduced us to each other at whatever ages we were when they happened: those things're over with, and gone.

'Tell Barbara Gleason that,' he said. 'Tell her you've talked to some people and the guy that's following Terry's a cop with an obsession. Guy that didn't change. Nothing more than that. Tell her that you talked to me, and I said to forget it. Those days are over with. Fred's an avatar, and he's out there all alone.'

31

At 5:20 A.M., Christina Walker awoke in apartment 2N at Waterford Village on Route 4. She got out of bed without making any noise. In the half-light that entered the room at the edges of the blackout drapes, she removed her short white nightgown and dropped it on the bed. From the top of the black steamer trunk at the foot of the bed she picked up a white bra, already fastened, stepped into it and pulled it up over her breasts. Bending again, she picked up white panties and put them on. She put on a tan cotton sleeveless sweater and faded blue jeans that she buttoned but did not zip. She padded barefoot across the thick yellow shag rug of the bedroom onto the thick green shag rug of the living room. At the door to the hall she picked up a large straw bag and put it over her shoulder. She opened the door silently, partway, and slowly removed the strip of duct tape she had put on the bolt of the snap lock the night before, allowing it to emerge gradually from the mechanism. She took a deep breath, opened the door further, dropped into a crouch in the hall, and closed the door as quickly as she could without making noise, wincing as the snap lock clicked home.

Holding the straw bag on her left shoulder with her right hand, she ran bent from the waist on tiptoe until she reached the back stairwell. Inside it, hidden from the lens of the television camera in the corridor she sat down on the top step and took another deep breath. She rummaged in the straw bag and found her Adidas sneakers. She pulled them on, tied them, stood up, zipped her jeans, and went down to the parking lot.

At 5:55 the clock radio in the dim bedroom of apartment 2N clicked on, midway through a performance of Bach's Third Brandenburg concerto. The music sounded at moderate volume in the speaker in the white van at the MediMart in the shopping plaza some seventeen hundred feet north of Waterford Village. Initially it made Michael Fitzroy stir fitfully under his trench-coat on the floor of the van. He fought off the interruption of his sleep for about seven minutes, working his dry mouth on the morning residue of the previous night's cigarettes and coffee.

At 6:03, Christina Walker parked her silver Volkswagen GTI outside the easterly wing of the Commodore Motel west of the Union Street rotary under Route 3 in Braintree. She fished in her straw bag again and came up with a tabbed key numbered 4. She got out of her car, locked it, and went to the door numbered 4. She opened it and entered the dark room. She closed the door and allowed her eyes to adjust from the sunrise to the gloom. She heard the shower running in the bathroom. She saw light between the bathroom door and its threshold. She went to the nearest of the two easy chairs set against the westerly wall and put her bag down on it. She dug into the bag again and groped until she found her toothbrush and a small tube of Crest toothpaste. She started toward the bathroom.

At 6:06 Fitzroy surrendered to consciousness and sat up on the floor of the van. He rubbed his eyes. He worked his tongue against the deposits in his mouth. He shook his head, his shaggy blond hair falling into his eyes. He said: 'Arr.' Gripping the equipment counter with his left hand, he cast off the trenchcoat with his right and pulled himself upright. He intentionally shivered his entire body. 'Ahh, *shit*,' he said, 'got to get *rolling* here.' He started toward the front of the van.

Christina Walker knocked before she entered the bathroom of the motel room. The shower was loud on the Fibreglas walls of the enclosure and she got no answer. She went into the room filled with lighted steam and tapped on the glass door of the shower on her right. 'Hi, honey, I'm home,' she said. The indistinct figure lurched against the enclosure.

The door opened quickly partway. Terry Gleason's red face under white shampoo lather and black hair peered out. 'Jesus, you startled me,' he said. 'Everything all right?'

She held up the toothbrush and toothpaste. 'Everything except I've got to brush my teeth,' she said. 'And also take a leak. Just go right on with what you're doing. I won't bother you.'

At 6:10 Fitzroy unlocked and opened the door of the van without interrupting his gargling of Scope mouthwash. Bending from the waist, he spat it onto the parking lot. Then he clambered down to the pavement, closed the van, and walked around to the back of the drugstore. He crossed the loading area and made his way into the scrub pine grove that bordered the brook in the back. He stood hidden from the road and urinated into the brook, farting once as he did so.

At 6:12, Gleason emerged from the shower. Walker was standing in front of the basin, scrubbing her face with a washcloth. Gleason took a towel from the rack beside the shower and began drying himself. 'Almost finished,' she said. 'You can have this in a minute.'

'Take your time,' he said. 'You're early as it is.'

At 6:14, back in the van, Fitzroy filled his mug from his Thermos of coffee, capped the depleted jug and replaced it on top of the steel box at the front of the van. He turned to the back of the van and sat down on the chair at the counter. He drank deeply from the mug as he focused on the TV screens. When he inspected the picture from the parking lot camera he said: 'Oh my *God*,' and put the mug down. He leaned forward and manipulated the zoom control to produce a close-up picture of Walker's parking space. It remained vacant. The speaker receiving noise from the apartment stopped delivering music and an announcer came on. Fitzroy put his head in his hands. 'Holy shit,' he said. 'Holy, holy, shit. Christ on crutches. Holy shit. Holy goddamned shit.'

At 6:17, Gleason with his towel wrapped around his waist finished shaving, wiping the last of the lather from his neck with a hand towel. Walker sat on the commode next to him with her pants down, urinating. 'Not,' he said, 'not that I don't admire your dedication and your zeal, all right? Because I do. But are you really that convinced? That they've got your place so bugged there's one in the toilet, too?'

'Look,' she said, finishing and reaching for tissue, 'I don't know, all right? So, better to assume there is, and don't use anything in there either.'

'Because they very seldom do that anymore,' Gleason said, applying English Leather aftershave lotion. 'If they're after the Mafia, maybe, but on your standard surveillance they don't bother. Because all you ever get is flatulence and rushing waters, and it's not worth the trouble.'

She stood up, pulling up her panties and jeans and fastening the zipper. 'I don't care,' she said. 'I know they're watching me. I just don't know how much. I'm going to make it just as damned difficult as I can for them. Maybe they'll still lock onto me. Maybe they've got some sort of bug on my car so they can find out where I go with an airplane or something. Maybe they have. But I can't help that. What I can help, I will.'

She opened the bathroom door and went into the dark bedroom. She turned on the lamp on the table between the chairs and used the switch at the door to turn on the two conical fixtures over the head of the queen-sized bed. The right side had been slept in; the left was virtually undisturbed. 'Huh,' she said, 'bet the maids in this joint don't find many beds like that one in the morning.'

Gleason in the towel was pawing through a blue nylon duffel bag on the luggage rack next to the open closet. On the rod in the closet there was a grey lightweight suit; a zippered suitbag was next to it. He found a tee shirt and jockey shorts in the duffel. He dropped the towel and pulled on the shorts and undershirt. 'I could've slept on the floor last night,' he said. 'Surprised I didn't, in fact. Time I got here I was too tired even to dream. All I wanted in the world was to get horizontal and remain that way for seven consecutive hours. No interruptions. No one next to me having nightmares, flailing around and grabbing me at two-thirty or so, whacking me with her elbows, kicking at me with her feet.

319

I've been on trial for thirty-eight days since Memorial Day. My client's a desperate man, in every sense of the word. For the amount of money that he's paid, he thinks he's entitled to his lawyer's full attention, and he expects that full attention to include complete alertness and enough presence of mind to protect his interests.

'Well,' Gleason said, 'I think he's right.' He took a white button-down shirt out of the bag and put it on. 'And even if I didn't, I would act as though I did. Because, like I say, he's a desperate man. In no mood for arguments. Which means I have to find some way to get enough rest to function, and that means I have to get myself out of that house.'

'But why this dump?' Christina said, sitting down on the chair nearest the door. 'Last time you had to do this, you were in the Parker House. Why come all the way out here, and then fight the traffic back in the morning?'

'Because,' he said, opening the suitbag and taking out the trousers of a dark blue poplin suit, 'while I charged Phil Iannuci a generous fee, I charged it last September, and since the first of May I haven't taken on any new cases. I don't mean I'm broke, but when you're two months into what looks like a three-month trial, more or less, you tend to look closely at the difference between a hundred bucks a night and twenty-four-fifty. Now, if Barbara'd do what I suggested, which was either we rent out the house in Chilmark if she wasn't going to go there, or else have her take the kids and go there and leave me alone here, there wouldn't be any need to think about it. Either we'd have the money coming in for the rental, which would be about fourteen hundred a week – plus the tax write-off next year because we rented it for profit – or she'd be down there, thrashing around, and I could sleep in my own bed in my own house in Canton.' He snorted. 'Christ,' he said, 'we spill more in a year now than I used to make.'

'Do you think she's crazy?' Christina said.

He picked up black tasseled loafers from the floor of the closet and took dark blue socks from the duffel. He walked over to the foot of the bed and sat down to put them on. 'Mildly,' he said. 'And intermittently. Not clinically, so she doesn't know what she's doing. But in the ordinary sense of the word? Yeah, she is crazy. She's never gotten over when you and I had our adventure, and she never will, either. She thinks I licensed her with that to do anything she wants to me ever afterwards. Whenever she feels like it, she punishes me again. And she's never going to stop.'

He stood up and returned to the duffel. He took out a blue and red striped tie and went into the bathroom. 'You should've divorced her back then,' Christina said. 'Whether we stayed together or not, you should've done it then.'

'I know it,' he said in the bathroom. 'But it's *now* that I know it. Not then. And if I had known it then, I was in no position to do it. Because I was just building a practice and I didn't have the dough. And now that I've got the dough, well, I still can't do it.'

'Guilt feelings?' Christina said.

'For hurting Barbara?' he said, coming out of the bathroom. He went to the suitbag and took out the coat. He put it on, shooting his cuffs. He walked to the table next to the right of the bed and collected his black wallet and stainless-steel Tudor diver's watch. 'No,' he said, snapping the watch bracelet around his left wrist. 'It wasn't anybody's fault that by the time that I met you, the marriage'd turned into a puppet show, with Barbara pulling the strings. Or if it was anybody's fault, it wasn't mine – it was hers.

'No,' he said, 'but am I afraid I would have guilt feelings, if I divorced her now? Yes, and with good reason.' He sat down on the bed again and leaned forward with his forearms on his thighs. 'I haven't finished with the kids. And I know I haven't. If I dropped out on them now, became an occasional visitor in their lives, I'd be taking risks that I know I shouldn't take.

'They seem to be in pretty good shape,' he said. 'Terry's grades're good, and he's not a bad ballplayer. He'll get into Tufts, I think, which is where he wants to go next year. Joanne went through a little punk phase last winter when her hair was green and spiked up and she was wearing about nine pounds of earrings, but at least she didn't shave one side of her head the way some of her friends did, and I think she's back on this planet now. Philip's got his problem, but otherwise he's a fine, nice kid. With some fairly expensive help, he should be able to overcome it. It's a mild case that he's got.

'Maybe I flatter myself,' he said, 'but I think I had something to do with all that. I didn't leave them, when I really wanted to, all alone with a woman whose system of values consists solely and entirely of social standing points and calculations. I know Terry's aware, responsible adults're interested in something more than the tennis ladder at the club and what's on sale at Bloomingdale's, who went to Hawaii last winter when you had to settle for a weekend in New York.

'When Joanne started hanging around with a group of kids who were headed directly for trouble,' he said, 'her father was home every night to work on her delusions, check her out for drugs, flog her about her homework, and generally make sure she had to work so hard to keep me satisfied she wouldn't have enough energy left to meet the demands of her peer group. She's going to be all right.'

He stood up. 'Philip,' he said, 'well, we'll see what the future holds. That's why I'm hanging around. This's his important time. Talk to me five years from now and I'll give you a report. He seems to be doing all right. Let's go get coffee. There's a quick-'n'-dirty up the road.'

She hesitated. 'Is it safe, you think?' she said.

He grinned. 'Look,' he said, 'the evasive tactics you've been taking, there's no way they can find you. And if Barbie-doll's got someone out looking for me, he missed me when I came here last night, because it was almost ten and I had the road to myself. No one was tailing me.'

She stood up. 'I hate living like this,' she said.

He grasped her upper right arm gently. 'So do I,' he said. 'But the reason that we're doing it is, the way we lived before.'

32

'The first three years,' Christina Walker said over the remains of scrambled eggs and her third cup of coffee, 'I didn't go to see him. There wasn't any need to. I knew how he'd react. I didn't like what my brother'd turned into, but I knew what it was, and what he'd do if I did something.'

Gleason sat across from her in the center of one of the three booths beside the northerly window of the Red Ball Diner on Mason Street in Braintree. Down the hill below them on Route 3, northbound traffic to Boston increased steadily. Outside the entrance to the diner, men in business suits selected newspapers from among the four vending machines, came in and took places at the counter; they folded the papers twice and read segments of several stories before refolding to new pages, avoiding encroachments into each other's spaces.

Two men and a woman in white NYNEX telephone company

hardhats sat in the booth behind Gleason; they talked about catching bluefish off Minot's Light in Scituate. 'It's all a buncha bullshit,' one of the men said. 'I grew up around this area. Used to fish Hull Gut. Get some stripers, get some mackerel, maybe foul-hook your stray flounder, let your eel gig get too deep. Then all a sudden: bluefish. Jumpin' inna boats. Got them out there fightin' for the first chance, take your hook. Now you read it inna papers: "Bluefish dyin' out. Must be the pollution. Prolly Pilgrim Nuclear plant." Bullshit: that's what I say. Nothin' but bullshit. Fish come in and fish go out. It's the fish, decide.' He stood up with his companions and dropped coins on the table. 'Either the fish or God.' They walked toward the register.

At the table behind Christina, a grizzled man in his fifties in a white New England Patriots tee shirt listened stoically as a man in his late twenties talked in a low voice about his wife's insistence on working, and his deep disapproval of it. 'I tell her,' he said, 'I try to tell the bitch: "Look, I married you because I wanted a wife. And I needed a wife. If I'd've wanted a goddamned sales clerk in Filene's, I would've gone down the goddamned plaza and gotten one of them. I didn't want a goddamned roommate that's so tired every night she goes to sleep before the goddamned news is over. I wanted a *wife*." And she doesn't listen to me, doesn't hear one word I say.'

The older man wore a blue and white nylon mesh cap with a panel above the visor lettered: 'Obviously you've mistaken me for someone who gives a shit.' He cleared his throat. He said: 'Well, I don't know. Your mother, she always said she wished she had a job. After you kids grew up. She didn't have nothing to do. I still think that's what did it, why she sits there all day shit-faced, staring at the wall. She didn't have nothing to do, after you kids grew up. Maybe, maybe you should just shut up and let her do it.'

'I knew what Jimmy thought of me, by then,' Christina said. 'God knows, he hadn't made any secret of it. It was bad even before you guys caught him and Sam, and I didn't happen to be there. Like the least I could've done was get myself captured too. I was afraid of him before that. Afterwards, I was really scared.'

'We didn't have a warrant for you,' Gleason said. 'We never had any case against you in The Friary.'

'But if I'd been there,' she said, 'if I'd've been in the camp in Deerfield, you, cops would've picked me up.'

'Oh sure,' he said. 'No question. But then we would've had to let you go. We didn't have any evidence you were in The Friary.'

'What Mom says doesn't matter,' the younger man behind Christina said as the older man got up and produced a wad of dollar bills from his left pants pocket. 'What matters's what she did. And she raised the three of us. Which is what I want Patricia to do. When the kids're grown up, that's different. Then she can get a job.'

'Your mother,' the older man said, releasing the elastic band around the bills and counting off four of them, 'your mother says that that's too late. That you can't get anything good by the time the kids're grown, because you don't know anything.'

The younger man got out of the booth and hitched up his pants. 'Doesn't matter what Mom thinks,' he said. 'Doesn't matter what she says, whether she's right or wrong. Doesn't matter what I think, either. Not to old Patricia. I want her to stay home and raise the damned kids. And she just flat won't do it.' He left coins on the table. They went toward the register opposite the door.

'Well,' she said, 'I wasn't. In The Friary. I was long gone by then. I, when it dawned on me they were serious about Emmy, that they really were going to off her, that was when I said: "Hey, no, this is too much." I raised hell with Jimmy about that. I said: "Hey, all right? You guys, you guys can't do this. I mean, the whole prin-ciple here, the reason we're all together and living like this, it's supposed to be because we're against people doing this to people, no matter what they do." Because that was how I could justify it, you know? The robberies, I mean. That nobody was getting hurt. That we were going in and taking what we needed and not hurting anybody, even if the way we did it was to make them think we're going to. With the guns and everything.

'And he wouldn't listen to me,' she said. 'He got mad at me, in fact. Jimmy was absolutely ripped, and I just couldn't figure it out. And I said: "Jesus, Beau, what is this shit? I mean, first of all, the first thing you do when I come in, when I get involved with Sam, the first thing you do is try to keep me out." And he did, too. He was in my face all the time. And I thought, you know, it was because I'm his baby sister and the sex thing bothered him. I wasn't even seventeen, and Sam was twenty-two, and even if Jimmy did think Sam was God and would do anything he said, he didn't want his god fucking his baby sister. I thought that's what it was.

'But it was also,' she said, 'those guys, I think about it some-times now, and it all seems so long ago and strange. Here it is, it's over sixteen years ago that I met Sam, and I can relate to that all right, because it seems like a century. Something that happened to somebody else, I couldn't possibly've done and Jimmy could not have done. Because none of it – you look back on it and none of it makes any sense. It didn't make any sense then, either, when

327

we were doing it, and yet if you'd asked us then, asked any of us, explain how what we did was something that was really good, we would've looked at you like you were nuts and said: "What's the matter with you, right? We're against fascist domination." And all that rally stuff. "And what we're doing's what we have to do to put an end to it." And that was enough for us.

'Sam,' she said, 'well, you've met him. It all made perfect logic when Sam explained the reasons. Andrea was the cookie jar, the cash box for the Contingent. And that was perfectly all right. It was the way that things should be. When we needed money, well, Sam or Beau would say to her that we needed some. And she would get it for us. Let me tell you something: If I ever get any money, and it's going to be for my kids, if I ever have any kids, I can tell you right this minute that those kids are not going to get their hands on a dime of it until they're at least thirty. Because all that money Andrea had, all the dough she gave to Sam – all she was doing with it was hiring guys to fuck her. Make her think that she belonged.

'You'd've asked her, you know, why she was giving Sam and them, forty, fifty grand a year, she knew all the lyrics and you'd get such a bunch of propaganda your ears'd ring for a week. And she really thought she was, that that's what she was doing – financing the revolution. Making amends for the way her grandfathers and her father and her poor dopey mother out there in Atherton'd been exploiting the lower classes and the powerless, all the years they'd been on earth.

'What a pathetic lot of shit,' Christina said. 'Would've been bad enough if she hadn't really, if she didn't really believe it. If it was just something she pretended because she didn't like the idea she was buying guys for sex and so they'd let her hang around. Feel like she was part of something. But she did believe it. At the time, she really did believe it. And as long as she kept on believing it, well, Sam let her stay around.

'Which naturally was how *I* could stay around,' Christina said. 'I used to sit around and think how pathetic Andrea was, because I could see what was going on. And I felt superior. I'd never do something like that. Not old Christina Walker, boy. Let anybody take advantage of me like that? Not this hip, smart chick. But of course the only reason I could do that, feel that way about her and myself, was because she was doling out the money. Then, when she got so serious about Glenn, and Sam and Jimmy began to think they couldn't trust them, either one of them, well you had a situation where something had to give. Because either way, it didn't matter. Either they couldn't trust Glenn because they had no respect for Andrea, and if he could fall for her then he must be a piece of shit that'd fink out on them some day, or else they couldn't trust Glenn because Andrea wasn't coming up with the cash the way she used to, and he must be the one talking her out of it. Telling her that Sam and Beau were playing her for a sucker.

'So it all came together,' she said. 'They started, they planned the first one there, the Danvers job, and when I caught on what they're doing, I said: "Hey," you know? I mean: "Protests and symbolic acts're one thing, but this here, using guns? I thought that's what we were against. People using guns." And they were furious. They said: "Hey, grow up, little girl. You're a woman now. This's the real world we're in. Takes money to operate. People do this all the time, only with laws and stuff. They decide what they need to oppress the masses, and they pass the laws to do it. See what they need and take it. And that's all we're doing here."

'And I went along,' she said. 'I didn't, I wasn't at the actual jobs, but the only reason I wasn't was because they needed someone to be in the catch car and switch the loot after the job. If they'd've decided, if Jimmy and Sam'd trusted me enough, or thought they had to have me at the actual hold-up, I would have been with them. I would've been scared, to be, but more scared not to be. I could see them, I could see the two of them, and one is my own brother, I could see them working on each other, playing off each other, feeding off each other. And I knew, or I started to know, these guys were getting crazy.

'I really believe that now,' she said. 'I really believe, I think when Jimmy started out with Sam, when he first came under Sam's influence – which was long before I knew Sam, when they were out there on the Coast – I really think it's possible Jimmy was just so caught up in the war and the whole thing that he really, and Sam too, probably, that they really believed what they were doing was right and noble and just. I do believe that. I don't believe Sam, when he was starting out, I don't believe he was out to manipulate people and just use them, any way he could. Not in the beginning. And I don't think he was thinking that, well, maybe he'd become the new Jesse James as soon's he found a way. I don't think that at all.

'What I do think,' she said, 'I think if you spend all your time thinking about ways to stop people from committing violence, nationally, I think what happens is it gets to you and fucks up your head. So it becomes okay, you do it, individually. And I think, I also think, if you're out on the barricades all the time, with the bullhorns and all that stuff, and the hecklers're yelling that the real reason you're against the war's that you're afraid to fight, I think that also does it. Like they decided, Sam and my brother, they decided they had to do something that involved them using guns and maybe getting shot, just to show it wasn't, that they weren't afraid of it.

'And they weren't,' she said. 'They sure proved that. But it was like, once they had proved it, they sort of lost their grip. And they became paranoid.

'I remember,' she said, 'it was when we were running out the money we got in Westgate Mall, and Sam said it was time, plan another job. And the way, the way we did them, you had to start getting ready quite a while before you went and did it. Because what they did, one the women'd get a job waitressing or something. In a doughnut shop or something where she could watch the banks and stores get their cash pick-ups and deliveries. Because nobody notices somebody like that, ever thinks a thing about them. And then when you know their schedule – that the truck drops off every Thursday night, or picks up Monday morning, there's a big weekend sale – whatever it happens to be, and you've got it down what the guards do – how many there are in it, and do they all leave the truck or's the driver stay in it? – when you got all that stuff down pat, then you can make your move.

'Well,' she said, 'Emmy was the one that did that, that got the job and watched and all of that shit, or she had been, anyway. Andrea was the first one that tried it, but she almost screwed up the Danvers one, and after that Emmy was the one. And this time she didn't want to do it. She said: "No, it's too risky. They, they've got to know by this time, that somebody gets a job like this and then she doesn't show up for work and the robbery goes down, and that's how we're doing this. And they're going to be watching for me, and they're going to nail me the minute I go in for the job.

And what am I going to say? What if they check on what I tell them, on where I went to school and do I really live where I'm telling them I'm living? What if they do that? Then they'll call the pigs, and they'll arrest me, and all you other guys'll just take off and split – you will disappear, and I'll be going to jail. And I don't think, I don't think I should always be the one who has to take the chances. I think either Jill or Kathie should be the ones to do it."

'And Sam went into orbit,' Christina said. 'He was just totally out of his mind. We had, we were all living in this dumpy apartment out in Northampton, me and Sam and Jimmy and this girl named Paula he was seeing that was a sophomore at Mount Holyoke, and Kathie and Jill, and Sam just went berserk. Paula, I don't think Paula was there that day. This happened in the morning and I think she had a class. She went to summer school. She was sort of a nice kid. I don't think she really knew, what was going on. Just that it was exciting, but they didn't tell her much. And Sam just exploded. Did you ever see a picture of Emmy?'

'No,' Gleason said. 'Not alive at least. I saw them of her body, where they found her, but I couldn't really tell from that what she looked like, she was alive.'

'No,' Christina said, 'no, you couldn't. Well, Emmy was really pretty when she wanted to be. Most of the time, see, she didn't make the effort, because that was another thing we all did; we all looked like we slept outdoors and never washed our hair, and never had any clean clothes to put on. Just go around in old shirts and pants and stuff like that. Showed we were sincere. Committed to the struggle. But when Emmy was going out, when she was looking for one of those jobs, she'd get cleaned up. And she really looked nice. She'd use bleach and streak her hair, and put some makeup on, and wear a bra, which she should've done all the time because she had big boobs, and naturally she didn't have any trouble finding a job. Because all she had to do was find someplace that had a man running it – which almost all of them do, managers – and he'd get a look at her and start thinking if he played his cards right he'd be in her by midnight. And they did, too. That was part of her mission: anything she had to do to get the job and learn the schedule, that was what she had to do.

'And she said, when Sam blew up, she said: "I don't care. I don't care if Jill and Kathie, if they don't want guys putting their hands on them, and that's why they won't do it. This's supposed to be a unit here. Everybody works together. And I don't think I should always have to be the one that gets down on her knees and sucks some married guy's cock because he says to work in his doughnut shop you got to like his cruller. I'm sick of putting out for these jerks. Find a place that some other dyke runs and let Jill or Kathie put out."

'Well,' Christina said, 'Sam was livid, and when Sam got worked up, so'd Jimmy. Jimmy got his cues from Sam. And Emmy wasn't very big. So Sam just said to Jimmy: "Grab her." And she's hollering and yelling, "No, no, no," and Jimmy's grabbing her by the arms and he's behind her, holding her, and Jill and Kathie're just sitting there cross-legged on the floor, taking it all in and enjoying it. Like two cats watching a birdbath and thinking about how they can catch what's in it. See, they didn't get along too good with Emmy, 'cause she wasn't one of them. And, well, they didn't like me all that much either, because of the same thing. But I was with Sam, and Jimmy was my brother, so they were sort of afraid of me and they didn't say anything about what they thought of me.

'And Sam says: "Jill, drop trou. Kathie, drop trou." And they both stood up, nobody ever questioned what Sam said, and very slowly they take their jeans off and they haven't got anything on under them, and Emmy's like, crying and struggling, you know? And he has Jill get down on her hands and knees, or her elbows, really, and he said to Jimmy "Kneel her down." And Jimmy did. And Sam said: "Emmy, lick Jill's asshole."

'So,' Christina said, 'Emmy's crying and saying she won't do it, and Kathie's getting all excited, fingering herself, and Emmy won't do it, and Sam just walks over to her and smashes her in the face. Right across the mouth. With his fist. And he did it about, I don't know, four or five times, cut her lip on her teeth so there's blood and everything, shoved her face down into the crack in Jill's ass every time he did it, and all this time, every time he does it he says: "Do it, Emmy, I'll kill you, you know. I'm perfectly capable of doing that if you don't. And you know I am." And I, here was this guy that was my lover, you know? And I was *terrified* of him, of what I saw him doing. And I said: "Sam, Sam," trying to stop him, you know? And he just turned to me and he said: "You stay out of this, Tina. You just stay out of this or we'll do it to you next."

'And I looked at Jimmy, you know, like I thought he would protect me? And I could tell just by looking at his face he wouldn't, just by looking at him. He didn't need to say a thing. Not a goddamned thing. Sam owned him, heart and soul. And that was, that was the beginning of the end for me, when I realized that. That as long as I stayed with the unit, Sam could do absolutely anything he wanted with me. And my brother wouldn't help me. My brother would help Sam. So that was when I started to decide that I would go back to school, and just sort of gradually disengage myself from them, you know? Because it had to be like that.

Nothing sudden. I did it too fast, Sam might decide I was a security risk and torture me like that.' She paused. 'He is the strangest man,' she said. 'He's got all these principles and stuff – no drugs, by then, like mescaline – except amphetamines if he decided to fly, which he did a lot more'n he admitted, even at the trial – and no booze or like that stuff. And, and yet this guy will hurt people, hurt them all the time. If he thinks it is right.

'So,' she said, 'Emmy did it. And after she got finished with Jill, blood all over Jill's ass, she had to do Kathie. And then Sam says to her: "Okay, that's your punishment for that insubordination. Now I'm going to tell you again what you're going to do on this job, and if you tell me again that you're not going to do it, we'll punish you some more. I don't care what you think, what you like or what you feel. We're gonna have discipline in this group, no matter what anybody thinks, because discipline, absolute discipline's the only way we can survive."

'And Emmy just nodded. I don't think she could talk. And about a week later, when her face'd healed – I don't think she came out of her room that whole week except to get some water or go to the bathroom, and she didn't talk at all, even if you spoke to her – she went down to Quincy there, all by herself, and rented a room and got the job, the Braintree plaza, just like Sam ordered her. Cashier in the clothing store. And then we did the job. Just like Sam said we would.

'And then,' she said, 'then about three weeks later, we're all scattered all over the place, and Jimmy and Sam were staying with a guy they knew in Deerfield, and they're going to get the house. Sam's teaching math in Brattleboro. That was his cover then. Emmy was still in Northampton. I, I was in school again down here, so I wasn't with them during the week, and I'm gradually cutting myself loose, but I went up on the bus one weekend and Jimmy picked me up. And I don't know exactly what'd gone on, but Sam'd evidently gone out of control again about something Emmy said or did, and Jimmy was warning me. And I made him stop the car. And I said: "Let me get this straight here. Are you saying, are you telling me you're going to kill that kid?" And he wouldn't admit it. He would not come out and say it. But I knew that's what he meant. That Sam was thinking about having Jimmy kill her. And that was why that was. And I knew if Sam told Jimmy, "Kill her," Jimmy would kill her. So I said: "Well, that's it, then. No more for me." And I got out of the car and thumbed a ride back to Northampton and got on the bus for home.'

'You didn't,' Gleason said, 'you didn't make any effort to warn Emmy?'

'I was afraid to,' she said. 'I was going to – that was my first impulse. Go and say to Emmy: "Run. My brother's going to kill you." But then I thought: "Wait. What if this's one of Sam's crazy tests? What if they're not going to do that, and I tell her and she runs? Then they'll know I told. They'll probably kill me. And besides, maybe even if they're thinking about it, they'll end up not doing it." All kinds of rationalizations. So I didn't, didn't tell her, and within the next couple weeks they tricked her into getting into a car with them, and brought her down here and killed her. Close to where she grew up. So, probably, people'd figure it was someone she grew up with around here.

'What I did do,' she said, 'the only thing I did do, I knew about that hotline number. The reward line. And I called that.'

'It was you,' Gleason said. 'John Richards thought it was Handley.'

'That's what Sam,' she said, 'I think that's what made Sam kill her. That, not that he knew anybody'd called the police, but he had this really good intuition. About when something was going on. And I think, I think he sensed, something might be going down. And that's why he killed Emmy. Because of what I did. When I was trying, to help her.'

'And that's what Jimmy's offering now,' Gleason said. 'Emmy's murderer.'

'That's what he wants,' she said. 'That's what he wants to offer. See, he hasn't done it yet. All he's done, there's this other guy in there that he knows pretty well, and this other guy knows the cop. Consolo? And Jimmy, what Jimmy did was have the other guy ask Consolo if Jimmy can get a deal, a commutation, if he tells them about Sam. And this cop, this cop is evidently thinking, well, maybe he can get Sam without making the deal with Jimmy. So he keeps having this other guy, the contact, he keeps having him go up to Jimmy and sort of tease him, you know? That Jimmy's got to make the case before the cop gives him any agreement. And that's what's going on.'

'And that worries you,' Gleason said.

'Well,' she said, 'yeah, it does. I mean, Sam beat the charge before, right? What if he, what if he beats it again, and then comes after me? I mean, I'd like to see Jimmy get out. He's not right in the head, I think. I don't mean he's dangerous, now – I don't think he is. But Jimmy, it's sort of like he's regressed, in prison. I don't know if he can cope. And I think Sam should be, that he should be punished. But suppose this cop can't find him? Suppose he comes after me, when he finds out they're looking for him? What do I do then? Is Jimmy trading me along with Sam, to get out? He doesn't mean to do that – that's not what I mean. But suppose he makes this deal of his, and the cop fucks up? Sam gets away? What do I do then?'

'Does Jimmy know where Sam is?' Gleason said.

She gazed at him. 'No,' she said.

'Do you?' Gleason said.

She toyed with her tableknife. 'I might,' she said. 'If I don't, I could find out.'

33

'Okay,' Gleason said in the diner where nine men lingered separately at the counter over coffee, 'three wishes.'

She laughed. '"Three wishes time,"' she said. 'God, how I miss that. Isn't that funny? There we were in that impossible, *awful*, mess, and there was no way in the world it wasn't going to end in a complete, fucking, disaster, no matter which way it turned out – and you say that and it almost seems like it was actually fun. "If you could have three wishes." I think that's what kept me sane.'

'Well,' he said, 'yes, but you're being kind. In the first place, you know, I was sort of teetering along the edge of the cliff myself. And in the second place, either you're being kind or maybe you never noticed, but you never, I never granted any of those wishes.'

'One you did,' she said.

He looked puzzled. 'Which one was that?' he said.

'Oh,' she said, '*you* never noticed. I never mentioned more'n *two* wishes. The other one was to go to bed with you, and I already had that. I did sort of have another one, that I also didn't mention and that I never got. But I sort of knew, I knew that one was a little more'n I could reasonably expect.'

'What was that?' he said.

She frowned. 'Oh,' she said, 'I was young then. And when you're young, you can know something isn't going to happen, and still sit there like a ninny, and hope and hope it will. I wanted you to leave her. To divorce Barbara and live with me. And I knew, I knew you wouldn't. So it was sort of voodoo I was doing. I wouldn't ask for it, because I wouldn't get it, but if I didn't ask for it, then maybe I would. Screwy, huh?'

'We were all screwy then,' he said. 'The time was out of joint. The players, the players didn't belong in the games that were going on. Guys like Sam, he should've been writing learned papers and getting a tenured chair at Caltech. Your brother should've been a high school teacher and varsity coach – football, maybe, or wrestling. Jill Franklin was a talented woman, crazed but talented. Her background, she should've been moving up the ladder of administration in some progressive public school system. Kathie, just as crazy as Jill was, she should've been organizing grass-roots political support for some up-and-coming young pol who'd be a senator today and being prominently mentioned as a presidential candidate.

'Instead,' he said, 'we were all embroiled in weird stuff. There I was, nose-to-the-grindstone young prosecutor, working homicides because I'd really learned my trade, and instead of hanging hitmen and real psychopaths, I was going after a bunch of people whose backgrounds weren't that different from my own. And whose natural inclinations, if no one'd disturbed them, would've been to do things very similar. But instead they'd gotten twisted. None of the rules applied. They'd all been abrogated.

'It was the oddest trial I'd ever had,' he said. 'Up till then and up till now, the very oddest trial. If it hadn't've been for the reason that brought us together, I could've been talking to Sam over coffee, or maybe having a couple of beers and discussing the news of the world. I was prosecuting, the people I was trying to convict of cold-blooded murder were much more like me'n the people I was saying that they killed. The children of privilege, on trial by the children of privilege, for killing people whose children were going to be of privilege, if their daddies' drug trade didn't get interrupted. That's unusual. It's pretty near unique.' He paused. 'And for sure, The Friary was the first trial I ever had where I ended up in bed with a defendant's sister.'

'Had any since?' she said.

'Ahh,' he said. 'No. I have had some trials since then where I encountered ladies whom I would not otherwise've met, but very few, and none of them related to defendants. By blood or marriage.'

'How many?' she said.

'Well,' he said, 'I consider that to be privileged information.'

'How many?' she said.

'Two,' he said.

'That surprises me,' she said.

'What?' he said. 'That there were actually two women who were interested? Or that there were only two. Say: "That there were only two." I've got a long day ahead of me, and I need bucking up.'

'That there were only two,' she said.

'Thank you,' he said. 'I appreciate it.'

341

'I'd think, knowing you,' she said, 'I'd expect them to hunt you in packs.'

He grinned at her. 'Meaning no offense, ma'am,' he said, 'most ladies of intelligence and breeding seem to find me less than thrilling. You were an exception. Since you were: three wishes.'

She sighed. 'I hate going there,' she said. 'The three years, the first three years that he was in there and I didn't go near the place, it bothered me. And then when I finally went, I found out staying away from it's nowhere near as depressing as going to it. No matter how guilty you feel.'

'I know,' he said. 'It's like going to a mass wake, but all the guests of honor're alive. They just might as well be dead.'

'I wrote to him,' she said. 'I wrote letters to him that he didn't answer, and boy, was that difficult. It takes a tremendous amount of effort to write to someone that you never hear back from anyway. But when the person who's not answering's in prison, what the hell do you say? Do you just ignore the fact that he's locked up? Write him happy little notes about how great your new job is, and how he'd love your new car? Rub it in, in other words? Or do you start right off with that, be "adult" about it? And if you do, what's your tone? Sympathetic or disciplinary? "Dear Jimmy, I'm really sorry you're doing life and it's hard to believe you won't be getting out for at least fifteen more years." Or: "Dear Jimmy, You dumb shit. I heard an old record the other day I'm taping to send you. It's called 'I fought the law, and the law won.'" So they were awful hard to write.'

'But you did it,' he said.

'Sure,' she said. 'Jimmy was arrested and convicted, but I was the one who felt guilty. I was afraid to go see him. I was afraid if I went there he'd either refuse to see me, and I'd be mortified in front of a group of strangers. Or else that he *would* see me, and he'd just humiliate me in front of all of them. So I settled for writing letters, and when I'd talk to my mother on the phone, you know, pick up what I could from her about what was going on. Without asking too many questions, of course – I never let on to her that he didn't write to me. She assumed he did – he wrote to her, and Dad wrote to him, after he recovered, and he answered them. He didn't tell them anything, as far as I could tell, but he did write, and that seemed to satisfy them. So there wasn't any point getting her all upset that he wouldn't answer me.

'Besides,' she said, 'I was always afraid, you know, that if she found out, she'd want to know why. So she could patch it up. Florence is completely feckless, but she doesn't realize that. She likes to manage things, run her children's lives. And everybody else's too. Especially if they don't want her meddling and her pointless damned advice – then, especially. She's one of those people that think once you see a problem, and discuss it, and decide how to approach it, the problem disappears. No need to do anything more, see? Just discuss it, and discuss it, and then discuss some more. Well, a big part of the reason Jimmy wouldn't write to me was my affair with you, which I didn't want to discuss with her, and therefore did *not* want her to know about.'

'Why?' he said. 'I thought, I thought she encouraged you, you know, to do as you wanted to do.'

'Oh,' Christina said, 'she did. I don't mean that. Florence told me when I was first with Sam, who as far as she knew was my first, she ... '

'He wasn't?' Gleason said.

'No,' she said. 'I was with a boy when I was fourteen. He was, I know everybody says the first time was awful, the pain and all that clumsy stuff, grabbing on and getting hurt, but mine wasn't – he was wonderful. He was only sixteen himself, and we weren't even dating or anything, but I was absolutely, I couldn't wait to try sex. I had to find out what it was like, and I knew Tommy, sort of – the school I was in was all girls, but Tommy's father was one of my father, mother's friends. Carl Oates? The correspondent? And so I'd met Tommy, and he was nice, so I asked him if he would help me. And he was just the sweetest boy. He told me he wanted to, but that he never had either, and you know what he did? He did research. He read a book or something, so he'd know what to do, and I wouldn't get pregnant, and then one afternoon I went to his parents' apartment and it was just wonderful.

'That was three years before Florence got around to telling me her father'd been just as strict with her as Dad was trying to be with me, and that she'd listened to him and now she wished she hadn't and I shouldn't listen to mine. "Just be discreet," she said. "Don't let him find out. Deceive him, to be kind, and do what you really want to do." So she was sort of stuck with it when I started going with Sam. She, I don't think at first she really thought that much of Sam, even though Jimmy just worshipped him and talked about him all the time, whenever he was home. "He seems awfully *intense*," she'd say to me. Which of course he was. That's a good part of what attracted me to him – that he was so driven all the time. And how could you be too intense about preventing war? And I said that to her. So she decided she liked him, and she wanted a lot to like him, because she agreed with him.

'But you?' Christina said. 'A married prosecutor, living with his wife and kids? Who put her son in jail? No, I think you would've been a little too much for her. If I'd ever told her about Tommy, that I went to bed with Tommy because I wanted sex so bad, that she would've approved of. But if I told her I went to bed with you because I wanted you, that would've really shocked her. Florence's always liked to think of herself as very progressive. Very much in tune with the times and all that. But what she actually is is sort of a prisoner of the times, whatever they happen to be. Actually, very conventional, but always careful to make sure she has the fashionable conventions. Whatever they happen to be. Florence thinks the city was named after her. She and Dad, up there on Sutton Place, if they went to a cocktail party in the Sixties that didn't have at least two Black Panthers and a few gay activists, she'd get all depressed – think they might as well've stayed home. And Dad was busy being eminent, so he just humored her. So when Jimmy brought Sam home, my father was a little less than thrilled, but he was in a trap because my mother was enchanted. Sam might not've looked like much, but what he said was chic.'

She paused. 'A few years later,' she said, 'after Jimmy was convicted and she found exactly how Sam'd changed her son, well, she wasn't very pleased with herself. Blamed herself, in fact, for Dad's heart attack, because she opposed him when he kept saying Jimmy was doing bad things, hanging out with Sam. "I didn't help your father," she says. "He was right, and I didn't help him." That's how she feels today. Although what she could've done, I don't know – she was powerless.'

'Remorse,' Gleason said. 'That's the way it always is. Saw it when I was prosecuting, see it more now, I'm defending. When they get convicted, the folks who get convicted do their best, persuade the judges that they really feel remorse. Because that's what the judges're supposed to be looking for, when they consider sentences. And some of them're telling the truth, although it's hard to swallow when this guy's been insisting for several weeks of the

345

trial that he didn't do it, and then he gets convicted and stands up in front of you and says in substance and effect: "Well, okay, I did it. I didn't think they could prove it, but they did, and so I did it. But now I'm really sorry I did it, because if I don't say I am, you're going to bury me."

'But there are people who are sincere, about remorse: the defendants' families. They may sit in your office and tell you the guy was trouble from the minute he came out of the womb, recite all the things they did, that didn't work, to get him straightened out, and they know it's not their fault. But all you have to do is look at them and you know it's not the truth. That they're blaming themselves for everything that's happened, and they'll go to their graves doing it.'

'It's very hard for her,' Christina said. 'I didn't want to make it worse, to let her think she was also responsible for Jimmy and me being estranged. One more thing to feel guilty about. So I didn't, I tried not to let on he wasn't answering my letters, and we'd talk, and she'd tell me as soon as Dad was fully recovered, well, she was sure they'd go up to see Jimmy. And I'd say the time Dad needed to heal would also help to let him come to grips with what'd happened. And I'd pick up a few bits of news that Jimmy'd written to her, and then I'd write to him.

'Well,' she said, 'after about two years, he started answering my letters. I couldn't tell from the first one he wrote how many of my letters he'd read, or whether he'd just ripped them up when they came. He seemed pretty distant, what he wrote, and he didn't really give me much information. But I could see, or I thought I could see, a definite change in his attitude from what it'd been when he went in. Just the fact he was responding – that alone was encouraging. So I answered him, and he wrote back, everything very noncommital and light, and we went on like that for about another year, me always holding myself back, thinking: "Don't push him. Take it easy. After all, he's got nothing but time. Progress is slow? Okay. Don't try to hurry things and end up ruining them." And then my mother called me up one Sunday night and said Dad'd been examined, and he was all recovered, and they were driving up to see Jimmy the following weekend. And she was all fluttery and anxious about it. And I was not to tell Jimmy when I saw him, they were coming up. So if Dad had a relapse or something, and they couldn't come, Jimmy wouldn't be disappointed.

'Now, you've got to understand Florence,' Christina said. 'My mother's known since she was a little girl what to wear to an opening night of the Philharmonic, and how to act when invited to dine at Lancaster House, or to the Queen's garden party. And my father's all brusque and efficient when it comes to white-tie receptions for Nobel laureates. Ceremonial occasions are familiar to them. But this one was something new, this reunion with their son. Neither one of them was what you'd call "familiar," with the protocols for visiting close relatives doing time for murder. No experience in that line. So she said to me: "Tell me what to do. Tell me what you do when you get there." And I was on the spot. I had to improvise, because of course I hadn't been there, and I said: "Look, Florence. I'm not sure the rules're the same for parents as they are for siblings. So when I'm up there this week, I'll ask, and call you back." And she said that would be "very helpful," and she thanked me very much.

'So that iced it,' Christina said. 'Now I had to go. And I called up and found out the visiting hours, and I picked, I decided I would go on Thursday because Thursdays and Wednesdays you

347

had to be out of there by five, and the other days you could stay as late as nine, and I wanted, I thought the first time I went it might be just as well if they, if I couldn't stay too long.

'I drove out there,' she said. 'It was one of those brilliant days in late September when the leaves're just starting to change but the air's still warm, and that year I had one of those rare pupils that you think when you start out teaching music, that you think all your pupils will be. In about a week you discover you'll be lucky if you ever get even one. Toby Leach. The nicest, smartest, hardest-working, most intelligent kid who ever played piano.' She chuckled. 'When he graduated last June he packed his bags and headed off for Annapolis. "Sorry, Miss Walker," he said. "My father says the sons of naval officers have to understand when there isn't enough money to do things they'd like to do."

'So,' she said, 'I was a little scared, going out there, but it was a beautiful day and One-A is pretty and my car was fun and all, and I came up over this rise and there was a, some kind of town forest or something on the right and then down on the left in the valley, there it was. And I thought at first, you know: "Oh, good. There it is. Now where the hell's the entrance?" And then it sort of registered on me, the white concrete walls, and the paint peeling off them, and the towers at the corners, and I thought: "Oh my God. This is where he is. Jimmy's in that place." It was like getting hit in the stomach with a hammer. It doesn't look like anything else, does it?'

'Nope,' Gleason said. 'It's a penitentiary, and that's what it looks like. They could put up signs out front that said "Holiday Inn" and "Hilton Hotel," or anything else they liked, and nobody looking at it would be fooled at all.'

'I went numb,' she said. 'I was just numbed. I found the parking lot and I went through the rigmarole of getting in there, and every-one was very nice, and then I was in this big sterile bleak room, sitting on a metal chair. And they told me, they said: "No touch-ing." "No contact." And I thought afterwards – because they make you so conscious of that, when they tell you that it's on your mind all the time you're seeing the guy – I thought afterwards, how hard it must be for wives and lovers, you know? And children. And the mothers of the men. There were little children there, seeing their daddies in jail. Because Jimmy's my brother, and we weren't on good terms, I didn't have a real strong urge to embrace him. But my God, someone's husband? Someone's daddy? Someone's lover? Must be terrible.

'And we talked,' she said. 'It wasn't bad. Well, it wasn't good, either – it wasn't as bad as I thought it might be. Leave it at that. He looked good. He'd been lifting weights, and running, and he said he hadn't used any stuff since he'd been in. And his eyes were clear and all of that. And I told him. I said: "The reason I am here," and I told him about Florence and Dad, and how he was not to tell them I'd told him they're coming. And he got this sort of strange look in his eye, and he said: "Nothing changes." And I said: "Beg pardon?" And he said: "Everything stays the same. I get thrown in here and it doesn't have the slightest effect on Mother or Dad," – and I thought: "Well, unless you count Dad's heart attack, that almost killed him," but I didn't say that, of course – "and here you are, come up here and sit there and sling me the same old shit you always did, always pretending you don't know what's going on and asking me to help Florence pretend, nothing's going on.

'"I'm not complaining," he said. "I know you can't help it, and she can't help it either. But my God, what'll it ever take to get the three of you to just face reality and deal with it, huh? Tell me that.

What is it, is there anything that's bad enough so when it finally happens, none of you'll be able to pretend anymore that it didn't? Is there such a thing? Would nuclear war do it?" And then he said: "Look, it's no day in the park, being inside. It's dangerous and it's boring and it really, really sucks. There's over eight hundred of us in here, and we're all in here alone. So I'd appreciate it, you know, if you want to stay in touch, and Florence wants to stay in touch, well then, fine – let's do it. But just do that, all right? Just write me the letters and I'll write to you, and that'll be the end of it. If I think of something, if I think of anything that any one of you can do for me, that would actually help, I will let you know. Otherwise, leave me alone."

'So it didn't go too well,' she said. 'I got the information Florence needed and I called her up and gave it, and then I said: "Mother, now let me tell you something. You can go there and you can see him, and Dad can see him, too. And he won't make a scene or anything. He'll come out when they tell him you're there, and he's not crazy anymore. But you're not going to like it, and Dad's not going to like it, and Jimmy's not going to like it either. It's going to be, it's just going to be another ordeal. For everyone concerned. More pain and everything for you. And for Dad. And for Jimmy, too, I think. And if I were you and Dad, I would not do it.'

'And she said: "I was afraid you'd tell me that." And I said: "Well, I just did." And, I expected an argument from her. And she said: "All right, we won't." And she hasn't mentioned it again.'

'That's too bad,' he said.

'I guess so,' she said. 'But I'm really not that sure. I didn't go back there for almost, well, I didn't go back there until this spring. In April. When he asked me to, I was surprised. And I wrote back and said: "What happened? You told me to stay away." And he wrote back and said he hadn't changed his mind, that he'd said he'd let me know if he thought of something I could do, and he had, and he wanted to see me. So I went up. And he told me. "Sam's getting out," he said. "Sam's getting out next month, I heard. I want to get out, too. I need you to help."

'And, it sort of bowled me over,' she said, 'what he was think-ing of doing. Because he'd always been so adamant, you know? So ornery and fierce. And I said to him: "I don't know. I don't know how to do this, how to make arrangements like that. And I don't know who does. And he said: "Your old boyfriend there does – Gleason. Gleason knows the ropes." And I said we, that we'd broken up, a long time ago. And he said: "He'll see you again. Call him up and ask." And I said: "I don't know if I can do that, either." And I didn't. And that's why I waited, why it was almost two months after that when I called you. I was getting up my nerve. But I did it.' She paused. 'So, what do I do now?'

'You want me to ask around?' Gleason said. 'See if they'll cut a deal to grab Sam again?'

'Yeah,' she said. She nibbled her lower lip. 'That's what he wants, at least. And he is my brother, so I guess I ought to help. Worry later whether I've ended up creating a lot more grief for myself. He's, Jimmy's a very pissed-off guy these days, Sam's out in the world and he's still doing time. But by myself, I can't, there's no way I can find out whether this guy Consolo's on the level, and can really make a deal. And also, if you can do it, I would like you to see Jimmy. Talk to him and make sure, you know, that I've got it right.'

'Ahh,' Gleason said, 'I don't know about that.'

'It'll be all right,' she said. 'He's over that. He needs some help, and knows it. When I mentioned, when he said I should call you, he didn't, you know, flinch. He was kind of nasty, but he didn't flinch.'

'What'd he say?' Gleason said.

'I'm not telling you,' she said. 'It was nasty to me. Not to you.'

'It's the same thing,' he said.

She smiled. 'Well, well,' she said, 'that's nice to hear. That was my third wish.'

Gleason took his paper napkin from his lap and crumpled it on the table. 'Okay,' he said, 'reciprocate. You see me tonight?'

'The motel?' she said.

'No,' he said. 'Maybe afterwards. Meet me first 'round seven, the old Station Tap.'

34

Christina Walker arrived at the Station Tap on the northerly bank of the Fort Point Channel at 7:20 in the evening. The dwindling sunlight made the surface of the dirty water a misleading blue; the black mud of the banks was shiny; three soiled, watchful seagulls perched on the listing pilings of a demolished dock and scrutinized the shallows for offal. She found Gleason in the high-backed booth at the southwesterly end of the restaurant. He was sitting at a table with a checkered cloth on it. He had a large frosted mug of beer. He had loosened his tie and unbuttoned his collar; he needed a fresh shave. 'You look worn out,' she said, sliding in opposite him. 'You look like you've been out cutting timber or something. You didn't used to look like this, when you were trying James. Is this something new?'

He took a deep breath and exhaled it loudly. 'It's a bad case,' he said. 'It's a very tough case to try. In the first place it's one of those damned RICO productions – racketeering-influenced, corrupt organization – and there's no damned *shape* to the fucking things. They basically amount to the prosecutor saying: "Here's a whole bunch of bad guys, folks, and you can tell Guy Number One's a hood because Guy Number Four and Guy Number Six broke some legs, under orders from Guy Number Three, directed by Guy Number Five, and Guy Number Five knows Guy Number Two, who once had coffee with One." Then they bring in the evidence in a front-end loader and dump it on all seven guys, and then they get convicted.

'There's nothing you can do,' he said. 'You sit there and you're absolutely helpless to protect your client. It's like fighting a swarm of bees. Once they RICO the guy, the rules of evidence're gone. There's almost no rules left. "Is this piece of evidence material, or even relevant, against Mister Ianucci?" "Well, yeah, because it's material against Mister Dinapola, over there, and relevant against Mister Greco, over here, and Mister Ianucci's Mister Greco's former lawyer." So you can't keep it out, get it ruled inadmissible, but at the same time you've got to object every time it happens, that they do that, because you've got to protect the record on appeal. Which means the seven of us're jumping up and down all the time, like we're the seven dwarfs and Snow White's out of town, and that in turn means that a lot of time gets wasted. Which in turn makes the jurors hate us, and therefore our clients, because the jurors're sequestered and they haven't seen their families or reported to their jobs since the end of May, and they're becoming quite resentful, quite annoyed with us.

'One of them,' Gleason said, 'one of them when we were impaneling, he said he couldn't serve because he retired from his job last year and this's the first year he's got season tickets, the Red

Sox. And the estimable Judge Reese got this expression on his face that those of us who know him well've learned to dread to see – he's got this evil little smile he uses when you've just asked him politely not to do something gratuitously nasty to you, that he doesn't have to do. And he's decided to do it. Not because he thinks he has to. Not because he thinks you're trying to mislead him. Not because leaving you alone would cost him anything at all, but because you've quite politely asked him to leave you alone and he's going to show you his power by doing the opposite.'

'Was he always like that?' she said. 'Was he like that, before, when you were working for him?'

'Oh yeah,' Gleason said. 'But he concealed it better. When he still thought he could be governor some day, before the voters finally convinced him that was never going to be, he tried to restrain himself. And he had buffers, then. Paul Green took the raps when Colin Reese stuck his dirk into some poor bastard's back. Andy Boyd, when Andy Boyd called some young assistant into his office and told him he was pink-slipped, and good luck in his future career, Andy and the kid both knew it wasn't because Paul Green'd decided to trim the fat off the criminal division staff – it was because the kid hadn't been shrewd enough to see that a five-hundred-dollar, purely voluntary, contribution to the AG's birthday party at the Park Plaza was in his own best interest, and Colin didn't like that sort of thrift. But Andy was loyal; he always blamed Paul. And Paul was loyal – he accepted the blame. So Colin was insulated from any culpability. Just like a Mafia guy. "Strictly staff administration," he would say if you asked him. "Paul Green handles all administration, all administrative matters involving personnel. This is a professional law office. I'm a politician, because I have to be, and that's why I stay away from that stuff: because the rest of you are not, and you shouldn't be."'

'And now he's a federal judge,' she said.

'Well,' Gleason said. 'They had to give him some reward. They couldn't just pat him on the back after he took the poison cup and ran against Teddy Kennedy. Say: "Hey, thanks a lot, Colin. Nice kamikaze job you did there. We appreciate it." You want the truth, my guess is that he got the commitment they'd appoint him to the bench long before he made that run. Would not've done it otherwise. That was Colin's price. Paul'd be satisfied with a parachute landing into a partnership at Baker, Gordon, Tye. And Andy got his tenure at the School of Law, where he can wow the students and use them for free labor, preparing the appellate briefs that bring those handsome fees. All of that publicity, and no overhead at all. But Colin, well, Colin likes the limelight too, but he likes authority more, and he likes being whimsical without doing too much work. So his price was the judgeship. But every man has one of those, and his was reasonable. Rather hard on working stiffs, and guys that paid eight hundred bucks for a Red Sox season ticket, the first year they retired, but still: not too much to ask.

'So, having asked it and received it, Colin got his little smile on and said to the helpless geezer: "If you're a Red Sox fan, sir, you have learned of disappointment. You're old enough, you were around, they lost in seventy-eight. Maybe I'm sparing you. But in any event, I'm sorry but I can't excuse you. You will have to serve."

'So as a result,' Gleason said, 'every time that I stand up, and John Morrissey stands up, along with all the others, juror number six glares at me and them, and blames us 'cause Hurst is starting and looks like he's solved his problems, and the Blue Jays are in town. I know what the juror's going to do to get even, and what his equally annoyed compatriots are going to help him do. He's going to convict Phil Ianucci of being a gangster, among other things. And also all the other guys, sitting there with Phil. It's really exhausting work, you know? Going in there every day, knowing what is going on, and what is going to happen, completely helpless to do a thing about it. All trials use up your capital, your energy, your brains, but trials you've got a chance of winning're at least enjoyable. This one's just fatiguing. Just exhausting work.'

'Well,' she said, 'I mean, is this guy a gangster? Really? Is that what he does?'

Gleason shrugged. 'Well,' he said, 'Phil has a small law office on Prince Street. One secretary. Almost no law books. Which lack he doesn't notice 'cause he's very seldom there. Phil drives around in a green Rolls-Royce with right-hand drive, that he imported from England. His regular glasses're pink wraparounds, and his suits're very sharp. He has a Cigarette speedboat and a house in Nassau, and he goes to Vegas a lot.'

'He's a gangster,' Christina said.

'Perhaps,' Gleason said. 'But he's also a lawyer, and an American citizen, and he pays all his taxes – many as he has to, at least. And he's good to his family, and really likes dogs, and pays his attorney promptly. He gives me no lip, and does what I say, and you can't ask for more than that. Not in my line of work, at least, and I selected it.'

A middle-aged waitress, chewing gum, approached with menus and put them on the table. She glanced at Gleason's beer mug, two-thirds full, then turned to go away. 'Excuse me,' Christina said, 'but could I please have a drink?'

The waitress interrupted her chewing and gazed at Walker. 'You sure you're old enough?' she said. 'We don't serve minors here.'

'You want to card me?' Christina said, moving her straw bag closer to her.

The waitress resumed chewing. 'Yeah,' she said, 'I do.'

Christina stared at her. 'You really think,' she said, 'you really think I'm under twenty-one?'

'I don't think anything,' the waitress said. 'I'm not paid to think. Fetch and get: that's what I do. Bring and clear away. I serve someone that I'm not sure of, then they get in trouble? I would lose my job.'

Christina brought out her wallet. She removed her license and handed it to the waitress. 'I'm surprised you haven't anyway,' she said. 'Gin and tonic, please.'

The waitress arched her eyebrows at Christina before she inspected the license. She handed it back. 'Some of the customers I get,' she said, 'sometimes I wished I did.' She sauntered, leaving the table.

Christina replaced the license in her wallet and the wallet in her bag. 'I assume,' she said to Gleason, putting the bag aside, 'I assume there's some particular reason why you come here.'

He snickered. 'It's the warm, homey atmosphere,' he said. 'The cheery hospitality, the expertly prepared cocktails and the excellent cuisine. Besides, it's two blocks from my office, open late, and cheap. You have trouble, finding it?'

'No,' she said. 'I had trouble, getting here. The Red Line was running late.'

'You took the trolley?' he said. 'Why'd you do that? The Red Line's been running so late so long now it's actually early. You take a train at six-forty today, that's supposed to've been six-twenty, it's not late at all – it's actually the seven-forty-five from yesterday, and your actual six-twenty today won't pull out until eight-ten tomorrow. Everybody knows that. How did you escape?'

'Well,' she said, 'that's why I did it, actually. To escape. I had a guy on my tail when I left my place tonight. He was in a car alone, just like he'd been all day. I figured, if I take the train, which I did in Braintree, this might not actually shake him, but it'll inconvenience him. And that's all I'm really after – make it difficult for them. It annoys me, having them, following me like they do. Anything that makes their life a little harder? That I'm going to do.

'After I left you this morning,' she said, 'I decided to go right to the school and practice for a couple of hours before my first student. And I was through at one o'clock. And they, there was a man waiting for me there when I came out to go to lunch. In the usual unmarked car. Wearing the usual Irish face, with the usual Irish scowl. He followed me down to the usual place. He watched me eat my usual lunch, egg salad and a Coke. Then he followed me back home and watched me go inside. I had a real temptation, you know, when I went in the apartment, to just sing out: "Hey, guys, I'm home. I'll be going out this evening, though. You'd better stay alert." But I didn't. Getting shy, I guess.'

The waitress brought the gin and tonic. 'Ready tah order?' she said.

Gleason looked at her. 'No,' he said.

'Wanna couple of minutes?' she said.

He looked at his watch. 'Ten,' he said.

The waitress nodded. "Kay,' she said, and went away.

'Does that mean we won't see her again? Ever?' Christina said.

'No,' Gleason said. 'It means that in precisely ten minutes, she'll be back. To see if we kept our promise to be ready to order then.'

'And if we're not,' Christina said, 'will she punish us?'

He smiled. 'Only with a look,' he said. 'A look implying we're not bright enough to choose our own meals from the menu and will need some help from her. Whether we want it or not.'

'Why'd you ask me here, this morning?' Christina said, picking up the menu.

'Because I knew two things this morning,' Gleason said. 'One: I knew there were some more things I'd want to know, before I decided what to do. And two: I didn't know what those things were. So, with a boring day ahead of me, listening to more accountants drone on about more records, knowing I could therefore count on lots of time to think about many other things, I asked you to meet me here at the end of it, so that we could talk.'

'Oh,' she said, studying the menu. 'I was hoping there was something else.'

'There is,' he said.

'Good,' she said. 'That's a help, at least. 'S why I left my car in Braintree, right near the motel. Now, is there anything here that I can eat, without regretting it all night?'

'Sure,' he said. 'The rule you follow in places like this is, avoid the complex dishes. The less they claim they do to your food before you get it, the better the chances that they won't do anything bad to it. John Richards taught me that, when we were running around all over the country, chasing your brother and Sam. "Occam's Razor," John said. "'Do not multiply entities beyond necessity.'" In restaurants or anyplace else.'

'I thought that was Thoreau,' she said. '"Simplify your life."'

'It probably was,' Gleason said. 'Just because William of Occam said it, and John Richards said it, doesn't mean Thoreau couldn't say it. I could say it too.'

'So, how do I do it?' she said. 'Here, I mean. Tonight.'

'Well,' he said, 'if you want to take a chance, with me, this's not the week they spawn, you could have raw oysters. Dozen fresh Cotuits with a little lemon juice and a good-sized glass of beer, do wonders for the sore of heart, and heal tormented souls. And the only thing the chef's called on to do is get the damned things open. Which at least up to this point he's always been able to do without badly wounding himself with the knife, or mangling the meat.'

'They only spawn one week a year?' she said. 'That doesn't sound like much fun.'

'It's worse'n that,' he said. 'They're protandrous. They all start off as males. Become females when they mature.'

'Definitely no fun,' she said. 'I would not like that at all. Sounds like Jill and Kathie to me. Maybe they were oysters, in a former life. Might explain their behavior, I never understood.'

'You have a linear mind,' Gleason said. 'That's what I admire. No bullshit and no fooling: that's the way to be.'

'Fine,' she said, putting the menu down, 'so let's not. Tell me what you want to know.'

'Let me tell you first,' he said, 'what I do know, that I didn't know this morning. This morning I didn't know if I had the appetite, for getting a man out that I after all put in.'

'Jimmy,' she said. 'he ... '

'No,' he said, 'let me finish. You're asking quite a lot of me here, whether you know it or not. You're pitting me against my old colleagues. I do what you want, I'll be at least tacitly telling them I've decided to turn coat. John Richards won't mind. June McNeil won't mind. They know what lawyers do, and they're at least resigned to it. But Fred Consolo will mind. He will mind a lot. And he'll be publicly talkative about it – if Sam is caught, and there's another trial.'

'I see,' she said. 'Well then, does that mean you're bagging out of this?'

'No,' he said, 'it doesn't. All it means is that this morning I wasn't sure, I didn't know whether I was ready to commit a symbolic act like that. I thought it over, and now tonight I am. I do know. I will help you.'

'Thank you,' she said.

'Maybe you won't,' he said, 'when you hear the rest of it. When you hear the price.'

She gazed at him. 'Try me out,' she said.

'It's a straight-player deal,' he said. 'You for Jimmy. I was thinking about what you said, what a rotten life he's got. And he has. Often happens to guys that kill people. Not as often as it should, but pretty often, still. And then I thought: "Well, Gleason, who you going to brag to? Your own life's not so hot. The only time you've had any fun in about ten years was when you were bedding Christina." And I didn't even kill anybody.'

'You could've kept on doing that,' she said. 'Wasn't my idea, having us break up. You're the one that wouldn't leave her – I encouraged you.'

'And I told you why I couldn't,' he said. 'I told you at the time. And those reasons, like I said, those reasons're still good. Will be for five years more.'

'I don't get it,' she said.

'I'm saying,' he said, 'I'm saying what I want from you is five years of being a mistress. Five years of frozen dinners alone at Christmas. Five years of sneaking around. Five years of putting up with me playing out a charade of a marriage that'll take more time to perform than I'll have for you. Then, if wretchedness hasn't gotten you by then, then when it's either clear that

Phil's out of the woods, and he's going to be all right, or clear that he's not coming out, and never's going to be – in either event, after I've given it my best shot with the kid, I'll leave her and live with you. But it's going to be awful hard. On you, this is, it will be rough – on me, well, I am drowning. I'm asking for a rope.'

'Will she let you get away with it?' she said. 'Won't she find out, and throw you out?'

'She might,' he said. 'I'd bet against it, but she might try that, yeah. She does, though, and the first thing she'll get in the confrontation is the news that I'm gonna fight her down to the cobblestones. That if she decides to file for divorce, I'll counterfile. That if she charges adultery, I'll come back with cruel and abusive treatment, and what amounts to sexual abandonment. And we'll see who wins that little tussle in the public eye.'

'She hasn't,' Christina said, 'she doesn't come across?'

'Now and then,' Gleason said. 'When the urge hits *her*, she does. She doesn't, I don't think she's really got a strong sexual drive. She accommodates me when in charitable moods. Once or twice a month's about all she's inclined to deliver. I think it's all that golf, all that tennis that she plays. Uses up her energy for everything else. Anything more often'n that, takes dinner, wine and candlelight, at Anthony's Pier Four. And God help the man who asks her to put something in her mouth beside a Diet Coke – she does it, but for the next six weeks it's monosyllables and wounded looks, until she grants parole.'

'Well,' he said, 'I'm paying for all of this. And I don't mean just financially, either. I'm paying for it in frustration, and annoyance, and short temper. And since I *am* paying for all her sporty rounds and chatty lunches; since I *am* the guy who foots the bill for the fun she'd rather have, instead of fun with me, I resent it. And I want something more. Which is you.'

Christina shrugged and smiled. 'Fine by me,' she said. 'You knew how I felt about you, a long time ago. Hasn't changed.'

'Beautiful,' he said. 'You're sure you can do this, now.'

'Oh,' she said, 'yeah, I'm sure. How's the old joke go again? "I figured you'd want money"? Talk about three wishes: wow. I think this is great.'

'Okay, then,' he said, 'now for the easy stuff. You really don't know, where Sam Tibbetts is?'

'No,' she said, 'I don't. But like I said, I can find out.'

'But you know what country he's in,' he said. 'That much you do know.'

'I know which country he *was* in,' she said. 'Was in a while ago. Whether he's still in it? That I do not know.'

'But you know how to find out,' Gleason said.

'Yes,' she said, 'I do.'

'If you were going to find out,' Gleason said, 'if you had decided, for whatever reason, to do that, how would you proceed?'

'I would send him a cable,' she said. 'Care of American Express.'

'Yes,' he said. 'And what name would you use? What name would you address?'

'Well,' she said, 'I'm not sure yet, that I want to tell you that.'

The waitress returned. 'Decided?' she said, producing her pad.

'Dozen oysters,' Gleason said. He tapped his mug. 'And another one of these.'

The waitress scribbled on her pad. 'How 'bout you?' she said to Walker.

'Dozen oysters,' Christina said, 'and bring me a beer as well.'

The waitress nodded, chewing her lower lip, and wrote '2' on the pad. She left the table.

'When do you think,' Gleason said, 'just so I can plan my day, when would be your best guess when you will have decided?'

'Probably after the oysters,' Christina said. 'Probably by then.'

'You know what's bothering me,' Gleason said.

'I can guess,' she said.

35

Gleason pushed the pewter platter with its twelve empty oyster shells one inch closer to the center of the table, regarded the wreckage with satisfaction and took a drink of beer. He put the heels of his hands on the edge of the table and straightened his back against the booth. 'Now,' he said, 'what is bothering me, or was, at least, is: I know Fred, and Fred's a nut, but Fred is not careless. Fred's a carbuncle on the ass of every life he touches, but he's thorough. Fred's so careful that when you're the lawyer on the case, you wish you weren't. The bastard hovers. Everything you do, you get the feeling that the next thing he's going to floss your teeth for you. Some guys, they make mistakes because they don't ask questions. Not Fred: he asks you questions when he shouldn't, like by calling in the middle of the night to check some obscure point of search-and-seizure law that'd never come up in a million years. That nobody but a Fred with nothing else on his mind'd ever even think of. He wants his cases made up like barracks beds, hospital corners so tight you can barely get under the sheets. Fred's going to law school nights now, in the wintertime at least, because after all these years of scouting around for a lawyer he thinks worthy of his trust, he's at last reached the conclusion that the only person reliable and precise enough to be Fred's lawyer is, guess who? You got it: Fred.

'This means that if Fred's got you bugged, and if Fred's watching you, Fred's already got enough evidence to've satisfied some young assistant that he buffaloed – or some older guy that just wanted to get rid of him – that he can prove a crime. And that prosecutor took Fred's bale of hay in before a judge, and the magistrate, who also wants to go off to the beach, gave him a search warrant. Betcha nickel whole thing happened on a Friday afternoon, when the only person in the whole world with his mind on his job in the summertime is Cowboy Fred Consolo, scourge of evildoers. Fred loves Friday afternoons. But anyway, he got it, and that was when he put the bugs in – everything ship-shape and no suppression worries down the line.

'Now I can guess who his primary source is,' Gleason said. 'It's one of James's pals in the pen. James's pal's your basic "reliable informant who in the past has provided information that has proved to be reliable." Meaning: "The guy's got a long history of ratting on his buddies in return for privileges." So consequently Fred can say that he believes the guy is shooting straight this time, without surfacing the fink.' He grinned. 'Which is a trick Fred learned from me,' he said. 'John and me and Doctor Frankenstein, 'cept the doc did it on purpose.

'In addition to the fink, though, Fred needs something more. Or he did, at least, before he could tap you. He had to give some reason to think that you know where Sam is. His informant's told him James is set to hang Sam, but James doesn't know where Sam is, so neither does informant. Fred in order to bug you must've provided something else that made the prosecutor and the judge think Christina does know.'

'Well,' she said, 'but after all, he knows I used to be with Sam. Would he need more than that?'

'Your average buckaroo might not,' Gleason said. 'Public record'd do it, trial transcripts and newspaper clippings, bang 'em in and bang 'em out. But our Fred's not an average fellow. Fred'd look at the stuff and say: "Yeah, but down the road some crafty bastard in a suit's gonna come into court and say: 'This warrant ain't no good, pal. That stuff was old hat.'" Fred maybe wins that one on appeal, but Fred doesn't like appeals – they're another chance to lose, after you have won. So Fred found something newer, left a little fresher taste.

'Which left me with my question: What did our Fred find, and how did he find it? Best rule, from my experience, is take the second question first. Work back to the first one. And the way you go about that is by saying: Has he done this before, and if so, how? And the answer is that he has, and he did by checking records back when we were hunting Sam. He thinks Sam's not in the country. He thinks you know where Sam is. Therefore: find out where you've gone, assuming you saw Sam.

'He did it through Customs and Immigration,' he said.

'How do you know that?' she said.

'Because that's what we taught him to do,' Gleason said. 'He called up Customs and asked them to run your name through the computer to see where you've been recently. And if that didn't work, and it often does not, well, he called in some chits with a credit card outfit. But one way or another, he found out you'd been somewhere he thinks that Sam might be. And that was what he told the judge, and how he got his warrant. And how he got into your hair and lair, and's now looking up your ass.'

'Okay,' she said, eating the last of her oysters, 'to this I say: So what?'

'So this,' Gleason said. 'I practice law in this town. It's how I make my living, which facilitates eating and staying dry nights when it rains. One of the things I have to be able to do is make deals. Almost everybody hires me, did what he's charged with doing. That's one the facts of this life. It was that way when I did the charging, and it's that way now, when I defend. It was true when Phil Ianucci's clients bought the ranch in the back room of The Friary, and I put your brother in jail, and it's true now, when the USA says Phil Ianucci's no good either, and he should go to the can.

'I can't try every case,' he said. 'I'd lose most of them. Clients can't afford it anyway, and it only makes sense when it's someone like Phil who's simply got to take a flier, 'cause if he pleads, he's ruined. So I belt the bastards out. And that means when I say something, to a judge or prosecutor, it'd better be the truth. It's the only way I can function.

'I get involved with helping your brother,' he said, 'what I'm going to be doing is saying to the prosecutor, not so far down the line, that James'll deliver Sam. Not only that Sam ordered Emmy killed; also that James or someone acting for him won't tip off Sam what's coming. So that he can run and hide. Because otherwise, James don't get out, and that's a natural fact.

'Basically what you're asking me to do,' he said, 'is trade your brother for Sam. And since I've now figured out that you know where Sam is, because Fred's figured that out, what I have to wonder is whether you're prepared to follow through. To make the trade, I mean. Because there's no reverse gear on these things. Well, there is, but you'd better not use it. It's like the automatic parking lots where the spikes come up after you drive through the gates – no backing up; severe tire damage will result.'

'I realize that,' she said.

'Good,' he said, 'I hope you do. My problem is different. I go to see James, and then cut a deal – you then have a change of heart and give old Sam the high sign and the bugger pulls a scoot, I'm out there in the cold wind with no pants on. Understand? James'll languish in durance vile, and you can go and frolic in whatever mists you choose, but I will get my ass chapped. Permanently chapped. Fatally, in fact.'

'I won't do that,' she said.

'You say you won't,' he said. 'But you've done it before.'

36

'I've never done it before,' she said.

'Begging your pardon, ma'am,' he said, 'but you've had a memory lapse. You've not only done it *before* – you have done it *recently*. After Judge Reese liberated us from the day's toil, after I'd spent most of my day thinking, I went back to my office and called John Richards. John knows everything. The habits of the animals, the progress of the seasons – you name it and John knows it. So I told John what I knew, and what I thought I'd figured out, and asked him to critique it. And he said what I'd said to him seemed pretty realistic, and it squared with what he knew.

'Now, John's retired,' Gleason said. 'John doesn't hack around with criminals and other riffraff anymore. But he still expects the folks who call him, and impose upon his time, to keep their grey matter alert, and use it as called for. So I said: "John, what is it?

371

What is it that you know, that I should know about?" And he said that he would tell me, and that is what he did.

'Substance of it,' Gleason said, 'was that Barbie-doll spotted someone trying to put a tail on me. She went to see Larry Badger, and Larry got Alton involved, and Alton talked to John. And the two or three of them figured out that who's watching me's Fred Consolo. Who is also watching you.

'So I said to John,' he said, 'I said, "Well, if they're watching me, because they're watching her, why are they watching her? Because that is where we start." And John said it's because you have been to see Sam, within the past six months.'

'Oh,' she said.

'Yes,' Gleason said. 'John knew this because Alton found it out, same way as Fred did. Although maybe not quite as legally. Alton poached on the government's computer files and put your name on the screen, and bells rang and whistles blew, and he found out you went to London in June. You were gone ten days.'

'Yes,' she said.

'Now Alton's a shrewd bastard,' Gleason said. 'Just because somebody goes to London doesn't mean she stayed in London. Maybe she went somewhere else. So Alton invaded the airlines' computers, which coughed up the information that you were in England for a total of about eight hours.'

'Yes,' she said. 'I was.'

'Just long enough, in other words,' he said, 'to make the connection to Casablanca. Which Alton discovered you did, by raping another computer that also told him about the car you rented there.'

'I suppose he got the mileage, too,' she said. 'When I brought it back.'

'That's correct,' he said. 'About fourteen hundred kilometers, at two-two *dirham* each.'

'I give the guy credit,' she said. 'When he was working for James, I thought he was a little weird, but I thought the guy was good.'

'That he is,' Gleason said. 'Having learned all of this, and keep in mind that my child bride hasn't paid him or his uncle a dime for it, but when he gets started on something, the more he learns the more curious he gets. Having learned all of this, he said: "Why does the single music teacher go to Morocco by herself?" That is what he said. "To meet somebody else," he said. "Let's see who might be there." And you know what he found out?'

'I could guess,' she said.

'And that's what Alton had to do,' Gleason said. 'Because Sam's still got his collection of passports, and he is using them. Doesn't do any good to type "Tibbetts, S.," into the terminal, because Sam's very seldom "Tibbetts" these days when he goes a-traveling.'

She sighed. 'He has a lot of them,' she said. 'I didn't know ... It never came up at the trial.'

'It never came up at the trial,' Gleason said, 'because in those halcyon days, when we were protecting Mackenzie, we didn't want it to. Back then Mackenzie said: "Eight." Would that have been correct?'

'It was at least eight,' she said. 'We used to, when Sam was really humming, one of the things he had us do was spend the time between the jobs filling up the passport-bin. And I think Sam had about ten. Go into some little town. Search the library collection of the weekly papers for the year when Sam was born. Get the birth certificate for some infant that died that year, soon after birth. Show it to a Department of Motor Vehicles, and you've got a driver's license. Submit it to the State Department with pictures of Sam. Presto, you've got a passport in another person's name, which person you've become. He had a lot of them.'

'Alton,' Gleason said, 'according to John Richards, Alton thinks Sam Tibbetts's probably the Raymond Hickcock that registered with the police in Agadir on May sixth, as an American alien, not seeking employment, intending to remain in that country for more than ninety days.'

'That's the name I used,' she said, 'when I got in touch with him.'

'Alton also surmises,' Gleason said, 'with the help of his computers and extremely fertile mind, that Sam Tibbetts is probably the Jay Cullinan who travels between Tangier and Zurich with remarkable regularity. And who is also registered with the police in Tangier as an American alien, not seeking employment. And that he is the same person who travels under the name of Francis Swift from Casablanca, on regular business to Athens. And that he's the Joseph Thomas who flies to Beirut from Marrakech.'

'All possible,' she said. 'The only one I know for sure is Raymond Hickcock. And the only reason I know that one is that I got the papers in Chester, Vermont, in nineteen-seventy-three, and Sam took them for himself. So that was the name I used. Used for him, I mean.'

'Why?' Gleason said.

She slumped in the booth. 'Why?' she said. 'Oh boy, this isn't easy.'

'You're the one that started it,' he said. 'Wasn't my idea.'

'Oh, shit,' she said. She put her elbows on the table and massaged her forehead with her fingers. She put her hands down on the table, crossing her arms at the wrists. 'Look, all right?' she said. 'I went because I had to. I had to go and find out. I called, when Jimmy asked me, I called up my mother. Because this wasn't just something that involved me and Jimmy – it also involved her and Dad. And I tried to tell her that. That it mattered, that she had to think clearly for once, and tell me whether she thought I'd be doing the right thing if I did what Jimmy wanted.

'And she wouldn't do it, of course,' Christina said. 'Oh, she was very nice to me, just like she always is, and I said: "What am I going to do, Mother? What do I do now?" And she went into that comforting voice she always uses when she's putting you off, ducking another decision of her own, and said: Well, that I was the only one who could decide that. And I said: "Can't you help me?" And she said: "The only person who can help you is yourself." And I said I couldn't, that I had to see Sam. And she said: "Then that's your answer. That's what you must do." And I said: "I don't know if I can do that." And she told me, she said she understood perfectly how I felt. That one of the greatest regrets of her life was that Sam, and Jimmy, that she hadn't been able, you know, to influence them more, because she was so impressed by what the two of them could do. The potential that they had.

'So, I did it,' she said. 'I was totally at sea. I had to see how I would feel. Jimmy knew what he was doing. He was getting even. I could see why he'd want to do that. I could understand. But me? I wasn't doing that. I didn't want revenge on Sam. I was a free agent. But Jimmy needed me to do that. What he wanted for revenge. Needed me to make it happen. And, what he was asking me? I knew what it was. It was absolute betrayal. That was what it was.

'I'm not good at this shit,' she said. 'I'm not used to moral questions. Not used to them, don't like them, run away from them. You want to play the *brio* passage *largo*? That is fine by me. I may not think that you should do that, and that it won't work out. But

I will sit and listen, and if you can make it work that way, well, that's all right by me.

'So,' she said, spreading her fingers on the table and looking down at them. She took a deep breath. 'So, James asked me to do what I'm doing. And he is my brother. And, for my father. He's old. Suddenly he's old. I said to my mother: "And that's another reason, why I may have to do this thing. Get James out of there." And she said all she wanted, all she wanted was to be sure, that I would be all right. If Sam got free, I mean. And I said: "Oh, Mother, just this once, at least, let's try to think of someone besides our two sweet selves."

'So I wanted to do what James asked,' she said. 'But I also wanted to be right. And I couldn't know, whether I was right, unless I went and saw Sam. So that is what I did.'

'You told me,' Gleason said, 'you told me a long time ago, it was all over. Between you and Sam.'

She nodded. 'I did,' she said. 'I did tell you that.'

'It wasn't true,' he said.

'I thought it was,' she said. 'At the time, I thought it was. If I misled you, well, I didn't mean to.'

'"Didn't meant to" doesn't count,' Gleason said. 'This's the adult world. No rehearsals and no retakes. You get me out there, swapping Sam's ass for your brother's, I'm gonna be in no position, if I make the deal, tell the guy agrees to it I really didn't mean it.'

'No,' she said. 'I know that. I know you can't do that.'

'So,' he said, 'level with me. What is going on?'

37

'When Jimmy asked me,' she said, 'when Jimmy got in touch with me, and asked me to do this, he was really cruel about it. He can do that, you know. He can be really cruel.'

'This is news?' Gleason said. 'You're telling me a guy that shoots people behind the left ear when they're nude and kneeling's got a mean streak in him? I sort of figured that.'

'All right, all right,' she said. She waved her left hand and looked down at the table. She raised her gaze to meet Gleason's. 'This isn't easy for me, you know.'

'A hundred thousand pardons,' he said. 'Let me remind you once again: this was not my idea. You came back to me. You did tell me the truth, but you didn't tell the whole truth. You left some things out.'

She put out her left hand and touched his right wrist. 'Terry,' she said, 'we met what seems like a long time ago, and we went through a lot. But you don't know me very well. I'm not, I'm not an ambitious person. My wants are fairly simple. The things that mean a lot to most people just don't seem to matter much to me. I have my little apartment and my little car, and my little life with my music. And I'm content with that. If I can just do my job, do what I like, and now and then make love with someone that I like, that's enough for me.

'My mother,' she said, 'neither my mother nor my father really understand that. They look at me with this puzzled expression on their faces, staring out of their elegant lives onto what looks to them like the craters of the moon, and they can't see why I am happy. They're *glad* that I am, I think, or at least they seem to be, but they can't really comprehend how I could be. No husband. No children. No social life to speak of. And, really, not so great a job. Teaching music to high school kids in Waterford, Massachusetts? The only man in my life is married, and bland, and he runs a record store? Shouldn't I, don't I, miss Sutton Place? The Upper East Side and Bloomie's? Don't I care that all of my friends in school are married now, a couple of them for the second time, and to men that get their names in the *New York Times*, not for being arrested? Shouldn't I've had a great career now, as a touring concert artist? Even though I'm not really, good enough for that? Don't I miss those things? Don't I regret them? Well, no, actually, I don't. And if that, if that baffles them, I'm sorry, but I really don't.

'But at the same time,' she said, 'at the same time I'm never completely sure that I'm doing the right thing. That I should be satisfied. That there isn't, really, something wrong with me, and they're the ones that are right. And that I won't wake up some morning when I'm fifty-two or something, and have it dawn on me that my attendance record in this life hasn't been good enough. That I'll realize I haven't taken the full course, and I'm not fit to graduate.

'So I do things,' she said. 'When I get uneasy like that, I do things. I make little adjustments in my life, tinker with it. Break up with the guy, if I'm seeing someone at the time, even though it hurts him and I'm really not tired of him, just to see if doing things a little differently will improve my life. And to see, you know, well, whether something that seems okay to me, something that's working all right if you don't push it too hard, whether it actually means that much to me. You know? And it almost never does. I get along all right, no matter what I do to change the way I get along. You see?'

'Imperfectly,' he said. 'It sounds like a pretty cold-blooded way to live. Almost suspended animation. Like you'd frozen yourself in one of those silver tanks of nitrogen they use to preserve rich dead California nutbags until the medical millennium. The way you *would* live on the moon, where your parents see you now.'

'It is like that,' she said. 'It's a lot like that. And I'm aware of that. So when something like Jimmy asked me to do this spring comes along, it's a real jolt, you know? I'm not used to dealing with decisions like that. Not just the specific, particular problem that happens to come along, but any kind of a major decision that might affect the way I see myself, and how I live. Because that is how I live – making no major decisions.

'So I get very cautious,' she said. 'I circle around things, and pick them up and handle them, and try to see what shape they are and whether they will keep that shape, before I put them down. And when Jimmy asked me to do that, well, that is what I did. I had to see Sam again before I could decide.

'So I went,' she said. 'I went to Morocco to see Sam. I went there in June. I took a BritAir plane to Heathrow, and I sat in the transit lounge with all the people with their yellow plastic bags full of duty-free perfume and booze, and I had two Bloody Marys and I bought three hundred Camels, because that's what Sam always smoked, and then in the late afternoon I got on another airplane, and I flew to Africa.'

'Yes,' he said.

'Yes,' she said. 'And I got wedged in between two fat guys, and Royal Air Maroc is six across in coach class, so it really is crowded. And I got to Casablanca and it's raining.'

'And Rick wasn't there,' he said.

'Rick wasn't there,' she said. 'Ingrid wasn't there. Claude Rains wasn't there. None of the usual suspects. Not even Dooley Wilson. And I went to one of the hotels along the beach where everybody swims in the pools and nobody goes to the ocean because the hotels pump their sewerage right out into the surf, and I waited there two days, and then I got a call. From him.

'And I did what he told me,' she said. 'I rented a car and I drove south to Marrakech and I checked into the Sahara there. And that evening I went down to the tables that they have around the pool and just sat there in the middle of all these French teenagers with their tight jeans on, dreaming up new ways to do the same old things that night, and Sam walked up and sat down.

'He didn't say anything at first,' she said. 'He didn't touch me, and I didn't reach out to him, either. We just sat there and looked at each other, and I guess we must've looked so odd, almost like we were in a trance, that one of the French kids finally couldn't stand it anymore and came up to me and asked if "Mademoiselle" could spare a cigarette. His English wasn't very good but I knew what he meant, and it sort of reminded me that I'd brought the

Camels for Sam and I had them in my bag, so I took out the carton, and it wasn't open, I hadn't opened it, and I pushed it across the table to Sam and told the kid he should ask "Monsieur" for his smoke. So the kid looked at Sam, and by now this poor kid is probably convinced he's struck up a conversation with a pair of lunatics, and repeats his question. And Sam opened the carton and took out a pack and gave it to him, without saying a word or even really ever looking at him. And the kid says: "Packet, M'sieu? Packet entire?" And Sam looked at him like the kid'd just stepped off a spacecraft, and nodded. And the kid made this kind of little bow and said "Merci," and went away. Like he'd been dismissed. Which, of course, he had.'

'The habit of command,' Gleason said. 'Imperial demeanor. Bearing. You're so used to being obeyed it never even occurs to the other guy not to do what you want.'

'Something like that,' she said. 'Whatever it is, ever since I've known Sam, he's always had it. He just radiates this damned assurance that of course you will do what he says, and he does it so well that half the time it never even enters your mind, that you could do something else.'

'So you went to bed with him,' Gleason said.

'Of course,' she said. 'Not immediately, I mean. But that night. And then the next day we got up early and got into my little Fiat rental and he drove down to Essaouira.' She paused. 'I don't know what I expected,' she said. 'From him, from the country, from the people – from any of it. But whatever, nothing was like I expected. We drove through these dry plateaus, where I guess they mine phosphate or something, and all the men in their brown robes were out there just standing along the road, absolutely motionless, and there'd be women and children sometimes with these little flocks of dirty sheep there, and I couldn't understand why they were there. Because there didn't seem to be anything growing in the sort of clumpy red dirt for them to eat. Some of the men were holding up bunches of asparagus, and some of them had strings of fish, and there were some that had live birds tied by their feet on a string – I suppose they must've snared them. And dogs. Ratty, scrawny, mongrel dogs.

'Then we got into the Atlas,' she said. 'The road is two-lane blacktop, and when you get into the mountains there are all these chicanes, and you get behind one of these lumbering old diesel lorries, Bedfords, that's hauling cattle, or maybe's loaded up to the sky with some kind of fodder or something, and you're behind it for miles, breathing the smoke, no way to get around.

'It was early afternoon when we got to Essaouira,' she said. 'He hadn't told me anything, so I'd just sort of assumed we were going to one of the hotels, but instead he stopped outside this white wall that had an iron gate in it, and he got out and unlocked it and then drove the car inside, and locked the gate again. And we were in this courtyard of this little villa, really. White, with a red tile roof. Like you'd see in Palm Springs, maybe – that kind of architecture. And he unlocked the front door and we went inside, and that was where we were staying.'

'Was it his?' Gleason said.

'I don't know,' she said. 'I didn't ask him. I had the feeling that it wasn't. That it belonged to somebody else who just happened not to've been there for a long time, and was letting Sam use it. Because it had that sort of closed-up, almost moist smell to it, like beach houses get when you've left them closed up all winter and then you come back in the spring and open all the doors and windows just to let some fresh air in. But I don't know, really. It could've belonged to Sam, I suppose. Maybe he just hadn't been there. He did know where everything was.'

'Including the bedroom,' he said.

'Yes,' she said. She hesitated. 'That was a lot of the reason I had to go and see him again,' she said. 'Before I decided, I mean. When I stopped seeing him, and keep in mind this was almost eleven years ago, long before I met you, but when I stopped seeing him, it wasn't because I wasn't attracted to him anymore. That I still didn't, that he wasn't still fascinating to me. Because he was. It was because what I'd seen him becoming was frightening. Because I was scared of him. That if I stayed with him, he'd not only destroy himself but everybody else. And I was afraid. But that magnetism he had, that he still has, like a power supply he can turn on any time, on anyone, he wants – that was all still there. So I had to find out ... before I did what Jimmy asked, I just had to find out myself whether I could do this to a man I really loved.'

'Spare me the suspense,' Gleason said. 'What did you find out?'

'That night we went to this hotel,' she said. 'The Hotel des Isles. We were late, and there was only one other person in the dining room. It's on the second floor with these big windows, and you can look out across the boulevard at the beach, and the ocean, and there's this big pink fort that guards the harbor. And there was only this one old woman eating dinner in there. She was European. German, I think. Wearing one of those silk dresses with lots of flowers on them, and lace at the bodice. And she had this napkin tucked in her collar and she was eating cracked crabs. Dipping the meat in mayonnaise and chewing so you could hear, and every so often putting her fork down and sucking her teeth, picking out the meat from between them with her nails. When she finished, she burped. And there were these three wizened old waiters, all pruned up – from the sun, I suppose – and they served us our dinner in silence. Then we walked out and along the beach in the evening. And he said to me: "Why did you come?"

'That was the first time he asked,' she said. 'It was the only time he asked. Here I'd flown across the ocean and traveled all these miles to see him, after almost eleven years, and he waited until the second night to ask me that. I said: "I'm not sure." Because, what could I say to him? That I was coming, I'd come to see if I could turn him in like this? Like Jimmy wants to do?

'And he said: "Don't you have memories? Can't you refer to them?" And I said: "Yes. But some of them frighten me, you know? They really frighten me. And I needed to know if you've changed."

'He said: "What have you decided?" And I said: "Well, I haven't, you know? I really haven't yet." And he said: "When do you think you will?" And I said: "I don't know that, either. You've got to give me some time."

'He said: "I can't. I can't give you too much. I've got to be in Tangier the day after tomorrow. I've got to take you back to Casa tomorrow." And I said: "Why? I can fly from Tangier. I don't care where I fly from. Why can't we just stay here?"

'He wouldn't answer me,' she said. 'I thought it was probably because he was either meeting someone there that he didn't want me to see, or going somewhere from there that he didn't want me to know. But it was probably the passport thing, like you said. He probably didn't want me to see who he was going to be when he took off from there. Security.'

'John Richards,' Gleason said, 'John Richards thinks, or Alton thinks, he's with the PLO. Or one of its affiliates, one of its splinter groups. He's still involved with that.'

'That could be,' she said. 'I asked him that, when I was there: "What are you doing, now?" Because he never could stand to be, you know, just idle. And he was very secretive. But I know, 'way back when we were together, he really did mean what he said about financing the revolution with the money from the trucks, the armored cars. And he made a lot of connections that he's probably still got. Those that aren't dead by now.'

'You know who they were?' Gleason said. 'Who any of them were?'

'Some of them,' she said. 'There was a man on Long Island that was supposed to be, he was in NORAID, the Northern Ireland Aid thing? And Sam was helping him buy guns. I know he went to Ireland, to the Republic, with him, and they went across the border into Ulster. But I don't know what they did there. I didn't go with them. And I know, he let it slip once in Morocco that he's got this friend named, he called him "Kiri," but that's about all he said. And that Kiri'd been with him in Casa when my message arrived, and told him not to see me because I'd be "dangerous." Which was why they made me wait two days, and had me watched, and then had me drive myself to Marrakech – to be sure I was alone. I asked him what he meant by that, by "dangerous." I said: "I never hurt you." But he wouldn't tell me. Just said, you know, that Kiri thought a man who'd disappeared, and wanted to stay disappeared, wouldn't take unnecessary chances. But that was all. Then he said: "I told him, when a man gets to be forty years old, he starts to slow down a little anyway. Gets nostalgic, maybe. Takes a little gamble that he wouldn't've at twenty. Kiri did not like that. He said I should play safe."'

'Uh huh,' Gleason said. 'Kiri was right, there. That's why Consolo's bugging you – 'cause Sam's been playing safe.'

'I don't follow,' she said.

'Badger ran the extradition codes through his machines when he found out where you'd been,' Gleason said. 'Morocco and this country haven't got a treaty. What they've got, what we have got, is a sort of attorneys' general accord, where we say and they say that we'll do our best to help each other get our evildoers back. But it hasn't been ratified, and it's mostly for hijackers and drug-traffic guys. So there's a real question whether Consolo can get him out of Morocco even if he does make his case, and get him charged with murder.'

'So why is he doing it, then?' she said.

'Two possible reasons,' Gleason said. 'Either what he's got in mind is catch him when he's visiting some country that does have a treaty with us, or else he's planning his own mission. Go abduct the guy.'

'He won't kidnap Sam,' she said. 'Sam carries a gun, and he's always watching out.'

'That wouldn't bother Cowboy Fred,' Gleason said. 'That wouldn't bother him.' He studied her. 'Question is: It bother you? That Fred might knock off Sam?'

She looked down. She worked her lips against her teeth. 'I don't,' she said, 'I don't think so.'

'Now that you've seen him,' Gleason said, 'now that you've made love again with him, you're satisfied you can betray him? Even to the point of getting him, maybe, killed?'

'I think so,' she said.

'Well,' he said, 'that worries me some.'

'Terry,' she said, 'this is hard for me. I'll keep my word, really.'

'Oh,' he said, 'I know that. What worries me is not your word.

It's that you had to see Sam again to decide whether to hand him his hat. And you did, and you are. And now you're seeing me – again. Hope there's no pattern there.'

38

At 4:15 in the afternoon, Det. Sgt. Frederick Consolo presided at a meeting in the offices of the Norfolk County District Attorney's office on Main Street in Dedham. He rested his haunches on the front edge of his grey steel desk and braced himself with his hands. Cpl. Peter Kelly sat at his desk to Consolo's immediate right. Cpl. Molly Dennis sat at her desk, to Consolo's immediate left. Tpr. Walter Davis sat behind Dennis. The chair behind Kelly was vacant and the desk was clear.

'I have some announcements to make,' Consolo said. 'The first is that Fitzy's been transferred, effective immediately, to the office of the District Attorney for Bristol County.'

'We knew that, Sergeant,' Dennis said. She nodded towards the empty desk. 'He was in here this morning, cleaning out his gear.'

'I know you knew that, Molly,' Consolo said. 'What you may not know is that Trooper Fitzroy was transferred against my wishes.'

'Oh, come on,' she said.

Consolo held up his hand. 'One the problems you have,' he said, 'not by any means the only one, but certainly among the more serious, is your tendency to presume facts not in your possession. Without considering the possibility that reality may not square with your presumptions. Which is the case in this instance.'

'Enlighten me,' she said.

'I shall,' Consolo said. 'Trooper Fitzroy was transferred upon receipt of my report at Ten-ten Com. It described his gross dereliction of duty yesterday. "Sleeping at the switch," was the old railroad term I used. My wishes, though, were that he be transferred to North Adams, assuming there was no opening at Ultima Thule, and that policy continues to frown on firing squads. Those wishes were not heeded, and that is why I say to you today that he is in New Bedford, against my preferences.

'Trooper Fitzroy,' he said, 'is an asshole. You, Corporal Dennis, have been something of an anus yourself. Corporal Kelly has nothing to boast about, so far as I'm aware. The result is that I spend my days trying to shine shit. I can't do it.

'Therefore,' he said, standing up, 'we are going to have a new birth of freedom here, is what we're going to have. Today, after this meeting, you, Pete, will drive me to Waterford and as soon as we know she's out of that apartment, we'll pull out the bugs and yank the truck.'

'Good,' Kelly said. 'We haven't gotten a goddamned thing out of it since we put the damned thing in.'

'That is correct,' Consolo said. 'It is also one small part of reality. The rest of reality is that the reason we haven't gotten anything is that you, and Fitzy, and you also, Brother Davis, have been inattentive, lazy and stupid. You've nonchalanted this project from the beginning, proceeded on the idea that it wouldn't produce anything – and therefore it has not.'

'Does that mean it's over, then?' Dennis said.

'Sorry to disappoint you,' Consolo said. 'It doesn't mean that. As war is the continuation of diplomacy by other means, so this investigation will continue. By other means. In which none of you will be required to participate.'

'Same thing, then,' she said, 'as far as we're concerned.'

He shook his head. 'You keep doing it, Molly,' he said. 'While your participation will not be required, it will be very much allowed. In other words, if your commitment to this project should for some reason improve to the point at which you think you might actually like to contribute something to its success, where it should have been all along, I'd appreciate your help.'

'Are you serious?' Kelly said. 'Are you actually *serious*, Sarge?'

'Certainly am,' Consolo said. 'I'm always serious. I'm not as hopeful as I'd like to be, that you'll think things over and decide to be serious too, but it is a possibility and I don't want to rule it out.'

'Why,' Davis said, 'why, the way you've treated us, would we do a thing like that?'

Consolo pointed his right index finger at Davis. 'Good point,' he said, 'good point. You have a good point there. It's time for an attitude check. Mine as well as yours. I think you'd want to pitch in, where you were holding back before, because I've been doing some serious thinking of my own about this investigation, and I've concluded – and this maybe will surprise you – but I've concluded some of your reluctance, just going through the motions, that I may have caused it. Some of it, at least. At least a part of it. Not intentionally. Not on purpose. But when you find yourself in a snafued situation like this, and you're the one supposedly in charge, one of the things you have to think about is whether you've communicated your goals clearly to the people you want to carry them out.

'Basic principle of management,' he said. 'You'll never get successful management if you don't analyze mistakes of unsuccessful management, especially your own, and see if you can find out what brought them about.

'Now,' he said, rubbing his chin with his left hand, 'I have tried to do that in this case. And that's what I came up with: that Fitzy's carelessness; that your chronic insubordination, Pete; and your mediocre handling of the Simone interrogation, Molly; that all of those events happened because I failed initially to articulate clearly exactly what I wanted to do here, and why I wanted to do it.'

'Hey,' Davis said, 'does that mean I'm off the hook?'

'Inflate the life raft, Pete,' Dennis said. 'Ship must be sinking if the rat is getting off.'

'Cut it out,' Consolo said. 'No, Walter, it doesn't mean you're off the hook. It only means that your responsibility for the lack of success so far is probably attributable to some omission to act at a time when you should have, so I don't know what you could've come up with if you acted properly.

'Anyway,' he said, 'this is what I'm going to do. I called Osgood down on the Cape this morning.'

'I'll bet June loved you for that,' Dennis said. 'You know how she feels about Dave being interrupted on his vacation.'

'Yes I do,' Consolo said. 'He hates it, and she hates it, and right now all they're thinking about's going to the beach today and then to the races next month. And that's why I did it. Why I called Osgood direct – so he'll do what I want when I want it, just to get rid of me. I said: "Look, I'll make this quick. Our guy is moving around. If I get a chance to grab him, I want to be in a position to take it. I don't want to be in a position where I have to ask Interpol to shadow the son of a bitch for two weeks until I can locate you somewhere for approval, and schedule some grand jury time, and then have to scrounge up some spare assistant DA somewhere that doesn't happen to be doing much of anything, and isn't on vacation, so I can present the case. By which time the bastard will've moved on somewhere else. I need to be ready to move out with a warrant in my hand, and take my prisoner."

'And he pissed and moaned, of course, but not for very long – because he wanted to take June to the beach with their shovels and their pails, and their delicious picnic lunch. So, Fern Schofield's presenting the case on Wednesday morning, which is the thirty-first and later'n I'd like, but that's the first day we can get the grand jury in. And we'll go with what we've got and hope to get more later. But we'll at least have a warrant, if we do stumble over the guy, and that'll be an improvement.'

'Have we got enough to indict?' Davis said. 'Have we actually made the deal? Cut the bargain with Walker?'

'We've got enough,' Consolo said. 'If I can't cut a deal with Walker by then I'll throw his buddy's statements in, and go the hearsay route. If I can cut a deal, then we'll put Walker in, get him immunity, and put him on the record, under oath, before we ask him the first question. Every single syllable, down on the record.'

'He'll want to see his lawyer,' Dennis said. 'The first thing he'll say is that he won't talk until he sees his lawyer. He picks the wrong one, Tibbetts'll get a telegram, and he will go to ground. We'll have our warrant, maybe, but nobody to catch with it.'

'It's a chance we've got to take,' Consolo said. 'We're not getting anywhere this way, proceeding as we have been. Time to try something new. He knows, most likely knows by now we're chasing him again. If he doesn't know exactly what for, or how we're going to prove it, if he thinks about it long enough he probably can guess. And Walker's not going to get anything out of it until he testifies at trial, so we lose nothing by making his deal now. Might even gain something, as a matter of fact – once he knows the only thing between him and the front gate at Cedar Junction's us capturing Tibbetts, he's going to be a lot more alert for any scraps of information that'll tell us where Sam is.'

'Yeah,' Davis said, 'but once that word gets out, you know, won't Sam try to reach in there, and make Mister Walker dead?'

'We'll isolate him if we have to,' Consolo said. 'Put him in the infirmary. But I don't think Tibbetts can pull that off. Not now. Too long's gone by. All his people've dispersed. He hasn't got the guns.'

'Who's gonna try this blinger, Fred,' Dennis said. 'Assuming we do catch this buzzard, who is going to try it?'

Consolo shrugged. 'I dunno,' he said. 'Haven't gotten that far yet. Catch him first, then worry.'

'Fern's a nice kid, Fred,' Dennis said, 'but she ain't no Gleason.'

Consolo showed a crooked smile. 'Yeah, Moll, you're right,' he said, 'but Dave Osgood used to be, and if we grab this SOB, he'll be chomping at the bit.'

'Okay,' Dennis said, 'where do we fit in, if you join this new campaign?'

'I don't know exactly,' Consolo said. 'As I've said, this is, we're entering a new phase. To a degree we're going to have to improvise, make it up as we go along. But one of the things we know – if we don't know exactly how we're going to have to react, we do know that we're going to have to react. So for now it's a matter of keeping our eyes open, staying plugged in to our sources around town, and being prepared to respond instantly if something starts going down.'

'I see,' she said. 'I think that's great.'

'I thought you would,' he said.

'You know how I lie,' she said.

39

James Walker's skin was the color of strong coffee mixed with a little light cream. He had a closely trimmed, black goatee, and he had shaved his head. His features were even. He wore rimless bifocals with stainless steel bows and he sat on a grey metal chair in the visitors' room with his arms folded at his waist. He spoke in a soft voice. At 8:13 in the evening, he told Gleason on the opposite chair that they could not talk there.

'No, we can't,' Gleason said. 'On the other hand, though, we can't get a counsel room because the guard looked in his book and he didn't find my name after your name as your lawyer.'

'Hey,' Walker said, 'sorry 'bout that, man. I had, I've been having visitors lately, want to see me private? Makes the other cons nervous. Other cons get nervous, I get nervous. I like to sleep on my stomach, close my eyes when I drift off. Other guys, you know, get nervous, think you're making deals. Doesn't 'matter who goes down, they don't approve of that.'

'Like who?' Gleason said. 'There's another lawyer on your case, that is fine by me.'

Walker held up both hands. 'Hey, no offense, man,' he said, 'no lawyers at all. Everything you heard is true – assuming that it was, that is, since I wasn't there.'

'Christina said you needed a lawyer, and you didn't have one, and she asked me to come,' Gleason said.

Walker nodded. 'Well, then,' he said, 'mind's at ease. That is what is true. Guys coming in to see me, what they were was cops.'

'Now wait a minute,' Gleason said, 'my understanding was you wanted to see a lawyer *before* you saw the cops.'

'Mine, too,' Walker said. 'Cops don't always care 'bout that, what the guy in the joint wants. They just drop by for a chat, any time they like. Yank him out of general pop, shoot the shit a while. Put him back in population – let the guy explain.'

'I see,' Gleason said. 'I probably already know the answer to this question, but I'll ask anyway.'

'Don't even need the question,' Walker said. 'Fellow named Consolo. Came out here back in April, told me what was on the way. Then came back here, middle June, asked me how I liked it. First time: "Sam is getting out." Second time: "Sam's out. I hear rumors maybe you'd like, you'd like to get out."' He shook his head and laughed. 'Strange man,' he said, 'a strange man. He thinks Sam's in England, 'cause my little sister went there.' He gazed directly at Gleason. 'You know she went to England, Gleason? Tina tell you that?'

'Yeah,' Gleason said.

Walker laughed again. 'Damn,' he said, 'that's something, ain't it? That is really something. Christina goes to England while I'm waiting on her call, and now Consolo and you both know, and she only just told me.'

'Yeah,' Gleason said.

'You know *why* she went to England, man?' Walker said softly.

'Yeah,' Gleason said.

'You *sure* you do?' Walker said.

Gleason sighed. 'Oh yeah, I'm sure.'

'To catch another plane?' Walker said. 'Isn't that what she did?'

'Could be,' Gleason said.

'"Could be,"' Walker said. 'Yeah, right: "could be." I couldn't get it out of her, either. I knew what it was, but I couldn't get her, say it. But I knew what it was. I've known Christina a long time. I know how she thinks. Oh, very sly, Christina. Very sly, she is.' He coughed. He mused. 'Consolo,' he said, 'he asked me, he asked what that meant. "That mean Sam's in England? He went there when he got free?"'

'What'd you say?' Gleason said.

'Said nothin',' Walker said. 'Thought plenty. Thought: "This guy's an asshole and I'm making deals with him? He don't know where she went after she left United States?" He's either too stupid to be dangerous, or too dangerous to be stupid, but it's one the other, and it don't matter which. Not from where I sit. I got to have a lawyer.'

'He's neither one,' Gleason said. 'Neither stupid nor dangerous. He is what he is. He plays strictly by the rules. If there's some rule that says he can't find something out, he doesn't find it out. That's all. Just plays by the rules.'

'Then he's stupid,' Walker said, '*and* he's dangerous. That is what I just said. He asked me: Did she tell me where she went when she took off?'

'What'd you say?' Gleason said.

'My friend,' Walker said, 'I said nothin'. Just like I'm gonna tell the boys when I go back inside from you. "Can't help if people come to see me, matter who they are. I ain't goin' noplace, Bro, I am still right here."'

'What'd he say?' Gleason said. 'Say to you, I mean?'

'Said he heard a guy I know say I would make a trade,' Walker said.

'Did you say that?' Gleason said.

'Did I say that?' Walker said. 'Sure I said that, man. Naturally, I said that. I been in here a long time. Got to find myself a way out. Got to get some air. Feel some sidewalk with my feet. Just do what I please. But I did not say I would deal directly with no cop. All I wanted was to find out, if the deal was there. And that is why I asked Christina, what I asked her to.'

'Okay,' Gleason said, 'you asked her, and she asked me, and now here I am. Wherever she went, in between. And I'm willing to abide by your decision. Christina asked me to come and see you, and I've done that. But I can't do much, I'm not your lawyer. And I'm not your lawyer now. Makes you nervous, take me on, that is fine by me. If you're satisfied the attempt's been made, then I certainly am satisfied, and we can leave it at that.'

'You understand my position,' Walker said. 'John Bigelow and I, I haven't seen him, or heard from him, in years.'

'I understand,' Gleason said.

'I'm going to,' Walker said, 'if I go through with this thing, I'm going to need a lawyer. Because I've been fucked over before by the law. As you know because you did it. And I learned from that, I did. I need somebody looking out for my ass outside. While I look out for it, inside. They got a habe on me for Wednesday.'

'That's fast,' Gleason said. 'Without a deal, they're habing you? Why they doing that?'

'Well, I don't know,' Walker said, 'but it doesn't make me glad. I think, what I think is that they're gonna try to get what I got, without making me a deal.'

'Well,' Gleason said, 'not going to do them any good, get you immunity. They can throw contempts at you for the next ten years, and with the time that you've still got, hell difference does it make? You can sit there like a stone, and smile and smile and smile.'

'Yeah, I can,' Walker said, 'but I don't want to do that. And also, the minute I go out of here that day, talk is gonna start. Talk that won't do me much good. Talk could get me killed. So, they're bringin' me in anyway, I should have my deal. Give the bastards what they want, so they isolate me.'

'Is that what you want me to do?' Gleason said.

'It's what I want somebody to do,' Walker said. 'I hope you're the guy. You, you knew how to do it, the other side. I hope you still do now. I got to look out for myself. Guys get shanks in their backs in here over cigarettes and candy. There're guys in here that never heard of the Bolivian Contingent, never heard of Sam, that if they knew what I'm doing, they would stick me just for that. For trading him for me.'

'But you're prepared to do it,' Gleason said. 'Betray the revolution.'

Walker snorted. 'Sure I am,' he said. 'Revolution betrayed me. I'm sick of it. Everybody else but me, Kathie and Jill, out having a good time. I'm still true to principles? Doesn't make much sense. I just woke up late – that's all. My life is going by. Sam isn't going to help me. Christina, by herself – Christina can't help me. Only way

I make bail from this place is by selling something, and I've only got one thing to sell the cops. Which is Sam's ass. Fair enough. But I don't want to make the trade, and then find out I gave away the only thing I had, without getting something back.'

'Reasonable,' Gleason said. 'You need someone you can trust. So: why pick me to trust? Like you say, I'm the guy that put you in. I'm the guy that's in the process, losing a big federal case. You say you're not sure you trust me, and yet I'm just the guy you picked? Then why'd you say, Come and see me. Why did you do that?'

'Because I don't have any money,' Walker said. 'I probably could get some money, if I asked my mother. Florence would do anything. Clayton? Maybe not, but Florence would do anything her baby boy asked her.'

'So, why not do that?' Gleason said. 'Ask your mother for some money. Hire a guy that you're sure you trust, can trust to get you out.'

'Because I don't want to, Mister Gleason,' Walker said. 'My mother is an asshole. I got in here without any help from her. I plan on getting out the same way. Right now, I'm sitting here, I owe a full fourteen years, the State. Good behavior time's all gone, all the self-defense I've done, and I am rotting here. But I'm not looking to get out and owe the next thirty, my mother. I'm getting out without any help from any goddamned reactionaries. Fucking fascist pigs.

'Think of me as the trader,' Walker said. 'What I want is out. What I got's two things to trade: Sam Tibbetts and my sister.'

'I'm with you part of the way,' Gleason said. 'The cops'll deal for Sam. But who you trading your sister to?'

'You,' Walker said.

'Me,' Gleason said.

'Yeah,' Walker said, 'you. You got a marriage sucking brown air. Christina told me that, man, a whole long time ago. You're about as happy as a big snake in the snow. Unhappy man'll do things. You've done them before. And you've done them with my sister, which I didn't like a lot then, but I do know that you did.'

'Yes,' Gleason said.

'So that's the deal,' Walker said. 'Her pussy for my life. My life out of here.' He laughed. 'That's a better offer'n you get, most your clients, I bet. Christina Walker's cunt, just for making a few calls?' He laughed. 'You really like that girl's ass, don't you? You'd do anything for that. Get inside those little panties, stick your cock in her.'

'I don't have to sit through this,' Gleason said.

Walker laughed again. 'Course you don't,' he said. 'You can get up and leave. You are a free man. You can stand up on your back legs and say: "Well, that's it, nigger. Stay and do what you're gonna do. Another fourteen years or so. That is, if you live." But you're not gonna do that, are you? No, indeed, you're not. You made a deal, my baby sister. And why'd you make that deal? Because old Christina, she knows what makes you happy. She knows how to get to you. And she did that the other night. Down at the motel. What's the room number again? Number four, is it? You saving water in the shower, taking one together? They get the dirty movies, there, the cable television? Does Christina know what you like? Does she? Tell me, huh, does she?'

Gleason did not say anything. Walker leaned toward him. 'Now you listen to me, white boy. You just listen to me good. There's only one thing in this world that I want, and that's Out. Out of this fucking place forever, fast as I can go. I need some promises to do that, someone ride my horse. I need someone to deal for me, with

401

this fucking crazy cop. Only thing I can tell you's that Christina will deliver. She really seems to like your cock, though that's not saying much – she's liked a lot of them. Just like her lovely mother, who's so smooth and so refined. There'd be a bounty on those women, if they didn't fuck. How long she will deliver?' He shrugged. 'That I do not know. But you will get your piece of ass. You will have your fun. You negotiate for me, you will have to lose her, or she will lose herself. Which of those two things comes first? *That* I do not know. But you should have a nice ride. Which is better'n I've got.'

'Brrr,' Gleason said.

'Ah, come on, what is different?' Walker said. 'What the hell's the difference, between what you did to me, and what I'm offering today? It's all a fucking goddamned deal. That's all it ever is. Cut the fucking deal, man, all right? Cut the fucking deal. Talk the people that you got to. Make sure it goes down. Locate Sam and let 'em get him. Then I will get out. Everything is hunky-dory. Everything is fine.'

40

Florence Amberson Walker was accompanied from the first-class cabin of British Caledonian flight 222 (JFK International to Gatwick) to the EEC gates of British Immigration shortly before 8:05 in the morning. She wore a grey silk Ungaro coat dress and a small round matching hat. She presented her UK passport in the name of Florence Amberson and was waved through. Outside Immigration a tall man in a grey uniform advanced toward her. 'Mrs Walker,' he said, 'so nice to see you again.' He offered his arm.

She took it gratefully. 'Wonderful to see you, Kenneth,' she said, 'I'm afraid I'm getting old.'

'Nonsense,' he said. 'You're looking wonderful.'

She rapped him lightly on the forearm. 'Lies, Kenneth, lies,' she said. 'You always were a liar. Or your eyes are going bad. I'm absolutely tottering. *God*, and to think I used to do this as a matter of course. The most primitive equipment, hours and hours in the air, propellers drumming away, stopping at Gander to refuel, and arrive fit for a scrum.' She sighed. 'No more, Kenneth. No more. Those days are past me now.'

He patted her left arm with his left arm. 'Well,' he said, 'into the car then, settle down. I shall have your things in order and we'll be on our way to a good lie-down for you.'

'Sounds wonderful,' she said. She dozed most of the way to London in the red leather back seat of the Daimler limousine, now and then sputtering a ladylike snore that made the chauffeur smile. Coming into Knightsbridge near the barracks, he adjusted the radio to concentrate the sound in the rear compartment, and very gradually increased the volume until she stirred, opened her eyes and then sat up. She flexed her facial muscles and rubbed her hands together. At The Dorchester Hotel she was ready to emerge smiling when the doorman opened the car. 'Mrs Walker,' he said. 'Lovely to have you back.'

'Lovely to be back, Dennis,' she said. 'Lovely to be back.'

'It really is the most ghastly thing,' Florence Walker said to Claire Naisbitt at tea in the hotel lobby at 4:30 P.M. Most of the tapestried chairs, couches and low tables were occupied: Americans with greying temples determined to be young wore dark blue jogging suits, tight jeans and running shoes; dark men from the Middle East swept through in white robes, their ladies in silk dresses. Three German men in severe dark suits sat near a rose marble pillar and drank red wine. At the far end of the lobby, a pianist in black tie overlaid the conversations with medleys from *Cats*, *Guys and Dolls*, and *Showboat*.

'There was never any trouble in the old days,' Florence said, 'booking a flight on short notice. And there were nowhere near as many of them, then. But now, now with all these damnable students, and tourists, and *families with little children*, absolutely choking the facilities, crowding onto the planes with their baggage and their brats, probably their dogs and cats – even if you did want to spend the whole night listening to their racket, you can't do it. Because you can't get on. No matter whom you call. And you *have* to fly first class – it's the only thing that's open. And you have to fly at night, because the day flights are all jammed. The businessmen seize those. Do you know, do you know that the Concorde was full? I tell you, Claire, I was tempted. I truly was tempted. When Christina called me yesterday – no, Saturday, it was – when Christina called me Saturday and dropped her little bombshell, I was actually tempted to ring you up and do it that way. Save this dreadful trip.'

'Well,' Claire said, 'damned good thing you didn't, Florence. Damned good thing, I'd say.' She wore a pale blue silk dress with pearls at her neck, a rose silk hat on her head and a grey flowered scarf on her shoulders. She spread strawberry preserve and *crème fraîche* on a scone. 'They're all microwave relays now, all the lines are, as if the cables weren't bad enough. Might as well send a cable, you want everyone on both sides to know what your business is.'

'It was still an ordeal,' Florence said. She drank tea. 'It was still an utter ordeal.'

'I'm sure it was,' Claire said. 'Neville said, when I told him I was coming down, he went into his usual performance, stamping feet and growling – What were the Fobeses to think, after we'd promised we'd come – and I had to say to him: "Oh for heaven's sake, Neville, do try to be sensible. If Florence thinks it's enough of an emergency that she's flying the Atlantic like this, it's a hell of a lot more important than the bloody damned Fobeses and their bloody dinner party. Now shut up and go yourself, and make excuses for me.'"

'Well,' Florence said, 'still, I am sorry to disrupt your schedules like this.'

'Nonsense,' Claire said. 'The only reason he was angry is that he didn't want to go himself, but he lacked an excuse. I was getting out of it and he didn't have a way.' She picked up her teacup and sat back in her winged chair. 'Now,' she said, 'tell me. Tell me everything.'

Florence lifted her hands and dropped them in her lap. 'Claire,' she said, 'it's such a nuisance. Such a damned nuisance. The effort we go to, to deceive the children into believing they've managed to deceive us, so they won't just make things worse? It's perfectly exhausting. Now here's Christina, all bound and determined that she's going to make this glorious sacrifice of her peace and quiet, in order to perform a noble gesture for her brother. Which will of course be at the expense of everybody else's peace and quiet, meaning Clayton's and mine – and God knows, there's little enough of that as it is.'

'Clayton's still not well?' Claire said.

'Clayton's drinking too much, Claire,' Florence said. 'He's drinking far too much. Over the years the accumulation of things has simply become too much for him, and now he's tired and wants his rest. But the heart attack didn't kill him. He trained his colleagues too well. They knew exactly how to save him. They assumed that's what he'd want. And at the time, he probably did. But if he'd been downed away from home, almost anywhere else in the world, and just allowed a few painful hours for matters to proceed too far, he would've had some peace. Far more than he's had since.

406

'He's stuck with his own nobility,' Florence said. 'Forty-odd years ago he struck his pose when I became pregnant by Gerald, and he was stuck with it. Well, that was his limit for one lifetime. Everything else, anything else that came after that was above his tolerance. And there have been many things. Many, many things. He's simply absorbed more punishment than he was constructed to endure. So now he wants to die. If his heart won't give out on him, damnit, well, perhaps his liver will.

'Now, James,' she said. 'James is better off where he is now than he's likely to be, anywhere else in the world. Clayton's better off, far better off, with James incapacitated from causing further trouble – he can pretend sometimes that he doesn't exist. But James and Christina don't think of such things. They flatter themselves that Clayton still expects James to amount to something – he does not; he's written him off entirely. And they like to think that of course I know nothing of the nature of James's situation. That I go around making my foolish, deluded best of things as usual, in my poor, deluded vanity, pretending that James's away at some school somewhere, or in some monastery. That I have no notion whatsoever of maximum security prison.

'Well,' she said, 'they're wrong. I do. Gerald's on the Judiciary Committee, subcommittee on corrections, and as infuriatingly stupid as that man can be, he does have his uses. I've read enough studies, and reports, and testimony, to qualify me to teach at John Jay. I know what those places are like. And that sort of place is exactly where James belongs. He fits the profile of the dangerous offender to a tee. He might as well've been pouring Drano in his ears, all those years he was on drugs. He was utterly without respect for authority before that, completely rebellious and wayward, absolutely impervious to civilized discipline. When he was a child, and a young man, he tested our limits and found he could flout them. Then he tested the limits at his schools, and found the worst they could do to him was throw him out. Then he tested the limits of the criminal code, and got away with that, too, for some period of time, and then he was caught. And now he knows there are some in authority who mean it – really mean it. And that there are other disciplinary cases who are harder than he is. This is the first time in James's life that he's ever been at close quarters with people that he fears. And that is the only set of circumstances in which he'll behave himself. When he is afraid.

'He doesn't like it,' Florence said. 'Of course he doesn't like it. After seven years in that company, he hasn't managed to intimidate everybody else into allowing him to do precisely what he pleases. He's become discouraged. He wants to get out.

'Until May,' she said, 'until this May, he couldn't do that. Oh, the means were there. The means he's using now. All he had to do was barter Samuel for himself. The police are just like everybody else. You offer them something they want more than what they've got, they'll be interested. But James, who never was too bright, even before the drugs, James was too *proud* for that. But then Sam got out. And James, dim as he is, began to see what a total ass he'd been.

'So,' she said, 'after spurning all Christina's overtures for years, refusing to write to her, reply to her letters ... '

'Really?' Claire said. 'I thought they were so close.'

'They were,' Florence said. 'They both hated Clayton, and they both scorned me. That was how Tibbetts acquired both of them – getting even with us. Until she had the wit to see what a fix they were all getting into, and cleared out. That's what James resented. That's she's smarter than he. And, more talented. Not a grain of sense in the child, of course. Scatterbrained as windblown chaff. But smarter than her brother? Yes. That's why, though she's been in less public trouble, in many respects – for me, at least – she's been the more difficult child. And that's what James disliked. But, after all those years of being just a total bastard to her, knowing she'd have to be talking to me, knowing I'd know at least the small amount he was willing to report about what he was going through, knowing that she'd have to dissemble to me, so that I wouldn't figure out that he'd shunned her utterly – after all that gratuitous cruelty, he called on her for help. And like the idealistic ninny that she is, she decided to prove it. She's going to get him out.'

'How?' Claire said.

'Well,' Florence said, 'that's another thing. Christina's mind is unformed. She's not at home with complexity, reasoning out all the probable consequences of her actions. When James called on her for help, she went back immediately to that Gleason fellow, took the matter to him.'

'I suppose it has a certain logic,' Claire said drily.

'Well, of course it's my example that she's proceeding on,' Florence said. 'Not that she even realizes it, or would, God forbid, admit it, but she simply set out to exploit a former lover just as I've done with Gerald. Known quantity. Unlikely to refuse her anything she asks.' She smiled. 'It's a rare man, Claire, and a bad one, who can reject a plea for help from a former maiden he distressed. And Terry Gleason's not a bad man. Rather a sad one, I gather, discontent, unsatisfied, and therefore even likelier to react favorably to a younger, pretty, former lover's pitiable cries.'

'Does she know you know all this?' Claire said. 'I thought you weren't supposed to know.'

'I wasn't,' Florence said. 'Back when they got involved, after the trial, and Larry called me up, he swore my oath in blood that I never would let on. And of course I didn't. But I wouldn't have in any case. Half the pleasure of a married lover for a restless young woman is the delicious thrill of imagining how shocked and angry her parents would be if they knew what she was doing. And I didn't want to spoil that for her. Besides, if she had reckoned that I knew, she would've become careless around Clayton. And he *would* have been angry and shocked. I'm sure he could not have supported the knowledge that his daughter was as adventurous as his wife had been. He would've thought he was under a curse.'

She paused. 'Maybe he is,' she said. 'Maybe we all are, always have been. The reason we're always coping – so successfully, we think – with one disaster after another, is not that we're resourceful, smart survivors; it's because we're accursed.'

'Yes,' Claire said, setting her teacup down. 'Well, that certainly would make life less demanding, wouldn't it? Just give up, and blame the devil? But I assume you didn't come all this way just to do that.'

'No,' Florence said. She sighed. 'No, I came because of course I can't do that.'

'Then what is to be done?' Claire said.

'Well,' Florence said, 'it's perfectly obvious that neither James nor Christina will be safe if young Sam Tibbetts is brought back to America and tried again for murder. If this time he's convicted, he'll be free in less than fifteen years. Sam's much more intelligent than James. None of those thugs and hoodlums who've managed to provoke James into prison fights will be able to do that with Sam. If he's incarcerated, and assesses his situation as one requiring him to enter into a homosexual relationship in order to save his skin, that's what he will do. If he determines that something else – becoming a reliable source of illegal narcotics, for example – will guarantee his safety, then he will do that. Whatever is necessary to enable him to get out in the shortest possible time, that's what he will do. I knew Sam only briefly, but I know him well. Several weeks ago one night, Clayton staggered off to bed quite early, and I found myself alone with the television set and cold cream on my face. So I browsed around until I found a film – *Doctor Zhivago*. And I sat there entranced until after three in the morning thinking every time that Strelnikov appeared – the Tom Courtenay locomotive driver? That Stalin ruthlessness? – "Sam Tibbetts" ran through my mind.

'He won't forget, Claire,' she said. 'Most men do, but he will not. Either he will be acquitted, and the danger will be imminent, or he'll be convicted, and it will be postponed. But in either event, today or tomorrow, once Sam is recaptured both my children are in hazard.'

'I've always preferred,' Claire said, 'I've always preferred to deal as promptly as possible with dangerous situations as soon as they're perceived. The Chamberlain experience, I suppose. Nip evil in the bud.'

'And much truer now than then,' Florence said. 'At least as far as we're concerned. Neither James nor Christina is equipped to deal with a menace like Sam. James fancies himself tempered by his severe experiences, but his letters reveal clearly the operation of a still adolescent mind. He might manage to protect himself, but he would do it in a fashion that would put him right back in the same fix that he's in now. Christina's personality would be entirely passive if the world would only permit. Action is not one of her talents. She might be able to bring herself to retaliate, though perhaps not effectively, but she's unlikely to have the leisure to do that, if Mister Tibbetts strikes first. Young Mister Gleason may be a resourceful person, but he may be back with his wife again by then – and anyway, I don't know him at all. I don't like to rely on strangers in important matters.

'You and I are dependable,' Florence said. 'But we are getting old. Larry Badger's still ogling mere slips, but he is aging too. Young Alton seems capable enough, and certainly Fiona shows great, great promise. But for the rest of us, every day that dawns without the thief having come in the night means that the chances of his arrival tonight have increased.'

'I agree with you,' Claire said. 'I don't suppose we can tidy up the world entirely, but it would be nice to straighten things up as much as possible before we go.'

'Precisely,' Florence said. 'I've not done very well by my children. Whatever resources I might've had to prevent harm from reaching them, those I have squandered. I think, to be on the safe side, I think perhaps I'd better make some kind of reparations now, for my omissions and oversights. And that is why I came.'

'Yes,' Claire said. She beckoned a waiter for more tea. 'Would you like anything else, Florence?'

'Yes,' Florence said to the waiter. 'I should like a large gin martini, please. With a lemon twist.'

'Just more tea for me, please,' Claire said. The waiter went away. She leaned forward. 'Now,' she said, 'the first thing we must think about is where it should be done. Do we know where he is now?'

Florence nodded. 'Larry says Morocco,' she said. She grimaced. 'Where Christina went to see him late spring, just in case, after James turns him in, he might otherwise fail to make the connections and identify the causes. I gather he's safe as long as he remains there. Legally, that is. Even after they charge him back in Boston. Or wherever it is. Something about treaties.'

'Does Larry say what he is doing?' Claire said.

'Um, running guns, he thinks,' Florence said. 'Dealing in arms. He's not sure, but he believes that's it. Apparently Sam travels a lot. Under various names. They think that is why.'

The waiter returned with the tea and the drink. Florence picked up the martini and sipped it. 'And after all these years, and all these times,' she said, 'every time I set about something like this, I have to screw my courage up.' She set the drink down.

'That should be easy enough, then,' Claire said. 'Just a matter of getting him into some country where he can be detained until something can be done. Fabricate some reason to trick him into travel. Collar him when he arrives.' She paused. 'Have you spoken to Fiona?' she said. 'Did you call the Embassy?'

'No,' Florence said. 'I was about to, and then I thought perhaps I should discuss it with you first. That it might be better. dearly as I'd love to see her, but that it might be better ... '

'Yes, I should think so,' Claire said comfortably. 'Much better not to visit with her just now.'

'How is her marriage?' Florence said. 'Her last letter seemed a little more strained than usual.'

'Well,' Claire said, 'just as I did, just as you did, Fiona's learning the burdens that come with being married to a man who thinks he's a warrior. It's exciting, at first, but then after a while the thrill subsides, and one becomes somewhat fatigued. She and Louis are still married, and the children are well. How long the marriage will last? That I couldn't say.'

'And Louis's still doing the same thing?' Florence said. 'He did seem a dashing young man.'

'Oh, yes,' Claire said. 'I don't know what they're calling it this week, or what it will be next, but he's still doing it all over the world, every chance he gets.'

'So, then, if Fiona,' Florence said, 'if you got in touch with Fiona ... '

'That's what I had in mind,' Claire said. 'Neville has a contact in Derry with the Special Branch. I believe they've had some success with one of their super-grasses undercover, trapping men like Sam. Shouldn't be too difficult to coordinate something there through Fiona here and Larry in Boston, so that the instant they have power to arrest Sam, we set everything in motion. And once we know he's coming, well then: Louis's expertise.'

'Such a wonderful cornet player,' Florence said. 'I think perhaps the year he toured with the Ensemble, I think that was the best series of pieces for brass that Neville's ever put on.'

'That was one of the better years,' Claire said. 'It's rather, I'm afraid we're rather thin this year, in the reeds. We've lost some good people. Graduations among the undergraduates. Better jobs elsewhere, taking faculty members away.'

'But you'll still be in America, this winter,' Florence said anxiously.

'Oh certainly,' Claire said. 'Neville's confident. He's always confident. He's set up a concert at the University of Missouri, Kansas City, and in California at Davis, and the Redlands, and some others. And we'll be at Town Hall one night. And of course, Neville's determined to do Tommy Oates's show. While we're in New York.'

'I warned you,' Florence said. 'That's not a good idea. I've known Tommy ever since I deduced he was the penis that started Christina on her lifetime of condescending to my intelligence. He's a charming young man, and a viper.'

'I know you did, Florence,' Claire said. 'He wasn't much of a musician, either. I reminded Neville of that. "You told me long ago," I said, "you said after he toured with us that was the last time you let anyone in just because you knew his father. You know how much trouble we had with him. How rebellious he was." And you can guess what Neville said. "I'm not afraid of Tom," he said. "I knew his father well."'

Florence nodded. 'They are such fools,' she said, 'such dear and blessed fools.' She picked up her martini and sipped again. 'But *I* feel ever so much better,' she said. 'Such a weight off my back.'

'You'll be here how long?' Claire said. 'Will you see anyone?'

Florence laughed. 'Well,' she said, 'I do have to stay long enough to buy some tweeds or something. Or perhaps a foyer rug. After all, I did tell Clayton, I was going shopping. I must buy something as well.' She smiled.

41

Claire Naisbitt sat at the southerly end of the burnished cherry table that accommodated ten in the Walkers' dining room on the first floor of their three-floor condominium on Sutton Place. She traced the beveled edge of the table with her gnarled left little finger. She nodded. 'Well, of course I agree with you, Florence,' she said. 'Of course he'll get in trouble.'

Florence Walker sat at the easterly end of the table. Her hair had returned to coal black, and was cut short. She wore earrings of rubies and diamonds; they dangled forward when she leaned, and caught the candlelight. Her white dress was cut low. Her breasts were abundant and smooth, and her chest and neck were unwrinkled. She wore two bracelets of hammered gold. 'Well, then,' Florence said, 'why on earth did you let him do it?'

Claire looked at her with amused, feigned disdain. 'Florence,' she said, 'really. You and Clayton have merely *known* Neville for forty years and more. I've been *married* to him. Have you or anyone else you know ever been able to forestall Neville from getting into trouble?'

A double steel door about sixteen feet wide and twelve feet high opened into the studio. There was a revolving red light over it, with a sign next to it that said 'No Entry. On the Air.' The guide opened the right half, preceded Prof. Neville L.C. Naisbitt, C.B.E., through it, and shut the door behind them.

It was very dark after the door shut. Naisbitt felt the youth slide past him in the gloom. 'Follow me, please, *señor*,' the youth said. Naisbitt hesitated for a moment while his eyes partially adjusted to the low light. '*Señor*?' the youth said.

'I'm coming,' Naisbitt said. 'Go ahead, I'll follow.'

The narrow, irregular and variable spaces left as walkways Naisbitt saw to be enclosed by large backdrops. The only lighting was residual, filtering down from twenty feet above under the steel rafters of the roof high above. The painted concrete underfoot was slightly moist, littered with fat black cables laid with no apparent pattern. The youth insinuated himself behind the scenery and scampered over the cables with facile familiarity, leaving Naisbitt groping slowly along behind him, his left hand held before his forehead to ward off collisions with unseen obstacles, his right arm bent at the elbow to hold the coat, the cane hooked over the wrist, hanging useless in the dark. He irrationally envied the guide's agility, straining but unable to hear the halting English being spoken to him from ahead. He ducked around a sharp upright at eye level to his left. He hit the ulna bone of his right elbow on a tall stepladder he was sure had been placed to ambush large, unwary visitors blundering through the sets. The shock radiated through him. '*Damn*,' he said, and stopped, lowering his left hand to massage his right arm. 'You're simply going to have to slow down,' he said in a louder voice into the dimness.

'*Que?*' the guide said plaintively, invisible ahead.

'More slowly,' Naisbitt said. 'Proceed more slowly, please.'

'Oh,' the guide said. 'I say: "you, make, the, tapes, music?"'

'*Shit*,' Naisbitt said.

'*No comprenez*,' the guide said, alarm in his voice.

'Oh, go on,' Naisbitt said desperately, using his left hand to make a shooing gesture he was sure could not be seen. 'Just go on. Get where we're going. Get this over with.'

'*Si, señor*,' the guide said, hurt urgent in his voice. 'Just a little further. We will be there soon.'

The lighting began to improve, brightening over the tops of the backdrops twenty feet above, and Naisbitt's vision had completed adjustment to its level just before the guide suddenly appeared silhouetted against strong direct light about fifteen feet ahead. Lurching forward out of the darkness, Naisbitt was again blinded momentarily by the illumination from the set fifty feet across the room. He stood blinking in the new light, his guide standing about six feet away from him.

'You okay?' the guide said. 'You okay, *señor*?'

'I'm fine,' Naisbitt said. 'I'm perfectly all right.'

'Florence likes to provoke me,' Claire Naisbitt said, making eye contact with Fiona Cangelosi, seated across from her at the center of the table. She shifted her gaze to Fiona's left, to a man with heavy jowls she knew only as 'Doctor Dan.' 'She calls it: "Drawing Claire out."' She glanced toward Clayton Walker at the westerly end of the table. 'Clayton,' she said, nodding, 'and Florence of course,' redirecting her gaze to Fiona's right and a white-haired woman with a vacant smile, 'know what a trial Neville can be. Even after all these years, he still has the capacity to amaze me. He really means what he says.' She turned to her left and used her right hand to pat Gerald Ward on his arm. 'Not only when he's in the privacy of our home. And it's not just a public show, either. As I'm sure you'll understand, Gerald, being a public man yourself, he is quite intemperate.'

'I'm not sure I do,' Ward said stiffly.

'Well,' she said, 'I simply meant ... When he left tonight, I said: "Now Neville, please don't get started about the Russians again. Killed Stalin, rearmed the Germans, sent them to the East. And how the Japs would've pitched in, and then when we were finished, we could've knocked *them* off. It's all very well for you to be a perfectly bloodthirsty old bastard, indoors among friends, but the public won't understand."'

'I'm sure they won't,' Ward said. 'I don't myself, as far as that goes.'

'Well, then, you see?' she said. 'That's my point exactly. He's a very awkward man. As awkward as a ten-foot ladder in an eight-foot room. And that's all I am saying. Absolutely all, and I know he's in a scrape.'

A woman wearing a scarf and a sweater and tight jeans emerged from the dimness behind the camera on the left. She was carrying a clipboard. She had a stopwatch on a cord around her neck. She peered toward them, shading her eyes with her right hand. 'Cesar,' she said in a sharp voice, 'is Professor Naisbitt here?'

The young man whirled toward the woman. 'Yes, he is here,' he

419

said, in an anguished voice. 'I am trying to ask him, I am trying to tell him ... '

'I don't care what you're trying to tell him,' the woman said, striding toward them. She extended her right hand to Naisbitt.

'Regina Fisher,' she said. 'Call me Reggie. Co-producer on the show? Your secretary and I've spoken. Several conversations. Awfully nice to have you here. Tom, well, he's excited. Tom's a great admirer. Having you come on the show was chiefly Tom's idea, and that doesn't always happen, that our guest's a treat for Tom.'

'Well,' Naisbitt said, 'and for me as well. All the exposure we can get for the Ensemble, well, we appreciate it. Tom's being very kind.'

'Well,' she said, 'you may not think so, after you've spent two hours under those lights. Why don't we go back to Tom's office, now, and ... '

'Two hours?' he said, holding back slightly. 'I understood it was to be one. I've seen Tom's show when I've been here. Visiting, you know. Thought it was very good, of course, or I would not be here. But I thought it was one hour.' He shook his head. 'I must be getting old.'

'It is one hour, on the air,' she said. 'And if it's good, that's a big part of the reason. One of the things in Tom's agreement is that we tape two, and edit down to one. But we'll break at least twice, at the end of each hour. And if that's not enough, well, then, three times, if you like. Any time you want. We're the last show taping tonight, so we don't have to clear out for anyone else. So don't you hesitate. Just pipe right up, for any reason, and say that you'd like to take a break, and that is what we'll do. And don't worry about it. We can splice anything. The breaks won't ever show. So stop us if you want to catch your breath, and we'll touch up your makeup, and make sure everything's okay. And then what goes out on the air will be the very best, that we can do for you.'

The five monitors now showed the set as having a pale blue background. Across the tops of the screens it appeared that a logo in silver block letters had been affixed to the blank backdrop. The logo read: 'Tom Oates: In Search of History.' In white letters at the lower center of the monitors was this legend: 'Tonight: Neville L.C. Naisbitt, C.B.E.'

'It's amazing,' Naisbitt said, as they moved toward the left behind the cameras, Fisher clinging lightly to his arm. He waved his right hand toward the set. 'I know how they do that illusion, superimpose the letters, choose any colors they want, but as many times as I've seen it done, I'm still always amazed. That it can be done. That, literally, one can no longer believe what his own eyes see.'

The center line legend disappeared on the monitors and was immediately replaced with another: 'The Atlantic Alliance – In Music.'

'I know it,' she said. 'But it's because, it's all so expensive, you know. So they have to use this set for eight other shows every week. If they had to have a different set for all of them, and pay the stagehands' union what they're asking for these days, well, the public couldn't support it, that's all. It would be out of sight. And we'd be dark most nights, or running endless reruns. So, thank God for illusion, that we can make things what we want to now, no matter what they seem.'

'I'm afraid we're laboring under a misconception here,' Ward said. 'If your attitude is that a person of strong principles should conceal them in public forums, then I have to say that we're in serious disagreement. I was the first black Congressman ever to serve this District. I became a Congressman when persons of color were still "Negroes." In polite circles, at least. When they knew we were around. And I can tell you right now, I didn't get there in the first place, or remain there all these years, by convincing the voters, both white and black, that I had no real principles, or would compromise them to win. Quite the opposite. No, my view is that if a public statement of your principles is dangerous, because they'll anger people, then there's probably something wrong with your principles. *That's* where the problem lies. Hell, the Ku Klux Klan, *they've* got strong principles. That's not what bothers me – it's the *nature* of those principles. That's where the problem is.' He turned to face Claire Naisbitt. 'I hold no brief for Tom Oates,' he said. 'I've seen him destroy too many defenseless people on that little show of his. But that show is his turf, not your husband's – if he behaves as you seem to think he will, he may be in for more trouble than he's dreamed of. Tom will eat him alive. And he'll deserve it, too.'

'Gerald, please?' Florence said. 'Would you like a little more wine?'

'Yes, Gerry, for God's sake,' Clayton said. 'Have another glass of wine.'

'You know, Congressman,' Claire said, holding her glass out for a refill as well, 'I very much doubt he's in real danger. My husband, that is. He got through the Blitz and a few other things. He can take care of himself.'

The first forty-eight minutes of the Naisbitt taping began with Tom Oates escorting Neville L.C. Naisbitt onto the set. Fisher emerged from behind the lights. She was wearing headphones with a microphone attachment. She had the stopwatch in her right hand. She pointed her left forefinger at Oates. The monitors emitted beeping sounds, went dark, and began showing vertical pictures of the spectrum, digitally displaying below the bands of color Navy time in hours, minutes, seconds, and tenths of seconds reading up from 20:18:05:09. At 20:19:00:00, Fisher said: 'And: ready. Tape's rolling. Sound up. Five, four, three, two,' and she dropped her left forefinger.

'And good evening again, ladies and gentlemen,' Oates said, leaning forward. '"When in the course of human events," as the revered old document states, "it becomes necessary for one people to dissolve the bonds that have connected them with another, a decent respect for the opinions of mankind" – and I'm not quoting now; I'm making this up, so don't bother to write in – demands that they recall with mutual affection that the ties that have been sundered do not include the ones of common history. So it was in seventeen-seventy-six, and so it remains today.'

He settled back in his chair. 'It remains so today,' he said, 'because it remained so in nineteen-seventeen, when the England that we fought back in the eighteenth century was under siege for the first time in the twentieth by the German attack. It remains so today because when the England that we fought in eighteen-twelve was threatened once again in the fourth decade of this century, we responded once again. Because that England, from which this country sprang, and the England of today, remains a place of heritage for us. The one ally with whom we have, "a special relationship."'

He leaned slightly to his right and stretched in the chair. 'With us tonight,' he said, 'is a guest from England with whom I have a "special relationship." Professor Neville L.C. Naisbitt. Honored by the Queen who named him a Commander of the British Empire. Treasured by the University at Ipswich which permitted him to accept the status of "professor *emeritus*" only on condition that he continue to enrich its student body each year with his Flagler lectures. Known to an amazing number of Americans as the founder and conductor of the Ipswich Ensemble, which has toured this country so many times since he started it after World War Two, to such rewards for all. Recorded as a valiant member of the Royal Air Force until he was seriously wounded over Germany in nineteen-forty-two. An extraordinary man who is also known to me, or was, when I was growing up, as "British Uncle Neville."'

Oates paused and smiled. 'My father served with him, in those long dark days of the Battle of Britain, back so many years ago. I have not known him all his lifetime, but I've known him all of mine.'

He turned toward Naisbitt, leaning forward, his hands clasped before him. 'Neville Naisbitt, welcome,' he said. 'Thank you so for coming.'

Naisbitt leaned backward in his chair. He extended his right forefinger to massage the lobe of his right ear. He smiled. 'Thomas,' he said, 'your debut for my eyes occurred in a crib where you were unhappy to be left. And so disrupted a dinner party. At the time I sympathized with your parents, who were somewhat annoyed. But after that introduction, I now wonder if perhaps they didn't err, and should've asked you out of it, to come and dine with us.'

Oates grinned at Naisbitt. He looked back to the center camera. The red light on the top came on at once. 'Since nineteen-forty-seven,' he said, 'the Ipswich Ensemble has been a regular ornament of the American cultural scene. Its members have traveled around the world, several times. Is that right, Neville?'

Naisbitt nodded. 'Eleven,' he said. 'And this visit is our thirty-eighth, to America.'

'Tell us about the Ensemble,' Oates said. 'What were its origins? What are its roots? Where did it come from? Thirty-nine years after, what do you think it's meant?'

Naisbitt crossed his legs. 'Tom,' he said, 'I have to go back to the beginning. To those frightening years when I met your father, when it seemed that the world might end. When the group of us were thrown together into makeshift barracks in East Anglia, and it seemed as though the fate of the free world hinged in part on what we did.'

'And didn't it?' Oates said.

'I believe it did,' Naisbitt said. 'I believed that then, and I believe it to this day.'

'Your specialty, sir,' Oates said.

'I am a mathematician,' Naisbitt said. 'I was trained to expect order. To insist on it. When war seemed inevitable, I was thirty-one years old. It made no sense, and yet it made all sense. Disapproved, informally, but disapproved nonetheless, for return to active service, I was remanded to ground service and invited to state my interest. I included cryptography, and I am very glad I did.'

'I want to get to that,' Oates said, 'but right now what I want to talk about was your specialty in the RAF.'

Naisbitt frowned. He steepled his fingers and rubbed his nose. 'Before I was hit,' he said, 'well, it's a little difficult to say, actually. I suppose you could say I was a sort of a forward observer. Reconnaissance. What in the infantry, or in the artillery, you Americans would have called "a spotter." My MOS, as you Yanks would call it now – Military Operations Specialty – my job was to select targets.'

'For later bombing runs?' Oates said. 'Troop concentrations and like that?'

'That's correct,' Naisbitt said. 'The Germans at the start of the war could afford to be profligate with their bombs, and waste them on civilians. We had to be more careful.'

'After you were wounded,' Oates said, leaning forward and grasping his right wrist with his left hand, 'tell us what happened then.'

'Initially I was in field hospital,' Naisbitt said. 'It was evident to me, even as a layman, that the wound was not healing properly. "Irksome damned thing," as my doctors referred to it. And there seemed to be a rather unpleasant possibility that I might lose the leg.

'I had met your father on one of our early missions,' Naisbitt said. 'That meeting, of course, should never have taken place, had Carl seen fit to obey the wishes, if not the outright commands, of his superiors here in America.'

Oates grinned. 'The network wanted him to stay on the ground, and he didn't think he could do his job of covering the war properly if he did that. So he didn't do it.'

'And lucky for me that he didn't,' Naisbitt said. 'We hit it off from the start. We became fast friends. Odd, too, when I think about it now – that we did become such friends. Carl was a daredevil, in many respects. Quite heedless of danger. He stood out, even in the company of other young men of an age, each of us convinced until forcefully taught otherwise, as I was, that he was personally immortal.'

He hesitated. 'You may not know this, Tom,' he said, 'and if you don't, perhaps I should not tell you: But your father phoned me, just before he died, and told me what he was going to do.'

Oates nodded. He pursed his lips. 'I did know,' he said. 'He called me up one day and asked me to meet him for lunch, and he told me the tests had confirmed it, what he had. And he knew what to expect. And he said to me: "I won't do it. I will not go out that way." And I understood.'

'Precisely,' Naisbitt said. 'The idea of Carl Oates submitting to such debility, of wasting away; as horrifying as it was to have to think that his refusal to linger meant that we would lose him sooner, the alternative was worse.'

Naisbitt grimaced. 'The hardest part of life,' he said, 'the very hardest part of it is saying "good-bye" to friends. I recalled, of course, after I talked to Carl that last time my mind was just flooded with memories, and I got out of my chair and walked across the room to fetch a steadying drink for myself, and I thought: "If it hadn't been for Carl Oates, you'd be doing this on a prosthesis." And I would have been almost certainly. Because when Carl came in to see me, one of those forbidden forays that he made, he took one look at me, and then he demanded my charts, and then he said: "This will not do. We're getting you up to the Eighth. Friend of mine from Columbia College's assigned there, on the surgical staff." And Carl pulled strings and got things done, and that was how I met Clayton Walker, thereby not only saving my leg but acquiring still another friend I've cherished all my life.'

Oates held up his hand. 'I'm going to interrupt you there, Neville, for a moment, if I may.' He turned to face the center camera. 'Our New York viewers, many of them will know that Doctor Clayton Walker is the chief of cardiology at New York Memorial Hospital. And that his lovely wife, Florence, is an indefatigable fundraiser for many worthy causes. For those of you elsewhere,' he said, turning to face the camera on the left, 'the Walkers are the kind of people who make the Big Apple shine.' He sat back. 'And now we'll take a short break, and then we'll be right back.'

Fisher appeared from the dimness behind the cameras. The pictures disappeared from the monitors. 'Can I ask you, Tom,' Naisbitt said, 'why did you do that?'

'I was going to say the same thing,' Fisher said.

Oates sucked his teeth. He nodded. 'Simple,' he said. 'I need a couple minutes here to think.' He looked at Naisbitt. 'I expected this to be intense,' he said. 'But not quite this intense.'

Naisbitt smiled. 'I'm sorry,' he said. 'Out of the great evil that was Hitler, some great good was made. The sense of shared peril that brought us together, bound us together ever afterwards. Those of us who survived grew accustomed to acting on our principles, whatever the other rules said, sure in the conviction that those principles were right.'

Oates stared at him. 'Yes,' he said. 'Let's see what we can do with that.' He stood up. 'Five minutes, folks.'

42

The camera operators removed their earphones and put them on top of the machines. Fisher said something into her microphone, removed it and her headset, placed that and the clipboard on the front of the platform, and said: 'Tom, do we know anything about a reception at Bill Wingate's tonight?'

'I don't,' he said.

'Shit,' Fisher said. 'The desk's got some garbled message about a reception tonight at Wingate's, after the show.'

'Well,' he said, 'you know how Adele is. All that rock'n'roll crap about spontaneity, and *life*. There's probably some visiting fireman in town at loose ends that she just found out about, so now all of a sudden she's going to have a party.'

'What should I do?' Fisher said.

'Couple possibilities,' he said. 'You can call her up and bag it. Tell her, as she already knows, that I don't go to parties on the nights when I'm working. That I'm tense and exhausted when I finish these things, and all I want to do is go home, and sit down, and have a couple good stiff belts and then get you in bed. Or, we can ignore the damned thing, pretend we never heard it, and if she ever asks, say we never got the word.'

'Is that a good idea?' Fisher said. 'She does have that big mouth.'

'So's the Midtown Tunnel,' Oates said. 'That doesn't scare me either.'

'I'm going to call her,' Fisher said. 'I'll tell her we'll be tied up here 'till late, and we're sorry we can't come.'

'Up to you,' he said.

She left the studio. He walked to front and center on the platform and stuck his hands into his pockets, the mike cord stretching behind him. He scuffed at the carpeting. He turned and faced Naisbitt. 'You,' he said, 'you knew there was a time when Carl and I didn't talk.'

'Yes,' Naisbitt said.

'You know why we didn't,' Oates said.

'Yes, I do,' Naisbitt said.

'You know what that did to me?' Oates said.

'Not directly,' Naisbitt said. 'I do know what it did to him. That I know empirically.'

'What do you think it did to me?' Oates said.

'I surmise,' Naisbitt said, 'and be mindful that I don't know you anywhere nearly as well as I knew Carl, but I surmise it hurt you. Bothered you. Troubled you. Whatever you'd like to say.'

'It damned near killed me, 's what it did,' Oates said. 'You know how I was about my father.'

'I do,' Naisbitt said. 'I also know it damned near killed him, as you put it. Because I know how he felt about you. I must say I was greatly pleased and relieved when he came to London, back however many years, and we met at Scott's for oysters and he told me that was over. The long interval you had. You meant a lot to him. More than either Donna or Carol, and he loved them a lot. In the beginning, at least. You were his posterity. It, your quarrel ate at him. I was glad to see it over.'

'You think you knew him so well,' Oates said.

'I did,' Naisbitt said. 'We were two of many people who would have been perfectly contented to lead ordinary lives, suddenly united by maximum danger. Our sensibilities, if that's the right word, were heightened forever by that experience. The world was under attack by a despotic maniac, a maniac with more than a marginal hope of bringing all of us under his heel, and grinding us to bits. Each of us believed he had some small part in preventing Hitler from doing that. We were proud, and we never forgot.'

'And therefore,' Oates said, 'when I started the Fulbright interviews; when I did the McGovern stuff; when I talked to Sam Browne and did all those other things that my father disapproved of, almost to the point of disowning me, he was right and I was wrong?'

'Simply put,' Naisbitt said, 'that is what I thought. He was right to be angry. You were employing his medium – he thought it was his, as he thought that every instrument he used was his – to contradict what he deeply believed. What he *knew*, in fact. That was his opinion. And he did not like that.'

'And you agreed with him,' Oates said.

Naisbitt sighed. 'Tom,' he said, 'Churchill was right. Roosevelt was wrong. Forty-one years ago, when Germany surrendered, my visceral notion was that the war in the Pacific should be left in its current condition, subordinate to the conflict in Europe, and that the concentrated strength of the Allies should be marshaled against Stalin, while we had him breathless. I've seen nothing since to change my mind.'

'He was our ally,' Oates said. 'We had a treaty with Russia.'

'The obligations of which were as sacred to Stalin,' Naisbitt said, 'as had been the obligations of Russia's non-aggression treaty to Hitler. Treaties are always expressions of hope. Nothing more.'

'You think nations have a moral right to attack other nations that have systems they don't like?' Oates said. 'Is that what you're telling me?'

'Not quite,' Naisbitt said. 'I think moral men and women have not only the right but the obligation to defend themselves and their civilizations against aggressive, uncivilized, savage adversaries who would crush them, regardless of the aggressor's ideology. Adequate defense against such opponents has often mandated pre-emptive attack. And if you wish to disagree with me, be prepared to explain to the shades of six million Jews, and five million gentiles of assorted religious and ethnic persuasions Hitler deemed insufficiently Aryan, vaporized by that monster because we failed to act as promptly as we should.'

'You lost someone, didn't you,' Oates said, in a softer voice. 'I'd forgotten that.'

'I lost many people,' Naisbitt said. 'I lost old friends from college. I made new friends in the military, and I lost them as well. I lost my first wife and my two children in the raid on Coventry that we knew was on the way, and I agreed with Churchill's decision not to warn the populace – because that would have made it evident to the Nazis that we had broken their codes.'

'In other words,' Oates said, 'you participated in their sacrifice.'

'I colluded in it,' Naisbitt said. 'Exposing them to the possibility of death in the bombing. Of course I hoped the possibility would not be realized, but when it was, I could not claim I hadn't meant that to happen.'

'And yet,' Oates said, 'knowing how you must have felt, how you must feel today, you can still argue that the war should've been prolonged, leading to vastly more deaths and atrocities? You can really say that?'

'Certainly,' Naisbitt said. 'Think of the problems that would have solved. Think how the map of the world would look today, if that had been done. The Allies would have a nuclear monopoly. The ultimate danger, nuclear war, which we never dreamed of back in nineteen-forty-two, would simply not exist.'

'Unless we decided to use it,' Oates said.

'Nonsense,' Naisbitt said. 'We would not do that.'

'After what we did in Southeast Asia?' Oates said. 'Can you say that, Neville?'

'Of course I can,' Naisbitt said. 'Not only say it, but mean it. America's sin in Vietnam was not what it did, but what it failed to do. It failed to win.

'The watermark of tyranny,' he said, 'is not the tendency to invade or subjugate other nations. That comes later on, after the character of the assassin has become clear. The watermark is the eagerness of the assassin to tyrannize and slaughter his own countrymen. In the Forties, some of *my* countrymen dismissed the possibility that fascism, denominated "communism" or "the dictatorship of the proletariat," remained just as brutal, aggressive, repressive and threatening in Moscow as it had been in Berlin and Rome. In the Fifties, otherwise clearheaded and intelligent Frenchmen excused weariness of the struggle in Indochina by uttering the rubric that Ho Chi Minh was his country's chosen

433

leader, and that although he was a committed, Stalinist Marxist, he would rule it benevolently once he got control. In the Sixties and the early Seventies, the virus was abroad in America, and the very people whom you presented by this medium as wise, compassionate and, above all, *right*, were totally unwilling to credit overwhelming evidence that a Viet Cong triumph would be immediately followed by transformation of the country into an abattoir. The triumph was permitted, and the bloodletting began.

'To blink history is always a serious blunder,' Naisbitt said. 'It is a blunder which the private citizen may permit himself, in the luxury of irresponsibility for outcomes. But for someone in your profession, and in your position in it, it's a luxury of intemperate price and appalling consequence. You educate people, like it or no. Just as your father did. When he saw you educating the public as you did, it horrified him.'

'He thought it was "despicable,"' Oates said. 'That's the word he used to me.'

'He was understating his opinion,' Naisbitt said. 'Being kind to you. It was worse than despicable – it was stupid. That's what caused his rage – and that was what it was. He met Claire and me on one of these trips that we made, out in San Francisco, and I recall we were having a drink at the Top of the Mark. Claire asked him about you. How your career was going. And his face changed. His voice turned into a snarl. "Oh, swimmingly," he said. "Absolutely wonderfully. He's more famous now than I am. Certainly more admired. And you know how he's done it? He's done it by identifying opportunity when it leaps up before him. He's found out about this little conflagration going on in Vietnam, and he's taken the pulse of his generation and from it deduced that many of his contemporaries *disapprove* of making war, and shooting guns and dropping bombs. They don't think it's *nice*. So, every chance he gets, and he gets a lot of them, he rounds up some other damned opportunist and the two of them go on the air and sprinkle some more gasoline on the issue here at home. I think he must've been switched in the cradle, the stupid little *fuck*. I can't've spawned this jellyfish. I've got a fucking *brain*, for Christ sake. This kid can't be mine.'"

The camera operators straggled back into the studio, carrying cardboard containers of coffee. Fisher returned after them, carrying a tray with two more glasses of scotch.

'And yet,' Oates said, 'yet when I saw you in those years when the two of us weren't speaking, when Dad wouldn't speak to me, you were always warm to me. Always hospitable. And you agreed to come on here, come on here tonight. Knowing how he felt about me, how could you do that? Wasn't that betraying him? Wasn't that disloyal? Wasn't that another form, what Dad called "shiftiness"?'

'Absolutely not,' Naisbitt said. 'In the first place, I disapproved of Carl's conduct. Not that I disagreed with the substance of his appraisal. I disapproved of his vehement refusal to have anything to do with you because, well, it amounted to a private decision to send a son to Coventry in the hope he would be hurt. No private disagreement warrants any kind of death – and banishment and exile, those are kinds of deaths. I told him he was wrong to do that. That he would cause himself to grieve, and that he should patch things up, no matter what it needed.

'And about two years later,' Naisbitt said, 'he came to London, and he told me that he had done as I had said. I said that made me glad.'

Fisher, standing at the edge of the platform with the tray in her hand, cleared her throat. 'Ah,' she said, 'pardon me, Tom, but, ah, are you planning to use that? Use that on the show?'

He turned and stared at her. He shook his head. 'No,' he said, 'no, I don't plan to. I'll use this instead.' He crouched to receive the tray. His hand shook as he took it from her, and some of the Famous Grouse scotch whisky spilled.

'Are you okay?' she said.

He stood up. 'I'll be all right,' he said. 'Once I get on the outside of this.' He turned and walked to Naisbitt. 'Restorative?'

'Very much so, thanks,' Naisbitt said, accepting the glass. 'This is demanding work.'

43

The digital clocks against the spectrum on the monitor screens read 21:07:04:00 when Fisher dropped her left forefinger for the second time on the evening of February 21, 1986.

'My understanding, Neville,' Oates said, 'is that while others have written and spoken at length about the Enigma machine, and the general work done by British Intelligence during the war, you still refuse to do so.'

'That's correct,' Naisbitt said.

'Why is that?' Oates said. 'The story's pretty much out. How could anything you might add harm any present interest of your government?'

Naisbitt chuckled. 'Well,' he said, 'perhaps that's part of the reason I decline to discuss my role in the matter – because it was so small, so ancillary to the accomplishments of the major participants, that I would seem ridiculous.'

'I doubt that,' Oates said.

'Well,' Naisbitt said, 'but then there's the overriding issue here. Which is that I signed an agreement binding me to secrecy in nineteen-forty-two, and so far as I know, not been released from it. Nor have I asked to be released from that pledge, or wish in fact to be. We lived then, and we live now, in a world filled with predators. To this point at least we've been able to fend them off.' He shifted in his chair. 'I just don't see any benefit in the revelation of secrets about national security, no matter how old they may be.'

'All right,' Oates said, 'we'll honor your reluctance. Tell us about the Ipswich Ensemble. How it started, who was in it, what its purpose was. And why you're here tonight.'

'Happy to,' Naisbitt said. 'After the war ended, and all the Yanks went home – most of you, at any rate – there was a curious sort of lull. An intermezzo, as it were, people hunting around for the pieces of the lives they'd discarded when it began.

'Now,' he said, 'in that almost post-coital depression that came after the war was over, I found myself in a situation where the issue of whether to rebuild my life had been made for me. I'd been on sabbatical from Cambridge when it started, doing some research and living with my family in Coventry, wishing I could afford to purchase one of the Jaguars made there and knowing I never could, looking toward an intellectually if not financially rewarding adult lifetime on the Cambridge faculty. And suddenly, if a span of six years can be called "sudden," it was all gone. My family were dead. I decided I'd had thrust upon me either an exercise in damage control or an opportunity, an adventure.

'I chose to treat it as an adventure,' Naisbitt said. 'I took an inventory,' he said. 'I don't mean that I did it all at once, sitting down with a tablet of paper, ticking off alternatives, "one from column A and two from column B." And I did rather rapidly conclude that I did not wish to return to Cambridge. It was home to me, and I still loved it, but I'd involuntarily sharpened my appetite for risk, in the war, and since I was without responsibilities at its end, I could voluntarily elect to continue taking risks. So, instead of returning to Cambridge, I chose to accept a most flattering offer to head the mathematics department at the new University of Ipswich.

'The effrontery of the founders, when you think about it,' he said, 'was positively astonishing. What they proposed to do was take a huge estate, out in the middle of nowhere, and convert it into a university on the American model. To make available to English students of the middle and lower classes the sort of educational opportunity that American institutions, aided by your GI Bill, were gearing up to offer here. It promised ferment, Ipswich did, excitement, enthusiasm, maybe even joy.

'We began making do with quarters in a huge old manor house, extremely grand, extremely draughty, and extremely unsuited to pedagogy. But the commitment and the money were forthcoming if not there, and the land around the manor was expansive, and the buildings began going up and the students coming in, and the faculty began to grow and it was inspiring. Just as I had hoped, it was an adventure.

'In nineteen-forty-six,' he said, 'Claire very much against her will visited the campus with her second husband, Cecil. Cecil Moody, his name was, and he was a fine architect. I was assigned to cultivate Claire, because Cecil's agreement to design new buildings was very important to someone or other who controlled a lot of money, and we were supposed to make them happy so that Cecil would agree.'

'And you did,' Oates said.

Naisbitt smiled. 'Well, I'm not sure Cecil came away at first quite as happy as Claire.'

'My first husband, Ronald,' Claire said to Fiona Cangelosi, 'picked me up at a recital I gave in the Young Players' Competition they used to have each spring at Carnegie. I was seventeen years old. He was forty-one. It didn't occur to me then that a girl of seventeen probably ought not to turn a fling into a permanent arrangement, nor did I step back and consider that marriage to a man with three marriages behind him might not be such an arrangement.' She smiled. 'He was just as fickle as I was. Nearly a quarter-century older, but quite as immature.

'He was in banking. There was, naturally, a scandal. This was nineteen-thirty-seven – if his family hadn't had a lot of money in the firm, he would've been cashiered. Since they did, he was banished. To the London office. Where almost immediately he went into the second of his two cycles: find a new pastry to replace the old pastry now his lawful, wedded wife.

'I was a spiteful little thing, but not stupid. I suppose he got away with screwing his new tart for about a month before I caught on. I was furious. We were having our flat redone and there was quite a bit of structural renovation required, and he'd retained this architect, Cecil Moody. Cecil lived in Montagu Square, lovely old barn near where Anthony Trollope'd lived, and he wanted to show me some of the things he had done to make it liveable, while preserving its character. So one morning, full of rage at Ronald who had not come home the night before until gone three or so, I went there with Cecil, and seduced him. He appeared only mildly surprised by the approach – told me later that he'd regularly shown his house to clients, and a few of them had taken the invitations as the same sort of opportunity it had seemed to me – but quite overcome by the performance.' She paused. 'I don't think Cecil had a strong sexual drive. Oh, he liked it well enough, wasn't defective or anything – thought it was quite pleasant, in fact. Something like a day's good shooting: bracing fun. But really, nowhere near as absorbing, as satisfying, as what he really liked to do. Which was think. Cecil loved to think. So, as much as my angry prowess excited and beguiled him, in the long term it would be no match for my competition – which was of course his work.

'By the time I met Neville,' she said, 'I'd been tied to this calm, thoughtful, kind, reflective man for more than six years. I'd stayed, an American in London when every Londoner who could was packing for America, and been spared not only death and dismemberment but even the loneliness that other wives suffered – Cecil's service was civilian, surveying damaged buildings for repairs or demolition. And consequently I was nearly mad with boredom. So we went out to Ipswich – after all those years of what amounted to nothing more than engineering work, nowhere near stimulating enough for Cecil – to see about this massive campus design project in the offing, and I met Neville. Who was no different then. Subject to enthusiasms, bouts of choler, great bursts of extravagant energy, always rushing about from one thing to the next, and I thought it might be interesting to bed this man. Just for a change, you know.' She laughed. 'It was that, all right; it certainly was that. And that is why, Fiona, I've stayed married to him ever since. Neville's interesting.'

'So,' Neville Naisbitt said, 'Claire and I were married in early forty-seven, and she came out to Ipswich to live, and we were both very conscious of the probability that she might find it a bit confining, perhaps dull, after her years of living in London, sharing Cecil's animated social life and all that sort of thing. So we talked about that, and she said to me: "Well, you know, we can't spend all our lives just seeing the same round of people for drinks tonight, and dinner tomorrow and luncheon the day after that. Which will be what will happen if we confine ourselves to this town and this faculty for friends, and we shall both go utterly mad. What we must do is involve ourselves in something we both find interesting, that will not only amuse us but get us out from time to time, and bring new people in." And music was the obvious direction.'

'Right,' Oates said. 'Now, as I recall, both you and Claire had been musical before you met. So there was that resource, that many wouldn't have.'

'Yes,' Naisbitt said, 'although I would have to say that Claire's virtuosity – and her ability, as far as that goes – far exceeded my own. In today's world, I think, Claire would probably have begun a professional career, but in those days that option was rarely available to a woman.'

'I was under the impression,' Oates said, 'I was under the impression that you also played trombone.'

'I did, by the time you came along,' Naisbitt said. 'That was another wartime acquisition. I had put aside my music while I was in the combat branch, "lost me embrochure," as one of my American colleagues phrased it, but when I took on the more sedentary duties of cryptographer, I felt the need of some form of relaxation. Three or four of the Americans had in fact played professionally before the war, and were extremely good. So several of us began to meet informally in the evenings, on the weekends, whenever we had a bit of time, and we were able to get one of those big, black, so-called "fake books," that violate every copyright in musical existence, and we began really to have quite a good time for ourselves. We played in the mess and we even got to the point where we'd go around and try to give the troops a little entertainment of a Saturday evening, relieve some of the tedium that service in the rear echelons substitutes for the unremitting terror of service in the lines. And we played in hospitals. It was all really quite satisfying, and an immense contribution to morale – our own, at least.'

'Now,' Oates said, 'this wasn't, this was not the classical repertoire that you were playing then, for these soldiers and so forth?'

'No,' Naisbitt said, 'although given the sheer hunger that our audiences had for any sort of entertainment that would get their minds off the war and the killing, I think it could have been. We cultivated our common strengths, and that was what we played.'

'But when you and Claire started the Ensemble,' Oates said, 'then you went in what I suppose many would call the opposite direction.'

'Well,' Naisbitt said, 'yes, and for approximately the same basic reason. Which was that Claire's talent was the commanding one in our household, and her experience and knowledge were concentrated in classical repertoire. To me it mattered very little what music we were playing, so long as we played it. And among the faculty, and the student body as well, that same preference dominated. So it was simply a matter of looking to the sources of our talent and combining them in such a fashion as to bring out the best performances. So that accounted for the orientation.'

'So,' Oates said, 'you were after excellence, and you intended to perform. For the public, I mean.'

'Correct,' Naisbitt said. 'The overriding purpose of going about this was to broaden our horizons, to keep us from getting provincial, and to allow us not only to acquire new friendships, but to keep up those we had made during the war.

'You see, Tom,' he said, 'before the war, international communication among private citizens in America and those in Britain was relatively non-existent. When the war came it was all very well for the British common soldier who'd known nothing of you Yanks and didn't like what he was learning, for him to express his jealousy of your troops' prosperity by denouncing them as "overfed, overpaid, oversexed and over here," because it didn't matter if the exchanges over some barmaid ended up in blows. But when it came to matters of greater complexity and urgency, especially in the field of intelligence-gathering and interpretation, animosity preventing communication, envy balking complete cooperation – well, we had to overcome those barriers, and do it damned fast, under fire.

'So a good part of our hope,' Naisbitt said, 'Claire's and mine, was that initiatives like the Ensemble, and many, many of them, would not only preserve but extend the network of friendships that had been formed in the war. The interests of the North Atlantic community are not limited to those comprehended by the NATO documents harmonizing our military preparedness efforts. There are many, many more of them, as critical to our survival as those of armaments.'

'And you believe, then, after nearly forty tours in this country with the Ensemble, that you've accomplished this,' Oates said.

'I'm certain of it,' Naisbitt said. 'Since forty-seven, no fewer than nine hundred and fifty-six people from Britain have journeyed to America under the auspices of the Ensemble. Their experiences have in many, many instances led them to matriculate at American graduate schools for study, to teach at American universities on exchange bases, and to see to it that American students are encouraged to enroll at Ipswich. And let me emphasize again that only a minority of our players have turned out to be professional musicians. The majority have been historians, mathematicians such as I, literature professors, biologists, chemistry teachers, economists, barristers, professionals in government – an endless variety. The ripple effects of that sort of thing are enormous.'

'I had no idea,' Oates said, 'that your turnover was so large.'

'Well,' Naisbitt said, 'our choral group of twenty-four voices has of course shown the largest amount – like it or not, the instrumental longevity of the human voice is considerably less than that of a grand piano, and there have been times when we have had to take an old and valued friend aside and tell him or her that the day has arrived to step aside for someone else. We've made it a policy to include as many talented members of the student body as we possibly could, which guaranteed the turnover in the orchestra. And there's been some attrition as well in the quartet and the chamber unit. People changing jobs, you know. Age catching up with nimble fingers, dental problems developing for those who play the brass. Claire's rheumatism three years ago relegated her to the sidelines, but she was very brave – she was the one who insisted that she should be replaced.'

'But you've been in place from the beginning,' Oates said.

Naisbitt smiled. 'Well, you see,' he said, 'from the outset I was crafty enough to perceive that the reservoir of musical talent at the university was fed by many springs much more bountiful than mine. I was a journeyman, at the very best, able to fill in if illness or some schedule conflict caused a temporary vacancy, but unable to take a permanent chair without not only depriving a more skillful person of his or her rightful place, but also lowering the overall quality of the performance. I know good musicianship, and I know how it is done. But I also know that God in His wisdom did not see fit to distribute to me the measure of natural ability that it requires. So I made a big public show of manfully assuming all the administrative drudgery of running the operation, doing the odd arrangement here and there, serving as conductor when the talent pool for some reason or another failed to turn one up some years, acting as music director, travel planner, and all that other detailed choring without which the thing couldn't run. So, by taking on an indispensable job that no one else in his right mind would have assumed, I made myself indispensable. And it's worked out very well.'

Oates hunched forward. 'Yes,' he said, 'let's get to that. You've orchestrated all these trips. You've secured guest performances, professionals, to appear as soloists, in – how many countries is it?'

Naisbitt laughed. 'I've lost track,' he said. 'When we started the Ensemble, we had no notion of the potential it would also have for contacts with other nations. We've toured Israel with Israeli soloists, Egypt with Egyptians, China with an extraordinarily talented young woman from Ipswich whose harp work was perfectly superb. Here in America we've enjoyed for many years a traveling fellowship program with the New England Conservatory up in Boston – each spring semester a Conservatory student receives all expenses and a stipend to accompany us on our annual tour. One recipient, as a matter of fact, was Christina Walker, an extremely talented young pianist who happens to be the daughter as well of the doctor who saved my leg, Clayton Walker. She went with us all across the country and down into Mexico back in nineteen-sixty-eight, or -nine. A beautiful young woman, only about seventeen or eighteen then, and truly a splendid musician. The campuses were troubled then, but we were enthusiastically received. I believe she's teaching now.'

'Yes,' Oates said, 'and that brings up an interesting point. As you've said, the logistics of transporting a chorale, a full orchestra of what, sixty, seventy members?'

'It varies,' Naisbitt said. His lips compressed somewhat. 'We've had as many as a hundred and six, when the talent was available. This year's group is eighty-three. Plus the twenty-four in the chorus.'

'And all their instruments, their baggage and all that,' Oates said.

'"Impedimenta," Caesar called it,' Naisbitt said. 'I know exactly what he meant. Latin's a useful language, when you think about it. "Professor *emeritus*," they call me – "e" meaning "out" and "meritus" meaning "deservedly so."'

Oates laughed. 'I doubt that's the connotation that they mean at Ipswich,' he said. 'But tell me something: Doesn't this all cost a lot?'

Naisbitt stared at him. 'I think I'd like to take one of those breaks I was promised here, Tom,' he said.

Oates stuck his tongue in his left cheek. He nodded. 'Okay, Neville,' he said. He turned to face the cameras. 'Reggie, shut it down,' he said. 'We'll take another five here, and another drink as well.' The monitors went dark.

'Mrs. Naisbitt,' Ward said, as Clayton offered port, 'you are an entertaining lady. Has it ever occurred to you how lucky you have

447

been, to have had enough money to have been so selfish, and so irresponsible, with impunity?'

'*Gerald*,' Florence said.

'I'm serious,' Ward said. 'I'm quite serious here, Florence. The charming autobiography we've all heard with such amusement – if you remove the factor of Mrs. Naisbitt's comfortable circumstances, it's physically the same story that the most abjectly frustrating welfare cases have to relate. The inability, or the refusal, to control their appetites. The only difference between them and us is our possession of resources sufficient to meet the bills for our conduct.'

'I think,' Fiona Cangelosi said, 'I think that's quite a difference, Mister Ward. And not the only one, either. It seems to me that the distinction's one of responsibility, more than anything else. The willingness, coupled with the ability, to assume responsibility for one's acts. If I choose to marry, have children, and then to divorce the father of those children – or he chooses to leave us – and I do not ask society to subsidize my decision, then it seems to me that I've been socially responsible. Whatever my private morality may be. But if I go to society, after making such decisions, and say: "Since I have done this, you must now support me. House me, feed me, care for my children, and so forth," well, then I think I've not been.'

Ward nodded. 'Yes,' he said, 'a popular view. You represent very well the position that your government currently takes, I'll say that.' He paused. 'Just about any position it takes, am I right?'

'I beg your pardon,' Fiona said. 'What else would you expect me to do? Undermine it? Would you want people on the staff of the Ambassador to the UN torpedoing American initiatives? Is that what the Congress has in mind, when it advises and consents to his appointment? Someone who will recruit people to sabotage our foreign policy? Act against our interests?'

'Not at all,' Ward said, accepting port. 'What we have in mind is that persons supposedly assigned out of Foggy Bottom Plans and Policy to ambassadorial missions – missions *anywhere*, I might add, not just to the UN – actually *be* State Department career employees, trained and experienced in foreign policy matters. Able and willing to evaluate proposals, whether ours or other nations', according to their impact on our broad national goals. *Not*, in other words, operatives of other agencies in no way designed or intended to determine such policy goals. Do you follow me?'

'I'm trying to,' Fiona said.

'I'll be plain,' Ward said. 'Covert enforcement measures are not within the proper scope of diplomatic responsibilities as this nation construes them. Whatever the Russians may do, rostering KGB agents as diplomats, we should not respond in kind. Our diplomatic delegations should have no place for misnomered agents working undercover, hand-in-hand with covert operations managed out of Langley.'

'I see,' Fiona said. 'You're under the impression that I'm with the CIA.'

'No,' he said, 'the FBI. You were with the FBI last summer, and you're with it today. Breveted you may be formally to State, all the proper papers signed, in the expected places, but what you are's Agent In Place. And in that capacity you are not fulfilling the nominal function of your position, which is to analyze policy proposals – you are surreptitiously carrying out plans formulated outside the State Department, even its back channels. And that's not what we had in mind, had in mind on the Hill at all.'

'It's often rather difficult,' Fiona said, 'for the outsider, at least, to ascertain what the Hill has in mind. In the meantime, the earth revolves. And as for your allegation, that I'm still FBI, I'd like to see you back it up. In fact, I will insist.'

44

Oates stood up and walked out to the front of the platform, stretching elaborately, watching as the camera operators left the studio. He relaxed, allowing his shoulders to slump, put his hands in his pockets, turned to face Naisbitt and grinned. 'Going well,' he said. 'You're a good guest, Neville. An excellent guest, in fact. I suppose it's all those years of teaching, right? And the tours as well? You're used to performing. Doesn't frighten you.'

Naisbitt stared at him. 'I suppose so,' he said, without any expression.

Oates shook his head and blew out breath. He arched his neck and massaged it with his right hand, moving his head back and forth. 'So,' he said, 'is Claire with you this time? I assume she is.'

'She is,' Naisbitt said. 'She's dining with the Walkers tonight. They're keeping a plate warm for me.'

'Nice of them,' Oates said. 'Very nice people, the Walkers. But I hope it isn't breakfast by the time you get to eat it. We've still got a long way to go here, 'fore we're finished up.'

Naisbitt brought himself forward in his chair. He moved his right shoulder. 'Perhaps not,' he said.

'Oh,' Oates said, 'sure we have. I mean, we've covered a lot of ground here already, but there's still an awful lot of stuff that I haven't asked you yet.'

'So I gather,' Naisbitt said. He sat hunched forward, his hands dangling between his knees. 'And that is what I meant.'

'Where the hell's Reggie gone to get that scotch?' Oates said, turning to scan the dark studio. 'Edinburgh, for Christ sake?'

'What I meant, Tom,' Naisbitt said, pausing until Oates had to face him, 'what I meant is that your questioning at the end there seemed to me tendentious.'

'I don't follow you,' Oates said, frowning.

'Let me explain,' Naisbitt said. 'Unless I'm very much mistaken, you were laying the foundation there for a line of inquiry that I don't propose to allow.'

Oates shook his head slightly. 'Line of inquiry?' he said.

'Yes,' Naisbitt said.

'That you don't propose to allow?' Oates said, his voice quizzical.

Fisher returned with the tray. Crouching, Oates accepted it with both hands, said: 'Thanks,' and brought it to Naisbitt's chair. Naisbitt took the nearest glass and said: 'That I don't propose to allow.'

Oates backed up to his chair and sat down, putting the tray on the table and taking the remaining glass. He sipped. 'Neville,' he said, putting the glass down and crossing his legs, grasping his left knee with both hands, 'forgive me if I'm presuming too much here, or if I'm getting the wrong idea, but are you under the impression that guests on American televised discussion programs have some sort of veto power over what's to be discussed? Because they don't, I can assure you.'

Naisbitt sipped his scotch. 'This one does,' he said.

Oates sighed. 'Well, look,' he said, 'I've known you a long time. I didn't have you on here to start an argument with you. We're both too old for that.'

'Oh,' Naisbitt said, 'I don't mind a good row now and then, if it's in a worthy cause. Keeps the blood up.'

'Look,' Oates said, spreading his hands, 'this's probably over nothing anyway. Chances are what I've got left to ask you'll be perfectly acceptable to you, and there isn't a problem at all.'

'Easily determined,' Naisbitt said. 'What do you plan to ask me?'

Oates put his head back and laughed. 'Oh, Neville, Neville,' he said, 'I remember Dad, how Dad would come home after he'd spent an evening, drinking and arguing with you, and ... '

'We seldom disagreed,' Naisbitt said. 'Your father and I almost never disagreed. We often became choleric discussing someone else, with whom we disagreed, but I can't think of three occasions, other than when you and he were not on good terms, when we failed to see eye to eye.'

'Well,' Oates said, 'all right: discussing someone else. But you get my meaning. Dad would say: "Neville Naisbitt's the bloodiest-minded man on earth." And now I know what he meant.'

'Carl's memory is precious to me,' Naisbitt said, 'but invoking it as you are doing doesn't palliate my concern about your intended line of inquiry. If, as you suggest, the questions will not trouble me to answer, then it can't do any harm to tell me now what those questions are.'

Oates shook his head. He took another drink of scotch. 'I don't do that,' he said. 'I've been at this racket quite a while now, and I learned a long time ago that the fighter doesn't leave his fight in the gym. The interviewer doesn't rehearse his guest. You do that and all the spontaneity, all the readiness of wit, all the freshness of anecdote, all of that is lost. And the viewers can tell. They can tell when you've canned it before you served it, and all over the city, all over the country, you can hear those channel zappers flipping somewhere else.' He picked up the glass and took a gulp, finishing the contents. He put it on the tray and gestured toward Naisbitt's drink. 'Better sink that one, dear Neville, if you would. We'll get rolling here, and see where we're going, and maybe we can get you out of here at a relatively decent hour for your visit with the Walkers.'

Naisbitt gestured toward his drink. 'You can go ahead and take it away,' he said. 'I think I've had enough to hold me.' He folded his hands at his waist.

'Okay, as you wish,' Oates said. '*People,*' he said loudly, 'going back to work now. Everybody set to go.'

The camera operators reappeared from the shadows and returned to their machines. Fisher climbed up onto the platform and removed the tray and whisky glasses, putting them on the floor in front of the platform. The monitors came on with the spectrum again. The digital clocks read 21:41:10:04 when she said: 'And ... ready. Tape is rolling.'

'This "impedimenta,"' Oates said. 'All the baggage. All the people. Not only must the logistics of transport be formidable – so must the expense. Who pays the bills?'

Naisbitt exhaled deeply. He picked up his cane from the floor beside him and placed it on his lap. He glared at Oates with his jaw clenched.

454

Oates laughed delightedly. 'Okay, Neville,' he said, 'let's try it another way. Would it be fair to say that the principal source of funds for the Ipswich Ensemble for most of its life has been the American Central Intelligence Agency, and its predecessors? That all of your gallivantings've been mostly for the purpose of maintaining an intelligence network against radical organizations, here and around the world? That the reason you've been such a frequent visitor to our colleges and universities, or were in the Sixties and Seventies, was that you were pre-empting and co-opting student radicals?'

'Tom,' Naisbitt said, leaning forward, 'it would be fair to say that history is a pattern of repetition. Every generation has sacrificed its children. And every generation has strived to sacrifice its parents, or at least what they believe. If we are, in fact, all outlaws, it has been of necessity. The Ensemble was our modest initiative toward changing that pattern. An effort to preserve international concord by acquainting the young early with the realities and people of friendly nations, and their goals as well. And when we have succeeded, when the friendships made have endured, our hopes for mutual assistance have, yes, been realized.'

Oates laughed. 'And yet, and yet,' he said, 'all this time, haven't you been aware? That you were collaborating in an enterprise strictly forbidden by American law? Didn't it, wasn't it the purest chance, lucky coincidence, someone's careless oversight to probe a little deeper, that accounts for the fact that the Ensemble wasn't publicly named among the CIA-funded fronts divulged in sixty-seven? Haven't you been, in fact, outlaws? For the CIA?'

Naisbitt cleared his throat. He gazed at Oates. 'I repeat: If we have been outlaws, it was of necessity.'

Oates laughed again, incredulously. 'That's Marx,' he said.

'That's Marx. "Ends justify the means": Isn't that what it is? Didn't one of your American alumni, young man named Sam Tibbetts, didn't he die under *very* suspicious circumstances in a London jail last year? Don't you have to answer such questions, at least to yourself, and your conscience?'

Naisbitt studied the rug. He looked up at Oates, who was still smiling. 'It would be fair to say, Tom, that I have much to answer for in this life. And one of the greatest blunders I ever committed,' he said, pausing as Oates leaned forward eagerly, his eyes shining, 'was the night in San Francisco when your dear late father called you a fucking jellyfish only with a smaller brain, and no ethics at all.'

Oates's eyes opened wide. Naisbitt detached the microphone clip from his tie, draped its cord over the arm of his chair, stood with difficulty and marched between the camera and Oates toward the stairs leading off the platform. When he passed Oates's chair, without looking down he said: 'Whelp.'

45

Gerald Ward sipped his port. He piled Stilton cheese deliberately on a small round slice of light rye bread and put it in his mouth. He drank from his *demitasse*. He folded his hands at his waist. He regarded Fiona Cangelosi. 'Ms. Cangelosi,' he said, 'you deserve your reputation.'

'My "reputation,"' she said. 'And just what might that be? And where?'

'For being formidable,' Waid said. 'And, in the halls of Congress.'

'The only times I've ever visited Congress,' she said, 'were when I was a little girl, and my parents brought me there, and then when I first came to Washington to work for the Bureau. And I went there on my own, one day of my vacation, because I didn't remember much about my first visit, and I thought I should.

'As for the "formidable,"' she said, 'I'll take that as flattery. I don't know how much you know about legats, Congressman, but when I was selected as one, and sent to London, I was very proud.'

'I know quite a bit about legats,' Ward said. 'That was my allusion to your fame – both individual and corporate – in the halls of Congress. We, I, at least, would have enjoyed the opportunity to learn even more than we already know about such distinguished employees of the Bureau as yourself. We would have admired the opportunity to benefit from your particular instruction last summer, for example. You would have been most welcome. But for some reason or other, you were unable to come.'

She smiled. 'I believe,' she said, 'I believe I was out of the country? At the time?'

'*Way* out,' Ward said, smiling back at her. 'Malta, wasn't it?'

'There'd been bombings,' she said. 'There was an order to reduce personnel to only necessary staff. And there was one person who was very necessary, but had a family emergency back home and they gave him a humane leave. So I went there for a while. But just to fill in. For a while.'

'Until the Congress took its Thanksgiving recess,' Ward said, 'and some of the dust settled down.'

'I don't know,' she said. 'All I know's that they really needed someone who could get there in a hurry, someone who traveled light, and I was relatively nearby in London, so I was the one who went.'

'And became, for all practical purposes,' he said, 'safely incommunicado.'

'I didn't feel incommunicado,' she said. 'My bosses knew where I was. They had no trouble reaching me.'

'Yes,' Ward said. 'Yes. That was the explanation for your sudden travel, I expect. They knew how to find you in a hurry, and ship you somewhere else. I admire your candor. Let me, as you put it, respond with some of my own.'

He leaned forward and rested his elbows on the table. He used his loosely clenched hands to prop his chin. 'I'm sixty-four years old. I've traveled around this country a lot and I've seen a lot of things. Perhaps it will not surprise you to learn that the things that have impressed me the most in the thirty-nine years since I left home were those involving black people.

'In the North as in the South, and in the West as well, I did not see moral differences in the ways that black and other minority people were treated. There were differences in the amount and variety of violence employed, to be sure, but those distinctions were not moral. There were subtler differences between the means of excluding black children from quality education in the southern schools than there were in the northern ones, but they did not rise to moral levels. The virtual exclusion of most minority adults from rewarding employment was morally the same in Los Angeles, where it was directed against Mexicans, as it was here in New York, where Puerto Ricans were targets too. But the plain, universal fact that I saw obvious wherever I went was that white people in this country had become accustomed – simply had a nasty habit – of monopolizing the better things of American life. And, you will forgive me for saying this, but I think they still do, if they could get half a chance to indulge it.

'Now you see, Ms. Cangelosi, that all conditioned me. When I got to the Congress, by the time that I got there, I had acquired a habit of my own. I study what I see. Any time I saw something I didn't recognize, that I hadn't seen before, I mentally sort of hunkered down, and studied it some more. Made sure I understood it just as clearly as I could. Because sometimes things that

459

look familiar, harmless and familiar, aren't that at all.

'Take the government, for example,' he said. 'The federal government. What I had seen of it from the outside was benevolent and kind, at least for the most part. And when it wasn't exactly kind or benevolent, it was still the best hope we had. The Kennedy Justice Department? Lyndon Johnson's legislation? Without them, where would we be? Still in the back of the bus, was where. I loved my government. Including, of course, your employer, the implacable FBI. It wasn't the county sheriffs who caught and prosecuted the killers of Viola Liuzzo, of Andrew Cheney and the rest. It was the FBI who stood between murderous racism and us. Oh, I loved my government.

'When I first ran for Congress,' he said, 'I said that publicly. I had to, you see, because I was having an awful time with Bobby Seale. Huey Newton, too, and Eldridge Cleaver – all of those fine gentlemen gave me a real hard time. I don't mean that they did it personally, ma'am. I don't mean that they came around and paid me any visits. Called me an Oreo, or a handkerchief head, or Tom – they would've done that, probably worse, if they'd paid any real attention to the way I addressed the problems of a black Republican trying to succeed a white Democrat in an affluent district. But I didn't catch their eye. What I mean is that what they did, and what they said, just played hell with my campaign. There I was, a nice young fellow, trying to succeed, and I needed everybody who could vote to vote for me. I had no margin to spare. White or black or spotted green – I really did not care. All I wanted from people was a fair hearing in the morning and a vote by evening on Election Day. And all those damned niggers out in Oakland, raising hell like that? All they did was torment me, 'cause I was the same color, and I could see the good white folks in what I wanted to become my district, looking out the corners of their eyes and thinking: "Most likely one them Panthers, another one them revolutionary bastards, gonna rape our women next."

'Well, I overcame it. Somehow. I wore a suit, and I talked soft, and I was most respectful. And I was very careful, too, to make it abundantly clear that I was disassociating myself from all those paranoid black folks shooting at policemen. Telling people to set fires, burn the cities down. Saying that the federal government was full-throttle out to get them, kill them and their families.

'But privately,' he said, "way down deep in my soul, I remained suspicious. Everything I'd ever seen'd taught me that when black people made some allegations about the government, and Whitey, they were usually telling the truth. So why were these Panther people saying all these bad things? Why were they making these wild claims, about my government?

'Well,' he said, 'I got to Congress, and I had some time, and some power to ask questions. Which I could make people answer. Those I could locate, at least,' he said, nodding at Fiona. 'And in the course of time, I found out that those rabble-rousers really had some points. They were not completely nuts. Were not all that far off.' He leaned toward her. 'In fact, they were quite right. I found out about COINTELPRO. Ever hear of that? "Counter Intelligence Program"?'

'Yes, I have,' she said.

'Well then, Ms. Cangelosi,' Ward said, 'then you must know what I mean. Here was the FBI, this fine investigative body, of which, no matter what you say, I think you're still a part – and I mean no offense by that, nor do you have to answer me – and what was our nation's finest doing to these folks? Why, they were carrying out the domestic side of the Bureau's habitual policy of ignoring its own charter. And any other laws or constitutional provisions that prove inconvenient to them. Here is this arrogant outfit, just as clearly prohibited from spying on its own citizens as it is from sending legats abroad to spy on foreign nationals, going right ahead and doing just exactly as it pleased. Opening their mail. Breaking up their marriages, and busting in their homes. Trying to get them, shoot each other. *Making* them rebel. Using *agents provocateurs* to drive them to those extremes. Making them paranoid. I did not agree with those folks, those Black Panthers, not at all. But out in public you've got people saying: "Work within the system. Make the system work the way that it's supposed to do." I'd been one of those people. I was saying that. And behind the scenes of that selfsame system, you've got people working fulltime to subvert what's being said. People in the same job you've got Ms. Cangelosi, now. Doing every evil thing that popped into their minds.

'Now, that's by way of background. That's just telling you. Telling you that I've got reasons. I think, because I have to think, that if we're going to tell people that this whole damned thing can work, those of us that work it have to play by the damned rules.

'Your status as a legat,' he said, 'the very existence of the job, is a violation of the Bureau's charter. It's against the law. You're an attorney, I think?' She nodded. 'You're sworn, you've been sworn twice. Once when you were admitted to the bar, and once again when you entered government. To uphold the Constitution and the laws of the United States. And yet there you were, breaking both your oaths, participating not only officially but proudly in an ongoing, defiant, systematic violation of the law. The charter expressly confines the FBI to the investigation of offenses against federal law, committed in the United States. Period. No international jurisdiction. No enterprises in espionage. No ifs, no ands, no buts. So what does the FBI do? It "detaches" agents for assignment, putatively by State – which somehow or other always spontaneously decides to send the particular legat where the Bureau wanted him – or her – to be, and there the agent does exactly the job of work that the Bureau had in mind. It's hypocrisy,' he said, 'and it's espionage.'

'It's not espionage, Congressman,' Fiona said. 'The work I did in London, whatever you may think about the propriety of my being there to do it, was not espionage. The work I did at Grosvenor Square was strictly confined to liaising with my British counterparts in order to assist American law enforcement officers working on cases arising in territories under their jurisdiction. I'm aware that in the past some overzealous Buagents have gone off on frolics of their own, playing spy and so forth, but that sort of foolishness isn't allowed anymore. Seat of Government was very strict on that point. If I'd done it, and gotten caught, I would have been fired.'

'Uh huh,' Ward said. He surveyed the table. He rested his gaze on the easterly end. 'Florence,' he said, 'I must say, you do give the most stimulating parties.'

'What?' Fiona said.

Ward looked at her. 'I merely said,' he said, 'that dinner at the Walkers' is always stimulating.'

'Oh no,' Fiona said. She shook her head twice. 'You all but called me a liar there, Congressman.'

'I did no such thing,' he said.

'Rubbish,' she said. 'If you responded like that to another Member's remarks in a floor colloquy, you'd be liable to censure. Now, with all due respect and so forth, I seem to recall

463

you boasting you're the fellow who plays by the rules. Well, that means you don't get to snicker at what I say, and then go run and hide behind some chivalrous decorum that says you can't answer me. You've impugned my veracity. You've been challenged, sir, for that. Respond.'

'Very well,' Ward said, leaning forward. 'I think you've broken your oath and the law. I think you personally have done it – not just as an FBI agent where the FBI's not supposed to be, but by committing specific acts. That you, as an official representing the United States, were deliberately instrumental in causing a man to die. I think that's hypocrisy, for our officials to act like that. I think it's evil. And I think when we – and I mean especially people like me, in the Congress – close our eyes – or what is worse: keep them open, so that we can wink – at behavior by our law enforcement people that is blatantly illegal, we in fact commission it. We tacitly commission it. And therefore by condoning it, we participate in the guilt, and I do not like that. Last August, August twenty-second, a young man that I knew, that I met in this house, last August twenty-second he was found dead in a British jail. I do not believe his death was accidental. I believe it was procured. And I suspect you were the functionary who handled that procurement.'

'Gerald,' Florence Walker said, 'you know all about Sam Tibbetts. You know how dangerous he was. He was a dangerous man. He was a radical, and he used heavy drugs, and he was crazy. A jury even said that.'

Ward nodded. 'I do know those things,' he said. 'I also know he was in custody. That he'd been apprehended by a ruse – which I guess I would condone, even though I don't generally approve of our government achieving its means by deceit – and he was in custody at the time of his death. And that's not supposed to happen to a healthy man in custody.'

'British custody, Mister Ward,' Fiona said. 'We formally requested that he be turned over to us as soon as he was captured at Heathrow. Our request was denied, pending extradition. We were prepared to hold him in maximum security at an American military facility. With all due safeguards. All the arrangements had been made. The Yard denied our request.'

'As they should have,' Ward said. 'If he'd been in some Air Force stockade, he wouldn't have lasted as long as he did. If he wasn't shot on the way to it, "trying to escape." So, since you couldn't get him into your clutches to kill him that way, you went around the other way and had it done by them. Contracted the murder out.'

'Congressman,' Claire Naisbitt said, placing her left hand on his right forearm, 'there was a very thorough investigation.' In the near distance a chime sounded. 'No evidence of foul play was found.'

'Oh,' Ward said, 'sure: "a complete investigation." The usual 'full-scale probe." "The customary whitewash" would be a fairer term, a little closer to the truth.'

'Congressman,' Claire Naisbitt said, 'really, you assume too much. The post-mortem examination was very thorough. A lengthy inquest was conducted. I think about thirty witnesses were called. No culpability could be found. No evidence to believe there'd been a homicide. But much to indicate that he had died by his own hand.'

'That he deliberately took an overdose of narcotics, was it not?' Ward said.

'Yes,' Claire said. 'Cocaine. And he'd been known to use cocaine. He had a history.'

Ward sighed. 'Mrs. Naisbitt,' he said, 'Samuel Tibbetts was taken into custody upon arrival at Heathrow. They'd been expecting him. Now you know how strict security's been at Heathrow ever since the IRA started acting up. Long before the PLO started leaving bombs around, Heathrow security was tighter than a Pullman window. Hell, half of America's movie stars and at least two-thirds of the world's rock musicians who use dope've gotten away with it for years, until they made the mistake of flying into Heathrow with their stashes. Then they got busted. And jailed.

'Now,' he said, 'can you tell me that a man arrested under security conditions even more extreme than those that are ordinarily enforced; can you tell me how a man who was strip-searched, body cavities and all, once at the airport and again at the jail, where his clothes were taken away from him – can you tell me how he managed to smuggle in enough freebase cocaine to give himself a lethal joint? Can you tell me that?'

'Yes,' she said, 'I can. The inquest found that the cigarettes containing the lethal dose must've been supplied to him after he was incarcerated. But the finding was that the one that killed him had probably been contained in one of the unopened packages from his luggage, and that he'd probably prepared the dose himself, just in case he was captured. But there was no reason to suspect anyone else of providing it to him. Only that in the future, to prevent such things happening, prisoners should not be supplied with their own cigarettes – only those from the interrogation center's supply. Negligence, yes, but very far from criminal.'

'Mrs. Naisbitt,' Ward said, removing her hand gently from his arm and reaching forward for his port, 'your trust in the authorities of your adoptive country is most admirable and sweet. But you've been too long away, from America. You've missed the

direct experience of the remarkable frequency with which enemies of our State, or those in control of our State, succumb to
suicidal tendencies. Are shot by demented assassins, always acting
alone.' He took another slice of bread and spread cheese on it.

'Some fruit, Gerald?' Florence Walker said, as he chewed the
bread.

'Yes, Congressman,' Fiona Cangelosi said, her eyes glittering,
'have a bite of the apple. You must need to replenish your knowledge of good and evil, after sharing so much with us.'

He stared at her. He put his glass down, removed his napkin,
placed it on the table, pushed his chair back from the table and
stood up. 'Clayton,' he said, nodding toward him. 'Florence,' he
said, again nodding. 'It's really been a most delightful evening,
and I'm sorry I can't stay. But I do have an early plane tomorrow,
and there's reading I must do. So, if you'll excuse me, thank you
very much.'

'You'll find your way out, Gerald?' Florence said, making no
move to rise.

'Oh, yes indeed,' he said from the foyer, getting his coat from
the closet. 'No trouble in that respect.'

Doctor Dan cleared his throat, awakening the lady with the
vacant smile from her reverie. She nodded. He stood up as Neville
Naisbitt entered the room. 'I have grand rounds in the morning,
Clayton,' the doctor said. 'Must be on our way.'

'What's this?' Naisbitt said. 'Collided with a fellow out there in
the hall, come in here and others leaving – must be my reputation.'

46

Shortly before 1:30 on the morning of February 22, 1986, Clayton
Walker rose unsteadily from his favorite leather chair in the study
of his home at 221 Sutton Place, and, slurring his words, informed
Neville and Claire Naisbitt, Fiona Cangelosi and his wife that
he was 'completely exhausted' and on his way to bed. Neville
Naisbitt drank the rest of his Glenmorangie scotch and stood up.
'Absolutely knackered myself, Clayton,' he said, taking Walker's
arm and steadying him. 'Think we both should bid the ladies to
sleep well, and we'll see them in the morning.' Clayton mumbled
something and made a half-hearted wave as they left the room.

Florence turned to Claire when they had gone up the stairs
to the second level of the condominium. 'Neville's such a dear,
Claire,' she said. 'Such a kind, decent man. He's always been so
thoughtful about Clayton.'

'He's thoughtful about Clayton because Clayton saved his leg,'

Claire said. 'And tonight, in particular, he's being thoughtful of Clayton because Clayton is drunk enough to fall and injure himself.'

'Oh, Clayton will be all right,' Florence said. 'He's just had a touch too much port. He'll be fine in the morning. As fine's he ever is.'

'Nonsense,' Claire said. 'I understand your, what must be your feelings of helplessness, Florence. But the fact that you have them changes nothing, and he will not be fine in the morning. He'll be suffering hangover, and he'll not be fit for duty. You should do something. Commit him, if necessary.'

'I refuse to do that, Claire,' Walker said. 'I've had one, my son was confined, and I have no doubt whatsoever that it finished him. I'll not do the same thing to my husband.'

'Sanitaria,' Naisbitt said, 'are not the same as prisons.'

'They are for men as proud as Clayton,' Walker said. 'Proud as he used to be, at least. And besides, it's too late. He's lived this long with his burdens? He's earned his anodyne.'

'It's still the business with James, I suppose?' Fiona Cangelosi said.

Florence nodded. 'I don't tell people that,' she said. 'When they comment on his drinking, I just say: "Oh, well, what Lauren Bacall said? 'I never knew a man worth a damn who didn't drink too much.'" Because it's too much bother, and too much pain, to explain. I just don't care to go into detail about James, now that he's out. I mean, everybody knows he was in prison, of course. They all know about the case. And they assume that he's not right, or he would be with us. Nearby, anyway. But I just don't care to discuss it with them, under any circumstances. And especially not when Clayton's around.

'When that happens,' Florence said, 'he goes on about how James is ruined. And then, unless someone manages, somehow, to get him off the subject,' she put the fingertips on her right hand to the bridge of her nose, shutting her eyes while she rubbed it, 'unless someone gets him off onto another subject, which is terribly difficult, sooner or later he goes back all the way to James's birth.' She opened her eyes. 'And when he does that,' she said, 'when he does that, I'm just *terrified*, especially when Gerald's here, that he'll start that business about how he knew, how he sensed, from the first instant he saw James in the nursery, that the child was damned.'

She looked pleadingly at Claire. 'You do understand, don't you?' she said. 'That it's not, that it's not because no one knows the story. Everyone knows. Everyone knows that Clayton had every right to throw me out when I became pregnant with James. Everyone, including Wilhemina, knows I offered to leave. They'd been separated, even then they'd been separated for years, and this was over forty years ago. I knew she'd never give him a divorce. I was willing, I was willing to go away.' She paused. 'And I should have, too. But Clayton, it was Clayton who wouldn't allow it. He pleaded with me, Claire. He wept. He begged me not to go and leave him. Said he didn't care what people thought. We would hold our heads up high and let them think as they wished, and I owed that much to him. To do as he asked.

'Well,' she said to Fiona, 'I did it. And one of the nicest things that ever happened to me was the day you came to me and said that you'd thought about what I'd told you – about never salvaging, never trying to salvage something that's damaged beyond repair, and that you were going to divorce Louis.'

'Your advice meant a lot to me,' Fiona said. 'If I hadn't been stuck with it, I would've given him his name back, too. But with Alicia and Tony in school, and all, all that tedious paperwork of explaining every year why the Cangelosi kids live with Miss Campbell – well, I said "The hell with it." But you were right, Florence. Once the air goes out of the balloon, there's no point in pretending.'

'Yes,' Florence said. 'Well, that's what I mean, Claire. Against my better judgment, I allowed Clayton to be gallant. As he wished. He formed this image of himself as the compassionate husband. The forgiver of transgressions. In time, in time we did conceive, and when Christina was born, well, I thought we had been healed. But then came that terrible business with James, when he was gone for so long. And then when he was captured and tried, and Clayton had his heart attack. Then: James convicted. Then in prison. Clayton thinking he'd been a fool. An utter, total fool.' She sighed. 'Odd as it may sound, given how he's lived his life, but Clayton's still a proud man. And he should be. He's a brilliant physician. Or used to be, at least, before all of this. It's hard for a man like that to look in the mirror and see what he believes to be a fool. A dupe. It's very hard.'

'Does he know,' Claire said, 'does he know about Christina? Now? What is going on?'

Florence sighed again. 'I hope not,' she said. 'I desperately do hope not. Christina, Christina's the only consolation that I think he has. He's very rigid, you know. Extremely rigid, morally. That was what was so astounding when I became pregnant with James. I was sure he'd throw me out. Maybe that's why I did it. But he didn't. And now, now if he had any idea what Christina, how Christina's acted, really, all her life – or since she was sixteen – I do not know what he'd do. I simply do not know.' She hesitated.

'No,' she said, 'that's wrong. I do know what he'd do. He'd call her a whore. And probably a murderess.' She laughed. 'Along with us, of course.' She leaned forward, clasping her hands before her. 'Isn't it wonderful?' she said. 'All of them, so fucking righteous? So damned sanctimonious? Gerald sitting there tonight, full of his usual blather about liberty and rights? And how vicious and unprincipled he thinks you must've been, Fiona, to do what he thinks you did?'

Fiona sipped from her port. 'If he knew the half of it,' she said, 'he'd bust so many gussets he'd have to wear a truss.'

Claire smiled. 'I've always found it best, with Neville,' she said, 'never to disclose more than about forty percent of the entire story. Strictly limit the details to those he absolutely has to know. Neville is the chamberlain of ideals and principles. No need cluttering up his mind with a lot of sticky, practical questions. They only get in the way of his thinking. They confuse him. Doesn't do to let men get distracted by petty questions.'

'Such as whether it's permissible to kill someone else's son, whom you don't know, in order to save your son?' Fiona said, laughing.

'Wasn't that *funny*?' Florence said. 'I could barely keep a straight face, when Gerald was badgering you. I wanted to say: "Gerald, Gerald. When did you get so pompous? You didn't, you never acted like this, before you went to Congress. If you had, we never would've had all this trouble, because I never would have screwed you. James would never have been born."'

'The cauldron does bubble, doesn't it?' Claire said. The other two women laughed. Fiona was surprised by a yawn. 'Oh, goodness,' she said. 'I'm really sorry. I think that means I'd better go. I hate to be a spoilsport ... actually, what it is, is that I hate to miss the fun. But Alicia's leaving for San Juan tomorrow morning, and I have to get her up and out to LaGuardia. You know how it is with the airlines these days – all the security.'

'She's going to see Louis?' Claire said.

'Well,' Fiona said, 'I hope not. I'm under the impression she's going with Mom and Dad to Caneel Bay. But you never know with Louis. He could turn up anywhere.'

'What's he doing now?' Florence said. 'I only met him the once, but he seemed a charming man.'

'What's he doing?' Fiona said. 'Or What are they calling it?' The other two women laughed. 'What he's doing, I assume, is what he's always done. Whatever needs to be done. What they're calling it, now? Well, now Louis's a roving consultant from the Department of Agriculture, and he's working with the government of Honduras on a ten-year plan to develop export crops. Isn't that cute? When he left London in such a hurry, he went to Sri Lanka as an expert on deep-water ports.' She laughed. 'Louis's a man of infinite expertise. You name a country with a really bad drug problem, or one that's genuinely looking for some help controlling people who blow up cars, and – it's the strangest coincidence, but Louis almost always turns out to be one of the logical choices of people we send to solve those other problems. If Canada sometime next year suddenly finds itself with a full-blown terrorist problem again, I bet you Louis's sent up north. To breed Huskies or something.' She sighed. 'He's a remarkable, charming man,' she said, 'but what a trial to be married to him.'

Claire laughed. 'Did you both get in trouble?' she said. 'After the Tibbetts affair?'

'Oh, no,' Fiona said. 'No, Louis was long gone and hard to find while Tibbetts was still alive. And, you have to keep this in mind;

Louis's genius is that he never, never does anything himself. Louis makes arrangements, and that's all he ever does. All I did, when I heard from you through Claire, all I did was mention it to Louis. And he said: "Well, when does Larry Badger say he's coming in?" And I told him what Alton'd found out, from his Cyclops, or whatever he calls it. That he'd cross-filed all of Tibbetts's aliases, and located a booking for Joseph Thomas from Morocco to Lebanon, and then one for someone named Swift out of Beirut, and then one for Jay Cullinan from Zurich to Heathrow, changing for Shannon. And Louis could just reel that stuff out of his head, without looking it up. And he said: "Yeah, schedules change next week. Marrakech to Beirut. Beirut to Athens. Athens to Zurich. Transfer to Swissair. Change to Aer Lingus. He'll be in the transit lounge at Heathrow around seven. Have the cops grab him then. Make sure they insist on all the formalities before they turn him over to us and this Massachusetts cop – who shouldn't even be here; must be a renegade. Yard'll have him in Paddington Green interrogation center by four that afternoon. Should be fairly easy. Swap his cigarettes while they're tossing him. Then just give them back, and wait for him to finish it. What's the bastard smoke?" And that was why I called you, Florence, to find out what he smoked. I told Louis, and three days later, Louis was on his way out the door. "By the way," he said, "that little matter with Tibbetts? All been taken care of. See you in a month." He was gone before I left for Malta. When I got back, there was a note – he'd gone to Sri Lanka. That was when I decided. It was fun; it was exciting, but it had to stop.' She shrugged. 'I hated to let him go,' she said. 'But I think *he* was relieved. Louis's really a sweet man; he would really like to be. But he loves his life so much that he just cannot let it go. Not for anything. I should've married Alton, that August in

Salzburg. But then I thought: "Alton is crazy." So I married Louis. Maybe I'm the one who's crazy. Maybe Louis's fine, and I've been unfair to him.'

'He's better off, dear,' Claire said. 'As, may I add, are you. The only thing worse than not being married to someone like that is being married to them. Wonderful people to know in a pinch, but hard to be married to.'

'As Neville would testify,' Florence said.

'Oh heavens, no,' Claire said. 'Neville has no idea. He saw the item in the paper – just a squib, really, that this American fugitive, whatever he was, had died of a drug overdose or something in Paddington Green. And he said to me: "Harumph, harumph, isn't that the young man that Florence asked about?" And I said, I believed it was. And he said: "Huh, strange isn't it? She was so concerned? That's what she told me, at least. That if he was recaptured he'd come back and do some harm. Very concerned. Wanted him out of the way, I thought. Wanted him out of the way. Gave me that impression."

'And I said: "Neville, really, I must say, you're worse than Larry Badger." And he said: "Claire, for heaven's sake, Larry can't even read."'

The other women laughed.

47

Terry Gleason in a white polo shirt, grey slacks and blue blazer sat alone at the round table facing the southwest windows and looking out on the docks of Little Harbor Marina in Sandwich. He watched the sailboats of the summer bitter-enders bob in the low wake of the harbormaster's Boston Whaler, churning slowly out toward the black-and-red buoy at the entrance. The maples interspersed among the oaks and pines on the steep hills around the harbor had started faintly to turn scarlet. He stirred his coffee absently.

Shortly after noon, John Richards in a blue polo shirt, blue blazer and khakis entered the restaurant, spotted Gleason, walked to the table and placed his left hand on Gleason's shoulder. Gleason looked up, grinned and started to rise. 'Siddown,' Richards said. He took the chair to Gleason's right.

Gleason reached into his jacket pocket and produced a

document consisting of four typewritten pages. He put it down on the plasticized chart placemat. Richards removed a case from his inside pocket and put reading glasses on. 'Reason I'm a little late,' he said. 'Couldn't find these things. God really isn't wholly fair. First he takes your sight away, so you have to wear glasses. Then your memory goes to hell; can't remember where you put them. Lemme see here, now.' He began to read. As he turned to page two, he said: 'John Morrissey thinks you should sign this?'

'Thinks I should think it over,' Gleason said. 'Very seriously.'

'Umm,' Richards said. He read quickly through the third and fourth pages. He refolded the document and put it in front of Gleason. He removed his glasses and returned them to his pocket. He nodded toward the coffee cup. 'Beer?' he said.

'Beer'd be good,' Gleason said.

Richards turned toward the bar at the easterly end of the room. He raised two fingers of his left hand. The woman behind the bar nodded. He folded his arms on the table. 'Recall I said to you, you called me,' he said, '"Big Mo's no divorce lawyer"? Sure you did the right thing, now, picking him for this?'

'Oh, I think so,' Gleason said. 'I didn't have much choice, you know, she hired Bigelow. Pretty obvious at that point, there'd been a slight miscalculation on my part. More than one of them, in fact, and not so damned slight, either. I didn't think Barbara'd come out swinging quite so hard. I definitely did not anticipate that she'd get John Bigelow to do the sparring – he's no divorce guy, either. But he does hate my guts, though, which part she had to like; probate soldier up against him in this case, he would eat the guy.'

The waitress brought two pilsener glasses of beer. 'I suppose,' Richards said. 'Just that, looking at this thing, have to wonder whether Big Mo didn't get your clothes stolen. What I read here smarts.' He drank some of the beer. 'You gonna sign it, you think?'

'I dunno,' Gleason said. He exhaled a deep breath. He tapped the document with his right forefinger. He drank some of his beer. 'Why I wanted to see you, maybe help decide.

'The kids're the first thing,' he said, 'and that's where the trouble is: that they are the first thing, Philip especially, as far as I'm concerned. And she knows that for a fact. So this is where the two of them, Barbara and Bigelow, really get very crafty.'

'The part about the kids?' Richards said. 'I mean, I'm no expert on this, but that looked pretty fair to me. "Unlimited visitation"? "Joint custody"? Where's your complaint on that?'

'I haven't got one,' Gleason said. 'That's what I mean by: "crafty."' The only thing that'd really make me fight this thing – well, the only thing *now*, that'd make me fight down to the last empty cartridge'd be if she tried some obvious little ploy to deny me access to the kids. And she hasn't done that.

'The support?' he said. 'Not a thing out of line there, either. I could say it's a little high, I suppose – four hundred a month per kid, plus tuition – but she's giving me the tax deduction, without being asked, and I was planning on the tuition anyway. I fight? Might get it reduced to, say, a thousand a month, plus the tuition – that's not worth a fight.'

'The alimony, then?' Richards said. 'Isn't that a little steep?'

'Well,' Gleason said, 'it's staggering, but not steep. You make the mistake of keeping wifey comfy, time you decide to divorce her, you're gonna regret it. She may not be able to keep you, but she does get the comfort. And there again, no indication they're trying any dodges: every buck I pay to her is one less I get taxed on.

'I figured she'd go for both houses,' Gleason said. 'Fooled again – she gets Canton, I get Chilmark. Mortgage's bigger on Chilmark, but then, so's the equity.

'No,' he said, 'there's no sniping going on in any of the places where you'd go and look for it. That fuckin' Bigelow – I bet shithouse rats learn cute from him. The kicker's in that innocuous little clause about "Children's environment": "At no time shall the children of the marriage be housed, entertained, or otherwise sheltered, in any domicile owned or regularly occupied by any person of the opposite sex with whom defendant husband has been or is having an unlawful relationship." It's a morals clause, all right? Until such time's I marry another woman, I've got to agree not to live with one, or let the kids see I am. Don't want Philip finding any bras or pants around, when he goes to take a leak.'

'Who's the judge?' Richards said. 'Who'd you draw on this?'

'You ever hear of Grace McCaffrey?' Gleason said.

'Oh, my,' Richards said. 'Norfolk County's answer to Calcutta's Ma Teresa.'

'That's the one,' Gleason said. 'She not only looks like the Pope – she sounds like him. Except not Polish, but more doctrinaire. Care to speculate a little, John, her views, adultery? Sex outside of marriage? Fornication, oral sex, all that kind of shit – all prohibited by law? Law's unenforceable, of course, but still there on the books. Sex outside of marriage is prohibited. Tell me what Grace'll say.'

'Happy to,' Richards said. 'And right after that, I'll make predictions which way you should look tomorrow, see the sun come up.'

'Right,' Gleason said. 'So, there's the zinger. All I have to do to see my kids for the next four years – unless I'm satisfied taking them out on movie dates and bringing them home again – all

I have to do's either take a vow of celibacy, or acquire another shanty where I go just to get laid. Nifty, huh? And, if I don't agree, then all bets're off. All the money stuff's reopened, also visitation, and John the Big gets to go in before Cardinal Grace, fulminate and filibuster about how my child bride wants to do the right thing, offered it to me, but I'm so randy I won't have it – I should be strung up.'

'And then Grace will block your hat,' Richards said.

'That's the way I figure it,' Gleason said. 'That's how I figure it.'

'Lemme ask you something,' Richards said. 'How'd they find this out? I realize you're separated, you and Lady Barbara. I realize you've had companions, reasonably enough. But years ago, you used to be, fairly swift yourself. You didn't go and flaunt your nooky, didn't rub it in. You don't show hickeys at your collar, haven't got the clap?'

'Nope,' Gleason said, 'no other vile diseases, either. I've been autoclaved.'

'So,' Richards said, 'we know they know – how'd they find out? Badgers and Bigelow were thick – they been tailing you?'

'They're better'n I ever saw, they pulled that one off,' Gleason said. 'Besides, they've got no motive. Barbara? Sure, Barbara's mean. So's Bigelow. But Barbara just assumes things, and he wouldn't go on that. Only place the kids've seen me, stayed with me, I mean, is down on the island – no one else was there. Someone gave them evidence, the Waterford apartment where I live with Chris. And that's what I can't figure out. Probably shouldn't bother me, all the difference that it makes, but things that I can't figure out – those things bother me.'

'Who's she told, then,' Richards said, 'she told anybody?'

Gleason snickered. 'Shit,' he said, 'she's more security conscious'n the Pentagon.'

'Anybody seen you with her?' Richards said.

'Seeing us would not do it,' Gleason said. 'Answer is, they have. Seen us at the Station Tap, seen us having dinner. But Bigelow wouldn't go on that. That's not "shacked up" enough. No, he's got something, he can prove we mostly live together. Well, we have been, anyway.'

'Then she has to've told someone,' Richards said. 'Where've you been with her? Where she'd meet someone she would trust, and tell them happy news? Or where you would've had to be sharing living quarters.'

'Only real excursion we've had,' Gleason said, 'only place we've been was to her father's funeral there. Back a month ago. I did go with her to that, because she asked me to.'

'And where was that?' Richards said. 'That down in New York?'

'The burial was private,' Gleason said. 'They, we flew down one morning, got met at LaGuardia. There's this funeral home, White Plains, where they burned the old man up. Shouldn't've had too much trouble igniting him, either, all the booze he'd put away. Bet he went in a sheet of blue flame, they lit the pilot light.'

'Who was there?' Richards said. 'Who came to pay respects?'

'Mother,' Gleason said. 'First time I met her. Son James was detained elsewhere. Saw no sign of him. Assumed he didn't want to come. Woman named Claire Naisbitt that the Walkers knew in England, apologizing for her husband, said he couldn't get away. Couple docs, the hospital, some black Congressman. Your old pal, Fiona there, from the FBI except she isn't anymore. TV pretty boy named Oates, I didn't recognize. Two or three more greybeards wearing suits that cost more than my car, and some ladies in fine garments that I didn't know at all.'

'Where'd you stay that night?' Richards said.

'In Waterford,' Gleason said. 'Took the last shuttle back. After the cremation, we went back the Walkers' condo, had some drinks and made small talk. Other folks gradually left, except the Naisbitt lady. Chris and I had dinner with them, her mother and Claire. Oh, and the Fiona person – very civilized. Everyone was very nice, specially the mother. Hadn't met her before that, and wasn't looking forward, but she seemed very nice and friendly – couldn't ask for more.'

'She knows you're playing house,' Richards said.

'Oh, yeah,' Gleason said. 'The Naisbitt woman and Fiona took Chris upstairs to talk, transparent strategy to leave me alone with Mom. And we had a real nice chat, everything hotsy-totsy. Most of it, she's warning me. Not about what she might do – just about how Chris needs help, and she hopes when my life's straightened out, I can give it to her. "Christina needs stability": that is what she said. I said I was very glad, we'd gotten back together. Said to me: "I'm going to tell her, if you don't object." I said: "Hell, no. I wish you would." Whether she did, I can't say. Did not stay long enough, I think, she could've on that visit.'

'There was another one?' Richards said.

'Two weeks ago,' Gleason said. 'Memorial service in the hospital chapel. Very dignified and refined. This time Mister Naisbitt came, delivered an oration. This time the TV kid did not – they don't get along.'

'Who else was there, you recognized?' Richards said. 'Anybody else?'

'No,' Gleason said, 'just the folks from the cremation. Course the Badgers, both of them, they were in the hall. Alton had to fly right back. Larry stayed around. Came back with us to Sutton Place. He left around eight.'

'You come back that night?' Richards said.

'Nope,' Gleason said. 'That was Friday. We stayed over, in the Walkers' pad.'

'Sleep in the same bed, did you?' Richards said.

'Of course,' Gleason said, 'why the hell not? That's not what Bigelow's using, that I fucked her in New York. I'm sure old Barbara doesn't like it, and I'm sure they probably know. But I'm not likely to take Philip, or Joanne, far's that goes, stay with Florence a weekend, when I've got visitation. No, Bigelow's not trying to, stop me getting laid – even Grace can't go that far. What he's shooting for is stop me, living with Christina. I can get my ashes hauled, but I can't make a life.'

Richards laughed. 'You didn't,' he said, 'I assume you didn't see Cowboy Fred lurking around, anytime you've been with her.'

Gleason grinned. 'No Cowboy Fred,' he said. 'What's he gonna do now, John? He gets out of school? Specialize in extraditions? "Fugitives Brought Back Alive"? Interesting specialty, that's what he decides to do.'

'Not much call for it, though,' Richards said. 'Also, discouraging work. Saw him maybe three months, four, after Tibbetts got it. New lieutenants' swearing-in? Decided I'd give him the leg a little, see how he'd react.'

'How did he?' Gleason said. 'I heard he was quite pissed off.'

'Very calm,' Richards said. 'Made out he was completely satisfied. More'n he would've been, in fact, if Sam'd made it back for trial.'

'He believe the inquest?' Gleason said.

'Of course not,' Richards said. 'He assumes that Ianucci, or one of your other druggie clients, wiped him out for you.'

Gleason frowned. 'So,' he said, 'Lieutenant Fred gets out of law school, most likely past the bar, some time down the road a piece, becomes a prosecutor and spends his life chasing me? That's something to look forward to. Phil Ianucci ever sees direct sunlight again, may have to get him to do something like what Fred thinks I have done already.'

Richards laughed. 'Calm down,' he said, 'you're worse'n Fred. Fred's not mad at you. His attitude's that you fixed things. Finally won Sam's case. Even respects you a little. Keep in mind what I told you: Fred likes symmetry. Sam's book was open 'cause you dropped it. Now Sam's book is closed, so Fred thinks you made amends. That's how Fred would handle it, he was in your shoes. Forget about the Cowboy – he thinks you did just fine.'

'Yeah,' Gleason said, 'just fine. I wish I had Fred's inclinations, I could be so *sure*. Must be wonderful, that feeling, knowing you're always right.'

'Well,' Richards said, 'what's the net effect, then? You gonna sign or not?'

'I got this thing a week ago,' Gleason said. 'I went into Big Mo's office, and he handed it to me, and I read it and he said: "Whatcha gonna do?" And I said: "Talk to Christina, I think. Only way I've got a dime, next ten years or so until the damned tuition's over, she gives up her apartment and I sell the Vineyard house, and we get something together. That's the only way I float. So, I think I better ask her." And I did. And she said: "Sign. Contest with your kids, I know: I am going to lose."'

'But that's the end of you two, then,' Richards said. 'All intents and purposes.'

'Uh huh,' Gleason said. 'And you know, I was relieved? Live with someone for a while, really find out who they are, it can take a toll on you. Going down her place, naturally the traffic's jammed, I'm rehearsing all the speeches. "It's just until the decree's final. Then we can get married. Then the kids can visit us. It'll be all right." And the trouble with the speeches is, it's not that they're not true. It's that I don't want to make them, even *though* they're true.

'I know her now, John,' he said, 'like I never did before. Fault's all mine, I didn't – she was always right up front. Told me, time and time again, showed me by her actions and confirmed them with her words. She drifts. The current changes your way, and that's the way she goes. The current shifts away from you, and so she goes away.'

'Short attention span,' Richards said.

'No,' Gleason said, 'no center. That's what made her so confusing, everyone she met. You look back on that crew she was with, and whatever else you want to say about that pack of animals, at least they had strong beliefs. And so did Fred, and so did you, and I had them, too. Theirs meant they could do things that the law said they could not. Ours said that the law came first, and that's how we all behaved. This old bastard Naisbitt, made the funeral speech, he got passionate about his subject, really emotional. "Clayton was a man of conscience." And while I never met the guy, I could believe him. Remember how his kid acted, on trial for his life? He showed the same intensity at MCI Walpole – in prison but unchanged. Had to get it from someplace. Probably his dad.

'So,' he said, 'and look at me: I never broke the law. But when I saw what I wanted, well, I went after it. How long did you work

485

that case? Well over five years? Christina doesn't do that, doesn't grab and won't hold on.

'Her mother told me that,' he said. 'That's exactly what she meant, and now I know that she was right. "I hope it does work out for you, for the two of you," she said. "But pray, as I will, nothing happens, that will frighten her. Christina never loses, never loses any fight. But that's because she runs away, before the fight begins. She's quite smart, Terry, quite smart, and she is most alert. I hope your life goes smoothly now – that's the only kind she'll have. That she will tolerate."'

'And it hasn't,' Richards said.

'And it won't,' Gleason said, 'because it happens to be real. What she wants is wonderland. That I cannot give.'

Richards stared at him. 'Lemme ask you something, Terry.'

'Fire when ready,' Gleason said.

'Did you say that to anyone, what you just said to me?'

Gleason shrugged. 'Her mother, sure,' he said. 'I said that to Florence Walker, words to that effect.'

Richards smiled and nodded. 'Then that's who told,' he said. 'Christina's mother sized you up, thought you wouldn't do. So then the lady turned you in.' He laughed. 'Lady's cagey,' he said. 'Fred should marry her. Two of them'd rule the world, and no one else'd know.'

'Be a different world, though,' Gleason said. 'I don't think I'd like it much.'